TERRA'S
SABBATH

DEAN PATRICK

2023, TWB Press
www.twbpress.com

Terra's Sabbath
Copyright © 2023 by Dean Patrick

This is a work of fiction. Names, characters, places, and incidences are either a product of the author's imagination or are used fictitiously. Any resemblance to any actual person, living or dead, events, or locales is entirely coincidental.

Edited by Terry Wright

Cover art and design by Markee Books
https://www.markeebooks.com

ISBN: 978-1-959768-16-6

Table of Contents

Dedicated To:

Joshua Nielsen, my brother, a Houston Police Officer, who is the inspiration for the protagonist, Marion Paul, and for his expert law enforcement expertise throughout the writing of this novel.

Alfiia Mankina, the cover model and friend who lives in Moscow, Russia, the embodiment of Terra Drake.

Finally, Lisa Montoya, my loving wife and best friend whose constant encouragement and love keep me pushing through every challenge that addiction presents.

PART ONE

"It is in dreams that I have known the real clutch of stark, hideous, maddening, paralyzing fear."

– H.P. Lovecraft

Chapter One:

School's In Session

arion's eyes snapped open like a focal-plane shutter set at 1/20-second speed. He knew instantly he was in a hospital bed, though everything that put him here was a blur. He tried to lift his head, but his neck strength wouldn't allow him to rise with any kind of power. Instead, he moved his head from side to side as he slowly blinked his eyes to sharpen their focus. Steve was nowhere to be seen. Marion's heart sank realizing his brother may not have survived.

His memories of that horrific night slowly became more vivid as his mind processed what he'd lived and experienced, like when he and his brother reached the last step of the stairwell that led down to Terra Drake's lair. Steve had told him she was the woman who had ceaselessly tormented him, that she was evil and had to be stopped before all of small-town America fell into chaos and ruin.

Hers was a lair of things Marion had never seen in all his years of gruesome homicide work with the Houston Police Department. He remembered a banquet hall the size of a Walmart warehouse, with a concrete block stage setup at the back that was equally wide and five feet high. The woman, Terra Drake, stood at center stage with another woman right by her side, both dressed as wooden puppets, their clothing fitted so tightly onto them that the garb looked more like varnish. They stared as if possessed over a child who was laid out before them on a Sacrificial Altar of some kind, and both women held large Bowie knives above the child's body.

He couldn't tell who or what was chanting or howling, or where the awful sounds were coming from, as every sound ricocheted about, too chaotically for only the women on the concrete stage, yet the sounds were an endless cacophony of joy and adulation. He saw the women were about to cleave the innocent child to pieces. His brother looked severely shocked, as he appeared to recognize all three people on the stage. Marion also remembered thinking, strangely enough, that there was no one else in the entire gothic scene of mayhem, as it had clearly been designed for a massive audience.

The others must have stayed in Hell for the night.

He slowly sat up in the hospital bed, being as careful as possible to check his physical strength as much as his mental condition. The room lay in deep shadows, and the quiet was unsettling, if not disturbing. He had a hard time focusing on anything other than the deep ache that was lodged in the atrophied muscles of his neck.

Better lie here and ease into this shit.

As he rested in the hospital bed, he looked around him at the vitals machines and their readouts. His blood pressure was normal; his heartbeat was fast but steady. He felt lucky to be alive. He couldn't see anything outside the window, but the glass itself looked filthy. As he looked directly in front of him at the whiteboard, he could see various names and phone numbers, but he couldn't make them out.

He wondered if one of those numbers were for any of the many bizarre characters Steve had told him he'd met as his world descended into terror and chaos. There was Burkenstock, a troll of a parking lot attendant, and a black couple Steve thought was possessed and following him for some unknown reason. Steve's hair stylists who became witches, diabolical neighbors, and the world's largest pig, bruised and beaten, on display at the County Fair. Where were they that final time in Terra's lair while Steve faced the two seductive puppets who had placed an innocent child on a Sacrificial Altar with the sole purpose to butcher her.

He remembered studying everything around them with his cop instincts and laser focus. His training kicked in. He had to save that child, so he pulled the gun from his ankle holster, took aim directly at the demon women on the stage of horrors, and shouted, "Don't you fucking move."

Both women stood straight up and glared at him. Their painted costumes highlighted every perfect demonic curve that Satan himself had sketched. That's what Marion thought, at least. Then, before he could mount any type of arrest, spectacular light beams burst out in such splendor and color it looked like the ceiling itself had exploded in a rush of stained glass panels, each one a hundred foot square, shattering in violent unison, and then from the floor arose a dragon of a man dressed in a cape and hood and wearing a giant fly mask of such detail it appeared to be his real head. The fly-demon lunged across the floor toward them, fully intent on killing them where they stood. Marion held his gun tight, pointing it straight at the beastly man to get the best shot possible, but the fly mask opened its mouth impossibly wide, and a scream from the depths of Hell assailed them: *"Get thee fucking hence from this house of thieves!"* and continued to rant about aimless gods, and limp and dying flesh. Marion damn near jumped out of his boots and pissed his pants, but the terror was coming at him so fast, his finger locked on the trigger, and primal fear stuck in his gut.

He shuddered, tried to open his eyes again to wake up, but he fell back into a deep coma with his body and mind being pulled away from the hospital room into a swirl of colors and tunnels with tube lights and strobe lasers that ricocheted in a thousand different directions that physically launched him into the opening of a large hallway that led to the entrance of a Stonehenge-like classroom.

At the front stood a spectacular stage designed as a replica of Stonehenge itself, except the pillars were made of a rich metallic material and trimmed in deep hues of scarlet. A massive transparent dome that looked like it had been perfectly cut from a block of glass hovered above some twenty feet and twitched ever so slightly. He could hear a long, slow hum that was in rhythm to the sphere's movement.

He found himself at the corner of Exit Stage Right where he had a full view of the stage and the classroom / auditorium. There looked to be a thousand seats, but only a few dozen were occupied by mesmerized children sitting in the first few rows. As Marion surveyed the place, he saw the back area where there stood a few dozen men and women so old they looked more like mummified mannequins than humans. Ancient men and women fully naked with pieces of their sheetrock skin falling to the floor. Each of them wore the same awful fly mask that Marion had seen on the demon that attacked his brother and him, just before he was blown into whatever world he'd landed in now.

Terra Drake walked down the center aisle of the auditorium. She was dressed in a black leather, a one-piece thong/lingerie getup, and six-inch stilettos with the heels finished in blood-red acrylic. She stepped up to the stage as a ramp appeared and descended to the floor. Marion sensed that she was more than just vile, but in a trance of witchery and focus so intense, he felt a rush of fear but couldn't look away. He now noticed she sported a light blue and pink ball-gag with a chrome chain that wrapped around her head. Her presence filled the entire auditorium with a wickedness that pushed Marion's fear into a panic so unnerving he wanted some way to call in backup from the

Houston Police Department.

Her sculpted legs were painted stone-white, she had talons for nails, finished in the same blood-red as her stiletto heels. Her pitch-black hair was ratted up in a nest of perfect chaos, and her lavender eyes were fabulously lit up, as if she'd just orgasmed and still radiated a glow of insane sensual glee. She walked up the ramp to the stage then faced the classroom of students, all aged four or five to that of her own age: endless, he assumed. He had no idea when the adults had been seated, but he made no mental effort to figure it out.

"Just play this out" he heard himself whisper.

The auditorium itself was just as endless as everything else Marion had seen. Designed as the modern Stonehenge replica, it was an enormous circular arena, giving Marion such a sense of foreboding he wondered what kind of terror was presented as classroom syllabi. The place had the overall sensation of a postmodern maximum-security prison created to enhance every one of the five senses. Maybe a few more, and the demon woman commanded them all.

A sudden blast of music pummeled from all corners of everywhere with Kiss's "Do You Love Me?" Paul Stanley's ragged and raging voice screamed so loudly in a surreal plea that Marion wondered if the entire universe could hear him. The woman's body moved insanely to the song's sexual vibrance, her hands to her mouth as if to lip-sync with Stanley, but Marion couldn't see her lips move around the ball-gag. Her hips and pelvis did the singing instead.

The music shifted into another Kiss mantra, "Makin' Love," so seamlessly it sounded like both songs were blended as the sound level intensified to ear-shattering levels. The woman's movement followed the pulsing rhythm like that of a sacrificial python. As the song ended in a blood thirsty rage, the audience of children and adults alike frothed at their mouths and "screeched" and "ah-haed" and "ewwed."

Marion looked at them in disbelief and shock.

The auditorium was filling up with men, women, and children all dressed or wrapped in paper sacks, their eyes peeled open in wonder and bafflement, their mouths perpetually smiling.

She pulled from behind her a razor-laced crimson whip, tipped with leather thongs and metal beads, which she swung around her head violently and cracked with a precision and speed that sounded more like an explosion and trumped the Kiss concert's volume coming from the walls themselves.

In unison with the whip's fierce crack, the Revolting Cocks' "Get Down" burst from the corners, creating a scene of witchery and a brew of deepening madness. It was a 14-minute techno song of frenzy that Marion remembered many times because he'd loved playing it during heavy workouts, but in the world he now watched, he knew it would certainly go on much longer. He covered his ears and wanted to cover his eyes, yet he could not stop watching the orchestrated chaos that panned left and right across the classroom.

Marion then noticed the seated children were far too young to witness such revulsion of the monster ball. He wanted to brace himself in front of them to protect their innocence from the demonic and strategic assault. The woman's walking epitome of perversion pulsated to the music in such obscenity, yet fully controlled, Marion felt as if his head would split.

"Why now you may ask?" the woman began as the violent music simmered to a slow-motion boil. A hi-tech headset suddenly grew around her head, a microphone attachment that looked like a pulsing eel slithered around her neck and finally ended just at the tip of her lips, erasing the ball-gag like a magic pen drawing over it with invisible ink.

"Here is the syllabus:

One. We'll start with the pole dance. How to use your pelvis to display the greatest sexual effect while grinding it against the pole as well as to swivel around it. How to turn your body upside down to gain the highest level of consistent arousal.

Two. Animal sex. With whatever animals you'd like. Especially the wolf.

Three. Anal sex with illustrations. All details are critical.

Four. Rim jobs.

Five. Gold streams of delight. Again, it's the devil in the details as we all know—"

"What is *fucking wrong* with you?" Marion shouted. "What in Christ's name!?"

The woman stopped dead in her tracks and looked directly down to Marion in such a rebuking stare that she didn't need to say a word. But that didn't stop her. "Silence from you! Don't dare speak further, and don't ever use that Christ name in this place again. I will hear no hypocrisy!" The woman hissed then turned again to the audience.

Marion said nothing, as he felt sick to his stomach and wondered what was the purpose of all this debauchery.

"Why all this mambo jumbo you may ask? This and all the gender trash-talk that's got everyone so tied up into tit clamps. Why is it so suddenly rampant? Because that's how it's supposed to be. That is how I want it to be. It's *my* agenda. *Our* agenda. Always has been. This is The Fuck All War, and it has been about since the beginning of time. Only this world is too silly silly stuck in drivel to see it as it's smacking them right across everyone's slippery cheeks!

"Can't you see everything running so fluidly? That everything is righting itself? That all you ever thought wrong is completely how it should be in the most rightest of rain showers? Can you not see that all you thought was good and wholesome and healthy is exactly the opposite of this because what you once thought should be is something that will never be again? Because I *want* it that way.

"And you wonder why it's all taking place now. Now this fine fine hour of our discontent. All that matters is your self identification...doesn't matter if it's a garden snake. Oh how I love them so. You're not even human anymore. You...you children, you are not boys or girls, you're snakes and lizards and bats, and I authorize you to behave as such, and there is nothing you can do about it, and the sadness only lies within you, for you little ones are nothing but the lies that come from your fathers' sacks!

"Yet you ask these silly questions 'why' but cannot see that I am inside every one of you. That I have been from the beginning. That your souls and bodies are mine. And how can *you* miss such things, cop?" The woman screamed directly at Marion. "*Detective* that you are and not see my possession of them to their genetic cores where I have their double helixes all to myself?"

Her voice hit him like a cannon blast, pummeling Marion to the floor. He braced himself to jump back up, but he felt her power command him to stay seated on the floor for the remainder of the show. That's all he could do as she continued, no matter how much he struggled to resist.

"What I say is true and just in a world where you still believe there is some hint of hope of truth and justice. But I am the one who drives all personal happiness right from the womb, and you cannot see that?

"But wait. The womb? Why the womb? Why not the ass? Why not the rectum itself where the tightness and strength of inner tissue better creates the growth of the *New*

Child? Want to see? Want to see? Do you all want to see?" she bellowed while turning toward the entire audience again, effortlessly commanding the auditorium. The audience roared in applause and cheers, and they had grown in number to where half the auditorium was filled with demon children mixed in with teenagers and the elderly so old they looked petrified.

Marion could hear the haunting cries of rape and murder sung by a chorus howling in the distance with Mick Jagger's voice complimenting it with stretched vocal cords.

"My dear children," she continued while turning to Exit Stage Left, raising her ivory hand and arm to point with a taloned index finger. "How can I deny you? Bring out He that we shall all see, whose birth of all that has ever been and all that you will ever see to come forth in a burst of violent and malignant purity! Bring out the freaks, for we are all freaks! Let all that was supposed to happen from the beginning of time come forth in a glorious spray of finality!"

The audience roared again in approval, standing and chanting and screaming for her to continue. A demonic mob scene where all rules of civilized peoples were destroyed.

Marion turned to where she was pointing to see a group of eight warlocks and witches all dressed in medical garb—deep purple uniforms with matching hoods and masks—roll out to the stage a full set of Operation Theater (OT) equipment with a grotesquely and obscenely bloated man strapped down on a birthing bed. Surgical headlamps, EKG machine, ultrasound machine, full anesthesia machine setup, pulse oximeter, back instrument table, oxygen table—all connected with hundreds of knurled wires that danced around the machines like some frantic massive spider with a thousand legs whose bowels had just exploded, trying to put them all back together again.

The demon woman walked in front of the entire

apparatus and directed her medical thugs to savagely open the man's legs. She turned to the audience of what had filled to every seat in the house of ravaging demons from infants to the ancient, all standing forward in frightful fascination.

Marion continued his struggle to stand again, wondering where and when and how so many had arrived.

She hissed at them to remain silent.

She directed the primary surgeon—or at least what Marion thought to be the leader of the medical abhorrence—to put the scalpel into the man's ass and hideously bloated gut, fileting him open as if he were a giant pregnant salmon.

"I am your god!" she bellowed again as the man screamed in an anguish Marion had never heard in all the years of the worst he'd seen in the police field. "I am your all-seeking online digital master of all that ever was! Open the beast up and let the final birth begin!" She raised both her arms high into the air, shouting in what sounded like a plea, for whatever reason.

The lead surgeon continued to cut the man across his awful belly right through to his neck and into his chin, then raised up the scalpel as the entire body split wide open. An explosion of thousands of brightly lit fluorescent insects that were fused with human eyeballs and tiny limbs burst out of the gutted man into a mushroom cloud of such a ghastly creation nothing in Marion's dreamscape could comprehend what had happened other than an instant spark of gratitude that he was still—hopefully—locked in the dreamscape and alive, for if it were reality he was witnessing, he knew that no one would ever survive. In any world.

However, the demon woman had not finished. Her lecture had not ended nor her presentation of the rapture of gore. With her arms remaining hung into the air as if in preparation to single handedly carry the weight of everything that had ever happened, or ever were to happen again in the endless space and time, she cast her eyes about to the audience. What came from her lavender eyes were thousands of pinpoint lasers that shot from her corneas in a single burst that looked like perfectly incised spider webs designed to strike directly into the eyes of every demonic attendee. The audience was struck dumb in a perpetual trance of worship.

The woman lowered her arms to her sides, palms upward, as the mushroom cloud of human-insect-limbed creatures that had burst from the gutted man began to swirl in harmony around her. A swirl that turned more into a sashay dance as every single creature buzzed in horrible unison to the woman's absolute control.

As suddenly as her eyes had turned into the dreadful laser-induced hypnosis, she blinked rapidly a few times and focused on Marion as she walked to the edge of the stage, the swarm of gore following her every move.

"This is going in one direction that I have commanded. It is now so." The medical team of witchery walked over to her, four on each side of her, and fell to their knees in a chant that seemed to compliment the awful buzzing of the swarm.

"What do you think I am, detective? *Who* do you think I am? Look upon me now to see my endless changes!" The demon woman then arched her head completely back so that her neck stretched so tightly Marion could see her blue veins pumping with vibrancy. She opened her mouth and howled the cry of a hundred tortured wolves, snapped back her head to face her wild-eyed servant audience as her eyes turned to massive yellow cue balls, her legs turned to elephant trunks, her breasts grew into bloodied troll heads whose mouths replaced her nipples. Her head split evenly into two pieces, then to four, then to eight, then to sixteen different heads with binary equations branded into their foreheads. Every angle she had, every POV facet, every flourishing woman's touch no matter how seductive or alluring it was when she first walked on stage, was instantly extinguished as she turned into what Marion knew was the Biblical Whore of Babylon.

In yet another burst of violent implosion that instantly shifted to exploded fragments of different flesh variants of the woman-beast, in a scene that flashed as if being filmed in reverse order and back again, the entire atomic landscape came morphing together back into her original appearance. She stood only a few feet in front of Marion.

She had changed her dress to a fitted transparent black silk bodysuit, barefooted to display snakeskin covered toenails, her body bent forward with hands and arms beside her sculpted core as if ready to spring upward from a diving board. Her face was gorgeously painted to brilliantly highlight her endless lavender eyes, yet also crimped at every edge of her porcelain skin that displayed a rage Marion thought even eclipsed what he'd just seen on stage. Even the violent horror that had been gutted from the pregnant man and the swarm of infestation that had surrounded her in joyous insanity was now superseded by a new rage. Her scarlet painted lips were opened wide and deep to show off a set of razor teeth that were far beyond human, as every other goddamn thing that had happened.

Hundreds of teeth that looked like perfectly sharpened ivory knives to compliment a mouth so hungry and ravaging with fury Marion knew that her scream would surely end whatever life he had left, regardless of what awful place some careless God had tossed him back into as he awakened from his coma sleep. The roar that came from the demon whore seemed to come from the depths of every betrayed and ruined soul that had begged for their revenge for a thousand lifetimes.

It was the sound of eternal damnation, a sonic boom that blasted Marion into another realm. The massive auditorium spun away from him as if the entire Stonehenge classroom building had been lifted from its foundation and swirled into what looked like a doughy saucer that equaled the mass of the auditorium itself.

It was another hellscape that quickly morphed into a glamorous burlesque restaurant where all the inside walls were spherical with transparent track lighting running up and down the walls in wild, frenetic paths that looked like spiny plastic stitches to keep the walls from coming apart. Had it not been for the dimly lit blood-red bulbs that were numbered in the tens of thousands, maybe the walls would have come apart.

The ceiling of the restaurant had at first appearance an imitation of the Sistine Chapel, but as Marion was able to inspect it thoroughly in the dreamscape, instead of the countless figures painted by Michelangelo—all the world's key players (Adam, God, Jonah, Jeremiah, Daniel, Isaiah)—were hundreds of human figures scored as a single cohesive orgy. The faces on all the figures looked possessed and starved.

In the middle of the restaurant's immeasurable floor sat a single twelve-foot table set for two. Chairs were a deep cherry wood, the table covered in black satin drapery. Two candles sat on the ends of the table that were easily six feet high with small torch flames spewing white smoke that lashed about like shredded pieces of cotton candy. In the middle of the table was a solid gold serving platter nine feet in circumference. Placed directly in the center of the grand dish was a massive bulb of flesh, twice the size of a human brain. A horrible tumor of a growth that looked like it had been cut from the side of an animal perhaps the size of a horse, or a rhino. The gore of the abscess shimmered in repulsive movement that Marion instantly knew it had to be some kind of infestation that his mind couldn't, or wouldn't, consider.

The same woman, Terra Drake, who had led the demon classroom and directed the horror cesarean birth was seated and waiting for him to take the seat across from her. Which he did in that awful hovering movement so familiar in nightmares. She wasn't dressed in the leather and ball-gag getup, but she was the same woman his brother had desperately tried to tell him about. That same woman who'd taken his brother for the wicked wicked ride into the never never land of his addiction.

And that's exactly where the fuck I am right now, dead in the middle of his insanity, and I have no idea when it's ever going to end or how I'll ever get out of here, wondering how long she will keep showing me the torment she'd inflicted on my brother.

Now she wore a roman silver dress made from heavy silk with deep cleavage. Her hands were painted in black acrylic, so deep and rich Marion couldn't tell where her fingers ended and nails began. Her black lacquer hair was wrapped tightly in an Egyptian bun. She was barefoot again, this time with toenails long and savage and painted in deep scarlet.

Maybe they're not toenails. Maybe they're claws.

"Who are you?" he asked, ignoring the thought, but completely transfixed as well as mortified. He noticed she held a stunning dinner knife in one hand, fork in the other. Before he could ask if she was about to dig into the hideous dish of tumored brain-flesh she spoke in a voice that was pure velvet.

"My name is Lilith," she said, just as transfixed, but so far from curious, Marion instantly realized she knew everything about him.

"That's not your name."

"Oh, but it is." She slumped back in her chair, taunting him with a sinister grin.

Glenn Campbell began singing in the background far too loudly, whereas two freakish ghouls appeared at either end of the giant table, wearing blowtorch goggles and moving in unison to "Country Roads" where the sound of

Terra's Sabbath

Campbell's voice was a scream in Marion's head. Ghouls whose mouths were plugged with long tubular hoses that were attached to creatures that sat at their feet—cradled at their feet was more like it—creatures that were not quite octopuses, not quite squid, not quite moray eels, but a grotesque fusion of the three that glowed the same deep lavender as the woman's eyes who sat at the table, looking at him as if the entire scene of repugnance was one of perfect order and harmony.

With each breath the ghouls took in from the hoses, each creature's sickly wet stomach would depress and indent with such dramatization Marion was certain the ghouls were draining the creatures' final moments of their own private hell.

"Pay attention when I speak," the woman who called herself Lilith whispered, as she slid lower down her chair and farther away from the table to where he could see her figure was just as explicit as he'd seen her in front of the classroom. She was lying, Marion knew. And though she whispered, her voice cut deep through the incessant blasts of Campbell's voice.

Thank God.

"Your name is Terra Drake," he whispered back. "My brother told me so."

"Pay attention. My name has been Lilith since the birth of time. At least the birth of time as you've known it." She was moving her sculpted legs back and forth, knees together, side to side while continuing to slump in the chair. Her beauty was such a contrast to the nauseating scene that surrounded him, he almost disregarded its barbarity.

Almost.

"You were just in front of that classroom hall lecturing to whatever the fuck it had become and cutting out some...some terrible, monstrous fuck of a mess from a man who I'm sure was just as monstrous, though I have no idea what—"

"Please, please, do shut up. You will shut your lips or I'll have them stitched for eternity. I *am* Lilith, and I swear to the ends of this insanity that you will still your tongue or I'll rip it from your throat and suck on it like a meat stick. Do you follow me?" She hissed while jolting forward in her chair with catlike agility. More than catlike; phantom to be exact.

Marion felt shaken enough that he wondered if Lilith's hissing scream would send him back to whatever reality he had once known, in a time that seemed long forgotten. He looked back and forth to the ghouls attached by hoses to the fused sea creatures, then back to Lilith, whose glowing lavender eyes seemed designed as a complete distraction. His brain began to pulsate in a rhythm that perfectly matched his heartbeat, his two life organs thumping in such unison he couldn't tell which one was which, but hoping that both could hold out just a bit longer.

"Maybe it's witchcraft you seek," she continued. "Witches and warlocks and ghastly priests of the night who'll give you those answers your mind so bleeds to know in despair. The howling of the graves that come biting through the ancient coffins that scream eternal hate. The Wolf's hate. The Viper's hate, and oh I know his hate so intimately deep, deep as his blood when it comes gushing inside of me after he's had me. I know him as my lover, my dear, he's been my eternal lover...for I am still his lover to this day. Since Adam kicked me from his bed—"

"What are you talking about?"

"*My* story. By the flesh of *your* god, I'll tell you the story of *my* god. I was Adam's first wife, not that silver little slut in the Genesis pages. Me." Lilith leaned forward in her chair, both her forearms now resting heavy on her knees, her legs open and braced as if she was about to lunge from the chair and rip out Marion's throat. "But I demanded sexual equivalence. I demanded to control desire. You can read about it. I know your doubts. The

Jews have a record. Some Muslims for that matter. But never mind that now.

"So...I left The Garden, but not for good. No, no. No one ever wants to leave The Garden for good. Just for enough time to track down the Viper and make the deal for all mankind. The deal that would seal all deals. As well as bed him for eternity.

"He wasn't easy to find. His anger was even greater than mine against Adam. You see, his anger had just been fueled by God, his father, rejecting his plan that would surely save us all. Humanity, that is. He was called the son of the morning. Did you know that, because I think you have some kind of idea what I'm talking about. You know the story, don't you? God choosing the other son's plan. Ha! Such self-righteous dribble! Nothing more than a fairytale, or a fairy's tale, that is. I told the Viper this when I found him playing a harp just outside The Garden in the middle of a damp and endless pasture of misery. That's right. Such places existed then, believe it.

"I told him to quit his bitching and whining and to join me hand-in-hand to go back to The Garden, that if he really wanted to get Father God back in spades, then I had just the thing. I knew Adam was just as filled with righteous indignation as the Chosen One, but that Adam's witless twit, his second bride, would be easy to convince so clueless she was of the whole affair of good and evil.

"The Viper hissed in glee when he heard my strategy, so off we entered back into Eden to taunt Adam's woman into betraying humanity for the rest of time. And she did. Oh she did it easily. It didn't take nearly the clever intake as scripture would portray—"

"I've heard enough!" Marion stood from his chair, shoving back from the table in defiance. Both ghouls looked to him, hoses still in their mouths, but their shoulders twitched as if something had burrowed deep under their skin.

Lilith slumped back into her chair in complete comfort and seduction. She looked up to Marion and stared at him. Her stare created a silence that felt so long that, for a moment, he'd forgotten he'd fallen into the perpetual ordeal that began in the classroom with the woman dressed in the ball-gag getup.

"Tssk, tssk, tssk," she taunted. "Sit back down, Marion. We haven't made our deal yet. I'm sitting here telling you all the glorious details of the deal I made with the Viper in The Garden, and you've not listened to a vowel or a syllable. Sit down."

"I'm not sitting in front of that for one more second." He pointed to the platter of gore.

"Fine." She stood and walked around the table to Marion's left, then gave a nod of authority to the hose-breathing ghouls, an okay for them to feast on the massive living growth on the platter. Then she reached for Marion's hand. "Let's take a walk."

"I'm good. I'll walk with you, but I'm not holding your hand."

"Says ye of so little faith."

As they walked a few steps away from the dinner table, Marion knew he could hear the ghouls begin to eat, but dared not look back.

"Don't worry about them, Marion. You've got a lot more to worry about right here with me."

"You don't think I realize that?"

"Sure I do. That's why I'm here with you. Take a look around, Marion. Where do you think you are?"

He saw that everything that was part of the spacious restaurant had swirled and shapeshifted into what became a spacious hallway with no ceilings. Just an endless hallway into a night sky that Marion had never dreamed possible, even though he was able to convince himself he wasn't going insane. It was his cop instincts—even in such a world—that had figured out he was somewhere between life and death, which had to have been meant as a warning as the two of them walked down the hallway that had no end that he could see.

"You want to know what happened to your brother. At least that's what you're going to want to know, and that's why I'm here. I want you to think long and hard about the lecture I gave those children when this all started. Consider every word I screamed at them. Why were they demons? Why were the ancient demons in the back of the auditorium the same as the children? Why the abhorrent cesarean, Marion?"

"I'm a detective and normally good at solving riddles, but this one escapes me, as does your motive for this shitshow."

"The world as you know it has documented evidence of alien metals and aircrafts that have speeds and abilities that far surpass anything on earth. And if it is alien...that it *is* alien, shouldn't concern you, because to the aliens there is no concern. It's because the science schools of the world have now chosen to teach your children, Marion, that they are no longer man or woman or even a *thing*. It is the science of alien life that will merge with the new science of earth life. And your god approved it by giving you free will. Ha! Free to do what? Free to choose to deny the alien life that now controls them—and you—and you don't even see it!"

"Now I know you're fucking crazy."

"That was my lecture to the demons, my dear. Nothing to do with the violent birth and transformation. Those children in the hall already knew it. That's why they're demons. *That* lecture was for *you*, you silly silly dear."

Marion stopped and placed his hand, palm out, toward Lilith to stop her from talking. "Just who the *fuck* do you think you are?" He kept his anger controlled. "No wonder my brother drowned himself in the drink."

All she did in response was take a step back from him in her endless seduction and hissed, "Is that what you think? Ask the witches. You'll find many answers, but I think you'll know who to believe though you won't like what you hear. If you ever wake up, that is."

"Are you talking about the innocent girl on the Sacrificial Altar?"

"It was her blood that saved you, Marion."

"And my brother?"

"Nothing could save him."

Marion's temper seethed, knowing he'd failed to save the child. He pulled back his right hand and braced his body to strike at her with all his power and ability but found himself paralyzed to do anything more than remain in an electrified and frozen state so filled with terror and revolt he believed he would certainly die that very moment. He pushed deep within himself for every bit of mental strength he had ever leaned on when he was stuck in the trenches of the most frightening and dangerous moments of police violence. And when that didn't help unfreeze him, he swore vengeance so heavy in its despair that his eyes fluttered, and he saw the vitals machine lights cast disturbing shadows on the walls, and frantic beeping echoed through his hospital room.

Terror would rob him of sleep, as his mind reeled with visions of aliens teaching Earth's children alternative science, alternative facts, and that the transformation had already begun, changing benevolent innocence to malevolence, cruelty, hatred, and malice. Terra Drake, aka Lilith, had to be stopped.

Yes, Marion Paul had truly awakened after four months in a coma that Terra Drake had sent him into, just before she ventured off to kill his brother, for which she would dearly pay.

Chapter Two:

Walking the Halls of Odessa Hospital

Marion bolted up in his hospital bed and moved around it with such discomfort and irritation that he briefly forgot about the horrible dreams of he and his brother in the demons' lair that was housing the event of a child sacrifice. He'd forgotten about the insanity of the classroom lecture hall in the modern-day replica of Stonehenge, the cesarean birth of thousands of severed human limbs fused with weird insect bodies; the grotesque dinner arrangement with the two ghouls and a gold platter that highlighted a ten-pound abscess that shimmered horrifically. All those visions he'd put on hold for a second or two as he tried to manage the sudden shift to a new reality. The real world and whether or not he'd taken the red pill or the blue one.

How did I get here? When did I get here? Where in Christ is my brother?

He continued pushing the thoughts aside, knowing that he had to get his shit together far more quickly than he wanted, for what he wanted was to lay back down and go right back to sleep yet again.

No, no, no, no, no, been asleep way too long, that's for fuck sure.

His entire being from foot arch to brain stem felt like it had been clogged with years of Ambien being pumped through his system. But instead of slumping down on his backside, he forced his mind to sharpen right off the cuff as he'd had done so many times in the field when facing life or death, and that's exactly how he felt.

Oddly, he thought back to a time when he was young and looking at an old cartoon church book. Back to the only time when he was ever tempted to get a bottle of whiskey and take a long deep pull. It was the cartoon of a young man dressed in all the familiar church attire: white shirt, polished shoes, blue tie. His hair was parted perfectly on the side. The next panel showed the same young man with his tie loosened a bit, his sleeves rolled up, his hair ruffled. The next panel showed him with his tie undone as if he were coming off a ten-hour shift from the office. Unshaven. Hair messy. Then in the next panel, said young man wore a stained white tank-top, hair unwashed for days, a week-long beard, and a cigarette dangled from his lips. The last panel showed what was once a proper young man turned completely unhinged.

God what am I thinking? Is that the story of my fucking life?

Marion shook his head and slapped his face a few times hard enough to cause a brief scream. He then looked at his arm and immediately knew that he could pull out the I-V needle and remove the wire leads from his chest that were keeping track of his vitals without much damage. He'd been asleep long enough...*coma, no question about it*...and escaped death, so pulling the shit out wasn't going to cause more harm than hadn't already been done. He looked at the whiteboard on the wall at the foot of the bed, hoping to see who was on duty, both technician-wise as well as the doctor's name. He knew the drill of every hospital in Houston, so wherever the hell he was now, procedures certainly wouldn't be much different.

"Let's see, let's see, room 2429...Doctor Pinault, and a Janet Stone, *On Duty.*

"Okay team, I sure hope the hell you're around in case I accidentally pull my own plug."

He rubbed his arms to ease a sudden nervous itch, then yanked the I-V needle out, put pressure on the wound, then ripped the wire leads from his chest, pulling hairs as the sticky pads tore free. The vitals machine flat-lined and emitted a solid tone. "Shit." He wondered how long it would take for the medical staff to rush in and throw him back into bed. Gently, he put his feet on the floor and eased to a standing position while checking his balance and the strength in his atrophied leg muscles. He could already tell he was a lot thinner than he'd been in quite some time, and worse, he was naked.

He looked around the hospital room for any type of clothing or covering lying around, even though he was willing to venture out into the hallway and escape the hospital, buck naked if that's what it took. In the closet, he located a hospital gown.

This will do just fine.

The room itself seemed off, tilted a bit. He'd noticed it the moment he got out of bed and began to walk around, taking each step with such a gingerly nature to make sure he had enough strength to put full weight on his feet. The fragility he felt enhanced the feelings of unease that seemed to permeate the room. A presence that was unsettling and thick, as if something evil had come in for a visit long ago and seeped deep into the walls, only to suddenly awaken as he had from his coma, a presence that didn't suffer the clog of the mind he was trying to clear, but something that had awakened with irritation and ugliness.

Whatever he was sensing compounded as he noticed the room had an odor that wasn't the typical sterile sickly smell that pervaded every hospital room he'd ever visited, and he'd seen plenty during his career. This was an odor of subtle decay that had lingered for ages, locked into the drywall since it was first hung. There was also a subtle over-cleansed aroma someone used to mask the nastiness underneath. The large window to his room was so caked with smears and dust that the view the window showcased was blurred out as if someone had turned on the *blur background effect* in a Photoshop project. He knew the glass was filthy when he'd first awakened, but what he saw sickened him. The blur-effect was literally feces and dead flies swirled together in the dust like some child's morbid fingerpainting.

The bulky television that sat on a wall shelf was so outdated Marion thought it was for decoration only, or for long-term patients who'd never need a remote, or a TV for that matter. The sink area was rusted and cracked. The floor tiles were yellowed and brittle; the visitors' sofa and chairs were dingy and faded.

Christ. Nothing in here's been maintained for decades.

The whole room had the appearance of being left behind from some long-forgotten era.

The door was left cracked open, so rather than try to call for anyone from the bedside phone, he opened the door completely to peer down the hallway to the nurses' station, hoping the coast was clear.

Second floor, second floor. Keep it together. Jesus.

He was extremely conscious of the gown that left his ass hanging out as it covered his groin, of all things.

Covered just fine, thank you very much.

There was no one in sight. No nurses. No janitor. No technicians. Computer screens all around the stations were alive and vivid with various animated screen-savers used decades ago. Long hallways stretched to each side of him, which most likely led around the hospital floor similar to a hundred others he'd seen on the many occasions he'd visited criminals who'd ended up handcuffed to gurneys to be stitched up or detoxed or having bullets removed from whatever the fuck violence had gone down that hadn't killed them. Hospital first, then county jail. He knew the routine all too well.

It was this familiarity that led him to venture out into the dimly lit hallway, regardless of his vulnerability and lack of proper clothing.

At first, he shuffled, stiff-legged, to the nurses' or techs' station that was right out front of his room. He wanted a quick peek at the computers and paperwork so he could possibly find more information about the hospital and staff other than the two names written on the whiteboard in his room. Anything would do: scribbled notes, hospital business cards, even a wayward cell phone, but even though he saw plenty of notes, and open notebooks and sticky pads galore nothing was of any help, and he found the abandonment of the station far too creepy to hang there for long, so he quickly decided to roam around the floor to find someone who could tell him where he was, what hospital, what town.

First things first. I'll check inside some of the rooms.

He walked down the hallway. Peeped inside every room that was open. Most were pitch dark with the exception of some with flickering tech lights from the vitals machines. He saw only a few patients out cold, the other rooms were empty until he came to Room 2411, where he saw an elderly woman sitting up on her bed, rocking her entire body side to side, so much so that he had to stop and watch to make sure she wasn't going to tip over. Had that happened, she would have ended up on the floor as her body sat so close to the edge she would have tumbled off. It was a wonder she hadn't fallen already and landed square on her tailbone, which would have surely busted it to peanut brittle pieces on the unforgiving floor.

Looking at her more closely, he saw that she was a tall woman, once a real beauty, in fact. Back and forth she rocked like an ancient puppet being maneuvered in precise, effortless tilts. The sharp pin lights from the vitals machines were just effective enough to give her an even more disturbing look than she already had with her slow, obscene tilting.

"Christ, lady, how long you been up?" Marion whispered as he stepped a foot or so into her room. He was alarmed at the sound of his voice, as if he hadn't heard it in ages.

"What was that?" the ragged woman asked. "You say something?"

Marion wanted to back away and keep moving at the moment he was caught snooping, but he didn't have the heart to ignore her. "Didn't mean to disturb you. You looked like you were about to fall over, and I was going to give you a hand. Not to fall over, that is. Sorry, I'll be on my way."

"No, no. Not so quick to scurry on. Come sit by me. Come, come. I won't bite. Well...maybe just a nibble. I've not seen or spoken to anyone other than hospital care in a long time." The woman spoke clearly with a shattered, trembling whisper that he couldn't ignore.

"Listen, I'm sorry. Really. I was just walking around—"

"Don't be silly. Please, come in and sit. I won't stoop to beg, and I sure know you'd not want me to."

She's got a point, but what the hell do I say?

"Did you hear me?" she persisted. Almost hissing.

"Yes, of course." He entered deeper into Room 2411.

The woman stopped her rocking and patted the bed area right next to her, indicating where she wanted him to sit.

Marion agreed to visit her, but had his limits. "I'll just sit over here in the visitor's chair, if it's fine with you."

"Well, well. That is perfectly fine." Her voice was so suddenly filled with glee that Marion bent over and leaned in closer to see if there was something more wrong with her than all the hell that had put her there in the first place.

No one's come by to see her since the cows came home, who the fuck knows when that happened.

Marion backed into the visitor's seat, never taking his eyes off her.

"Don't get too comfortable. As long as I love what you have to say, you're welcome, but you can't stay long, sunny boy. She'll be making rounds soon enough, and if anything's not in order...well...we don't need that, is all I'm saying."

"*Who* will come around to make sure things are in order? What do you mean?" Marion's cop instinct for elder-abuse was as instant as it was alarming.

"Never you mind that. Why don't you tell me a story?"

"You just said I can't stay long, right? No stories. Not now, anyway. Not before you tell me what you meant and who you are afraid of."

"Ha!" the woman screeched.

"Shhhh! Not so loud. Just whisper. What did you mean just then?"

The woman licked her charred lips with a tongue that was just as bad. Marion could tell she was on the verge of losing her teeth but wondered why, since that kind of thing in the hospital could only mean she'd been severely neglected.

She and every other goddamn thing in this place. I'll find out what the fu—

"The doctor on call tonight," she said. "Don't know what kind of medicine she practices. Not medicine at all, if you ask me. Then again, witch doctors don't practice medicine, am I right? Not real medicine."

"Well, *I'm* asking about it. I'm asking about everything you've said."

The trodden woman looked at Marion with sudden emotion tearing in her eyes as if she knew he was being as genuine as anyone she'd seen in decades. Family included.

"She's a reckless one, that one is. Reckless with these broken souls. Can't be reckless with a broken soul. No good can come out of it. You look like you know all about that kind of thing. And let me say I know about such things, young man. I know about the darkness of a man's heart. Or a woman's in this case. It's always a woman who holds the real power, am I right?"

He looked at her and knew what she said came from someone who had experienced and suffered a life gone quite bad. "What's your name? If we're going to sit here and talk about it, we may as well know each other's names."

"This is true. I'm Alice Parker. Well, I used to be, anyway. Goldman now. Alice Goldman, but...also Alice Parker. I've been married, you see. A few times. Neither of mine made it. Ex-husbands that is. Both of them had a real time of it, if that makes sense. First ex seems too long ago to remember if it was real or not. My second, well...he had a hell-on-wheels woman come over one day and do a real number on him. Maybe you've heard about all this, you look like a smart one. Hard one, too, yes? You a hard case, mister...?"

"Paul. Marion Paul." He tilted his head in recognition of her story, though he couldn't pinpoint exactly where he may have heard it. "I'm sorry I don't know anything about your exes. But I've been away for a bit."

Need to Google the shit out of all this, that's for sure.

"Paul you say?"

Christ. She knows my brother.

"Yeah. Listen...Alice. How long have you been in here? Never mind that. Sorry, that's not what I wanted to ask. I want to go back to what you said about the night shift doc on duty."

"Tsk, tsk, tsk. Why do you care, Mister Paul? Of course you don't. But I can't say more on it. Feels like I need to lie back down again. All this talk has gotten me deeply tired. Wait! Wait a minute...Marion Paul? You happen to know of a Steven Paul?"

"I do, actually. I'm his younger brother. And I do care about what you said. Anyway, how do you know Steve?"

"The last time I saw him I was at a fair of some kind. I was helping with a booth. A terrible booth, to be honest. When he came by, he wasn't right, wasn't right at all."

"No, I'm sure he wasn't, Alice. He was drunk most always."

"I liked your brother, though I didn't know him all that well. But I can't forget the last time I saw him. Are you looking for him?"

"I will be. I've been in this hospital a long time, but as soon as I get out, that's the plan. I'm not even sure if he's alive."

"Oh, that's a shame, that *is* a shame. I hope you do find him. At the very least find out what was going on with him, because something was terribly wrong. I think I need to lay back down."

"That's the best thing for you, Alice," came a striking but cutting voice from Alice's doorway. Harsh and throaty, it was one of no compromise. "Stop all this carrying on, lay back now and get some sleep."

He looked to his side to see who had to be Dr. Pinault standing in the doorway with eyes even more striking than her voice, focused on Alice so fiercely Marion looked back and forth between them several times, wondering how Alice would respond regardless of how tired she felt.

"Yes, Dr. Pinault." Alice scurried under her covers.

Before the doctor could say another word, Marion cut in, a skill he had honed to perfection with twenty years on the force. "Hey. I was talking to her."

"You have no business in here."

"I was walking down the hall, and her door was open, and she's the only one I could actually meet and talk to. I've been out for quite some time, and I really don't appreciate—"

"I know that, Mister Paul, I wasn't talking to you, nor

do I care what you do and don't appreciate."

Who the fuck does she think she's talking to?

"How do you know my name?" Marion felt the flush of embarrassment for having asked the obvious as soon as he'd said it, and he wondered why he hadn't spoken his mind instead.

"Who else would you be? I know every patient on this floor."

Marion started to see immediately what Alice had meant about the doctor. "You're right, and I'm sure you do. But I wasn't trying to break any hospital rules. Just looking for some needed company and conversation."

"Is that right?" she snapped back.

"Yeah, that's exactly right. She's got nothing to do with me being here. Not like she invited me." Marion tipped his head in Alice's direction.

"I'll be the judge of that," the doctor snapped again. "Miss Parker, you get some rest. That's what you need. I don't want to come by here again and see you sitting up in bed, rocking on your ass. And you, Mister Paul, if you need so much human attention all of a sudden, come with me and take a walk. You're not like Miss Parker. You don't need any more rest."

"I think she goes by Goldman now, not Parker," Marion said with authority. He stood from the visitor's chair to go with the doctor, but walked to Alice's bed first. "You take care now, Alice. Okay? I appreciate you talking to me tonight. I will make sure we talk again, rest assured of that."

Dr. Pinault cut them both off quick. "That's enough wordsmithing to Alice In Wonderland, Mister Paul. Let's be on our way."

"I'm not so sure she's the one in Wonderland, doc."

"Let's walk down to your room and go over what was left behind and a few other housekeeping items, shall we, Mister Paul? Let me fill you in on as much as I can. My, my, you must still be so groggy. Like you're still in a deep trench coat fog, yes?"

"I'm not the sharpest tool right now, that's for sure, but sharp enough." He gave the doctor his sharpest eye possible under the circumstances. "First off, my brother. Steve. I was with him before I landed here. Do you know where he is?"

"Yes, about him...he was found dead a few months ago at The Odessa Hotel. I'm sorry to be so abrupt, but no reason to skip around it. I don't have all the details, but I know that's your area, investigations, and I'm sure you'll learn all you want soon enough."

The bad news didn't hit him in the stomach as hard as he'd expected. He and Steve hadn't been close in so many years he couldn't remember when they were. Still, he was his only brother. And what they'd faced together that knocked him into a coma, and most likely was a contributing culprit in the killing of his brother, was as real as any shit Marion had ever seen. And she was right in that he could easily get as many details as he wanted from the local police. They'd certainly know all about what happened to Steven Paul.

It was also better she'd told him the truth right off. He was still far too thick upstairs to begin to feel any weight of his brother's death.

That would come later.

"Okay then...did he leave anything for me? Do you happen to know that much?"

"I told you we're going to walk down to your room and go over some housekeeping items. That's certainly one of them, Mister Paul. Shall we?"

"Sure. That's fine. But let me say this. I'm not Alice, or like any other goddamn patient here. You don't mean a thing to me, and I'd just as soon put you on your pompous ass than listen to you try and give me one more moment of strongarming. I just got out of a coma, and you tell me my brother's dead after pulling me out of Alice's room, who, by the way, didn't deserve how you cut her off. I'm not one you can bully, lady, is that clear?"

Better to show as much force as possible no matter how fucked up I feel.

Dr. Pinault turned her head a bit too far toward her shoulder, making her look like she had no idea what he was talking about. Then she yawned as if what he had said was not only boring, but completely harmless and without any meaning, and then she dismissed him by walking slowly back to his room. He followed her and took heed to leave Alice be.

"For now, Alice. For now, but I'll be back around soon, make no fucking mistake about it."

The doctor was a solid five foot nine, with alluring red hair, full lips, throaty voice, with a swimsuit model figure.

"You know, doctor, come to think of it, I'm in no mood to go back to the room where I've been asleep for four months."

Dr. Pinault stopped and turned around in dance-like grace as if she were mimicking a ballerina. "There's no line in the sand anymore. Have you noticed that? No lines are drawn up. No boundaries exist...with anyone really. But not with you. I can see that. You are one of those few who immediately draws a line. How refreshing, too, I might add."

"What are you talking about, lady? Lines in the sand? What does that even mean? I said I don't want to go back to my room, and you start in on lines—"

"Because you're a cop. That's why I say what I say."

"You don't know me from the jolly damn green—"

"You hush your mouth now. Never you mind a bit, Mister Paul. Just conversations in a dead hospital."

"Lady—"

"Shhh. I said hush now, and I mean it. You need not get so upset so soon after such a bad bad sleep from a bad

bad fall. Or blast in your case. Isn't that what happened? You're just trying to figure out what's normal and what's not. I know you're thinking about...well, just about everything. But what's considered normal now is nothing like it was just a few seasons ago. Evil is perfectly accepted now, but you've not seen that yet, or have you, officer?"

"I'm a cop, lady. Like you said, I've seen shit that's been accepted as normal for years."

"Not this kind of normal. Not this kind of witchery. And the witches shall rule, my dear police lover officer. When a child is faced with warlocks and demons and thugs in the classroom, their tiny tiny minds go into pure confusion and fear, but that's now normal. It's demanded to be normal. But I'm sure you were always too busy to notice such things. Oh. Wait. You're defunded and de-validated. The acceleration of evil is designed to never stop. You know that, don't you, Mister Paul? Did you know just the other day a cop in Thailand massacred some fifty children just because he was in a bad mood and found them to be in his way? Perfectly normal, wouldn't you say? Almost no news coverage. Funny, it really is. Kids were no older than three."

"Why don't we just cut the shit. Okay? Why don't you tell me just what the *fuck* you're talking about?"

"You silly silly boy," the doctor said in complete dismissal and boredom. "You know a Burke Macey? Professional fighter. Owns a local boxing and martial arts gym?"

Silly silly boy is what I heard in my coma, I'm certain of it, but not from her.

"I'm having a real hard time following you, doc, that's for sure." He certainly remembered Burke. His brother trained with him for years in boxing and jiu-jitsu. One year when Marion had come up for a visit, his brother had even paid Burke to give him a one-on-one lesson. It was one of the best gifts Marion had ever received, and one of the best self-defense classes he'd ever attended.

The guy is one of the deadliest fighters I've ever seen.

"Yeah, I know him. Good friend of my brother's. What does he have to do with *anything*?"

"Not a good enough friend though, right? Never mind that piece. Mister Macey brought over your brother's laptop a few months ago. Said your brother said it was important that you have it before you have anything else. Before anyone around here thought about trying to hack into it...eh! Mister Burke called back a few days after he dropped it off and said that if you were to ever awaken, or *when* you did...his words...that the logins for it were in a letter your brother was going to leave. The letter's here, by the way, in case you're about to ask."

"That still has nothing to do with whatever the hell it was you were talking about."

"Sure it does. Perspective. History. Everything's interlaced and intermingled."

Marion looked at her, dumbfounded.

"Still too foggy for any clarity? Not to worry, and we won't go back to your room just yet. Let's walk out into the larger areas, get a little freshy freshy."

"I'm still in this gown and don't feel too open to leave the floor. And can't you speak normal? What's wrong with you?"

"You're covered up enough, and you've been just fine talking to me in your 'gown' as well as with *how* I've been talking."

With that, Marion followed the doctor into one of the waiting areas, took a seat on one of the vinyl sofas, as the doctor sat in another one across from him. She crossed her legs seductively while pulling up her skirt high enough to completely distract him. She'd even unbuttoned her medical blouse a few buttons down to show off perfect cleavage. She wore a fine silver necklace and a strange pendant depicting an even stranger and deformed figure that looked like it was moving on its own.

She knows what she's doing in the distraction department. I'll give her points for that. Wouldn't matter what she's wearing, even that weird pendant.

"Now, about that letter. Mister Macey said it would be something you'd need to look over before getting into the laptop. More secrets I suppose. He said to not worry that he'd read it or not, because he didn't, but just wanted to have us be specific about it."

Marion shook his head a bit, trying not to stare at the doctor's flawless legs or imagine what she was wearing under her medical garb.

Witchcraft, Alice said, maybe this is all part of it, this doctor putting on some kind of weird show.

He let out a deep breath that he'd not realized he'd held in. "You wanted to bring me out here to talk about this letter? Is that it? You couldn't just tell me you had it and then given it to me, wherever it is?"

"Mister Marion Paul, don't you want to know more about Alice? Because I think you do. I think you have a very keen interest in our Alice in Wonderland. Don't you?"

That was enough to pull Marian away from his brief sexual fantasy. He knew he had to entertain the good doctor and keep things going for more intel, regardless of his foggy mind. "Sure, doc. If you want to tell me more about Alice, that's fine. She's certainly lonely enough to have someone care to say something more, even if it's you. She doesn't care for you, as you must know. But I know all the rules, okay? Doctor patient confidentiality. The works."

"Yes you do, smarty smarty, of course you do. And I'll not be breaking any of those protocol pieces. I thought this may be good information to know purely on legal terms, you being legal and all."

Marion thought it best to play this out.

Chapter Three:

Alice's Past According to Dr. Pinault

D r. Pinault, in full sexuality, let out a deep breath of her own, and one that Marion could smell. It was a sweet, thick aroma, but also one that was masking something sickly just as he'd smelled in his room. She licked her lips slowly and tapped her long nails on the faux pa wood arm of the sofa. "Our dear Alice in Wonderland was an abused woman. Savagely so," she began, taking in another deep breath and letting it out just as seductively.

Marion was all ears. In fact, he had all his senses ready, on full cop alert, and he was grateful for the years of training he'd mastered.

"It's an abuse that's been lifelong. Has been lifelong on both accounts of her exes. It's a tale that began long long ago when our dear Alice was first married to a beast of a man. A very beast of burden you might say. You know The Stones' song?"

Irritated, Marion nodded and twirled his index finger at her, a signal for the doctor to carry on.

"Of course you do. Anyway, this beast Alice was with was someone far greater than what Alice ever imagined. Because of his greatness, he expected much. Far too much more than Alice could give. She didn't have what was needed, what he craved, so he did what all men do. He went to someone who could quench his every need and desire. Someone who could match...even outmatch, you might say, the insatiable and unbridled release that our

Alice could never fathom.

"So Alice did only what *she* could do. She began to dabble in wasted time. Doing nothing but worry and panic and worry and panic when a buildup of such tension began to create within her pure hysteria. A constant paranoia. This disgusted her temporary lover. But make no never mind about that, as he found the whore he wanted and knew so deeply. Yes he did. But he still expected Alice to do her duties. So she'd abide him as he took her whenever he felt the need for extra. He would take her from behind, take her to the left, take her when she least expected it. All men do such things, right, Mister Paul?"

Marion stared at Dr. Pinault for what felt like a full minute, trying to follow her story, but he had far too many questions right out the gate. "I've known my share of turds, that's for certain. And before I met up with my brother and went through whatever the hell it was that happened, my last few years being a cop, well, let's just say I found myself having no faith or trust in humanity. I'm not arguing your point. Who is this pig?"

"A pig?! How clever. He's the Lord of Pigs, you might say. And even more."

"The Lord of Pigs?"

"May I continue?"

"You're the one who stopped and asked me questions."

"Touché, Mister Paul. You're so black and white. I'm not so sure that's going to be your best way forward."

"Why don't we just carry on with the Pig Lord story?"

Again, Dr. Pinault took in and let out a deep breath, recrossing her legs at the knees. "He's much more than that is what I was saying. And Alice couldn't keep her end of the bargain. So off she went into the deep dark passions where so many of those like her went, to delve into the bellies and trenches of black magic. Such a pity when her man has been the maker of such blackness since the dawn of your God's vision."

"My God's vision? What is that supposed to mean?"

She leaned closer to Marion, licking her lips again. The color in her eyes died as her stare turned to an unmoving and unflinching set of black saucers. Marion felt pinned to his chair. He'd seen plenty of all the ugly the doctor was spewing, but what he felt from her as she leaned in with dead eyes was what he'd felt while in the coma and sitting across from the demon woman who called herself Lilith while two ghouls sucked down through their hoses on their mutated sea creatures. Yet he was awake, and what hit him from the doctor was no dream.

What ever the fuck this is, I've gotta keep it together.

"What are you on, lady?" he whispered with as much strength as he could muster.

The doctor sat back as her eyes changed once again with deep amber-colored wire bands wrapped around the black pupils, creating a disturbing solar eclipse effect. Marion was never one to lose his cool easily or show a trace of weakness when he knew an opponent would seize upon it. Especially not fear, regardless of how scary a situation became, and he'd known plenty. He knew then and there that the woman or doctor or whatever she was had something within her that did far more than just dig into his skin. He was rattled and wanted the discussion to end and would have said so, but he thought he heard music in the distance as he struggled to keep his emotions together, pushing his internal mettle more than he'd expected. Maybe it wasn't music. Maybe it was the sound of animals being tortured, being strangled, mixed in with a million pots banging against each other. Farther away...much farther away maybe, the cries of anguished souls pleaded for mercy.

What am I hearing? Sure as shit's not make-believe. Maybe this is just a continuation of the goddamn coma.

"I'm not on anything other than what life's given me,"

she continued, her voice more throaty, more controlled. "Time for you to let me finish my tale. I don't care about your past, or who you are, or what you've seen or done. I'm sure, right here and now, that you know you've met your match. And things are just beginning."

Marion nodded in silence.

"Back to our Alice, Mister Paul." She leaned back deeper into the lobby sofa, letting her medical garb skirt move even farther up, knowing exactly what she was doing to keep the tension at a level where Marion continued his internal struggle.

"As I suggested, at first she had no idea who she was with. So, she kept at her wasted time of spells and potions and learning all the tricks that she could, in secret, and with the others, of soothsaying and ancient priest-crafts. Tsk, tsk, tsk, when all along she was getting plucked by the master of all these disguises.

"One night while she was hollering and chanting with the other ladies who found themselves in similar fates, inside an ancient church, her lover burst into the chapel, as he'd been looking for her. He was ravaging for release, but with him was his demon whore, the insatiable one. The savage couple burst into the chapel fully naked. Fully aroused, frothing at their mouths, their bodies sweating blood and stink. Alice and her coven couldn't bear such a sight. And our Alice? She knew she'd lost her lover forever.

"But it was worse than that, Mister Paul. Things can always get worse, am I right? What Alice hadn't known, nor any of her coven pride, was that her lover and his demon whore had been planting seeds of evidence in the minds of all the townsfolk leadership so they could congregate and decide that they'd get what they deserved. Everything needed to create an emergency that the town had to address, to create the hunger of a staunch, wound-up small world, all the reason they'd need for a mass execution. To root out evil with evil.

"That's Alice's history. Salem, Mister Paul."

"I see. That's quite a story. Just who the *fuck* are you?" Marion whispered again.

"Maybe I'm the Grand Inquisitor. You know that tale?"

It was like she'd suddenly given Marion permission to be relieved of the awful pinning he'd been fighting. Permission for the dread that was overcoming him to leave the foyer and go back to his room and stand in the corner. Excused from class. He let out such a sigh that the first thing he feared, and the last thing he wanted, was for the nutcase doctor to see fear all over his face or the weight it had carried sitting on his shoulders. And his shoulders were powerful.

"I remember it. Back in college. Dostoyevsky."

"Ah, pay no attention to that Russian pest. What I'm talking about far exceeds the *'great author.'* I'd never dream of taking any credit from my own master."

"At least he wrote about it, and he...wait, *your* own master?"

"A minor chapter, and never mind. What I'm talking about sits right here in front of you in a seduction you've never known. But I'm in no league with the demon whore."

"I really don't know what the hell you're talking about, lady. You're telling me Alice is somehow related to what happened at the Salem Witch Trials, is that what you're ranting about? Are you crazy, is that your problem? I get it. Insanity and rambling about nonsense is nothing more than part of what I do for a living."

"Maybe so. But I had you strapped in. And I'm not quite finished. Alice's second ex, of course, was no match for her first. You'll know that soon enough. But her second go-round was enough to cause her to forget her past. And by god the demon whore would have none of that. This one you can Google all your want, officer. One strange day she and your brother's neighbor came driving by in her hell-on-wheels red mustang. They pull right up to Alice's home, and give Alice's husband a good ole fashioned talking to. One of those kinds that Mister Grady told Jack Torrance about in The Overlook Hotel's ballroom restroom. When Grady told Jack that family members sometimes need 'correcting.'" Dr. Pinault said it in the perfect imitation of the rolling r's Grady used as Nicholson's Jack Torrance listened in fascination and horror of the butchering of The Shining Twins.

"I may remember my brother saying something about it. Don't recall anything related to 'The Shining.' But I'm done with this conversation, lady. I really am." Marion was rather impressed with himself that he found the strength to resist her. Or maybe it was just another moment when she allowed it.

"Did he tell you how Alice's second husband was beaten to a saucy pulp? Did he give you all the juicy details?"

"I told you I'm done here."

With that, Dr. Pinault stood and took a few steps toward Marion where she was almost standing directly in front of him, forcing him to look up at her. She placed both hands on her hips and leaned over far enough to where her face was about a foot from his. "So you say, Mister Paul, so you say. I'm glad you think you're done. You'll find the letter in the bottom drawer in your room below where the television sits. Just remember what we talked about tonight. Remember it good and well before you start playing night watchman to Alice in Wonderland. I'm sure we'll see each other again. Small towns and all."

She didn't walk back into the patient room area, but down one of the long corridors toward one of the exits to another section of the hospital. Marion watched her until she was gone before he stood and went back to his room.

He avoided Alice's room all together.

Chapter Four:

A Brother's Letter

My dear brother Marion,

Just to ease your mind a little, I couldn't come by to see you. As many times as I wanted to, that is, before I knew I'd either drink myself to death or that Terra Drake would kill me. But I wanted to see you.

As soon as we were blown out of the building where Terra had said she was staying...whatever had happened there that put us in the hospital, yes, I ended up leaving you there. We were placed in the same room right after it happened. As soon as I awakened, I had to leave, and I knew that you'd be okay regardless of the circumstances. I had gotten you into this shit and the first thing I needed to do was to get you out of it some way, somehow. For whatever reason, I think you'll have an idea of what I mean by the time you read this.

It was about a week later, maybe two, when I called about you and was told that you were in a deep coma. No idea when or if you'd come out of it. That's what they said. I didn't even bother calling your ex-wife because the moment I was on the phone with one of the head nurses they told me your ex had already been told everything and that she'd make sure you'd be taken care of regardless of the outcome. There were a few of your long-time friends from the force who also found out, and of course I knew you had the best insurance through HPD.

So I stopped worrying about it because I had bigger issues. As selfish as that sounds, I did. And I can tell you now, Marion, that if you do come out of your deep sleep, you can rest assured I am dead and gone. I was dying anyway, as you probably saw when I first came to visit you in Houston. Maybe that's why you came all the way up to Snow Crest to find me that awful night we found Terra and one of her she-thugs about to sacrifice that girl. I hope to Christ you find out something about her. Who is she? Why was she such an obsession with Terra?

Enough of the opening formalities.

Let me start with this: I'm leaving you all that I have. I have left the keys to my truck and home with the hospital, and they assured me they'd be safe in their keeping and that they'd hand them over to you when you came to. If you came to. Asked my friend, Burke Macey, to leave my laptop with you—you may remember him. I needed that to be with you right off. You'll see plenty of notes and links that I put together as evidence, and that will make sense to you, this I know. Username is SPaul2938, Password is the same. I pray to God you come out of this, because you have to. You have to come out of it, Marion, because you're the only person in this godforsaken world who can find out all there is to know about Terra Drake. You have what it takes to find out what is going on around here. And it's not just the small town of Duncan, although that is where, for whatever reason, everything about this demon woman seems to come into play with everything she does.

Everything she will do.

Check shit out, Marion. I have no doubt all your cop wisdom will see exactly what I mean, and what I was trying to warn you about. Things are not right. Look close enough and you'll see things wrong around every goddamn corner.

Terra's not all, Marion. Whatever it is that you do, remember when you awaken to never forget what came at us, and what put you in the hospital in the first place. That monstrous beast is no joke, and he's not some fucking fantasy. None of this is from the never-never land. None of it. As drunken as I am now writing this, I'm hopefully clear enough in my words that you will not dismiss me. Course I wouldn't blame you. God knows I'd lost credibility enough times.

Now, I'm sure you're asking, "why this letter?" Simple enough. I'll not be alive for more than another week. Maybe less. And in that time, I'll make one last push to find Terra, and she'll either kill me because she has no more use for me, or my body will give way to all I have put it through. Maybe a combination of both.

Find her, Marion. Find everything out. Check out everything in Duncan. Take close watch of everyone you see. Whatever witchery you'll find, it's of the most awful kind. Find the priest I was seeing. That little art shop just down from the house. You'll have to look deeper, but that's your specialty, and you don't have the demon drink to cloud you. Please remember all that we had talked about when I came to Houston. Should even check out the Downtown Hyatt where I used to stay every other month when I'd fly down and do the medical writing for the Orthopedic Center. There was some strange shit going down there that I am sure is interconnected with Duncan.

I love you, brother. I know I failed you in so many ways, but that doesn't take away our life as brothers. I've also left you what's in the safe in the house. Combination is my birthday.

Farewell and Godspeed,

Steve

Chapter Five:

Janet Stone

Marion put the letter back into the envelope and held it in his hands gently as he could see the level of pain his brother was in when writing it. He knew all the hospital protocols of getting his belongings. A set of clothes he'd had on when admitted, wallet, cell phone. He retrieved it all quickly enough from the nurse on duty, Janet Stone. He also knew that a representative from the Houston Police Department would have retrieved his gun long ago while he was still slumbering in coma land, so he was either going to buy one quickly in Utah as it would take less than a hour to do so in the state with laws much like Texas, or fly back and get his own. Better yet, he hoped that his brother had left a gun or two lying around. He hadn't decided yet. He hadn't decided on anything other than he awakened from the insanity he faced in the coma, to the insanity he just witnessed with the good doctor.

And Alice, something tells me I'll need Alice.

Because it was still in the middle of the night, he was out of the Odessa Hospital more quickly than he'd ever dreamt of getting out of any Houston hospital in the city's overwhelming Medical Center, a place the size of most U.S. cities, including Utah's capital. It hadn't taken long to find Janet, to have all checkouts done quickly and efficiently. He was relieved there was no sign of Dr. Pinault.

Terra's Sabbath

"Will there be anything else, Mister Paul?" Janet said as he shuffled about getting himself together as best he could.

"Yeah, Janet. I almost forgot my brother's laptop. It's supposed to be here, as well. At least that's what the doctor told me. That a friend had brought it some time ago."

"Let me get that for you. I would have forgotten it myself," she jeered.

Marion thought it was an odd and inappropriate tone. *Probably just way too much coffee.*

She came back a few minutes later with a laptop bag that Marion recognized from when Steve had come to visit him.

"Here you go, Mister Paul. Is there anything else I can do for you? Anything at all?" She handed over the laptop and leaned in closer to Marion, suddenly striking him much the same way Dr. Pinault had. She wore a familiar silver pendant that dangled just above cleavage that was every bit as desirable as the good doctor's.

Is it a requirement around here to look like a porn star? Christ.

"There is. I'm guessing it's too late to find an Uber or Lyft in these parts, so does the hospital have a shuttle service? Or what?"

"Well let's see...hmmm. It will be tough getting a ride, you're right, but if you'll give me just a few minutes, I could run you somewhere. Where is it you were thinking?"

"I don't know, to be honest, as you can appreciate."

"Head still clogged up?" Janet giggled one of those seductive giggles a woman used when she knew her looks were hypnotic enough to instantly distract.

Maybe it's a lot more than just coffee she's hitting.

"Well...you sure that's a good idea, Janet, to just leave your station?"

"You don't see anything going on around here, do you? Hospital this time of night is fairly self sufficient.

Dean Patrick

This isn't the big city, Marion. We do things a little more comfortably around here. And convenient. Besides, it's the least I can do...*we* can do, the hospital and all, for what you've gone through. I'm sure Doctor Pinault told you about your brother and all, which was a shame to be sure. Anyway, it helps with our Yelp reviews. If you'd ever like to leave one that is." She giggled again.

"I see. And what about Doctor Pinault?"

"She's gone for now. She'll certainly make no fuss. I'll make sure someone's notified. You don't have to worry, Mister Paul, Alice will be fine. Alice and all the others."

"What do you mean by that?"

"Mister Paul, do you want me to give you a ride or not?"

Don't be stupid. She's just trying to help. Looks like I'm gonna have to keep playing shit out, no other way around it.

"You know what, Janet? Why not? You're right. It's not been the best evening. Shit can't get any stranger than it's already been. Jesus."

"Don't be so sure about that," Janet retorted in a teasing manner as she leaned away from Marion and began toying with the familiar pendant on her necklace. Janet was an inch or two shorter than the doctor, a few years younger, and every bit as striking.

There's not a goddamn thing I'm sure about at this point.

"Whatever you say, Janet. I guess I won't worry about protocol."

"No need...no need at all to worry your little head. We know what we're doing around here, Big City. You can meet me down in the main floor lobby. I'll be out front in one of our vans. Can't miss me."

"I doubt anyone could ever miss you."

Not more than ten minutes later, Marion saw the van

Janet was talking about pull right up front where she said she would. He took a look around the hospital surroundings, took note that it was just past 3 a.m. and that he was feeling far more exhausted than he'd thought possible after being asleep for four months. He exited through the automatic sliding doors of the hospital entrance, walked around the shuttle van, and hopped in, now noticing just how attractive she was as she turned to him, cocked her head, and winked.

"So...where to, Mister Paul?"

"I hadn't thought about it. Especially after Pinault hit me with all the news."

"She's a trip, right? I'm sure she told you quite a bit. When you arrived here, when you and your brother were found and both were brought here, you'd both been found up in Snow Crest City. Lucky you both weren't dead at that time, or you'd never be sitting here with me. Funny how shit works, isn't it? But I'm well aware they found your dead brother at the Odessa Hotel, so I doubt you'd want to go back there just yet. Or maybe you do?"

"My dead brother? Don't you mean that's where my brother was found dead?"

"I know it's been a hard night, no reason to clog it more with semantics."

No, no, no. Dead brother has an entirely different meaning than finding my brother dead—

"All I was saying is that particular hotel is probably not the best place to take you. Only thinking of your feelings, okay?" Janet recovered from her abrasion by lowering her head and leaning closer to Marion in an obvious advance.

"Yeah, no, you're right. Look, I'm a bit on edge. Thanks for your concern. I know there's a few cheap hotels around the same area, but I don't want to stay in some shithole."

"What's so complicated?"

Marion looked at her and wondered how much he needed to tell her, as she seemed to have known quite a bit about him. She'd been nice enough, and not as dangerous or weird as Dr. Pinault. *At least not yet.* He needed to get up to Duncan to check out all that his brother said he'd left him, according to the letter.

"You know, Mister Paul, if it's Duncan you really need to get to, I could take you up there. Not a big deal. No reason to stay in a hotel if it's only for a little rest before you need a rental or whatever. I need to make a quick stop at my place first, but I don't mind. Really."

"You're reading my mind or something. How'd you know I needed to get to Duncan?"

"Well, your brother's place...it was all over the news when he was found at The Odessa. Everything about him, and you. Not hard to put two and two together. But it's more than that. You have to know that, right? I mean everyone who's been watching over you this whole time has gotten to know everything about you. Some of us more than others. We all want to help. I mean, I looked up everything about you, hope that doesn't bother you. Big city cop and all is quite fascinating. I mean, we get a lot of cops from Odessa and even a few from our own big city lights, but nothing like a Houston big timer. You've seen quite the world, Mister Paul."

"Alright. I get it. Let's just get going then. You said you needed to stop by your place, and I'm tired. If you really want to take me up to Duncan, we can talk all you want, but can we do it while driving, please?"

"Sure we can, officer."

With that, Janet Stone pulled the van out of the drop-off and pick-up area, turned onto the main street from the hospital drive. Marion instantly remembered all the surroundings of Odessa. He'd been here plenty of times to see some of his extended family years ago, and of course the trip up to see his brother before the bottoms of hell seemed to fall out and were somehow still falling.

When she drove past The Odessa Hotel, Marion almost made her stop but decided against it, as she was speeding right along Odessa's main street called Washington. All the main streets in Odessa were named after presidents, and all ran parallel to each other. Impossible town to get lost in, but for Marion even more so, as the town wasn't even the size of most neighborhoods in Houston that he'd battled in as a hard-case cop.

Some fifteen blocks past The Odessa, Janet turned down 4th Street and into an area of town that was a shithole within the shithole of Odessa itself. "This oughta be a lot of fun," he said under his breath as they passed by house after house that were far more like shack after shack.

"What was that, officer?" Janet turned to him. She hadn't said a peep the entire drive, and her voice sounded striking and vibrant in the silence of the deep early morning.

"Are we close?"

"Right there. House with the red door. Cute, right?"

"Adorable."

Janet pulled into a driveway that Marion could see, in the headlights, was broken to the point of being destroyed. She pulled under a cheap aluminum carport held in place by two-by-fours that looked too fragile to support themselves, much less the aluminum roof. The house itself looked condemned. It was far too dark to see what the yard looked like.

Christ. What kind of place is this?

Marion said nothing as Janet shut off the engine and turned toward him again. "It doesn't look like much from the outside, I know. But it's mine, and inside's a lot more pleasant. At least I think so. Come in with me. I won't be long, and you can have a drink, or...whatever."

Marion followed Janet to the front door, which was indeed painted a deep acrylic red. The moment he entered, he felt a chill creep around him and slip beneath his skin. He couldn't tell exactly what was so unnerving, but the living room area was a start.

Painted completely in different shades of scarlet, the walls and ceiling gave the room an instant feeling of being compressed and restricted, even though the room wasn't nearly as small as how he'd perceived the house from outside. In fact, it didn't seem possible to be so large. Thick, plush carpet covered the floor so loosely Marion could see various ripples and crimps throughout. To Marion's right side sat an old couch, faux pa leather, cracked and oily; to his left was a cheap particle board entertainment center that had every shelf filled with paperbacks, magazines, and papers that were stuffed in and around the books. On the left side of the top shelf leaned a large portrait of a woman with jet black hair, porcelain skin, and dark hollow eyes. On the right side sat a bizarre and morbid sculpture of a skinny figure with a big hooded head and twisted limbs that Marion recognized from the pendant Dr. Pinault and Janet wore. One large domed light in the middle of the ceiling glowed in a faint amber hue.

The smell of the room was thick with incense, but of no scent Marion had ever remembered. A kitchen area was connected to the living room, painted entirely lime green. It was dimly lit in such a way that created shadows that were deep and long enough to cover the paint in various areas. On the cheap backing of the kitchen cabinets that faced the living room was the stuffed head of what looked like a wolf or large jackal. Its mouth was obscenely wide open displaying a set of razor teeth that were decayed and broken. A ragged, black tongue hung from the side of its mouth like an overaged strip of thick jerky. The obscene display of taxidermy caused Marion to grimace, but to also stare in disbelief.

What in the fuck have I just walked into?

From his peripheral, Marion could see a long hallway

that led to what looked like at least two bedrooms. One of the bedrooms was visible enough to see Janet's bed and bookcase.

"Have a seat. I'm going to change and then we can be on our way. Or...feel free to see what's in the fridge. Can't remember what's in there, to be honest. I eat out a lot, but I'm sure there's something in there to eat...if you're starved enough. I'm sure you're ravaged with hunger, right?"

Marion looked away from the canine head and turned to Janet. "I'm not hungry."

I'm not sure how anyone could have an appetite in this place, but I've got to keep my shit together because it could be slipping.

"But thanks anyway."

"Suit yourself, but the offer is open if you change your mind."

"Who's that?" Marion asked, nodding toward the macabre portrait of the dark-eyed woman.

"That's my mother. Stunning isn't she? So alluring. Such a wicked temptress."

"I see. You don't look much like her. And that sculpture? Guess you'll tell me that's your father?"

"Ha! That's very very funny. You are so *so* funny. Funny that you said that. Exactly something you'd say. Such the clever one, you are."

Janet finished her comment as if she'd been cut off. She looked dead center at the space between Marion's eyebrows, avoiding direct eye contact all together in that disturbing way so many do in intense conversations. She had a smirk that looked carved into her face. Marion suddenly wished he'd had a gun with him. He had always favored a Colt .45, a heavy handgun that fired so smoothly it always felt like it had been something attached to his hand at birth. He'd even settle for one of his automatic knives. He felt completely vulnerable even though he outweighed Janet by at least a hundred pounds, and was certainly triple her strength. Or was he? Marion had been blessed with alarming strength, and he was professionally trained in years of martial arts and boxing. He'd been a star athlete in both basketball and baseball, and even towered over the woman some six inches, yet at that moment, even if he'd had a weapon, he began to feel more and more like he was in a bad spot, and throughout his career he knew the feeling all too well.

Don't be stupid. Get your shit together. It's the coma still lingering.

"Yeah, well...a sense of humor's important, right?"

"Go. Seat yourself. The couch is quite comfortable." She commanded it rather than suggested it, turned from Marion and walked down the hallway to her bedroom. He shuffled to the worn sofa and sat, looked down the hallway to her bedroom to see she had switched on a single lamp that was so brilliant it cast deep colors as well as long shadows, giving off an effect of a kaleidoscope that swallowed the hallway and everything around her.

Her body was superimposed on the colorful array in her room. She made no effort to close her door, just left it wide open then pulled down her standard med skirt and dropped it at her ankles, slipped out of her nurse's shoes, toe-to-heal, toe-to-heel, and pulled her blouse over her head, revealing bikini panties, perfect breasts, and no bra.

The outline of her body enveloped by the darkness of her room and hallway was hypnotic. But rather than give into the feeling of wanting to stare at Janet's bewitching figure, he immediately stood up and went into the low glow of the lime green kitchen. He began to feel as if he was in the middle of the Genesis scene when Potiphar's wife went after Joseph, but feared that the sexuality being displayed in Janet's house was far more dangerous.

Christ. How am I getting out of this one?

He attempted to open the fridge as she had said he could. It was a rusted, metallic fridge that looked more like an old ice box used on fishing trawlers. Even had a metal lever that was locked in position. He pulled on it a few times and knew he'd have to use quite a bit of strength to get it open. The hinges creaked, and a black light winked on...a black light of all things, and what lay on the wire-mesh shelves were bags and bags of...worms, twenty-lb. bags or heavier. The worms were enormous, the size of small snakes. The purple casting from the black-light lit each one—of what must have been a thousand or more—which created a terrifying sight of whatever horrid shit Janet was into.

Jesus fucking Christ. What kind of diet is she on?

"The door tends to stick sometimes, but I see you got it open."

Marion jolted up and turned to see Janet facing the kitchen as if she'd just appeared out of thin air. Her carved smirk still in place, she had put on a long-sleeve button-down shirt, open enough to where Marion could easily see half of her nipples and then some, all the way down her body. He forced himself to make eye contact as well as to not shift about nervously. He turned from her and slammed the fridge door shut with his right leg, then turned completely toward her.

"Yeah. Need to get that fixed. What the fuck is with the worms?"

"Hush now. Not your concern. We're all different in our own ways, right? I'll be ready in just a sec, anyway. Why don't you go back to the couch and settle down? Looks like you really need to just relax."

Marion walked by her as his heart began skipping way too many beats. His breath was rushed, yet he managed to conceal it as much as possible. As he walked across the thick carpet, he thought he saw movement in some of the bunches and crimps and wondered if it was the worms he'd just seen in the nightmare fridge. When he turned to sit down again, Janet was right there in front of him, looking down at him, her sexuality breathtaking, but her presence was more disturbing in a completely opposite direction and feeling.

"Do you know who Percy Shelley is?" she asked. "Or was? Husband to Mary Shelley. The Frankenstein Lady?"

Marion let out a deep breath. "I read her book, not much on him, though. Why?" He asked the question to remain focused, as this conversation was sure to become more and more disturbing. Janet's advances were what any man would ever want, but what was belying the sexuality was something darker than he'd experienced. Everything else was hitting him between his skipping heart beats besides just the worms: the portrait of her "mother," the freakish sculpture of some being he thought was inhuman, the head of the jackal-wolf and its opened mouth and leathery tongue, and the incense growing in strength with no incense candles anywhere in sight. Janet's beauty also grew to an intensity that Marion knew was an anomaly to the point where he wished for his gun again, thinking a knife would never do the trick. Music had also been turned on from Janet's' bedroom, now playing something heavy, but he couldn't tell what it was other than some kind of instrumental house tech number.

"What's the scariest thing that's ever happened to you, Mister Paul?" She put her hands on her hips, opening her shirt more as her hips slowly moved from side to side.

What's going on right now has gotta be right up there with bizarre.

Marion let out another deep breath. "Don't know if I have seen just one scariest thing." He instantly knew his voice had to move beyond a forced whisper to have the best chance of getting things to move along and get him to Duncan.

"Percy Shelley once said religion and morality compose a practical code of misery and servitude...the genius of human happiness must tear every leaf from the accursed book of God so that man can know his own true heart...that morality must look at herself in the mirror to see her own disgusting image to figure shit out. Something like that. And when I first read that...well, it was my mother who read it to me, I think *that* was one of the scariest times I'd ever had. But those kinds of moments can also be exhilarating, right, officer? Like what's happening right now?" She continued moving her hips.

Stand up to her, goddamn it!

Marion did as his brain screamed, and stood up so he could look down at her and perhaps turn things around a bit.

Gotta play this out. That's the best plan.

"I'm flattered, Janet, no question. But I'm also exhausted. If you can't give me a ride like you offered, not a problem. I'll find my own way. I'm pretty resourceful."

Janet backed up a few steps, making sure her full sexuality was on continued display, hands on hips, her shirt open completely. She had not a single flaw. She was also clearly irritated, and that was the part that scared Marion most. "Just giving you options to consider. I promise I'll be ready in two shakes to a lamb's tail." She said this in a perfect imitation of Uma Thurman's same line to John Travolta in the Jack Rabbit Slims scene from *Pulp Fiction*.

Janet turned back to her room, the sense of dread that he was feeling mixed with the high heat suddenly simmered to something else Marion couldn't understand or recognize. But at least his focus was returning.

Nice work. Let's just get the fuck out of here.

As quick as she said she'd be, Janet was back in the living room dressed with the long sleeve shirt still halfway unbuttoned, but now in liquid tight jeans and white tennis shoes, her hair ratted on top of her head.

How the hell did she pull that off so quickly?

"Let's go. I know you're spent."

Marion said nothing as he followed Janet out the door

and back to the shuttle van. He paused before opening the passenger door, looking back at Janet's red door, then back to Janet—who was already behind the wheel and ready to drive—then he opened the van door and climbed in.

Janet slammed the van in reverse, causing it to shoot out of her broken driveway, then slammed it in Drive, pinning Marion against the back of his seat. He thought to complain about her driving, but didn't say a word as she careened onto the canyon highway toward Duncan.

Last thing I want is for this crazy bitch to drive us off one of the fucking switchbacks and down a cliff.

She was still agitated, maybe a bit more.

Just before they entered the tight canyon curves, Marion decided to try a smooth-over. "Listen, Janet. I know everyone's into their own thing. You know? I get it. I've seen it all, and whatever your thing is, it's your thing. But you have to realize all the crazy shit the doctor was talking about just after I'd met Alice. Who also, by the way, seemed way off. Then I read a letter from my brother that he'd left, which told me about more weird shit, then hearing about his death—"

"Hey! I get it," Janet hissed, looking dead ahead into the black morning, mountains from the East Canyons coming up on them faster than Marion wanted. "A lot's been piled on. It's a lot to take in, I get it. But don't pansy out on me, not after all I'd learned about you while you were in your comatose state. And yes, that, too. Coming out of a coma and all. Plays tricks with the noggin. I do get it, and my place was just one more rattle on the snake, I'm sure."

Marion looked over at her, keeping his peripheral laser sharp. "Yeah. It's been a lot in such a short time. I came out of everything just before midnight and the sun will be up soon enough, and I feel like I lost another year in my life."

"Ha! I've had plenty of those kinds of nights! But

wow have you got discipline. You didn't even want to fuck me. Never seen that before."

Marion swallowed hard and let out yet another deep breath. "It wasn't that, Janet. Had you kept on you'd have probably put me back in the hospital. I'm just trying to figure out a lot of shit in way too short a time."

"Keep talking. I'll just listen. Helps me focus in this canyon, especially in the dark."

"Yeah. Driven it myself plenty of times when visiting family. Well, not plenty, but I know it can be a tough drive." Marion decided it was best to do exactly what she said and just start talking even though chit chat was something he'd never liked or wanted as it had always seemed like a waste of time. Yet it was chit chat that he thought would keep him the most safe while Janet raced up the canyon switchbacks.

"Truth is I'm not sure what to think of my brother and what happened before I was knocked into another world. That's the best way I can describe it to you. I mean, yeah, something terrible had happened that knocked me into a coma, is what I mean. And I thank God we were found and I ended up in the hospital and not dead. He was in some kind of awful panic about things going on around here, to the point he'd even taken a trip down to Houston to talk about it all, only I didn't see completely how bad off he was. Then I ended up flying up here to see him again and met him up at Snow Crest City. That's another story.

"So, when I read his letter, he told me...reiterated to me what he had been telling me late last year when he'd come down to Houston. He was a mess. My brother was a fierce alcoholic, but he'd managed to stay sober some nine years or so before he'd clearly relapsed and was in the middle of something that was killing him. *Did* kill him. At least it was part of what killed him, but what he talked about in his letter was the exact thing he'd come to see me about. That he'd met some wild fucking possessed woman who was tormenting him. Tormenting everything and everyone around her is what he said, not just him. Probably the last thing you want to hear about, but that's what's been hitting me since the moment I put my feet down on the hospital floor."

"No, no, no. It's fine. Keep talking. Get it out. Sounds *fascinating*."

The way she said fascinating caused Marion to pause.

I don't know what's so goddamn fascinating about it, but then again she has bags of giant worms in her fridge...

"Tell me more about the letter, more about his visit. I mean, there was a lotta shit on the news about you two, but you can't ever know much from the news these days."

"Okay. He came down to see me because he was getting an MRI, of all things. He was worried something serious was going on. He was a professional writer, my brother, Steve, and one of the clients he'd written for was a surgeon in Houston. Is a surgeon, that is. One of the best. So my brother called this doctor and asked for a favor to get an MRI done by someone the doctor knew because he trusted him, you know? But when I saw Steve, he looked like he'd been emotionally tortured, and it was at the MRI clinic where I came to get him. Took him back to my place. He ended up leaving, flying back. Here, not even saying goodbye. You probably know the rest of the story if you had read about it all."

Janet looked straight ahead completely focused on the canyon roads. "Not completely. Not everything. What happened next?"

"I flew up here to find him, like I said. We ended up hiking a trail in Snow Crest City and into this woman's freakshow of a house when we were ambushed by..."

"By what?"

"I don't know. Can't remember a lot of it. I remember having my gun out...then something horrible came at us, and that's it. Next thing I know I'm waking up in the hospital then dealing with Doctor Pinault and you, and here we are."

"Yeah. Here we are, officer. Almost there and I'm suddenly tired, too."

"I'm sure you are."

"So tell me about the letter. Still have a little more time before I drop you off."

"It wasn't like something he'd normally write."

"How's that?"

"It was troubling. Paranoid. Scared...like he was scared for even me and how I'd feel once I read it. He really urged me to find out about this woman. About the town."

"Then maybe you should, Big City. I mean, that's your plan, right? Find out everything that happened to your brother and hunt down this big bad wolf and bring it to justice?"

Marion looked over to Janet again, then back to the road. They didn't speak further until Janet took the Duncan exit and turned down one of the main streets, State Street, that led to Steve's address.

"You take a right by the rock church just ahead. Just a mile down to the left, past the creek. At least that's what folks around here have always called that church if I remember."

"I know the church, trust me. What was the woman's name, the one who fucked up your brother so bad?" Janet asked as she turned by the church that was indeed designed and built with large slabs of granite up and down the sides of the building, giving it a unique look in an area where there was a church on nearly every corner, and every one of them looked like replicas.

"Terra. Her name is Terra Drake."

"Really?" she said, turning her head to him for the first time since they left her place, with a cocksure grin across her face.

Dean Patrick

"You know her?"

"Ha! Oh I know her. You've got your work cut out. Are we close?"

"Just up there to the left," Marion said as they crossed the bridge over the creek. "See the silver truck out front? Weird seeing it abandoned there."

"Not anymore it's not. Looks like a dandy!" Janet drove a few yards past the truck then did a U-turn, pulled beside the truck to drop Marion off so she could take off straight away. "Out you go, it's been fun, Mister Paul."

"You know her," he said as he stepped out, but he didn't shut the door. "Who is she?"

The passenger window rolled down, signaling Marion to go ahead and shut the door. "Come closer."

He leaned to the open window.

"Yeah. I know her. She's...sort of a mother figure. Catch my drift?"

"No. Not really. What's that supposed to mean?"

"Gotta run, Mister Paul. Thanks for the chit chat."

"Yeah. Thanks for bringing me up here."

"Pleasure's mine. Really."

Her voice changed again to the hiss she had before they left, except her tone turned back to the seduction she'd assaulted him with back at her place. She kept looking at Marion as she rolled up the automatic passenger-side window. She smiled, licked her lips, then her face, with a long slithery tongue that was split at the end in two even strips. Janet then flicked and lashed the snake tongue at Marion as she spun the van away into the final moments of the fading dark.

Marion Paul stood in shock while watching the van until it disappeared from his sight.

Who the fuck are you, lady?

He had no idea what he had awakened to, no idea what he'd just seen, no idea what in God's name was going on since he stepped foot from his coma bed. He felt a sudden relief to be alive, and knew that it was all connected. Somehow. Some way. That Steve's letter was perhaps *the* connection to it all, and that what his brother had gone through was something Marion was going to figure out.

All of it, brother. I'm going to find out every goddamn thing there is, whatever it is.

He headed toward the front door to Steve's house.

Guess it's my place now.

Chapter Six:

Marion Takes Over Steve's Place

The sun was going to come up soon enough, and Marion hoped that would in itself shed some light on at least his mental state. But no matter how exhausted he felt or how tired he told Janet he was, sleep could wait. He knew that the minute he had stepped foot in Janet's living room, knew that when he finally reached Duncan that he was going to start digging into his brother's death.

His plans were to fire up Steve's laptop, look around the property, start the Ram truck to warm up the engine, open the safe...all of it, but not in that order. It was time to be a hard-case cop again.

Pronto. Slept enough, I've slept enough.

His inner cop radar was on high alert to whatever fuckery that was afoot as he unlocked the door and set down the few things he'd brought from the hospital, plus the computer bag. As soon as he turned on the lights, he walked around the living room to give the place a quick once over, then following the letter's instructions, discovered just exactly what Steve had left to him. He remembered the layout of the house from years ago when visiting. Steve was still married to Anna, the one woman Steve had been with who Marion found to be more than just a gem.

"But you fucked that up too, didn't you, brother?"

It was a three-bedroom home with fifteen-foot high

ceilings that made the place feel much larger than its 1,200 square feet. One room was the master bedroom, one for a study, and another where the safe was located and a massive bookshelf. In fact, the entire house was lined with bookshelves and hundreds of books that Steve had collected over the years. The house sat on an acre of land with a barn that sat in the middle of a corral that was surrounded by a solid oak wood fence, painted chocolate brown. Marion loved the place the moment he stepped foot into the spacious but quaint area that made his own place in Houston seem like an endless hammering of noise pollution.

He walked into the master bedroom first and instantly noticed it had a scent that was most certainly a perfume from someone who had to have been in the room not too long ago. But how was that possible? Unless there'd been other sets of keys given to other people Steve had known. Marion didn't know much about perfumes of any sort, but what he smelled was a scent that was alluring and strong.

Most likely some expensive shit.

Rather than mingle around any longer, he turned the lights and ceiling fan on and off to make sure they worked, then went to the room next to the master bedroom. The safe room. The room itself was as spacious as the master bedroom with the safe placed to Marion's left when he entered. It was an impressive Liberty Gun safe that had to have set Steve back many thousands.

"Nice thinking, Steve, no one's getting into this one."

The room was adorned with Snow Crest Film posters that Steve had collected over the years, as the town hosted one of the most prestigious film festivals every January.

Just as the letter said, Marion punched in the numbers on the keypad using his brother's birthday, and the safe door opened on the first shot. Inside were four guns that Marion immediately recognized: a .308 rifle, a Benelli M4 semi-auto shotgun, a lever-action Henry rifle, and a single shot .410 shotgun. He rummaged around the safe to find the valuables Steve hinted at in the letter, not taking long to find the getaway bag, a heavy denim bag with a thick silver zipper. He unzipped it and counted some twenty-five thousand plus dollars in hundreds, fifties, and twenties. The keys inside the bag consisted of an extra set for the house and truck, and a small key that opened a small fire-resistant safe that sat on a lower shelf of the Liberty. He counted another ten grand or so in gold and silver coins and bars, the deed to the house and the truck title, his brother's birth certificate, and some other assorted papers.

Also inside the denim bag was a Beretta .9 mm handgun, and seven or eight assorted knives, fixed blades mostly, but also a couple of fast clip knives that always came in handy for either everyday knife tasks or wicked street fights. Marion took the one he knew he'd use most, a Police Spyderco with a serrated edge, and of course the Beretta. Like any police officer in the country, he could legally carry and use any handgun he wanted in any state he traveled through. No questions asked. In fact the only place he would ever have a problem carrying a gun would be on an airplane, and even that wouldn't require much authorization.

He was set, and had plenty of money to do whatever he wanted while sorting out all the fuckery he was certain was lurking around every goddamn corner of Small Town America, Duncan, Utah.

He put back the gold and silver and all the cash except for a grand or so he'd use for immediate needs, shut the safe, walked into the kitchen, and looked into the fridge where the shelves were stacked with twelve-packs of beer. He opened the cabinets above and around the fridge to find half-empty assorted whiskeys and vodkas and gins. He slammed the cabinet doors shut, screamed out a long and throaty, "Fuck you, Steve!" then wept for a good five minutes before wiping his eyes dry and accepting that his brother's lifelong war was certainly part of what happened to him.

But then again maybe it was simply a way to deal with what Marion felt when sitting next to Alice just before Dr. Pinault arrived in all her witchery.

Time to get on the same page, brother, and I can't do that sulking in rage.

Marion went into his brother's study after getting his shit together, sat down in front of the large pine desk, plugged in the laptop and logged in while admiring all the hundreds of books his brother had in the walled shelves and separate bookcases.

What popped up on the desktop as soon as the password was accepted were two Houston homicide stories: one that had taken place back in 2007 about a Robert Demille's ghastly murder, and the other about Dean Corll, the infamous "Candy Man" Houston serial killer who had killed twenty-seven young boys from 1970 to 1973. The latter was a case that Marion was quite familiar with, as it was with most Houston cops. Candy Man Corll's murder spree was the worst in the nation at the time. The stories were clearly left open for Marion to read, and saved as .pdf files as well as links to the online data.

"What the hell is all this?" Marion said as he eagerly scoured the articles. He knew most of Corll's story, so he dug into the one he was not at all familiar with: the story of Robert Demille's bizarre murder at one of Houston's finest Penthouse buildings, One Park Place.

***

Dean Patrick

Local business executive murdered in elite One Park Place Penthouse

William Sparks, *Houston Chronicle*
October 21, 2007

Skyline of Houston's One Park Place

The Houston Police are still puzzled by the murder of local business executive, Robert Demille, who was found dead in the early hours of October 21. It was a grisly scene, as upon arrival, the police found Demille's naked body torn apart on the entryway marble floor of a Penthouse IV model of Houston's elite One Park Place.

Detective James "Butch" Macintire, a 20-year veteran of HPD said, "Never seen anything like this in all my years on the force. It was like a wild animal got hold of this guy. But make no mistake, it was a human being who did this, one with immense strength and obvious rage."

3-D Overview of Penthouse where Robert Demille was found murdered

What makes the scene even stranger, the penthouse was owned by a woman, and, according to One Park Place management, a woman who was never seen with anyone other than a few boyfriends here and there. Police have not released her name as no charges have been filed against anyone. "This isn't the kind of gruesome violence that we've ever encountered from a woman. That, and the fact that we can't locate her, or even determine her relationship with Demille, at this point, adds to the mystery," said Macintire.

Demille was Vice President of Marketing for the Houston start-up company, Digital Ventures, funded by venture capitalists David Woodbury and his twin brother, Terrance. No one from Digital Ventures has made a comment.

Dean Corll, aka The Candy Man, aka The Pied Piper

One of the more bizarre findings thus far in the investigation, according to Macintire, has been an out-of-print book on the notorious serial murders of Dean Corll, also known as The Candy Man and The Pied Piper. Known as The Mass Murders of Houston, 27 young boys were murdered from 1971 to 1973. There were also a few books on Truman Capote who, at that time, was looking to write his next *In Cold Blood,* but had dropped the project altogether due to health issues.

"I couldn't help but think there has to be some kind of connection here. These kinds of brutal murders always have some kind of connection to the ugliest side of humanity. I mean, why was that book lying around in Demille's master bedroom? And why was research about Truman Capote, who started the whole process of true crime books, there too? Something doesn't fit," said Macintire.

Eddie Henrickson

The Dean Corll murders, at the time, were the most brutal serial murders in the history of the nation. Within the span of a week, the bodies of 27 young boys had been found, ages 13 to 20. Dean Corll and one of his psycho accomplices, Eddie Henrickson, viciously tortured, and mutilated them, possibly 28, as there is still to this day an unidentified victim.

More intriguing still, the murder of Robert Demille is especially gruesome in that it looks to have taken place while Demille was having sex with someone. "This is another twist to this one. A sick twist of things in that it [the murder itself] looks to have happened while Demille's lover was on top of him and committed the heinous act during sexual intercourse. But the nature of how his chest and body were torn to pieces in the foyer makes absolutely no sense."

One thing that Macintire did say is that he would do everything in his power to find the killer, that he didn't want Houstonians walking around again in fear of yet another murderer on the loose.

***

"I'm with you, Detective, and why have I never heard of you? Why haven't I heard of this one before? And just what in the fuck did you find out, Steve?" Marion said out loud. "Got a feeling I'll be calling you, Macintire, that's for sure."

He then read the next article Steve had left open, material that Marion knew all too well. His brother had pieced together different sections from a Texas Monthly piece, and actual HPD recorded transcripts from the book, *Mass Murder in Houston* by John K. Gurwell, published by Cordovan Press Houston in 1974, the book that had to be the one referenced in the Demille writeup that had gone out of print.

Knowing his brother's whole life was professional writing, Marion opened up the Notes app and the Stickies app on the laptop. He also fired up the Mac mini so he could use multiple screens for faster navigation. Since the Stickies app had no Recent Files to open or browse, he kept the Notes app open. "Probably wouldn't have used Word for all your thoughts, so let's see what we can see."

Sure enough, Marion saw one of the notes that presented a variety of thoughts from the Gurwell book and the Houston Chronicle clippings. He could see his brother was working late into the night so whatever he'd been trying to piece together had been something that kept him from sleeping. "Probably kept pounding the sauce while you were at it, too. Let's take a look at this one, brother."

Connection notes to consider from
Gurwell and Chronicle - Microfilm 2020 – 21

I need to run this stuff by Marion, as he could use his investigative expertise to find a connection between Terra Drake, Houston, and Duncan and discover why she targeted me, to destroy my life, my town, and all of Small Town America.

I think he should take a deep look into the J. K. Gurwell book, Mass Murders in Houston. It contains details about Mass Murderer Dean Corll and his accomplice Eddie Henrickson, whom I believe have a connection to Terra Drake, or were possibly influenced by her, especially Henrickson, who turned against his mentor, Corll, and put six bullets into him. I don't know what this has to do with Terra and myself, but it's worth looking into.

After I read a 2011 article in the Houston Chronicle, I suspect, as the writer noted, that there's a connection between Corll, The Candy Man, and the Boston Strangler, Ted Bundy, and even Berkowitz, but that connection eluded him. Every bone in my body tells me Terra Drake is the missing link. I know she murdered my neighbor, Stan Smitts, and I saw her create chaos all across Duncan and beyond.

Worse, she's got an allure, a sexuality that makes me think she was in cahoots with Henrickson in a

Dallas porn ring. Hell, she may have even been the leader. He had a mother-in-law that's never talked about. What if she was Terra herself who'd taken Henrickson as a child and turned him into a sadistic killer, put him with Corll to hone his craft. I think that has a connection to what's happening to me now.

I am a drunk, and I may be crazy, but my gut tells me Terra Drake has her manicured fingernails in more debauchery, ruining more lives, more people, than just little ole me in Duncan, Utah, of all places.

Marion read over the notes until he had them memorized, stood up to stretch, then sat right back down again, wondering just how deep he was prepared to follow the rabbit trail. He closed out the documents and began searching for more files his brother may have left as clues.

Steve's Notes app had hundreds of entries just as Marion suspected. Too many to get into while he was then feeling the exhaustion of everything. As much as he wanted to keep his word that he had slept enough, he could no longer ignore his body. One of the few things he ever took to heart while seeing his shrink, Sarah Williams, was during a particularly grueling session when she noticed that his exhaustion was at a dangerous level. He had been working a case of a higher-ranked officer's side gig: pimping young girls for blackmail. Sarah told him that the body was the scorecard: it showed everything.

He stood from his brother's desk and decided to hit the living room sofa for a quick nap. "Just a few hours, that's all, then back at it," he whispered. But just as he turned for the living room his eyes caught yet another heading of one of the notes that he couldn't ignore. It was dated a little after a week later from the first note and just as late into the evening, or early morning. He leaned over instead of sitting back down and opened it.

Terra connection notes 2020 – 21

1. Who is she? That's first. WHAT is she? Since she came into my life, I've never felt such power from one person. She seems to know everything about me, and everything about everything.

2. Why is the whole goddamned town suddenly possessed? How did she manage it?

3. What is her relation to Adrian Cain/Kane. I've seen both names here and there, as well as the Hooded Darkness.

4. What about the murder of Robert Demille? He was ripped to pieces in a Houston penthouse Terra Drake owns. Why the limited press coverage? The story got buried, even covered up. No surprise, but this one was grisly and nobody seems to care.

5. What is her connection to the child trafficking ring in Dallas? I think it goes deeper than that. She's stealing children and 'turning' them into demons. I've seen it with my own eyes.

6. What about Dean Corll's step-mother. I can't find one damn thing on this person. Who was she? Where did she go after the murders? Is it possible Terra knew her, groomed her, and sent her out in the world to one-day raise havoc?

7. What of all the recent shit with all the exposed sex rings and black books from the Reginald Edward scandals? The private

locations and private meetings with Presidents and Ambassadors. Are these just conspiracy theories, or was Terra in on all of this shit? Wouldn't surprise me one fucking bit.

8. If she has so many connections in Houston, she could have them everywhere, for all I know. Serial killers and sexual deviates are running amok across this country.

9. I suspect she's a witch or something more wicked, but she's got me, and I have to keep that in mind no matter what's going on in Small Town America. She's out there and she's out to get everyone.

10. What does she mean by 'turning' me? What and how? I'm a goddamned drunk. She can't hurt me more than I've already hurt myself, my family, my wife, my neighbors, my friends, for God's sake. It's like she's under my skin and I can't shake her no matter how much I drink, no matter what's already happened.

11. I've got to make time to tell Marion everything I have seen and all that I think is going on. America and its children are in great peril. He's the only one who'll believe me.

The last bullet on the list, of course, hit him the hardest. "Nice work, brother. I wish we'd been closer. Jesus hell. I'll get to all these, Steve, but I'm useless without some rest...also with you on the 'turning' thing whatever that means because you were toast when we last met up."

Marion walked into the living room, turned on the

television for background noise, as it had always helped him fall asleep more quickly, and let his body crash deep into the leather sofa.

It was one of those instant dreams where he knew he was dreaming but refused to wake up out of the need for continued sleep no matter what disturbance or strangeness he was seeing or participating in.

He found himself in a similar hallway that was perhaps part of what had led to the Stonehenge Classroom while in the midst of his final moments of the coma dream. He was following the demon woman down the hallway that led to a system of different buildings where all those in power had resided since the beginning of time. Marion also felt the steps of countless known people who had been following him for quite some time, but he never turned around to see who they were or what they wanted.

She wore a single piece gold leather suit with matching full length leg boots on 8-inch spiked heels. Her hands were long strands of thick wires that were connected to bizarre devices that rolled beside her, the wires leashed around the devices. With each step, she increased her distance from Marion by more than twice his own steps as he fell farther and farther behind.

When she suddenly stopped and turned to face Marion, her feet were parted in a power stance that highlighted every facet of her seduction as well as control. Her wired hands stiffened as if electricity suddenly powered them into full force as she was braced to take on anything that would ever come her way. The devices she was connected to raced away from her on each side, and the wires shrunk and morphed into hands that looked mutated and distorted, as if someone had molded them into something unfinished.

She slowly leaned forward, bending her legs slightly as her lavender eyes struck him like two lasers he could not turn away from, and he felt a sense of hypnosis mixed with paralysis. To each side of her, an opening appeared that looked like a beach ball-sized funnel, and now Marion believed a wormhole would appear if it were that small and sudden. She reached into both openings and quickly jolted back straight up, arching her chest forward while pulling out two massive jelly-like abscesses that were giant mutated tumors attached to a single mass of gore. Endless tentacles and knuckled structures dangled from the terrible abscesses deep into the wormhole openings as if she were holding two deformed mutations of Portuguese Man O' Wars. Either that or she'd just pulled apart the heads of some unknown hellish creatures that were trapped in the wormholes.

Marion remained dumbfounded.

"It's crucial you understand and know who you are dealing with. I control everything. Everything in your world is mine. It is through these two masters, Commerce and Sexuality, these two gods you've always served, as I hold their heads out high before you." The demon woman raised both torn mounds of gore above her head as she looked back and forth to each one in complete admiration, and even...honor. The swirling floor openings began to clog and churn with hundreds of thick strands of rope that were moving and latching onto the dangling bloody strands that hung from the abscesses. It didn't take long before Marion knew the awful clogs were not cut strands at all, but thick worms that were reproducing exponentially.

"Commerce and Sexuality," she continued, eyeballing each of them as her lavender eyes moved side to side in a wigged out semi-dance. "You know them well, only you've never known how well I've used them. Dickens was on the right track with his Want and Need, with the boy-girl thing in his Christmas delight. I've just taken it full-tilt boogie.

"And now, my dear officer, I use them for all the children. Every exploited binary-charged gender leach out there, it's Commerce and Sexuality. I rip them away from you while you sit on the sidelines and do nothing. Riding the fence in blind neutrality. Disengaged while I am full-throttle, high-heels clamping down the pedal to the metal! I buy them and exploit them for a purpose as old as my romps around Eden with The Viper as he bled into me. Commerce and Sexuality *are* the children! And I have no consequence. Look around you, look down these halls, look behind you and above you. All but followers who do nothing!"

Marion did exactly as she said, looking up and around the dreamscape that had become all the buildings and institutions of leadership and privilege that he'd ever personally seen, and every one he'd ever read about. In his peripheral, he could see that she was also looking in all the directions he was.

The demon woman then dropped the two masses to the floor as Marion saw the miniature black holes seal shut. They landed in a wet sickening sound of absolute death as the giant worms remained in their horrible reproduction, burrowing into the abscesses' mutated heads and knuckled tentacles, sucking down the pieces in ferocious starvation. The sound of the worms eating into the mess before him was a hundred thousand slurps and swallows so vile and filthy he awakened in a sweat and screamed as he heard the demon woman cackle in a roaring laugh. Marion jolted up from the couch and tumbled down to the living room floor, covering his head and ears at first as he fought off the dream.

"Jesus fuck." He picked himself up and shuffled into the bathroom to drench his face in Utah's ice-cold tap water, then looked in the mirror to make sure he was still awake. "Every time I fall asleep it's a new fuckshow," he whispered as he tufted his hair about, checked teeth and gums. Before going back to the study, he checked his phone and saw that he hadn't just fallen asleep for a few hours, but that it had been a few days.

Holy Christ. I've got to shake this thing.

He went back into the bathroom and splashed more cold water on his face but decided that wasn't enough as he turned on the shower, left the water cold, stripped down and let the icy water do its number.

Feeling his body and mind were at last refreshed, it was back to the study to open up another story his brother had highlighted.

Of course, the whole world knew the dealings of Reginald Edwards and his connections with politicians, religious leaders, musicians, actors, and European Royalty. Marion wasn't surprised that Steve wanted to make an Edwards connection to what was going on with him, personally, but everything that Steve had left behind story-wise was making more and more sense to Marion; the Edwards' piece was no different.

Reginald Edwards' possible "John Doe's" begin to surface one sickening number after another; connections to children and Satanic Church made

Cary Blair, *Digital Accomplices*
November 18, 2022

It seems that Reginald Edwards was involved with what many have probably already suspected. In our darkest dreams that is.

While researching the recent murders that have ravaged the country, there has been speculation that Edwards, and some elites who ran in his circle, had indirect involvement due to ulterior motives. "Look, we've known about his outside operations for a long time, years, but pinning anything down with someone who's so heavily connected can sadly be an awful process," said Detective James "Butch" Macintire of the Houston Police Department.

Macintire was the lead investigator into the Robert Demille murder back in 2007, and when providing some of the details of

that case to some of the police who were involved with Edwards' arrest, Macintire said he started connecting the dots, and something seemed off. "There were a few missing pieces in that case [Robert Demille] that have bothered me from day one, and still do to this day. The way some of the items were left and how they were found, and the mystery of the owner's whereabouts that complicated the investigation itself. I'm not making any further comment until I have things lined up, but the connections, at least in my mind, are startling."

In another breaking story, revealing yet another alarming connection, Macintire believes that Edwards was also involved in large contributions to the Satanic Church where, says Macintire, those contributions were made for the purpose of bringing children "into the fold."

"There was a piece I read about a year ago when I suspected that

Edwards had donated money to one of Lucien Greaves' head ministers of his church, The Satanic Temple. Greaves was the founder of that church. When I was reading over an interview Greaves had given a few years back, he had this to say about Satanism itself. 'I think people should feel differently about Satan, actually. We view Satan as metaphorical, so obviously we believe the idea of Satan is up to subjective interpretation. The fact that we put forward a different conception of Satan underscores that point. People can think differently about these things, and you don't need to agree with the evangelical agenda to be a good person. We are good people. We disagree with evangelicals on issues like gay rights or other basic civil liberties. We don't need to demonize the other side. The witches of the witch hunts never existed. The satanists of the Satanic Panic never existed. And I think having the presence of people who self-identify as satanists, showing kids that people can have productive and moral lives, sends a positive message. The labeling of the After School Satan Club is a positive message. It would be a bit of artifice and concealment if we were to come in calling ourselves something other than the Satanic Temple. We're decent people with whom you can have a dialogue.'"

I asked Macintire to further explain what was so sinister about his findings as what was spoken by Greaves didn't seem anything other than a difference in accepted belief systems. "It's my belief, my thinking, that the minister who was dealing with Edwards was someone who was taking, and who I believe is now taking these seemingly harmless beliefs Greaves spoke of to a level where Satanism is part of a much bigger plot to buy children for the sole purpose of slavery. The so-called 'clubs' that Satanic churches were promoting a few years ago and trying to push forward a certain innocent agenda was only a façade for what Edwards planned to do before he was arrested. And The Satanic Church itself is also just a front. A pawn really. What these people really want is to come after our children and to use them in a way that will completely destroy the world."

"How?" I pressed.

"By literally creating within children a desire and even strategy to overthrow and destroy every principle that was ever known to be wholesome and good."

Terra's Sabbath

Marion read over the article again and again, feeling something way off about it, as well as something disturbingly familiar from recent news reports. He put the laptop aside and began flipping through TV news channels. Ironically, one station's headline was that of a Satanic cult member who had cut up his girlfriend into tiny pieces, dicing her up and storing all the body parts in his fridge in Ziploc bags. Another station then reported what had happened at a Colorado gay night club, how some whack job had gone in, guns blazing, killing at least nine patrons and wounding many others.

Back and forth Marion flipped, watching the highlights with laser detective eyes, seeing and feeling things that were not part of what any civilian could possibly see or feel. Or sense. That was the real edge. Marion could sense relationships and clues so he could focus on what caused his senses to go on high alert. Looking for details that would connect the dots and put together a pattern that made sense even when everything appeared so senseless. It was those stories on the news that triggered him to keep looking deeper into the stories that his brother had left behind in his laptop.

Again, he looked at the laptop and the Edwards' story, then flipped quickly back to the news stories of the butchering's across the country. Then back to the laptop, then Googling images of as many shots as he could find where he could zoom in to find that one connection that would begin to open a door to some clarity.

"I'll get to you, Macintire, and pick your fucking brain in due time."

As he looked over photo after photo after photo on the internet, Marion was convinced the tattoos he thought he saw on the mass killers looked—in his opinion—similar to a point that was disturbing. From what he could zoom in on, the tattoos were of some bizarre character. Again, similar for sure, but he couldn't peg it yet. It also struck his thinking that they looked similar to the pendant he'd seen Janet Stone wear on her necklace, as did Dr. Pinault. *How the fuck is that possible?* But he couldn't make a case out of it; just a hunch.

He again went to his brother's letter and what Steve had said about looking closely at the people and the goings-on in Duncan. So that's exactly what Marion did next. While he looked over all the material Steve had left, he also spent the next week with housekeeping issues, checking out the immediate surroundings of the house and property and Duncan itself, firing up the lawnmower and weed eater, buying groceries, checking out the local gyms, and he was surprised to find a few of them. He made a call down to HPD and spoke to his Captain about what had happened, letting him know he didn't know exactly when he'd be back in town. All in all, just gathering his bearings.

One day the idea hit Marion to drive down to Duncan's Main Street where there was an Exxon station and hotel just before a tiny shopping area where Marion wanted to visit the town's state liquor store. If there was any place in Duncan where Steve probably frequented the most during his slide back into hell, it would be the liquor store. More intel gathering.

Marion parked in one of the few slots right in front, opened the heavy glass door, and entered the smallest liquor store he had ever seen. The place had no more than two rows that carried the wine, one wall shelf for the whiskeys and ryes and vodkas and gins, and the wall shelf behind the cash register where the smaller units of all liquor were sold. The store looked more like the inside of a small log cabin.

"Hi," a woman shouted and suddenly appeared from the back area that housed coolers for cold cases of beer. "Good to see you! What is it here I can git for you?" She looked to be in her mid-40s, sturdy build, greasy blond hair, missing a few teeth, and wearing bleached overalls.

Behind her stood a much older man who looked just as greasy, who said nothing but stared straight into Marion with crazed eyeballs.

"What the hell you been on your whole life, pal?"

"Nothing. You can't get me anything, and you don't know me." Marion looked the woman up and down, checking her out closely as he immediately sensed things being off the way they'd started with Janet and Pinault.

"It's always good to see folks come in. Yippee!"

"Excuse me, lady, is there something wrong with you? Why are you yelling?"

"She's not a yeller." The older man behind the woman now stepped closer, and Marion could see he looked ancient, to the point of rotting. "She's just giddy, is all. Not a damn thing to mind, mind you!" His voice was phlegmy and raw.

Marion took a few long steps close to the weird couple, making sure they saw he was entering their space with a clear purpose. "Then why are you yelling? You both hard of hearing, is that it?"

"Oh stop it and just let me give you a few suggestions if you don't know whatcha want. We have a few new selections that came in this week. Want to see 'em?" the woman shouted again as if Marion hadn't mentioned a word about hers or the man's tone.

"No. I don't. And you stop—"

"We didn't start anything. You did! We're just trying to be friends!"

The last thing Marion wanted or needed was a confrontation with the weird couple. He figured they'd been together since the dawn of time, and that time itself had aged them into something disturbing. Sinister. But he also wanted information.

"I don't drink."

The ancient man walked up to the counter just a few feet in front of Marion and leaned on it with both arms, looking up to Marion. "Then why in His Holy Name are you in here?"

The woman remained where she was, her eyes staring off into space.

"And whose holy name would that be?" Marion looked right back into the ancient man's crazed dead eyes, keeping absolute focus. He'd looked into plenty of sets of eyes that had gone so far south that they'd never return home to normalcy, but what Marion saw in the liquor man's eyes was different, as were the eyes of the liquor woman's. They were somehow sicker, as if decay had come inside their skulls and pumped death throughout their brain tunnels.

Still, Marion knew that to turn away eye contact was to give away the scene, whatever scene was needed.

"Never mind that. Look, reason I'm *here* was to ask about someone who I'm sure came in here a lot earlier this year, late last year."

"You're no cop from this town. We know 'em all, each and every one!" the woman shouted. She'd pulled herself out of her brief trance and moved to stand next to her partner.

"No. Not from here. I'm a Houston cop and here to ask about my brother. That's why I came in."

"Town drunk, he was. We've had plenty! Praise be, have we had plenty!" The woman said, as it was her partner's turn to stare off into space.

"His name was Steven Paul. Died a few months ago. Back in early spring. Found dead, that is."

The woman went silent and the man remained spacy.

Marion waited a few moments before he knew she wouldn't speak again until pressed. "Clearly you knew him, so...I'm wanting to find out a bit more around town, is all."

"Let me tell you something, son," the man said. "It's time you be on your way. There's not a single peep we have to say about your brother. Make sure you hear me clear. Clear as a boil on a baby's ass. It's time you be on your way." He had snapped out of his trance to speak to Marion in a voice that was filled with as much clarity as fear.

His cop instincts remaining on high alert, Marion knew any further conversation would go nowhere. It was indeed time to leave. The weird couple's sudden loss of skin color as well as the man's instant frightening assertion told him everything he needed to know.

He backed up all the way to the liquor store's exit before turning to open the door, getting into the Ram, and heading back, all the while knowing that his brother's letter was spot on.

Before he had five minutes to wrap his head around the liquor store's freak showcase, as he was about to cross the creek to his new place, he saw, what had to be, every Duncan police car and an EM unit parked on the bridge and on the street just before it, just before what he was now calling the Duncan Ranch.

My place now. It's my place now. Gotta get that in my head.

Police hadn't yet blocked off the bridge, so Marion inched past all the chaos and looked to his left to see that a white pickup truck had ended up in the creek about fifty feet downstream and directly behind the back wood fence of his own corral. Just how in the hell a truck happened to land in the water there was baffling.

After he parked the Ram, he walked out to the street to get a better look as fire trucks arrived on scene. Instead of jumping right in to assist, which he knew he could, he decided to head to his corral and to the back fence so he could get a closer look at the truck itself.

The truck was halfway sunk into the shallow creek water. Emergency crews had several lines of tow cable tossed out in an attempt to hook onto the truck's bumper or axle, anything solid would do. Marion stood on one of the bottom boards of the fence to get high enough to oversee the truck and the surrounding area to determine some kind of cause for the accident. He saw nothing inside the front seats as water blocked any decent view. The truck's smaller short cab backseat had what Marion believed looked like a few large trash bags, some tattered clothing, large rusted tools and whatnot. "I'm sure the locals will pry into this, at least that would be the first protocol," he whispered as he looked over to the bridge again and the growing effort to get the truck out of the water.

Standing by the iron rail of the bridge's walkway, leaning over with one arm resting comfortably, was a wiry steel man who easily stood over seven feet. He wore a ragged leather cowboy hat with matching tattered leather vest. Black jeans that were sand blown and filthy. Cowboy boots with rusted spurs that were patterned and worn for years. His skin was as leathery as his clothing. He wore a six-gun shooter on his hip as if to dare any soul to make mention. Canon of a gun, most likely a .44 Magnum. Marion could tell the lanky husk of a cowboy could handle himself and anything that would come his way with relative ease. He also saw the man's eyes when he looked over to Marion and tipped his hat, half ash cigarette hanging from his lips, eyes that were gaunt, black, and piercing. Demon eyes. Warlock's eyes. Drilling into Marion with an instant "Do Not Fuck With Me" sign that hung around the cowboy's neck like a fresh war-scalping.

Marion didn't look away or flinch no matter how much his gut suggested otherwise. Instead, he took out his phone from his back pocket and took a quick photo of Cowboy Jack.

"Or whoever the fuck you are."

He stepped down from the fence rail and jogged back out to the street to talk to him on the bridge, but he was gone. The local police and firemen continued working on the truck in the drink.

Marion's presence attracted the attention of law enforcement. "Hey, are you taking over Steve's place?" one of the cops shouted.

Instead of answering, Marion looked all around the bridge area for the cowboy Jack, but saw no sign of him. "You see a tall cowboy type over here just a second ago?"

"Who's asking?"

Marion looked at him like he was stupid. "I'm his brother. Now tell me. Did you see a tall cowboy a bit ago?"

The cop glared at Marion with a not-too-concerned expression. "He took off. You best stay clear of that guy."

"Why's that?"

"Look. We've got a situation here—"

"Who is he?"

"He lives next door to your brother's place. Used to be Stan Smitts' spread. I don't know if your brother told you much about him."

"I don't recall—"

"He was found murdered at one of the local bars late last year. Easy to read up on, but only reason I mention it is because that cowboy you saw now owns the Smitts place, but no one sees him much, if ever. So him being here just now gives everyone pause. His name is Kane, with a 'K' as he's told townsfolk. Adrian Kane. Said he changed the spelling so people wouldn't confuse him with the Biblical character."

"Kane, huh? My brother may have mentioned him."

"Whatever. Look, I gotta tend to this shit."

"Any idea if anyone's been hurt?"

"Just happened. Have no idea."

"Yeah. I see things look a bit out of control. Need any help let me know. I'm a cop. Out of Houston. Be glad to lend a hand to the local force."

"I'll keep that in mind. And now I know who you are. Marion Paul. Of course. Your brother spoke a lot about you. I'm Jim Evanston."

Marion nodded. "Jim. A pleasure. How well did you know Steve?"

"I was his probation officer. Years and years ago." Evanston had quickly changed his tune and walked up to Marion to shake his hand. "I'm stationed up in Snow Crest City. You know of it?"

"Last place I saw my brother."

"Let's catch up soon. Duncan's PD station is just down the way about a mile to the left of the rock church, and I could always meet you there. I was in town when this wreck was called in, and I'm around Duncan often enough."

"I can come up to Snow Crest. There's a lot there I need to check out, but that's for later. I'd love to catch up. Probably necessary."

"Yeah. About your brother...and every other goddamn thing, if you feel me."

"Actually, I do. I'd like your take on some things my brother was putting together."

"Let's do it. Let me get at this, and I'll talk at you later."

Marion didn't press for any further information, shook Evanston's hand again, nodded in agreement, then headed back to his new home. He'd have plenty of time later to check out the area where the truck had to have traveled before it hit the water. It was time to check out the photo he'd taken of Cowboy Jack, aka Adrian Kane, nice and thorough.

Back at Duncan Ranch, he sat at his desk in the study and viewed the photo on his phone with intense scrutiny. Kane looked as hard as a chunk of granite, the surface weathered and cracked with what seemed a timeless age. He cast the photo to the large desktop monitor, zoomed in and panned the photo, looking for any markings or tattoos of any kind, but it was Kane's skin itself that was unlike anything Marion had ever seen.

Chapter Seven:

Bridget Magnus

Marion had been at the Duncan Ranch a week or so, his brother's place—my *place now*, and spent the time reading *Mass Murders in Houston* on the Internet Archives' site, only stopping to shower and take a few naps in between his researching. He'd not slept a single night in Steve's bedroom, his and Anna's bedroom was more what he wanted to avoid. It just felt too invasive. That, plus he hadn't been able to get used to the perfumed scent of the room, which seemed to live in the walls.

He went back and forth and over and over every detail of the murder cases his brother had found so disturbing, as well as so oddly connected to each other, as evidenced by the images Marion saw of the tattoos and jewelry pieces, both in photos as well as on some of the Duncan townsfolk, and most certainly on Dr. Pinault and Janet Stone. He looked for clues to this connection in the Houston Chronicle and excerpts from *The Lost Boys.*

One late afternoon, as he studied Kane's skin up close on the phone picture he'd taken, he decided to take a drive before catching a heavy case of cabin fever. He needed to allow his thoughts and connections to percolate while away from the computer screen and all the stories and notes his brother had left as bread crumb trails to who knew where. On the way into Duncan, he drove past a sign that advertised a local event in Utah called The Duncan Maze.

Always thought such events were held on Halloween.

Still trying to wrap his head around everything since coming out of the coma, he decided to drive down the canyon to the Odessa Hotel. His brain felt like it was lobbing around in his skull, sloppily hitting the insides of his cranium like it was a heavy, deflating floatie toy. The dream of the demon woman lecturing to the demon children that ended in the violent finale of the cesarean man birthing demon insects in that dreadful arena was still so vivid and so alive inside his every thought, he believed the entire ghastly scene was somehow attached to his brother's death and all the dread his brother went through. His thoughts had proven even more true with all the research his brother had left behind, and with what he'd seen from Pinault and Stone and the freakish Duncan townsfolk.

His cop spirit was determined to find out everything possible. He knew the last time he'd seen his brother, the two of them had gone on a late-night hike deep in the mountains past Snow Crest City where they found the woman who had been tormenting Steve during the previous year. Marion was pleased he'd met Deputy Evanston who had known Steve quite well. "I'll be coming up to Snow Crest soon enough to talk more about my brother, that's for sure," he said out loud as he sluggishly remembered he and his brother exploring the woman's freakish place where they'd seen her and her freakish partner doing awful deeds. But that was all he could remember when he awakened in the hospital just over a week ago.

He blasted the stereo two octaves too high, as the live version of Kiss's "She" was the cut. Of all things, Kiss.

How were their songs the backdrop of that fucked up dream? And now here they are on the radio. Good song, at least.

Marion then noticed a bludgeoned carcass of a deer on the side of the road that was fresh enough in its gore that he thanked God someone else had hit it.

Must have been hit by someone going a hundred miles

an hour to do that kind of damage. Christ.

When he approached Duncan's city center and another event sign, he noticed something odd on it—or odd *about* it—odd enough that he did a doubletake. He could have sworn he saw an emblem on the sign that looked similar to the pendant, of all things, that he'd seen Pinault and Janet Stone wearing. *What the fuck was that?* However, he drove by it too fast and had to go back to take a closer look. He whipped a U-turn, but traffic caused him to miss the chance to stop, so he drove up the road where he found plenty of space to turn around. A reckless driver damn near hit him when he slowed to get the look he needed. Sure enough, there it was, the gnarly figure he'd seen on the tattoos and pendants...the connection he was looking for. The Duncan Maze.

Shaken, he drove a mile or so into Duncan and pulled into the local convenience store. Local Exxon to be exact. Full-service diner included. It was dusk then. Almost the start of June. A spring chill hung in the air.

Maybe someone here knows what the Duncan Maze is all about, and the wiry figure on the event sign...what it means.

Once inside the station, Marion immediately decided he needed a smoke. A vape at the very least. The only time in his entire life when he'd ever smoked was some twenty years ago while a college freshman when he decided it sounded like a fine thing to do while he was getting drunk with the frat boys, also his first and only time for that nonsense. Marion had always played the straight-laced kid who refused to go down the family path of addiction that had ruined so many in his extended family. Including his own brother.

I wonder how many countless times Steve had been in this place. And Christ, here I am.

The gas station's interior had such a feeling of abandonment that he also disturbingly wondered why anyone would ever stop at this place for food or gas. It was far too dimly lit, in Marion's opinion, far darker on the inside than any convenience store he'd ever visited, come to think of it. In the middle of the cash register area stood a rather fragile looking man or woman (he had no clue which) on a small stepladder, restocking the cigarette case. Marion watched the nightshift clerk long enough to where he eventually cleared his throat in irritation to capture a simple acknowledgment.

The clerk stopped moving instantly and dropped all the cigarette packs on the floor with as much irritation as was Marion's attention seeking.

Stepping down and around rather quickly...too quickly, stood perhaps the most ragged and torched looking women he'd ever seen over the years he'd spent scouring the underbelly shitholes of Houston. The woman stood no more than five feet, her skin rampant with aged crevices that looked more like gashes, caked in filth, so raw and weathered she looked like an ancient cowhide suit had been stretched and sewn onto her rickety bones. Something far worse than years of meth or crack had taken a fierce scourging to her. Her bulbous nose was red and runny, her eyes sunk deep in sockets that looked like they'd been gouged out with a spoon, and her hair was a ratted mess the color of mildewed straw.

Her appearance was so strikingly hideous that Marion found himself struggling to not give away his instant repugnance. With as many times throughout his career he had faced the most awful creatures of the streets, he found it alarming that he felt such unease.

"Good evening," Marion said, careful not to say more until he could hear the hag's voice.

"Is it?" she replied.

Marion looked over his shoulder back toward the Ram, making sure the sun had set, as it was just going down when he went back to get a better look at the maze event sign. Either she questioned whether or not the evening was *good,* or she'd completely lost track of time and hadn't noticed the sunset.

"Yeah. It's been weird but good, that's for sure." Marion stared at the woman's black eyeballs, so black he couldn't see any movement that everyone's eyes made during any conversation. Just two large shiny black globular slugs stuck in place. He knew he was staring into something he'd never seen before during any interrogation.

"My day just dipped right outta sight, hmm, hmm. Just dipped away into that awful pit of nighty night nighttime."

"Whatever the fuck that means," he muttered, wondering if she'd ever had a look that resembled anything normal or decent.

"What waz dat?" she spewed out a broken mouth that displayed in full horror glory-rotted teeth that were spaced apart and protruding from both gum lines that looked charcoal-black and rubbery. He had seen more than enough crack whores and vagrants over the years, but the hag's mouth over-grossed-out any of them. Her voice was so clogged in phlegm, he wondered if her lungs had drowned in the shit long ago. Her service station attire was as tattered as the rest of her. Sickly blue rayon shirt with the top two or three buttons missing that exposed a veiny, shockingly white chest. Frayed rayon black slacks. Black walking shoes that had walked across a million service station floors. Marion could see no name tag but did notice the background music so familiar in most places, suddenly changed to a cryptic and acidy folk sound he'd never heard.

"I'm just here for some information."

"Gas outside, Copper!"

"What?"

"In here is other nifty knacks and saddle cracks and gimmicky kicks and such! We're fresh out of information." She walked up to one of the two cash registers with such a pronounced limp, he thought she'd topple over.

"What did you call me?" Marion took a step closer. No matter his caution, he still knew stepping up would show immediate authority, and it was indeed authority he was suddenly needing to display, not just feelings.

"I said *nifty knacks*—"

"Before that," Marion interrupted, certain the hag had coughed up a few inches of the shit that was buried inside her when she spoke. "Copper?"

The woman closed her mouth and frowned such an upside-down crevice her beak of a chin crimped upward as if some opening in her face could swallow it up. "No matter. You're the Coming One. Coming in with all your questions and concerns and all your whatnots. Thinking about all those landscape dreams of horror. You sure got the deeper looks of one who came out of dreamscapes. Eh? Ehhhh?! Here to talk about all the gremlins and ghouls and—"

"I don't know what you're talking about, and that's not what I asked?" Marion shot back, not giving her a second chance to keep ranting, looking up and down the hag as well as scoping out all the surroundings. He picked out the corners of the store, the restroom sign, the back area of the station where the diner area was closed, the empty chairs, the sunglass rack, the water-stained foamboard ceilings. All of it in his camera-eye peripheral. His decades-long and wisdom-deep cop senses immediately kicked in, homing in his laser sharp caution as well as discernment.

Still, how does she know of any of this?

No response. The hag just stood there, halfcocked as if she'd never had an inkling of understanding of anything, much less the frightening prophecy she just vented. Just a ruined smile that formed up and around her entire torn face, so precise in its etching it had to have caused even more torment the ancient woman had somehow escaped during all the years that had come down upon her. A ruined smile to mask the life that was hanging around her decrepit neck like a final helpless thread.

"You said *Copper*. That's what you said. That's what I heard. That's what I'm referring to."

"Ah! Eh, eh, eh. You a cop, ain't ye?"

"It's that obvious?"

"You got the look for sure." Her head then nodded up and down far too rapidly.

"Quit that! Christ, you'll snap something. You hadn't even seen me while you were stocking the cancer sticks."

"Didn't have to see. Don't ever have to see. It's my good sense that's always so keen. So keen from the ages and ages of—

"Stop. Doesn't matter. Yes, I am a cop. Never mind that you seem *out* of your mind. Look...listen for a sec, can you? I was wondering about that sign. It's the actual reason I came in. Sign about the Duncan Maze. Thought for sure anyone working here would know about it. Local event, isn't it?"

"Don't have to whisper. Cain't hear much, Christ knows. And he does. Rest assured."

Marion hadn't realized he was whispering. *Was I? Why?*

"Speak up!" the woman croaked.

"Jesus! Sorry. I only wanted to ask you about the Duncan Maze, the weird figure on the sign and the event."

The hag tilted her body to the other side, halfcocked again, sporting the same sick frown. "Hmmmm. Clearly new to these parts. But maybe not so new, eh? Ha! Hmmmmm...what about that sign got you so peaked? What it said? Or how it was said? It's design? What!?" Her tongue then slithered out from the corner of her crevice in a bleak attempt to lick the dry corners of her decayed mouth. Her tongue itself looked more like the butt of a whip that had been cut off and sewn inside her throat. "What is it you need to know so desperately?"

"I'm not desperate, lady. Just curious is all."

"Hmmmm. 'Bout everything I just said, that's a certainty. Curiosity killed the cat. Slit its throat, it did—"

"I see where this is going, Miss...I'm sure your name tag fell off your shirt during all your restocking..."

"Bridget Magnus. That's me. Bridget Magnus. Hmmmm." She rubbed her knuckled hands across a scarred neck so ripped in overgrown tissue Marion wondered what she could have possibly gone through that had destroyed her body, yet kept it alive, if just barely.

Looks like she's been hanged a hundred times over. Name sounds familiar, for some reason...

Always keep things serious when shit gets real was one of Marion's mottos that he'd lived by throughout the years of facing murderers, rapists, butchers of any kind. And for as frail and decrepit as Bridget appeared, every honed sixth sense Marion possessed thought she fit such a bill to a T.

"Don't run off so quickly, Scare Dee Cat. No, no, no. You came all this way to seek what you seek, may as well seek it here and ye shall find with me as I tell you a tale. You've got no place else to run run run away to, Copper, eh? Time for a tale or two?"

Marion took a deep breath and let it out with complete control and patience. Of course, he had no place to go, no place to be. No place he belonged, in fact. He'd awakened from a coma in the Odessa hospital some three months after his brother's death. Had roamed that empty hospital in horror of that emptiness. Had been given the title to his brother's truck and the deed to his property soon after. All he wanted were answers to his brother's death. All he was receiving was an opening of perpetual insanity where Queen Hag Magnus wanted to talk tales of deeper madness.

"Sure. I can stick around for a chat. Why not?"

"Mercy me, oh mercy me! That's the spirit, Copper.

Let me grab a few stools." Which she did. She also came back with a half-empty bottle of whiskey that she began pulling on the moment she sat down, her bony legs crossed and so razor thin that it looked like her frayed black trousers were kinked down the center of her rangy frame.

"Want some, Copper?"

"No thanks," Marion said in irritation. "And stop calling me Copper. You've got a name, so do I."

"Hmmm. Hmmm. Give it up, then," Bridget said while dry-licking her upper lip.

"Marion Paul."

"Paul, you say? Hmmm. Tad familiar to be fair."

"Yeah, well, you've probably been here long enough to have heard of my brother, Steven Paul."

The hag said nothing, but her sickly coughed giggles said everything.

"What do you want to talk about, Bridget? I'm committed to listen. You knew my brother, fine. Or of him. Whatever it was. That's why I'm here."

"That's why any of us are here, Mister Paul. Here just looking for others we've loved. Others we've lost. And doesn't it stink up ripe like in small towns, eh? But it's also the small towns where all the answers lie if ye just listen deep enough. And long enough, too. That sign had your attention straight up with your hairs nailing into your backside, eh? So let me tell you little bits and pieces about it. How its operated mostly. But more than that, *who* operates it. The whore of Babylon who ripped through your comatose slumber!"

"I'm all ears." Marion knew he'd whispered that time.

"Eh ye, eh ye, ye old gadget of sloppy crow bait! Sure, it's true!" The hag cackled with such ferocity that Marion thought she'd just been surged into an adrenaline plug any athlete would envy. She took another deep pull on the bottle, easily draining it an inch lower. "Before I get to the maze, let me go back a few seasons long long ago it was. Long enough to where the winds I heard whisper that night seem like a long slow whine from Father Time. He fixes all things, you know.

"It was deep in the mountains. Pitch deep. Miles past Snow Crest City, 'bout seventy miles north of here, when I was up and around with one of my partners. Saintly man, mind you. Hard for you to believe, ain't it?"

Marion just looked at her with his cop eyes laser focused on her every word.

"His name were Dan, and we had one of them rare moments of getaway time, for time was no longer Dan's friend. Friends of his gave us keys to a cabin deep in those mountains. Little time for privacy and silence. Telling stories. Cooking dogs by a fire. Cold as my goddamn nipples, it was, but ain't stop us from enjoying the vast beauty of nowhere nights.

"Rumor had it back then some giant wolf had been killing not only the locals' animals, but even some locals themselves. Look it up, Copper. Looky, looky, you'll see. But no goddamned wolf was to take away our last moments in time.

"One night...think it was just the night before our last...hmmmm..." Bridget then looked up to the ceiling as if caught in a sudden trance, her globby black eyeballs wobbly in their deep bony sockets.

"I'm still listening, Bridget," Marion said to get her back on track.

"Anyway, one night we were out on the patio deck of the cabin. Deck faced directly into the eastside of the mountains. Could see up to the tips of the tops as if they'd be tickling the bottoms of the stars themselves. The quiet? *The quiet?* It was that of death. Could hear the soul of death leave the body, by Cain. Hmmmm."

Marion cleared his throat loud enough for Bridget to pause. She remained in the trance-like focus, so focused that a bit of actual life seemed to breathe back into her skeleton body.

"What do you mean 'by Cain'?" He leaned forward a foot or so.

"Eh! Don't ye stop my tale, you pee pee boy! You seek answers, don't ever stop the flow! Seek and find, seek and find!"

She was right. Whatever she said and whatever she meant made no difference at that moment.

"I won't interrupt again."

"Be best you *don't*," she hissed back with such a force that Marion felt the kind of dizziness that sometimes came over him during severe distress.

"We'd all heard of that wolf. We'd all known the stories of its size and ravenous hunger. What it had slaughtered. But Dan...bless his innocence. And his ignorance. I'd be the protector over him but he didn't know no better. Still...he had his rifle on him, and that made him feel safe. That plus the safety of the deck. We turned to go back inside for the night when a wolf's howl—*the* wolf I was certain—tore across the silence as if space itself had been ripped asunder. In the haunted, blue-colored filters of the mountain realm, I could see all color drain from Dan's entire being. I held his hand firmly as we both looked out toward the howl. It was so close, the wolf had to be within the perimeter of the cabin's backyard area."

Bridget paused again, in trance, but instead of saying anything or clearing his throat to keep her on track, Marion felt himself in a similar trance, wondering why the hag's voice and speech sounded so eloquent when telling the tale.

"My eyes were far sharper than Dan's, so I scoured all around, not dare asking Dan to find any binoculars that could have been inside. Then I saw it. A ghastly phantom shadow that looked as much like a giant human as it did a wolf. Maybe it were *both*...I looked at Dan to silence him further when I saw his own eyes had fastened onto something to the right of the wolf's shapeshifting shadow.

Dan's eyes were more horror struck than had been triggered by the wolf. I followed his eyes.

"There was another cabin to the southeast of where we stayed. Never thought much of it as we hadn't seen so much as a candle lit at the place during our entire stay. As I looked where Dan was focused, I stopped in terror as I saw what would surely stop Dan's heart. Maybe my own. Walking from the cabin toward the giant wolf's shadow was a woman. Fearless in her approach. A shapely, striking woman dressed in such stark black that she seemed to glow in the blue night. Her walk then turned to panther-like strides as she pounced into the wolf's immediate space. There were trees lined up and down the area, and with an effortless leap, she jumped onto the tree closest to the wolf, anchored herself with both her legs and left arm, then outstretched her right arm and screamed at the beast in such a ferocious ear-splitting pitch I thought my own eardrums would burst. The scream sounded...alien. If an alien made sounds, that is. Hmmmm. And her eyes. I could see them. Two frightening pinpoints of lavender that could be seen from the howling moon. This woman had attacked the wolf in such a way that I believed I was watching something otherworldly. Something far more powerful than the wolf itself had ever known, for when the moment her scream blasted forth, it jolted back in its own high pitch whimper and ran off into the night in as much terror that had overtaken my Dan and me.

"Never seen such a sight. In all my ages on earth...a lot. It's a lot. Never seen such a sight."

Bridget leaned back on her stool as if to crack all the bones in her spine, and she took another long, deep pull on the bottle, swallowing just as long and deep. The silence she spoke about in the mountains began to lengthen in the gas station as they both stared at each other.

"That's quite a story," Marion said. He was as genuine as he was creeped out.

"Eh! It is that! Eh! Now what's it to do with that maze you want to know?"

"Yeah. I don't see the connection yet."

"Course you do! All those dreams you had in the coma! Those endless days of dreams where she came in through the other side to scream at ye! By the likes of Cain and God in hell, what do you think I was preaching at ye! Did you not hear a lick from my ticker?! Ye head into that maze...she'll be there. She'll be there." It was Magnus who was then whispering.

He huffed. "I've been bullshitted by professionals and you're full of it, Cain and God in hell, dancing around the mulberry bush with all of it. Why can't I get a straight answer from you? You think I'm playing here?"

With that, Bridget bumped herself from the stool so effortlessly she had become an entirely different creature. For she looked like a creature. Hobbled and rickety and in shambles, yes, but also with a newfound strength that alarmed Marion as he, too, stood off his stool to face her. Boxing style as he'd trained so many years in the sport, and all the street brawls any Houston cop must face. Yet he kept his hands down as to keep things as neutral as possible.

Bridget circled Marion even more hunched over, with her hands out as if to claw him in defense, but rather than striking she just circled around slowly, Marion following her lead, but all the while focused on her every move. In front of the cash registers, they had just enough room for a close-range sparring match.

"In all my days on this godforsaken earth I have lived, never before have I seen such wickedness, such ghastly power and furious anger, and in walks you, Mister Paul The Cop, in walks the likes of you just out of your comatose bleach, seeking the answers to all your loss! Doubting me! Yes! I knew your brother. I knew his demise. He let her in and she took it all as she has done so endlessly before. But you! You! You saw her in your dreams with the demon children! Didn't you?! Didn't you!?" Bridget hissed in fury.

Marion couldn't grasp how she knew what she knew, but that didn't matter. He'd heard a hundred thousand tales in his career that never made much sense but always contained some piece of truth in them if he dug in deep enough. His first rule had always been to ask the obvious.

"Why don't we stop this faceoff, Bridget, if that's what this is. Sound like a plan?"

"I've already given you the plan smack in the middle of your own tickler!"

"Okay then, why don't we settle down anyway. Because I know you don't want me coming in on you, and I sure as Christ don't want you any closer."

"Ha! Think you're funny, eh?" and with that she stopped moving as did Marion, following her lead.

"How is it you know about me so much? My dreams? Coming out of a coma?"

"You ain't been listening, pee pee boy. No matter you listened or not. Tale I told is truth. Now...all of a sudden I'm feeling too weary to carry on. At least for now. Make no never mind I'll be back at it soon enough! But you better scurry on out now 'fore you end up as your brother. Scurry on now, Mary Mary. Scurry on before things in here get a lot more than you'd ever want to handle. You'll need to have a deep trust in that."

Marion had no reason not to believe her story. It chilled him more than he let on, of course. Especially the lavender eyes Bridget saw on the demon woman who screamed down the big bad wolf. True or not, all of it began to resonate within him strong enough that he had grown just as exhausted as the hag said she was. He may have looked it, too, for all he knew.

He walked back a few steps from Bridget, turned to the station's glass doors and left. Just as he was about the shut the driver's door, he looked up to see the hag standing right in front of the truck. She was a shocking sight no matter how much he thought he'd gotten used to her looks.

"You'll see me again, Mister Comatose! Best you know that! And sooner than you expect!"

With that, Marion slammed the driver's door shut and off he drove, away from Duncan on the canyon highway heading west toward Odessa. He needed to drive around more to keep thinking things through.

He fired up the radio again to the same rock station. Iron Maiden's "Number of the Beast" filled the truck's cabin with exactly the recipe he needed. The darkness was so dense he kept the brights on constant, didn't matter if he pissed off drivers in the oncoming lanes.

No one's on the road anyway, so who gives a good goddamn? I've gotta see.

In fact, Marion was far righter than he realized when thinking to himself as he saw no signs of life in his own lanes behind him or ahead leading the way, none on the opposite lanes heading back to Duncan. Bruce Dickinson's full-throttle operatic tenor wailed on into the deep night drive as Marion wished the brights of the truck had another 50 lumens so he could see more than what was immediately in front of him.

Just as the song about The Beast ended, Marion suddenly could make out something in his headlights on the side of the road, twitching. More than twitching. He knew enough about roadkill that whatever it was, wasn't small game. He hit the brakes and turned onto the shoulder to position the headlamps for the best view possible of what was to be seen.

He knew how horrible it truly was before the horror had a chance to creep in enough to cause Marion's keen reactions to slow. Remarkably, yet also a perfect marriage to what he was seeing, the freeway lanes remained completely abandoned. Whatever gruesome savagery he

Dean Patrick

was about to face, the frightful night had left him deeply alone.

He opened the driver's door ever so slowly and carefully, knew he had no gun, nor a knife, only his hands to take on whatever assault that could come his way.

Fully lit up by the truck's headlamps was a hideous creature of obscene movement, devouring the shredded gore of the dead carcass of an unfortunate deer. The feasting creature's back was distorted and twisted in such a perversion of normalcy, Marion wondered if the thing was somehow insect in nature. Its legs were much thinner and smaller—with just as much distortion as its back—than its front legs, which were not legs at all, but jagged and metallic arms. Arms that tore into the dead carcass, shoveling the chunks of ruined meat and guts into the creature's face. A face Marion couldn't quite make out.

Then he could.

Fuck is that...What the fuck is that?

Marion's thoughts were so loud he believed he spoke, but instantly knew he was too stunned to speak just yet.

He never did speak.

It wasn't the creature's mangled features that terrified Marion to his marrow. It was what the creature was wearing. Shredded as badly as the carcass's remains, but still hanging around the beast's neck, shoulders, and waist to be perfectly recognized as the Exxon service station attire Bridget had worn. Same sickly blue top; same rayon black pants; same cheap faux pa black leather walking shoes. Only the shoes had been torn through by the creature's massive feet that looked more like the talons of an ostrich.

In a split moment, the creature stopped eating the carcass gore, stood up on its wiry legs, turned directly to Marion and the truck lights. The moment then turned much slower in motion, as the creature's limbs and feet and head sank in as if something was being poured on its entire frame, causing it to melt into Bridget Magnus herself.

"Ha! What of it now, Copper?! You think you've seen it all, but now I see you've not seen anything! Who are you to pass judgment? For I've been judged the centuries long since Salem, ye God fearing wretch! Hung until the maggots ate into my eye sockets, skull fucking me long before you were in ye's pappy's sack! Never forget this night, Mary Mary Paul Paul. Never forget what ye seek and what I've shown you during our show and tell. I do only *her* bidding. Only *her* bidding! The lavender-eyed demoness!" Bridget screamed in a voice so ragged and graveled only a witch's throat could bear the burden. "The lavender-eyed demoness! And ye shall fall to her feet, too!"

Marion had had enough for one night. Long known for his patience of Job, Marion's final patient knob was turned as far right as it would go. He jumped back into the truck and raced down the freeway with both the truck's front windows down, hoping the fresh air could snap him back to sanity. He *needed* to race back down the canyons that led to Odessa, perhaps to the Odessa Hotel, to root out all possibilities of what had happened to his brother as he swore to his own God he could hear Bridget Magnus cackle like a monster hyena long after she had disappeared from his rearview mirror.

Chapter Eight:

House of the Witch

H e drove hard and reckless right into the Odessa Hotel's parking lot. It was almost empty, and the town was blanketed in the silence of night that resonated with Marion's shock from what he'd just seen.

What am I doing here? What am I going to find here? What the fuck just happened?

As Marion debated back and forth with himself, he knew, of course, that he had to go back to the Duncan Exxon station. Had to go back to Duncan immediately. Had to find out more about Bridget and every other goddamn thing he'd seen. Yes, what he'd experienced with her had certainly eclipsed what happened at Janet Stone's place, what had happened at the hospital, and all the strangeness and witchery his brother certainly meant to warn him about.

He decided to wait around Odessa until stores were opened up so he could get a few changes of clothing and whatever else he needed, which was just about everything.

He ended up walking around the only mall in the area, the Odessa Center, wrapping his head around the horror he'd seen on the freeway in the middle of the night. Marion was a cop, and a hard case one, at that. He'd learned the skills of handling terrible events with ice in his veins, yet everything he'd seen since the hospital release had shaken him more than he'd ever experienced. Marion knew he'd awakened into a world where demons roamed the streets. His world had always been one of violence and betrayal, of murder and rape and robbery and pimps who whored out the innocent as detached as eating cereal in the morning. He'd seen the sickness and rot of police corruption where sacrificing the innocent was done as effortlessly as playing a hand of solitaire. All manner of evil he had seen and battled on the unforgiving concrete of Houston's hottest boiling cauldrons.

And here the fuck I am in Small Town America where evil is more literal, if that's even possible.

Later that afternoon, after buying all that he'd thought he would ever need for the next few months, Marion drove back to Duncan and stopped in the Exxon Station to find out where Bridget Magnus lived. He ended up speaking to a young man who was stocking the shelves. His nametag read *Devon.* "Hey there, Devon. What's up? Do you happen to know where a Bridget Magnus lives?"

Devon chuckled at first. "She's a character, that one. A hoot to be honest," Devon said, paying more attention to his products than Marion. The stocker was probably eighteen years old, twenty tops, gangly and heavily pitted in the face from awful acne that surely caused him a lot more trouble than just the scars.

"Yeah, well, not so sure about the hoot part, but she's a character. I'll give her points for that."

The comment was evidently enough to cause the young man to stop his duties and look Marion square in the eye. He was as tall as Marion but weighed a good eighty pounds or so less. "You new around here, mister?"

"Yeah. Steven Paul was my brother. I inherited his place down by the creek."

"Sure. I knew him. Nice place, too."

"About Bridget?" Marion prodded in his practiced way of interrogation. "Where's her place?"

"She's no longer here. No longer works here, I mean. She moves around from place to place up here, never staying at any one place more than a few months."

Dean Patrick

"You mean other gas stations? Convenience stores?"

"Yeah. Her way of trying to leverage more money with each move, only she's worked all of 'em up here. There's only a few."

"She must have just quit then. I saw her last night."

"Yep. Called in this morning, said she's taken a job down at Henderson's. You know it?"

"No."

"It's about ten minutes down the old highway, five if you take the freeway."

"I'm not interested in where she's working. Just want to know where she lives."

Devon scrunched up his nose as if what he was about to say was going to stink. "It's not only a shithouse, but the surrounding land is some three acres of garbage heaps and hoarded junk that's run afoul of the city for decades. The property is set deep off the main road, and you should have no trouble finding a spot to stake out the area from the comfort of your truck. If that's what you're thinking."

"Somewhat. Where's her place?"

"Simple enough. Head back to your place and go to the stop sign, hang a left, and it's on the left about half a mile down."

"Thanks, Devon."

The wiry kid looked at Marion with concern. "Listen...you oughta be careful going over there, looking around and such. I mean, I've known Bridget before I worked here. Few years. Whole town knows of her, at the very least, and I know what she looks like to folks who've just met her. Ragged and all. Broken down. But she's got a coarseness to her that's...well, it's different than just being ornery or mean. And different than even how she looks."

"You mean besides her abilities to transform into something that eats roadkill on the side of the highway in the middle of the fucking night?"

"I think I know what you mean. She struck me that

same kind of way, and then some. I'm Marion." He reached out his hand for a shake. Devon responded with a far more aggressive grip than Marion expected. "Nice handshake, Devon. A lot of kids your age have lost that courtesy."

"We're men, right? No reason to ever shy away from that, that's my thinking. No matter what my generation acts like."

"Good attitude, and I appreciate the intel."

"Intel? Isn't that cop talk?"

"It is. I'm out of Houston. Though I've been away from the force the entire year."

"Sabbatical?"

Marion looked over Devon and up and down and had completely changed his mind about the young man. He sized up Devon to be the exact type of character who could be trusted when things got ugly. He could feel it. "Something like that. That's another story, and one I wouldn't mind sharing with you sometime."

"I'm easy to find, and wouldn't mind at all, but take what I said seriously. Be careful when looking around Bridget's place. I've never spent any time over there, but I know a lot who have. It's the kind of place that gives off all kinds of bad vibes. And lately...well, lately there's been a lot of bad air around. Lot worse than you'd ever think, if that makes sense."

"Perfectly, and so noted. Thanks, again. I'll be seeing you. Rest assured."

Devon reached out to shake hands again, then hit the stocking duties as Marion headed out for his place, the Duncan Ranch.

***

At the ranch, Marion cleaned up, ate a quick bologna sandwich, and caught up on Facebook posts from HPD. He waited until it was nearly dark before venturing out. As he was backing out his driveway, he noticed a small light aglow at his new neighbor's place, which alarmed him, as he remembered what Deputy Jim Evanston had said when the white pickup truck was being pulled out of the creek. The long tall hard-case cowboy who had looked at Marion with a stare right out of hell was also the new owner of the Stan Smitts property. Adrian Kane, Evanston had said, purchased the place after Stan's murder, after Terra Drake had done the deed, but Marion hadn't noticed anyone coming or going, and he wasn't the type who let things slip. "Perhaps Kane is connected to Drake," he muttered a note to himself. "I'll have to check that out later." He pulled away and drove the directions Devon had given him to Bridget's place: left out of his driveway, left at the stop sign, and then half a mile down on the left.

Five minutes later, Marion drove by the house a few times, back and forth, turning around in reconnaissance, until finally picking a spot where he felt confident no one else was going to park. The vale was about as off-the-beaten-path as he'd ever seen, and the darkness was deeper and more enveloping than he'd ever felt in the monster city of Houston with its billion lights and dominant skyscrapers.

He'd found just the right spot where he could get a perfect view of the side and front of the house, lit by a dim lamppost, and most of the back area that was indeed littered with garbage and junk ranging from 55-gallon barrels (he could see at least 10) to ruined tires of every size, to piles of furniture and piles of scrap-wood that looked like all of it had been there for a hundred years. The ground was mostly dirt and gravel and overgrown with mounds of weeds and vines.

It wasn't that the house was run down, or that it was almost in ruins that gave Marion such pause to look around the place. He'd seen plenty of impoverished homes that were more like shacks in Houston's worst ghetto areas. MacGregor in the city's Third Ward. Fifth Ward.

Sunnyside. There wasn't a single place in all of Utah that threatened the kind of dangerous reputations those parts of Houston had attained. And Marion had done plenty of war-against-crime on those mean streets. Still, as he watched over Bridget's place, the sensation that rushed over him could have emanated from a large scarecrow with a sign around its neck: "STAY AWAY."

Marion took out the binoculars that Steve had left him in the glove box for a closer view and surveyed the area behind Bridget's property and beyond. There were acres of grassland and cornfields, but it was far too dark to observe any detail, and he wasn't quite sure what to even look for as he swept the binoculars back and forth, waiting for whatever the hell he hoped he would find. He could see a few dim lights from within the house, but not a trace of movement.

The silence and darkness began to feel oppressing until a creaking sound resonated from the house and echoed across the night. It came from the front door hinges as Bridget Magnus stepped out to the wreck of a sagging and splintered porch, talking on her cell phone. He could hear the grate of her awful voice but couldn't make out the words, as the crispness of the high mountain air allowed sounds to travel great distances but without clarity.

She walked around the front yard, cell phone to her ear, then walked to the back and stopped at one of the 55-gallon barrels. Cradling the phone to her ear with her shoulder, she lit a match and tossed it in the barrel, creating an instant burst of high flames. The trashcan fire lit up the area in wild deep shadows and undulating glows. She did the same to five more barrels, and before Marion knew it, the acre or more of Bridget's trashed backyard was alight with the giant candles.

Bridget remained on the phone for a bit longer as Marion focused his binoculars on the fire-lit fields connected to her yard. He could see movement that caused his skin to goosebump. It didn't take long before people strode from the back fields and onto Bridget's property. All women, and Marion counted ten to twelve of them, then twenty when he spotted Janet Stone. His breath hitched and his heart shuddered and his throat swelled.

Another woman appeared from directly behind the house, so she must have come from the fields on the other side. Her face and hair were painted a dark candy-apple red. She wore a silk suit that was the same color as the facial paint, with an open collared shirt (also red) and carried on her hips two children who were also painted the same red. The children were naked, Marion could see.

He thought the painted red woman looked like Dr. Pinault, but he couldn't swear by it, even with the binoculars. He continued to scan the area back and forth as he felt in his bone marrow something stranger was about to happen, and when it did, his grip on the binoculars tightened to the point his hands became sore.

Out of the cornfields from a center pathway that emptied into Bridget's backyard area, a line of orderly and full-suited men began to enter. From that single entryway, the men broke off into two evenly dispersed sections, to the left and to the right, in equal numbers they walked around and encircled the women, who had then spread out around the trashcan fires.

Marion adjusted the zoom on the binoculars to see each man was holding a hymnal. Each man wore a three-piece suit and tie, making the scene look as if a group of fifty or more business developers were gathering for a presentation.

Except for one other piece of attire on each man.

Each one of them wore a massive strap-on artificial penis with a deep black shine, either from the heavy rubber the dildos were made of, or they were painted in such a rich black enamel as to cause the sheen. The strap-ons were connected to a chained belt that wrapped in between the legs and up and around the waist in a snug fit. The men were singing a chorus of strange renditions of hallelujah that were in praise of different names Marion couldn't decipher.

What. The. Fucking. Hell?

He adjusted the binoculars for an even closer zoom, as he knew there was something else he needed to dial into. He focused on one of the men who had first come out of the cornfields, one who looked to be the leader, if there was such a person. When zooming in as close as the binoculars allowed, Marion saw an image etched into the strap-on's shaft, in gold, and knew that every man had the same. Though still too far away to capture any detail, he could see the images' outlines were similar in shape as the pendant figure he'd seen on Janet's necklace.

He had to control his breathing and remain calm, had to manage his increased heart rate. "I don't know if you saw anything this fucked up, Steve, but I'd wager that you did, holy Christ."

When all the men had entered from the cornfields, they created a complete circle, spread apart some six or seven feet from one another. The women inside the circle who were now gathered in an organized fashion around the trashcan fires, had already stripped down completely naked. Marion hadn't even noticed their unclothing, as he was too stunned and focused on the men's outerwear. The woman holding the children had also stripped off her clothing, her body painted the same red as the children's. She walked with the children on her hips into the center of the circle and turned directly toward the cornfield so Marion could only see her back and children's backs as she continued holding them perfectly still while they rested in peace on her hips.

The suited men, still singing in chorus, began to sing a little louder, and the naked women began to do squats around the trashcan fires with their arms out in front of them as if to warm their hands.

A sudden booming sound, more like a machine-cranking sound, as if large metal gears had suddenly burst to life, startled Marion to the point he put down the binoculars as he watched an enormous drive-in movie-sized screen appear from the ground behind the group. Or in front of them depending on perspective. It rose slowly and evenly, and when it stopped, it blocked his view of a large portion of the cornfields behind it, as the screen had to be at least eighteen feet high and fifty feet wide. The group of men and women remained where they stood, a large circle of men, smaller circles of women, but their heads all turned to the screen as a projector blasted from Bridget's house, filling the screen with a spectacular image of the woman Marion recognized from the portrait that stood on Janet Stone's cheap entertainment center. However, this time her eyes glowed lavender, and he knew who it was.

The enormous picture of the woman showed her arms high above her head, holding on to thick iron chains that were dangling above from some unseen rafter or ceiling. Her hair was worn down, long and flat with the sides pulled behind her ears. She was dressed in a one-piece leather-and-chains outfit highlighted with full-length leather-and-chain boots and matching full-length arm gloves. The boots had spikes instead of heels, the gloves had long taloned ends, and her lavender eyes were so vibrant and rich that the lights from them alone showed across the fiery trashcans of the wicked group below like two powerful flashlight beams. On her head she wore a crown of thorns buried deep enough into her forehead and above her ears that long streams of blood trickled down the sides of her face, past her eyes and nose, to the corners of her mouth. She had a wide crescent grin, her lips full and painted as black as her hair.

The massive image of the striking woman dressed in sexuality and mock-Christian suffrage was enough to cause

Marion to jolt back a bit in disturbance.

He also had no idea who was controlling the projector but saw that Bridget had chosen to stand by the trashcan fire closest to her house. She tilted her head back and shouted, "Begin!" A sound system of considerable power that must have been located and operated somewhere near the projector, began to play Black Sabbath's "Disturbing the Priest" at a near-concert level, causing Marion the instant reaction to look around to make sure no one else was up here. It was a song from the album *Born Again* when Ian Gillan had taken over the vocals, providing the band with a far more ominous and frightful sound than they ever had before or since. The song mixed with what was happening below created an effect that was as riveting as it was brimstone with Gillan's tortured vocals screaming about the falsehoods of religion and the glory of mockery.

A tall wiry man walked out from behind the house with another woman following him. She had him on a short chain leash. The man was naked except for the same strap-on the other men wore, and the woman was fully dressed as the men were dressed, only her suit was a fine black silk. She wore a half mask that covered her eyes and forehead, her jet black hair tightly braided and loose like long black strands of rope.

She led the man to the center of the ghastly scene, right in front of the painted woman and children. She screamed out in a deep throaty torn voice what Marion recognized as scripture.

"For the commandment is a lamp, and the law is light, and reproofs of instruction are the way of life, to keep thee from the evil woman, from the flattery of the tongue of a strange woman. Lust not after her beauty in thine heart. Let her not take thee with her eyelids!" She ended with some awful war-cry he'd never heard before. "Shemlemlafesh! Shemlemlafesh! Shemlemlafesh!"

As she shouted this a few times, the man arched his

back and opened his arms, stretched out as if to embrace the entire crowd before him as well as the massive screen picture that was moving just a bit due to a light wind. He arched his neck and threw his head back and roared into the fiery night. A barbarian yawp that Whitman himself had to have dreamt. Marion watched the man's body begin to go into controlled and twisted convulsions. His back began to buckle and bend in impossible ways as Marion saw his very spine, hips, and all joints protrude and even begin to break through the skin.

That was enough for Marion. He could no longer watch and did what he knew had to be done, jumping out of the Ram with the Beretta chambered and ready, safety off. He raced down the small embankment a dozen feet or so until he knew he could be seen perfectly by the wicked crowd below. "Lady, get those children out of here. If any other one of you motherfuckers move, I will gun you down without fucking notice." But the effect he created was nothing that he had expected, as every single one of the men turned and looked up to face Marion, then turned away and bolted around each side of the gigantic movie screen and back into the cornfields.

The naked women around the trashcan fires also turned and ran, not to follow the men, but toward the back of Bridget's house, disappearing into the fields to Marion's right as the house gave them cover.

The painted woman turned toward Marion, still holding the painted children calmly and seductively. The freakish man keeled over, slumped to his knees, elbows covering his body as if to hide. The woman who had him on a leash simply stood where she was and looked up to Marion as calmly as the painted woman and children.

"What the fuck is this shitshow?" Marion kept the gun on the woman and the leashed man. He had lowered himself enough to where he knew they could hear him without shouting.

"Nothing here concerns you, cop. We've broken no laws. This is simply a ceremony of a different sort. Nothing more." It was the painted woman who spoke, the children on her hips remained just as calm, which took Marion off his guard. The leashed man stayed put in a horrible fetal position. The woman in black remained silent.

"I know you." Marion's voice began to quiver.

"But you don't. And now it's time you leave. Time for all of us to leave as you have spoiled everything."

In what Marion was hoping to be a fantastic as well as heroic save of the innocent, the calm that had remained within the group below, children and all, disarmed him both physically and emotionally. He lowered his gun and clicked on the safety. His breathing was hard, his heart thumping relentlessly in his chest, his mouth slightly open, his eyes moving quickly over the group with a hard focus. He took deep breaths to control himself.

"I don't believe any of it. Anything you say." Marion's voice was ragged, but more in control than he expected. His eyes quickly darted over to the front porch of the house as he saw Bridget Magnus talking, once again, on her phone, avoiding eye contact of any kind, to anyone.

"Leave us now to clean up," the painted woman said again as she kissed the cheeks of both children. The leashed man remained on the ground; the woman in the mask and black suit remained iron stiff, and Marion was positive her eyes were laser focused on every move he made, though he had no clear view of her eyes behind the mask.

"I'll have a close eye on this...the whole lot of you. Believe it." Though he wanted his voice to have the conviction behind the words, he realized the group below shrugged him off. He put the Beretta in the back of his jeans and stepped backward to the Ram, never taking his eyes off the group, specifically the woman in the mask and suit.

Marion drove off, completely baffled and horrified.

Chapter Nine:

The Last Diner on Earth

All of what had happened in such a ferocious assault and speed since awaking from the coma had taken more of a toll on Marion than he realized. He was a big man, powerfully built, no matter if he was carrying more weight than he wanted, or was in top-athlete shape, Marion's training both in the police force and outside with other sports such as boxing, basketball, and baseball made him a formidable opponent to anyone and anything. But he'd never trained to take on the likes of such witchcraft and mayhem that seemed to be waiting around every Duncan corner to come out and rush him with an attempt to rip out his throat.

He was more tired than he wanted to be after just a few weeks trying to settle in. He'd taken many trips into Odessa to buy even more clothes, workout gear, and even a pair of the latest and most advanced walking and hiking boots. He took such trips to spend money and walk around simply to keep his mind away from madness, to purposely avoid shit. One night, while pacing back and forth from room to room, his restless mind unable to find peace or sleep, he decided to take a drive.

It was nearly 2:00 a.m. on a Saturday, and he needed to clear his head and take a walk.

The walk came first in the pitch night as he strode around the corral area. He was heading to the barn to check inside, as he hadn't yet taken any time to do so, when he looked up and saw that the sky was moving, undulating like a boa constrictor, and the longer he watched the massive phantom, the more he began to recognize it as some kind of spacecraft, its propulsion energy waves distorting the machine with the same effect as heat waves on the desert floor. The entire night sky was moving in unison as if it were an endless glowing snake with iridescent purple and red lights. He couldn't see the edge of it in any direction.

How can there possibly be such a ship that's this...big? What the hell is this fucking thing?

He had taken one of the many flashlights Steve had left lying around—a powerful USB C flashlight that was as bright as any police light he'd ever used—to walk around in the night. He shot it straight up into the air to whatever was slowly moving across the sky. It was useless, of course, so he turned it off and stuck it inside his back jean pocket, pulled out his phone and zoomed in as close as possible, looking into the phone's camera lens and saw that it picked up just enough detail to convince him it had to be some type of spacecraft, though he still couldn't see any outer edge for as far as he could see.

Has to be the biggest UFO ever...what the Christ?

He quickly pocketed his phone again to ditch it for the flashlight, turning it back on to walk out of the corral and to the Ram. The movement in the sky remained constant and consistent enough to cause Marion's terror alert to begin sounding off just as constant and consistent. He started the truck and ventured out toward the freeway to The Stones' "Symphony for the Devil," Mick Jagger's high-pitch howl perfectly embracing the blackness that consumed Duncan.

Marion ended up finding a diner, of all things, a few miles past the train tracks, some eight hundred feet higher on the mountain side about a mile east of the Exxon station and Duncan liquor store. He had a strange urge to stop at the Exxon to see if Devon may have been working, but decided against it as it was probably far too late. He'd grown to like Devon and had come by to visit him on a few occasions as he wanted to tell him the story of what happened at Bridget's place, and every other goddamn thing that had been going on. Devon seemed the only person he could trust. He and Evanston, that is, but Marion hadn't made time to meet up with the deputy. "I need to remedy that and see them both, and how long has this fucker been moving, and just how big is it?" he said out loud, turning The Stones down a notch.

He continued glancing up intermittently at the massive object while looking for a place to park. Just as he'd seen while standing in the corral, the object had no end and no beginning, as it filled the entire sky as massive as any full-blown storm over Houston during hurricane season. Marion noticed its lights had changed from the deep reds and purples to sharper yellows and warm whites. Deeper, more holistic. Lights that even shimmered as hauntingly as the object itself.

"It's not from this world," Marion muttered.

The diner's sign read: *The Dog Pound Bar and Grill*, lit up in a neon red that blasted into the endless pitch of night and seemed to reach up to the moving leviathan above. Designed in the same 1950s Norman Rockwell nostalgia, the diner looked as if it were the last place on earth to order a home-cooked dog or burger. He found the diner and all its brilliant windows to be as startling as the massive object above.

As he parked the Ram, he saw a few other lonely hearts had parked spaciously apart in the diner's parking lot. Along with everything else, he was also trying to clear his mind of the nightmare of the demon woman dressed as a whore with a whip and ball-gag, preaching unrestrained obscenities to demon children and ancient men and women, naked except for their grotesque fly masks.

He opened the glass doors and walked into a place that was lit up with even more brilliance than the building's outside neon. Marion had to shade his eyes to prevent an instant headache as he peered around the joint. The booths were all pasted in purple plastic, the floor tiles a beaming black and white checkerboard with a knuckled and protruding finish that he felt through the soles of his boots.

Large disco balls hung from the shocking white ceiling. To Marion's left as he entered, he saw a few women in white robes and bare feet, walking around a few of the diner tables in a trance and humming something quite familiar. To his right, and what caused his heart to skip a few beats, he saw at the far-right corner a table where lookalikes Joseph Stalin and Adolf Hitler were sitting across from each other, engaged in what surely had to be a conversation any fly on the wall would love to overhear.

This has got to be a residual part of the coma, somehow, that's gotta be it. No way they're real...or are they?

A piercingly light yet gravelly voice interrupted any and all thought. "How do Giddy Up?!" a woman said who stood behind the booths and bar seats that were evenly spaced and bolted down as the diner's centerpiece. She was dressed in a wicked powder blue vest with rusted oversized buttons on each side, torn down the front to reveal stunning cleavage. Her makeup and lipstick were smeared like a drunk clown's. She was tall enough that Marion saw she wore a heavy plastic belt that sat just above her pelvis, with a heavy plastic gun holster on her right hip that had to hold at least a .357 Magnum revolver.

Second sideshow I've seen in a month, wearing hip shooters.

Marion looked around the inside of the diner a bit longer before replying. He noticed, back to his left, sat a few young people dressed in rags who had clearly stopped talking—if they were ever talking—the moment the hostess greeted him. The robed mumbling women didn't stop shuffling or mumbling. On each side of the diner also sat monstrous television sets, each one playing a show Marion had never seen. So big were the TV sets, and so primitively designed, they looked more like giant wood and glass cubes. He then walked up to the diner bar area and sat down on one of the candy apple red stools. He looked over again to Stalin and Hitler, then straight into the hostess's eyes. Marion knew instantly that it was crucial to speak to her as if all the levels of bizarre that were neatly leveled in the diner were in perfect order. "You see what's been going on outside tonight?"

"Can't say I've had a chance to get out, as it's just little ole me here, takin' charge as the sitter of All Oddities Are Us." She leaned over the counter to purposely highlight a perfectly sculpted body that was an instant, though brief, distraction.

Marion looked around the diner again to survey all the scenes taking place in case he needed to make any drastic moves. He had started carrying the Beretta everywhere he went. Kept it in the truck's glove compartment for easy access and storage. He was grateful he'd taken it with him and had it tucked perfectly in the back of his jeans, ready for anything he thought the witchery of Duncan could beset upon him. He then looked at the hostess and took a deep breath. "I think things will be fine in here without you for just a minute; you need to see this, and you're clearly the sanest one in here. Your makeup needs a little touch up, but still, I need to know *I'm* still sane."

"Ha! Don't like my getup? Wow!" The hostess instantly pulled out a hand mirror from under the bar area and looked at herself quickly and dismissively. "It's been a long night, for sure." She put back the hand mirror, after doing just enough lipstick repair to take away the clown look but making herself look more like a cheap escort. "Can you imagine the conversation between two of the world's richest heathens, talking about an App Store issue, of all things, while I've got what I've got going on in here?"

That came completely out of the blue.

Still, the question seemed to suddenly make perfect sense to Marion's stalk from insanity. "You've got a point, I guess. But you've got to see this."

"Okay, okay. Hey, you two!" she yelled over to the Stalin-Hitler Party. "Keep an eye on the joint. I'm checking outside with our newest guest."

Both despots stopped their conversation and looked over to the hostess and Marion, said nothing, then went straight back to their intense conversation.

"Let's go, come on, be quick about it." The gunslinger hostess walked around the bar and over to the only door in or out, walking past Marion as if he'd never walked in. "Are you coming out or not?" She looked over her shoulder back to him in irritation.

Marion said nothing as he nodded in agreement and walked outside again, the both of them walking a few feet into the parking lot. He looked up to the sky as the hostess started vaping. It was a sickly sweet smell that Marion never liked over actual tobacco. "What's your name? I don't see a name tag."

"Rebecca. What am I supposed to be seeing?" She was aloof, holding her vape pen between her manicured fingers like a sophisticated madam in a 1920's speakeasy.

"Look up and see. You can't see that movement? There aren't any stars or clouds, and we must be more than six thousand feet up."

After taking a long drag and blowing out more of the sickly vapor, Rebecca tilted her head up. Marion was standing close enough to begin memorizing her features and filing them away for instant access when needed. She had a model's body with a leathered demeanor, wearing several rings on each hand, a few silver necklaces, and perfume heavy enough to compete with the vapor's stink.

"Yeah. I see what you're spatting on about. Even looks like an edge of it over the mountains." Rebecca pointed farther east.

Marion followed her arm and index finger. He could indeed see what looked like an edge that separated the moving object from the sky. He also noticed the ring she wore on her index finger; it had that same familiar image etched on the face of the wide silver band. "Let's go back in so you can tell me about that ring. The one that's got the weird figure."

Rebecca put her long slender hands to her seductive hip line in over exaggeration. "I thought you wanted to talk about the moving sky." Marion said nothing as he stepped back inside. Rebecca followed right behind. In fact, she walked briskly past him and right back to where he'd first seen her. He took a seat on the stool that faced the register, looked over to the Hitler-Stalin gig, over to where the robed women were still doing their act, then settled his eyes on Rebecca. "Now tell me about that ring."

She held it up and admired it as if it were the Hope Diamond on her finger. "Pretty cool, huh."

"It's weird."

"Everything in here is weird, if you haven't noticed."

"What's going on with the Hitler and Stalin comedy team? Who do they think they're kidding?"

"Their stories?" Rebecca made a finger gun and pointed to the robed women. "Or theirs?" She pulled the trigger and blew on her fingertip.

Marion remained speechless.

"Tough call for sure."

"Why don't you fill me in? Cut the shit."

Rebecca leaned into the bar with her left hand and rested the other on her holster. She was every bit the beauty of Janet Stone or even the good doctor, but Rebecca differed from them both in that her demeanor didn't seem to pose an immediate danger. "Cut through all the shit that's connected? You have to see some of those dots lining up by now, right?" She tapped her hard nails on the butt of the gun and winked at Marion while licking her lips.

Marion swallowed hard but kept his demeanor a hard stance with cool breathing.

Rebecca walked around the bar to Marion and took the seat on the stool next to his. The giant television that hung on the wall behind the robed women cut to a white noise screen as the diner music turned techno and pulsing, but played at a low level that intensified the feeling of everything going on in the diner. Like Marion's hearing of everything else around him. He could even hear the voices of Hitler and Stalin but couldn't make out what they were saying. What he did know was they were speaking in English, not their native tongues.

As much as he wanted to take a longer view down Rebecca's cleavage and over her crossed legs with how close she was to him, he turned his back toward what she called the living history Ted Talk. Hitler and Stalin were in a deep discussion with such penetrating eye contact that Marion thought they were perpetually locked into a stare contest with only their lips moving. The giant television screen behind them displayed closeups of the robed women on the other side of the diner who had sat down and were deep into their own private discussion.

About all kinds of hell, no doubt.

"You ready to listen?" Rebecca's voice cut through all the noise like a fresh razor.

Marion nodded.

"Wildcats and hyenas, wildcats and hyenas...they shall meet, and the goat demons shall greet each other. Greeting and speaking as if it's the most natural event you'd ever seen. And there, too, will be Lilith, dancing about wildly. And Lilith will find it all as a resting place. That's straight out of the book of Isaiah. Give or take a few lines I may have altered."

"What the fuck are you talking about?"

"This. All of this. How it all connects." Rebecca raised her hands above her head and moved them around with her body slowly spinning the stool in animation as if everything in the diner was something she had created herself. "What you've seen outside when you came here. Those you may have even seen since being here, because you're not from around here, let's be honest."

Marion looked at the woman as intensely as he could, focusing his eyes and looking into hers as deeply as possible. He wanted to understand. In that instant, he tried to wrap his head around all of it, all he'd seen and what she just had then suggested. He remembered the demon woman in his coma dream calling herself Lilith and his debating her that he thought she was Terra. He tried to tie in some kind of relationship with Dr. Pinault and Janet Stone. And the worms in the fridge. The horror of Bridget Magnus and the fiery devil dancing and worship he'd seen at Bridget's hellish hoarder place of ruin. Then it hit him as he looked Rebecca up and down her sultry body and into her eyes again. She was there that night dancing alongside the others at Bridget's place.

"You were there, too, weren't you? I know you were."

"Shhhh. Hush now."

He was about to spout off a few ideas about the notes and the letter from his brother that were indeed a connection to everything he'd seen and felt deep in his cop gut. He was about to really lay into Rebecca that he'd seen her at the Bridget Magnus witches' dance, when the diner door opened and in walked a tall gentleman dressed in a light tan suit, no tie. His hair long and thick. Perfectly shaven as if in preparation for an important presentation or speech.

Everything and everyone in the diner fell completely silent.

"You mind if we go take a seat in one of the booths

and have a talk?" The stranger directed this to Marion.

He didn't look at the man as if he were crazy, but he wanted to. "Sure. May as well." Marion noticed how instantly uncomfortable Rebecca looked. "You want to come join us?"

"I just want to talk to you," the stranger said. "I have no business with her or anyone else in here."

Marion chuckled. "Kinda rude, isn't it? I've been talking to this woman for a bit now, and you walk in and ask to talk to me, then you're rude to her. Sorry, I don't operate that way, no matter what level of crazy we're in. If she wants to come sit with us, she's more than welcome. You cool with that, Rebecca?"

The stranger glared at Rebecca with a set of eyes that commanded silence.

Marion turned to her, noting that her eyes were homed in on the stranger. "Rebecca?" He leaned in closer. "Hey. Rebecca. You want to join us?"

Still nothing.

"What's wrong? Hey, what's wrong?" Marion gently shook her knee. She finally looked at him. All the color had drained from her face, which didn't seem possible, as she was already porcelain white.

"I'll sit this one out. You go ahead."

"You sure?"

Rebecca nodded.

"Alright. I'll be right over there, I guess." Marion pointed to a booth that was farthest from the door. "After you," he said to the stranger with an inviting arm gesture. As he followed him to the booth, he looked over to the Hitler-Stalin debate and saw them looking at the stranger with their piercing black eyes. He then looked over his shoulder, back toward the robed women and the couple in the corner, all of whom had their hands linked together, watching carefully as if to see who was going to blink first in some kind of showdown.

The two of them sat across from one another. Marion leaned in to make sure his presence was felt and not just seen. "I've got years and years under my belt, dealing with weirdos. What's your play? Do you know what's going on around here? Have you seen what's going on outside in the sky? I come in here on a late-night drive, and I see those two fucks." Marion tilted his head toward Stalin and Hitler. "Why are they here?"

"I met your brother once."

The comment cut straight through the quick of all the bizarre surroundings. Marion went silent in his mind as he kept his police composure on full display. "I see."

"I sometimes step in when people are in over their heads."

"That doesn't even make any sense. Everyone here is over their heads, but then again, the shit I've seen lately, nothing makes sense. When did you see my brother?"

"Late last year."

"Yeah. So did I. Then New Year's. That was it. What's your story? You know who I am, clearly. Who are you?"

The stranger ran his hands through his thick hair, so thick it was more like course wire. "You can call me John."

Marion scoffed. "Okay, John. Let me lay it out for you, even though I think you know exactly what time it is. When I last saw my brother, I came to help him with some heavy shit he'd been going through with someone who I now know is as wicked as anything I've seen, and I've seen it all. I just came out of a coma a few weeks ago. Since then, I've seen the kind of witchery that's brought you here tonight, including what is going on in this diner from hell, and out there in the sky, in case you've seen it."

John looked bored, but his eyes were far too deep with wisdom and far too kind for such disrespect. "Have you ever heard of Lilith?"

Marion's coma dream came rushing back as if he'd

just awakened from it again. He let out a deep breath. "I had a dream about her. I think."

John leaned in over the table, his hands under his legs. His eyes suddenly turned from the deep kindness and wisdom to something coarse and hooded, which caused Marion to press against the back of his booth seat to brace himself. "Well. You're gonna meet her. And she's looking for something to eat."

Fighting a panicked heartrate, Marion leaned in toward John. "What am I supposed to say to that?"

"When I met your brother, he was already too far gone. But he still had enough left in the tank for me to show him the possibility of a way out. She was with him. He didn't heed my words. You're far from gone, Marion. You're just getting started. That's why I'm here. Feed her. That's your strategy. Your brother couldn't do that, not in his shape. Whatever you dreamt, she'll take it to you tenfold. You've only seen the previews. Go with it."

"You're talking in riddles, John. Feed her what?"

"You'll know when the time comes." John stood from the booth and held out his hand for a shake.

It was a handshake that Marion had never felt or known: gentle, but clearly withholding as much power as a cast-iron bench vise.

After John left, Marion stood and walked back to Rebecca. Hitler and Stalin resumed their discussion, and the robed women and young couple went back to their insanity.

"You have any idea who that was?"

"Some. You should leave now." Rebecca said this with a similar coarse look John displayed just before he told Marion that the demon woman would be looking for something to eat.

He left without a single word. It was nearly 5 a.m. as he drove back to his new place in silence. Whatever had been moving across the sky was gone.

Chapter Ten:

The Duncan Maze

A few nights later, Marion sat down on the leather couch to catch whatever movie was on television. He had the lights dimmed. It was early evening and far too quiet.

He'd gone out every night since returning from the diner to see if he'd find any movement in the sky. No such luck, but he knew what he'd seen, and he knew the others who'd seen it knew what it meant. At least Rebecca did, and he was sure that John knew just about everything. "Whoever the hell you are," he whispered as he turned the television on.

Only a few of his Houston cop friends he'd worked with had called, probably to see how things were going, that they'd been calling for ages and had about given up. It wasn't that he didn't have any friends who stopped trying to stay connected after his divorce a few years back, but there were still a few friends who were once neighbors who'd left messages over the months when he was comatose. It was more that Marion had told all those in his inner circle that he needed a good long sabbatical, that he'd made the decision to go find his brother and give him some help with whatever disaster had befallen him, and told everyone he really didn't have any idea when he'd be back.

Over the past month or so while staying in Duncan he'd only given his phone number to two people: Devon and Jim Evanston. He still didn't know Devon's last name.

He'd been thrown into a witch's brew after fighting through a coma for four months, but for all he knew that entire length of time was spent inside a dreamscape specifically designed by forces that wanted him planted front-and-center of the actual designer. He had been recounting every word his brother had written in his final letter until he could cite it backward and forward. Steve was right. From everything Marion had seen since awakening, madness seemed infested in every corner his brother had ever roamed.

What he'd seen and what his brother wrote caused Marion more determination to solve a crime, and only God knew how many had been committed that were directly linked to something he'd never thought possible. Since his Rookie year in Houston, when he faced the giant city with a profound fearlessness to single-handedly end crime all together, Marion had never felt such determination to get to the bottom of something that he knew was a horror with no end in sight. What John had said in the diner also stuck in his craw. He had to bust apart every last door with his bare hands, as knew how bad things had been for his brother because of how bad they were becoming for himself.

When his phone rang, Marion still hadn't gotten used to the sound of it. It took him listening to it ring ten, twelve times to become more familiar with the sound itself, as if he were still in the coma, trying to clear his way out of the fog. His phone displayed the instant irritation of "UNKNOWN CALLER" flashing on the screen.

May as well answer. I've got every other goddamn thing going on.

Marion: Marion Paul.

Terra: Hello, Marion.

Marion: Who's this?

Dean Patrick

Terra: I think you know exactly who it is, and I think it's long past due that we finally meet. In person, that is. You were recently asking around about the Duncan Maze, being so early in the year, and all. Prodding innocent folks with such intense questioning. You've seen and met some...curiosities. Is that fair to say? My little friend, Bridget, for example. Heard she got your goat. Janet? Rebecca? And the Woman In Red?"

Marion: They're different sorts, that's for sure.

Terra: Ha! How clever. Well, dear Marion, there's no longer any need for all the ravaging around our Little Town of Bethlehem—

Marion: That's where you're wrong. I'm just getting started, and if you think you're—

Terra: Don't you interrupt me. Oh no you don't. Don't you dare be rude with me. That's my role. I'm not like the others. I'm *not* the one!

Marion: Fair enough. Who are you and where do you want to meet?

Terra: You get right to the point, as I do. I think we'll get along just fine. I'm Terra, but I'm sure you're aware of that.

Marion: I don't think I've been more aware of anything in all my days, to be honest. Everything that's been going on—

Terra: I really don't care to hear about it. Why don't you take a drive down to the Duncan Maze you were asking about. We can chat there.

Marion: Fine. I'll be there shortly.

Terra: You hurry on, now. Best not to keep me waiting.

Before Marion could say a word back, she hung up. He stared at his phone then glanced at the movie on TV. *The Devil's Advocate* was playing, and it was at the scene when Al Pacino's devil was lecturing to Keanu Reeves that God was an absentee landlord.

***

The Duncan Maze was an annual event, usually held from the end of September until All Hollow's Eve. However, as soon as he'd seen the sign that led him to the horror of Bridget Magnus, and the ghoulish freakshow in the backyard of Bridget's witch house, he knew he would enter even more freakish territory. He fired up the Ram and headed to the cornfield a half mile down from the Exxon and across the street.

She said it was time to meet, so let's get on with it.

It was a five-minute drive, tops, like most drives to any place in Duncan, but when Marion pulled into the massive dirt parking lot, he was astonished at the size of the cornfield itself. He saw what looked to be at least a half mile in each direction, east and west, ten-foot corn stalks where visitors could roam around in weird delight, trying to find their way through a maze and back out again. If they were lucky.

But it was the end of June and everything about the place was indeed amiss.

The dirt lot had exactly three trucks and one car

parked smack in the middle. A red 1969 Mustang to be exact. Convertible. Mag wheels, dual exhaust. "Gotta be her car, and whoever else works here is with her," he whispered as he pulled up next to the muscle car and looked around the area to scope things out. He hesitated to shut off the ignition, as he wanted to hear the end of AC/DC's "Whole Lotta Rosie," as loud as he could stand it, and Angus Young's blistering guitar solo hitting the peak of the final segment.

Just before the song ended in its shattering final guitar riff, Marion turned off the truck, restoring peace and quiet, then hopped out and walked toward the ticket box, which looked to be a trailer house that was used for all transactions.

There she sat, in an over-sized oak wood rocking chair directly in front of the Duncan Maze entrance, just to Marion's right of the ticket counter. Terra Drake. Her hips and torso looked to be slowly writhing—almost grinding— to the pounding rhythms of AC/DC's anthem. Maybe she had heard it through the dead quiet evening that was slowly falling into place.

Her arms rested comfortably on the chair's arms. Her hands dangled at the wrists, displaying a set of nails that looked like three-inch scalpel blades painted a rich silver. Her sculpted legs were crossed in authority and sexual command, and she showed them off completely as the heavy leather skirt she wore was hiked all the way up. She wore a black velvet cowboy hat and black ankle alligator boots with chrome tips and matching spurs. Her jacket was fluorescent dark pink with embroidered zig-zag patterns of crucified lizards.

Christ almighty.

"I'm here to chat, so let's chat."

"You'll need a ticket first," she said in a soft voice that was sultry and breathy. Her right boot toe tapped up and down, causing the silver tip to cast a sharp spine of light at Marion as he continued to look Terra over.

"Right. A ticket."

He walked to the ticket counter where two large hillbilly types stood behind the plexiglass counter windows.

I could take both of them, no problem.

"One adult please. How much?"

"How much did the lady say it'd be?"

Marion looked over to Terra, who was looking him over, up, and down, then back to Hillbilly One. "She didn't say, and I don't see any prices listed anywhere, so why don't you just tell me what it is so we can settle up. That okay with you, buddy?"

"Buddy? *Whoa* there, stranger. I don't know you from Teddy Goddamn Roosevelt and his wire-framed spectacles," Hillbilly One bellowed. He had a mouthful of rotted teeth that dotted his gum lines, a large black nose ring that was cracked, and mangy hair tucked inside a filthy ball cap. Hillbilly Two looked even more ragged and gangly as he leaned closer to his partner while giving Marion a wide-eyed stare that could have only come from months of meth use, or even crack.

"Okay." Marion leaned into the plexiglass, resting his left arm on the outside counter, and his right hand rested on the Spyderco clip knife that he carried in his right jeans pocket. He knew the instant his hand reassured the presence of the knife that he'd left the Beretta in the truck.

Fuck.

"You want to play it that way? We can, but you better believe I'm not the one to fuck with. Not for one second or I promise you we'll do this right now, and it'll be as ugly as you've ever seen."

The hillbillies were big boys, no doubt about it, but Marion was not only close to them in size, he had his gifted strength from years of Houston street battles that had matched him against the meanest of the mean, when shit got wicked and real. He'd been shot a few times over the years, had shot a few shitbags himself, and he'd been in countless brawls in Houston's underbelly, experience that gave him at least a chance against Duncan.

I'll need every chance I get.

However, he'd seen his world turned on its head, post-Bridget Magnus era. And John had said he'd only seen a preview of the shit to come.

Maybe Houston's mean streets have met their match here in Duncan. It's best to just go with it.

Marion was beginning to realize, perhaps, what John had meant.

"Touchy," Hillbilly Two said in a high-pitched squeal, showing off a set of rot in his mouth that made his partner's look dental fresh. "So, so, touchy are we? Cost to get in will be twenty bucks even. No tax. No hidden fees. No fine print. Just a single Jackson or credit card. Debit, too. No checks. You in?"

"Yeah, I'm in. All the way." Marion handed the hillbillies a twenty-dollar bill, put his wallet back and made sure the knife in his front pocket was still there, even though he knew it was.

Better safe than sorry with this bunch, and I sure as fuck should have remembered the Beretta.

Marion walked away from the ticket counter and the hillbillies and back to where Terra was sitting, rocking her in chair without a care in the world.

"Looks like you just came wakey wakey from a bad bad dream, Big City. One of those kinds when you're running around in the wilderness and find yourself trying to ward off a giant war pig. Big tusked beast that was let loose that *you* yourself was part of letting loose. Big ole war pig babirusa boar! And *you* let it out!"

She spoke in the most striking voice he may have ever heard, but it was the comment that took Marion completely off guard and knocked down all his cop defense strategies, as he had indeed awakened the other night from such a nightmare.

"How the fuck do you know about that, lady?"

"I don't know what you're talking about."

"Of course you do! That's why you're here, is it not? Come down to the maze to find your way out? Find your way out of everything you've been lost in, just so you can find your way back to everything you once knew? Don't plan on that taking place just yet. We're just starting out. Your current disposition, I'm sure, will remain your constant navigator."

"Look, we were just on the phone a bit ago and you said this is the place we should meet, so whatever it is you're—"

"Now, now. You're trying to tell me you weren't running around in your dreamscape again, this time playing tricks on your whole family by letting out that giant war pig to hunt them all down while you giggled in trickery? Is that what you're telling me?"

Marion remained silent. That war pig was indeed part of his dream the night before. In some strange land—as all dreamscapes created—he had released a massive babirusa into a wild forest to hunt down his family and friends, family that had died years ago, family he hadn't remembered in years. He pushed himself forward to snap out of it, but Terra popped off the massive rocker and stepped instantly into his space with panther-like grace and power. In her boots, she stood eye-level to Marion.

A little taller, and why didn't she talk about this when they spoke on the phone?

"You better think this right on through to the other side, Big City. I know you saw your mother running away from the war pig. Screaming at you. Screaming and ranting and wanting to know why you did it, and why you wouldn't save her. Why did you do it? Why? Because you wanted that war beast to mow her down, her and all the rest of them, mow 'em down and tear them to pieces. That's why.

And that's why you're here, the *why* of it all."

He focused on his breathing as he realized that would be critical. "You know something, lady, why don't we just get this started, whatever *this* is," he said with as much strength as his inner spirit could muster, and he thanked God under his breath that he still had it.

Stay with me God, so help me.

"If you're praying to your God, well...if that's your strategy, then...by all means, God help you. No pun." Terra winked at him. "You see behind me here? Tonight the maze is just for you. One entrance. One exit. I had it all designed just for you." She turned toward the massive cornstalks that looked endless and foreboding.

Hillbilly One and Hillbilly Two had come out from behind the ticket counter and were just a few feet from Terra and Marion.

Again, he sized them up. They were even more filthy and repulsive than he'd seen before, and he suddenly halfway expected them both start to yelling at him and ordering him to squeal like a pig.

If it ain't God who'll get me through this, then it'll be my acid wit.

It wasn't the hillbillies Marion sweated. No, no. He knew every drop of blood he'd spill would come courtesy of the stunning demon beauty who was clearly in charge of everything.

"Inside the maze are several miles of pathways. You could be in there for hours, but knowing your background and all, I suspect you'll be out in no time."

"You're not going in with me? Isn't that the whole point of all this?"

"I'll be here when you come back. I'm not going anywhere. I've got these two here to keep me occupied. Unless you want *them* coming along?"

"Thanks. I'll manage." Marion made the quick decision to go along with everything. No reason not to.

He'd played along with plenty of games throughout his career to find answers, search for clues, figure shit out. If that was one thing he knew was most needed, since his feet touched the floor of the hospital room, it was the need to figure out what in God's name he'd stepped into.

Remember what John said: Feed Her. Go with it. Yes, witchery's afoot. No other goddamn way about it.

"In you go, Big City. See you on the other side."

Before he could retort, Terra had turned back to her grand rocking chair, her body more alive than any woman Marion had ever seen.

He walked into the cornfield maze and, within a few minutes, felt completely lost. Never any good with directions, Marion always used his GPS, always had his phone Maps app on. It was his one weakness in the world of policing, and now he was feeling it far too quickly. His phone was useless. No signal. *Of course not.* If being directionally challenged was his greatest weakness, his lack of panic and ability to remain cool under pressure was his strongest.

Still, something was beginning to feel as off as what he sensed when first talking to Dr. Pinault, and to Janet when he walked into her living room, and to Bridget before he saw her go full-ballistic horror.

He began to move faster as well as more focused, wondering why he'd agreed to such a stupid stunt, when suddenly the path he was on led to a wide open spacious area where a glass and wood octagon-shaped housing unit sat as if it had just been placed there not long ago. *But how?* That's all he could think to ask. Large wood paneling lined the outside with thick glass mirrored panes. The roof was steep and chiseled. Marion didn't hesitate to enter.

Good a time as any to sit down and think this shit through.

Inside the octagon were long iron benches painted in a deep amber lacquer. They faced a smaller octagon glass replica of the overall building itself that was housed for what looked like some kind of showcase display unit that was sometimes featured in more elaborate zoos like in San Diego or Chicago. Its ground was pure sand.

What the fuck is this doing here?

Marion took a seat on one of the benches to view the strange glass housing. As soon as he did, he saw the floor inside the building open in various places where cement pillars rose from below the ground. Standing and crawling on the pillars were toddlers with the heads and faces of aged men and women. Faces and heads that looked sewn onto their little bodies with catgut stitches. He saw they had teeth that were long rusted needles.

All in all, as they entered the building, stepping and crawling off the pillar platforms onto the sandy ground, there had to be easily twenty or more miniature human creatures that began moving around the building, looking confused and frightened. Some remained on all fours, crawling, others shuffled about with their stubby hands and arms reaching outward as if they were blind.

Every single one of them had fistfuls of worms. Some were eating them, others just looked at them in confusion.

"The fuck is this shit?" Marion whispered. "My God." He stood up from the bench and walked up to the front glass pane for a closer look. Not only were the miniature human creatures shuffling aimlessly, he could also see in their eyes something that had taken away their very souls long long ago. Eyeball sockets that were bored out and ruined. Blackened. Their heads were all bald and each wore a different tattered covering around the waist.

Thank Christ.

As Marion continued watching in a trancelike horror, he noticed the ceiling of the glass housing open, as well as the wooden ceiling that covered it. When he looked up—all the while his peripheral remained as focused as possible on every human creatures' movement—a large spherical array of light came from the roofs' openings like an upside down funnel. He looked up at the top of the funneled light and saw Terra Drake lowering herself from above in a spectacular effect where Marion could see nothing technology-wise assisting her.

She was fully naked, her body glistening with sweat. Except for the black velvet cowboy hat.

As she lowered herself farther down from the funneled light, she spread her arms from her side just a foot or so, palms out as if to welcome and protect the abhorrence below in a revolting display of power over the mini humans who were then looking up to her in worship. She stopped herself perhaps four feet from the ground and hovered above them, giving them a full display of her nudity and mockery of Christ. Far more disturbing and raw, she had crucifixion markings on both hands, her feet, and a slash just below her perfect right breast.

Marion felt faint, as if he was going into shock, yet he forced himself to look at her face and eyes as she looked down upon the miniature beasts. Terra turned her head toward Marion and lowered her chin as the tip of her black felt cowboy hat remained just a tad above her glowing lavender eyes. When she spoke, her voice came through the speaker system of the octagon. "Now that you know what you're up against, it's time for you to leave this maze as I tend to my flock."

The wounds from her hands and feet and side then closed up as if by Hollywood movie magic as she lowered herself completely to the ground. Every mini-human creature was on its hands and knees, faces and heads turned down as if commanded to no longer look upon Terra's perfect beauty that contrasted a malevolence so venomous that Marion wanted to slap himself to keep the shock from overcoming him.

He had been a brilliant detective. One who always knew that when he was outmatched in any way that it was best to back off and come up with a different strategy moving forward. Reassess everything and go back at it with a different angle. It hadn't happened often in his career, but such a strategy always ended up giving him the final edge to win the war. There in the octagon facing Terra Drake and her flock of freaks he felt more outmatched than he'd ever known. Whatever feelings of dread he'd overcome with all the fuckery he'd faced since coming out of his coma were nothing in comparison.

He slowly backed away from the glass, not giving up eye contact, not yet. When he was close enough to the exit door, he turned his back on Terra and the freakshow, left the octagon, and moved through the cornfield maze paths as fast as he could with as much focus as possible. All his previous dispositions of ever being lost or needing a GPS to find a place, vanished. He was out of the maze in less than ten minutes, only to run smack into Hillbilly One and Hillbilly Two, both of them standing and facing the maze's entrance and exit. Hands on their hips, standing guard.

Marion quickly pulled out the Spyderco clip knife, not hesitating a second to move into their space as if to strike. "Back off. Back way the fuck off or I'll gut you both right here!"

They both did exactly that, but not without grinning their repulsive faces off in defiance. "Whoo hoo. Still touchy, I see," Hillbilly One said. "We won't get into anything here. Go on your way. You've seen what's needed. For now that is. Go on now, git!"

Marion backed away from them, knife held out in front of his body, ready to slash any movement that would come at him. When he knew he was at a safe distance from the hillbillies, he turned and jogged back to the Ram, fired up the engine, and peeked down where his face was just above the steering wheel as he looked over the cornfield maze. The light from where Terra had come down was still there, toward the middle of the maze like a centerpiece, flashing and strobing like a massive retro club special effect.

"Whatever this fuckshow is, I'm in it. I'm not going anywhere, just need time to reassess," Marion said in a voice that was a bit shaky, but also fully alive as he turned up the stereo and drove back to his new home, Duncan Ranch.

He had no idea what lay ahead but knew everything had changed forever.

PART TWO

"And Darkness and Decay and the Red Death held illimitable over all."

– Edgar Allan Poe

Terra's Sabbath – Adrian Kane's New Home – Title Fight at Macey's MMA

Chapter Eleven:

Terra's Sabbath

Terra had plenty to do after she'd driven Marion out of the maze, leaving him more than just something frightful to think over good, long, and hard. She told her hillbilly thug slaves to go home, that she'd call on them again when needed, soon enough she assured them. Such thugs who were mindless and under her control needed constant reassurance they were useful, though her actual plans for them was complete abandonment after they'd served her purpose.

Back to Snow Crest City she went to her timeless world of spiritual warfare to get things just right for those who challenged her in any sort. Everything was becoming crucial.

A week after her personal introduction to Marion at the Duncan Maze, June was midway through the openings of Summer. Terra had grown tired of her red mustang, so off she went to Lake City to trade it in for a 2021 Ford Bronco, white with a black trim package. It was loaded, as she wanted serious 4-wheel drive with maximum power and speed. She wanted something that she'd love to use to run shit down while not having to worry about much vehicle damage. The Bronco had the power and speed and looks that matched her own.

It was an early afternoon on a Friday when she was planning an evening for Marion on that following Sunday. She fired up her new lover, the Bronco, and headed over to the mall outlet center to shop for a few items. Lipsticks. Nail polish. Hair products. New jeans and slacks and miniskirts and matching tops. She had plenty of shoes and boots. Along with shopping for such items, she had also decided the best way to deal with Marion was with some help. She needed strangers to coerce into a plan. She'd preyed on the weak and vulnerable since the dawn of time, always finding them ripe for wicked transgression. Rather than think it through, she knew such pickings would find their way to her.

She dressed in a pair of black denim short shorts, the same ankle boots she'd worn at the maze, a fitted black halter top with the turquoise lizard vest and cowboy hat she also donned at the maze. She ruffled her hair into chaos before putting the hat on for a perfect fit. When she walked into a specialty shop for modern stylish fashions, called Forever Trim, she was greeted by one of the shop's attire specialists who looked to be in her early 30s, wore a fitted cream suit with pumps, her hair pulled back into a tight professional ponytail. Her tone was so phony in its high-pitch squeal it instantly unnerved Terra.

"Why do you sound that way? What's wrong with you? I'm quite certain that's not your normal tone of voice."

The woman was clearly taken aback. "Hmmm. Nothing at all. Just wanting to provide some assistance." Clearly Terra's instant rebuke caused the lady to lower her pitch.

"Sounding like a hyena? Do you even realize how ridiculous you sound?"

The woman looked as if she'd been slapped but did her best to keep her composure. "I-I didn't mean anything. I'm very sorry. I'm not sure what I said, but please let me know if I can assist you in any way." The woman was polished enough in her career to know when it was best to walk away from customers who were dead set on being antagonistic. Just as she was about to walk away, Terra kept at it.

"It's not what you said. It's how you said it. Your shrill voice that's so forced and obnoxious it's a wonder anyone comes in here to stay and shop. Do you really think I have a need for someone like you to hound me the second I step foot in the door before even taking a minute to see what's on the racks?"

The woman began to shake a little but still held together her dignity as much as possible. "I was only trying to help you, doing my job—"

"Your job? It's your job to violate private space the moment a customer walks in? Is that handbook material? Or some HR twat's latest customer service bit that you're forced to watch on the company's app on your phone? Or maybe this place still has videos in the back for training."

The lady folded her arms across her body and placed one foot in front of the other, a clear stance of defiance but not one that was in any way threatening. "Listen, I don't know what's wrong, but is there something I can do to make this better? Because that's what I'd like to do, make things better." The woman then placed her hands to her hips in as much control as she could muster.

Terra walked right into the woman's personal space, inches from her face. "What's wrong? Is that what you're asking me? And to make things better? I'll tell you...Nina, is it? What's your last name, Nina? Let's start there."

"Frost." Nina took a step back, as she was now afraid of the woman in black alligator ankle boots and denim shorts that highlighted legs that even *she* envied. But it was the black cowboy hat and turquoise denim jacket that Nina felt most alarmed about. In her experience she'd learned that what a customer wore many times was part of who the person was overall. She'd never seen such bizarre lizards in a crucified position embroidered on anything, much less worn in public so fearlessly.

"Nina Frost. Hmmm. That is such a nice name. Do you realize how sexy that name is? Never mind. What's wrong with *me* is people like *you*. Going about your routines and spewing off phony introductions you never mean and only say because you're under contract. I've spent an eternity dealing with it, and you've pulled my last wire." Terra's tone of voice was filled with controlled rage just under a hiss, her lavender eyes turning to a pinpoint thin ring as her pupils filled her corneas with cold blackness.

Nina continued to hold composure regardless of the fear that began to grow. "Miss, I only wanted to see if I could help you find some items that would complement what you're wearing now. That's all. What you're wearing is...well, it's so fabulous. And I mean that. I don't know what has upset you so, Miss, but I do know my business, and what you're wearing is quite unique. I assure you I was only doing whatever it takes to provide you the best customer service. But more than that, the best experience." It was always Nina's best defense when taken off guard by rude customers, to bait them with compliments. Only Nina truly meant what she said, as she'd never seen such a stunning woman, nor her clothes that were so alluring.

Terra took a step back to look over Nina, taking note that she truly was a real beauty. She was ripe for the occasion. "Is that right, Nina? I like that. Maybe I could use you, after all. Use your help that is, and you've not backed down, which is rare. I know I can be a little ragged around the edges, or a little too sharp, depending on the occasion."

"I understand, I really do. We all have bad days, Miss, so why don't I show you a few pieces that I think you'd love."

"Please, call me Terra, and why don't you do that, Miss Lovely Nina. Nina Simone I may call you."

"Who?"

"She's a singer, dear. Lead the way. I'll follow. Seems

you've won me over. That's also rare." Terra was more than satisfied in her knowledge that they would always find their way to her. Preying on Marion was all that mattered, and Nina could be a perfect addition to the plan.

For the next hour, Nina showed Terra a variety of hot skirts and tops with different mixes and matches. Terra picked out her own various sets of panties and bras and lingerie pieces, all in her mind the pieces that would fit her flawless body to perfect nasty delight. After Nina rang up the purchases, a few grand in total, Terra pulled her to the side for a private.

"Nina, please allow me to apologize, again, for the earlier version of myself. You have clearly had to deal with a lot of bad players and you kept such a professional composure. I'm highly impressed."

"Well, Terra, I'm just glad we could find such nice things together. I accept your apology and appreciate your business. I mean that."

"I know you do. Glad to do my part. This isn't an easy business, is it? Listen, I'm having a small gathering this evening at my place. Just above the last ski lifts from the mining resort. Cannot miss it, Miss Nina. Nina Frost. I think it would be right up your alleyway. Please. Do come. Here's my card. Address is on the back with the phone number." Terra had a card in hand already, as it was part of her agenda, all along. Nina delicately took it, looked it over for a moment.

"Never seen a card like this. Just your name. May I ask what you do, Terra? Miss Terra Drake it says."

"Misses. Misses Drake."

Nina hadn't spotted a ring. "Oh."

"I dabble in pleasure, but it's not what you think. I'm an entertainer. *The* Entertainer is more like it. My name is everything and anything, and this is something you'll love. You'll fit right in. I will count on you then?"

Nina took in a deep breath as she was still uncertain of

everything that had taken place since Terra entered the shop. "What *kind* of *gathering* is it?"

"The kind where new friends are made and new stories are shared. Movies. Drinks. I need you there." Terra's voice turned deep and authentic, one where Nina could sense more truth than she ever expected no matter how strange the woman sounded. She also knew the woman wouldn't take no for an answer, and with all the merchandise just purchased, Nina would make a handsome commission. It would be hard to say no to a friendly invite.

"Well...since you put it that way, needing me and all...I haven't anything else going on this weekend. I don't see why not. I'm not really a night owl, but...sure."

"I promise not to keep you up past your bedtime. I will expect you early evening before the sun goes down. Do be on time, dear Nina."

"Is there a *specific* time?"

"Send me a text when you've arrived or call me if you happen to get lost, but you won't. We will see you there!"

***

As Terra was driving back to her witch's ship quite pleased with her purchases, but far more so with her discovery of Nina Frost, she took note of a vagrant who had just crossed a walkway that led to a corner convenience store and Chevron station. He was bald, wore a heavy coat, pants and boots, as many homeless do regardless of what the season, as they're the only items on earth they own. The man's skin was leathery and weathered. He stopped in his tracks and began to shout in furious anger. Terra knew the reaction well. His entire body jolted in violent shakes as he thrust his arms up and down with his fists clenched. He looked as if he were screaming at an audience with as much physical animation as his body could produce for the greatest effect. Terra knew the man was utterly alone in his own mind and suffering in great mental anguish and torment.

She pulled the Bronco up next to where he stood in his lonely world of either mental illness or absolute lost hope due to addiction. Probably both. One of the drivers behind Terra laid into the horn, letting her know she was in the way and blocking traffic. Terra rolled down her window and gave the driver a high and mighty middle finger. The man was in his early 30s and driving a blue Ford pickup truck. He pulled right in front of Terra's Bronco, got out in his own fury that matched the vagrant's, and marched toward Terra's Bronco. A different rage than the vagrant's, but just as sincere.

Before the man had taken a few steps toward her, she was already out of the Bronco and in the man's face. Without saying a word or to stop and give any warning, she backhanded him in a strike that was as powerful as a bear's, knocking him down to the ground with such force he stayed down, wondering what the fuck had just hit him. Dazed and shaken, he looked up to see a woman dressed to kill, but had to have weighed no more than a hundred twenty pounds. Tall, lean, so how in god's name could she have delivered a blow that he knew had caused internal damage.

"Get up, you fuck, you cheeky cunt, you... Get up now and get the fuck out of here before I kill you. And I will kill you if you take one moment's pause to think about what's going on. I will tear out your throat, cowboy, and suck down everything before it spills out on your dapper digs."

The man didn't even consider talking back to her, as he felt he may need to go to the hospital. He did his best to get up and get back into his truck, holding his jaw and head as he felt certain the woman had broken something. He was of decent size and strength, as he worked concrete, but had never in his life been struck with such a force. He felt scared, and did exactly what she told him. Other cars then drove past the scene more slowly, wondering what had just happened. Terra knew a few had seen her display of power, but didn't give the whole event a moment's further notice as she walked over to the vagrant.

He was still completely locked inside his personal rage, and had no idea what was going on around him or what had just taken place in the street next to him. Had no idea about any other world but his own that was trapped inside the emptiness and chaos of insanity.

"My, my, and dear me, what is it that troubles you so? You look as if you need some comfort, Lovey?" She changed her tone of voice to one that sounded as if it were filled with an understanding of complete empathy and consolation. It was a tone that instantly reached the man, cutting through all his turmoil and fear. Right to the quick.

He looked at her and felt his body ease up as if being bathed in some glow of healing ointment, even if it was just for a moment. The sudden rush of tenderness caused him to tear up. He stared into her lavender eyes, eyes of a beauty and trance he'd never seen before, wondering if it were possible to belong to anyone human. He didn't want to turn away from them.

Terra placed her right hand on the man's face in a petting gesture when she spoke to him. "What has you so upset?"

"Everything. It's everything." He felt his head shaking in an attempt to understand what was going on. The touch of her hand on his face felt as if he were being touched by his mother for the first time.

Terra continued to stare back with her hand now pressing more compassionately on the man's face. She could tell he was in his early 40s, Latino, most likely from Spain, not Mexico. He was powerfully built and had clearly gone through everything that life's rough edges could rake across his leathered skin.

"I understand. I understand everything." She tilted her head to one side then the other while slowly studying the man's face and eyes. "What's your name, soldier?"

The man wondered how on earth she knew he was a veteran, but none of that meant anything compared to what he felt in her warmth and comfort. She was also the most beautiful woman he had ever seen.

"Isaac."

"Isaac what?"

"Santiago."

Terra removed her hand and folded her arms across her chest, smiling at him. "Well, Isaac Santiago, looks like the universe has finally given you a break. Why don't you come follow me and let me give you solace." Terra motioned for Isaac to get into the Bronco. He looked at the vehicle in disbelief but pushed through anyway. He stopped shy of opening the passenger door as he continued looking at the stunning woman. Her beauty and compassion was striking, yes, but Isaac was always a man who'd trusted his gut more than anything else. Especially in combat, both on the battlefield and the unforgiving streets of homelessness. For whatever reason his mind felt like it was clearing itself, something he'd not experienced in years. After years on the streets and after losing everything due to his constant need to bury all his horror in the drink, Isaac's gut still had a strong enough radar to sense when things could become dangerous. Especially with a clearing head. He didn't know why, but he sensed, just briefly, that the woman could be as dangerous as she was consoling, so he parked the doubtful thought as best he could.

"It's okay, Isaac. Get in. You're not gonna find anything better than what I have to offer. Trust me."

Isaac looked around his surroundings again and knew what she said was true, regardless of his inner radar. He'd faced hand-to-hand combat with artillery shells whizzing by his ears; what she was offering couldn't hold a candle to such peril.

He opened the passenger door and hopped in the

Bronco just as Terra had shut herself in and fired up the engine. He couldn't help but stare at her legs, regardless if she knew he was staring. He'd not seen a woman up close in years, especially one so revealing and bold. He couldn't stop staring until she called him on it.

"I know it's been quite some time for you, Isaac, and I'm flattered, but keep your eyes straight ahead as we get going. I don't like the distraction, and I don't care if I am one."

Isaac felt embarrassment to the point of shame. Her tone changed so quickly from the warmth when inviting him to follow her to what sounded like the dangerous bit he'd briefly sensed when sizing her up. "I'm sorry, Miss. It's just—"

"No, no, no. No need to apologize. I realize this is all a bit fast. But you're suffering. And you've been suffering. I'm here to help. But you're going to need to be polite. Fair enough?"

"Yes, ma'am. Of course. That's fair."

"You don't speak with any accent. Education does that. Or it can. I'm sure no one else has seen that in you in quite some time. Tell me, sir Isaac, where were you schooled?"

He lowered his head, still embarrassed.

"Don't look down when I'm speaking to you. What school did you go to?"

Isaac looked back to her the moment she directed him to. "Believe it or not I went to Rice University."

"Ohhhhh, Houston! One of my favorite cities, and I believe you. No reason not to. In fact, I doubt that you will *ever* lie to me. And you'd better not. Do you understand me? Don't ever lie to me, Isaac."

Her stare changed to one that was filled with as much gravity he'd ever seen on any commanding officer. "Yes, ma'am. I understand, and I really appreciate this. I just don't know what this is." Isaac spoke to her queries the best his mind could offer.

"Better than what *was*. Right?"

"Yes, certainly better than what was."

"Oh, I'm right. You don't have any place to be, do you? No place to really go, I'm assuming? You've been on the streets for a minute from the looks of things." Terra turned her head from Isaac back to the road and turned on the stereo at almost full volume. "Dream Weaver" filled all corners of the Bronco. Gary Wright's haunting voice and lyrics funneled into every emotion Isaac was feeling as he realized they'd not taken off yet. Terra then shifted her body in the driver's seat so that she was nearly facing him with her knees turned into him, giving him the feeling that all her attention was his.

She said nothing as the power ballad intensified, creating a moment for Isaac that was as deeply melancholy as it was filled with a longing for something he hadn't known in so long he couldn't remember. A time that was once innocent and bound to an endless hope that nothing on earth could touch him. A time before he'd gone to war and lost his soul in the killing of hundreds he'd never imagined killing, other than it was for the freedoms of a country that he now couldn't recognize.

Terra turned down the stereo just enough to hear the song still dance along but didn't over play her voice. "Isn't this a nice tune? I loved it the first moment it was released and began to be overplayed almost overnight. Airwaves everywhere couldn't get enough of it. Has such a vibrant ability to pull you in and make you want to sooth all of your body to its slow pulse of comfort."

"I haven't really thought about it. But...yes, since you've put it that way, it really is nice." Isaac spoke carefully as he knew the woman couldn't be more than thirty years old and in no way could have first heard Wright's mid-70s hit when it was released. But why would she say that? She was far from one to misspeak.

"You've had a long hard run on the streets. Long and ugly. Maybe this song is ours for whatever reason...that I'm the dream train here to make all your worries go away. Don't you think you've come to a place where you're due?"

Isaac thought the days that he'd ever be due anything again had long passed him by, yet he was now suddenly taken over by an event so unlikely he knew one thing was certain: he had to play it out. With the woman who invited him a reprieve from the blistering loneliness that was killing him far too quickly, he had to play it out.

"I'll tell you something, lady, if that's okay?"

"You're free to speak to me your mind and thoughts, my dear. I'm on this dream train as much as you."

"You're right. Never for a fuck's second did I think someone like you would give someone like me a chance."

Terra slowly put her long index finger to her lips. "No need to feel those things any longer. This is all part of a bigger plan. Let's go, shall we?"

Isaac nodded in agreement as Terra grinned at him in mischief, turned the stereo back up and took off toward her place to continue her preparation for Marion as her second stranger had been placed in the palm of her taloned hands, as if by answered prayer.

***

When Nina pulled up to what looked like an enormous, abandoned mining station, she texted Terra immediately, as the place could in no way be the home of the woman she'd met at the shop earlier that day.

> **Nina**: I'm outside in what I think is a driveway but don't know if this is UR actual house. I went to the address by GPS, and I'm here, but it doesn't look... I don't know it just looks off, I think? Oh, it's Nina btw.

Nina watched the bubbles on her phone that would indicate if Terra was texting back. When they didn't appear right off, she started looking around the place as she leaned over her steering wheel of her 2013 red Subaru Outback. The warehouse-looking place was nestled deep into a wooded area just above one of the least popular ski resorts of Snow Crest City because of its seclusion and relatively few ski runs compared to other resorts the town played host to.

> **Terra**: It's not off at all, you're at the right place. I'll be down in just a moment. You can pull your car up closer into the lot area just outside the entrance.

> **Nina**: OK. Glad to know it's the right place. Lol, hard to tell these days what's good and what's bad when it comes to places.

Nina watched for more bubbles but, of course, there were none nor did she expect them. It was out of habit that she watched for texts that were incoming.

She started up her Subaru again and pulled in closer as advised by Terra, parked, got out of her car with much hesitation as the closer she was to the building the more its ominous appearance began to feel a lot more than just ominous. So much so that she started to get back into her car when the massive front door of the building opened and out walked Terra looking as if she had been expecting to see Nina standing right there, front and center.

Terra was wearing a royal purple fitted evening dress that highlighted every curve. The dress looked more like purple paint and had such a revealing boldness it made Nina blush. Terra's long purple gloves and black satin boots completed the ensemble along with hair done up in a tight French bun.

"I feel way underdressed, maybe I should come

back?" Nina's discomfort was cut short the moment Terra spoke.

"Underdressed? Please, please, dear Nina Frost. There is no such thing at my place. I was simply feeling a little mischievous and overly ladylike and had to put on something that you'd think was fabulous. I know you didn't sell it to me, but I couldn't help myself."

"Where did you get such a dress?"

"I found it just before I came to your place."

"Well, wow. That's a wow."

"Please, do come in. So glad you are here."

Nina followed her down a hallway so long and so enamored with paintings and illustrations of demons and demonic scenes of distorted clowns and circus freaks dancing and mangled in bloodied forests of war, she felt far more unnerved than she did outside. She wasn't sure if it was such wicked portrayals painted in such spectacular detail that caused her to begin feeling dizzy, or if it was something else altogether. Her breathing felt quicker and heavier.

The longer she followed Terra the more the vertigo came from both what she was seeing as well as how the overall design of the place created a sense of imbalance. The hallways were endless, the ceilings higher than they ever should be, and the floors as spacious as needed to connect all the geometry. The entire place looked alien, like something Nina would imagine as the decor of a spaceship. She even wondered if it was a spaceship, as the thought didn't seem such a stretch.

The artwork hung by the dozens on each side of the hallway and was splashed across the marble floors. In her dizziness when arching her head back while pushing forward to follow Terra, the ceilings, too, no matter how high, were also painted in the same ghastly art, only on a grander scale. Everything about the place was on a grander scale than anything Nina had ever seen. A more frightening scale.

Although Nina noticed there were various connecting hallways that led to other rooms of the building, the hallway she followed Terra down spilled into a fabulous grand room shaped like a diamond. There was no centerpiece anywhere. No table. No sitting arrangement. Just a spacious diamond where standing in each of the corners was a twelve to fifteen foot pillar that had a ceramic snake wrapped around from the base of the pillar to the top where each snake's head faced the center of the diamond-shaped floor.

Nina had also never seen anything like that. She also decided that she didn't want to.

Terra stopped and turned to face her. "What do you think, dear Nina Frost? This is just the beginning of the home, but what an entrance, yes? This is where we will be spending the evening. Dining on far more than just food and drink."

"I'm not sure what to say about it." Nina was whispering while keeping her head arched up in amazement as well as uncertainty.

"Of course you don't. Please, follow me. Let's head to the actual dining room area where the other guests are seated and waiting for your arrival."

Terra walked across the grand room and down another long hallway, one that had glass walls, but from what Nina could see, there was nothing behind the glass but blackness. She wondered what on God's earth could be behind them, giving the place more and more an alien effect that was seeming more plausible with each step. Step after step after step.

Finally, Terra led her into what had to be the dining room. It was bigger and more spacious than the first grand entrance room, with a center dining table that was at least twenty-five feet long and eight feet wide. Nina looked it over long and carefully and could see, from what she could understand at least, that the table was a single sheet of glass that had to be six inches thick. She wondered instantly how such a thing could have been placed in the room. She couldn't comprehend the weight of it, let alone how it was maneuvered, regardless of the room's size.

At the center of the table, to Nina's left, was Rebecca, Janet Stone, and Dr. Pinault. On the other side sat Bridget Magnus, sitting alone on her side. At the far end of the table sat Isaac Santiago, who was looking just as astonished as how Nina felt. She could tell that Isaac, even though she had no idea who he was, was in fact as much a visitor and as new to such events as she was. The women sitting across from each other looked perfectly calm and collected, other than Bridget being what Nina thought was a hundred years older than the other three. Maybe older.

Bridget was wearing an eggplant-colored denim dress, the three beauties on the opposite side were all dressed similar to Terra. Same colors. Same sculpted fit. Their hair was also done up the same as Terra's. Bridget's hair was in chaos.

"I would like you all to welcome Nina Frost. She's our other newcomer. She will sit here, on this end, facing Isaac. Such a delight to have both of them with us this evening." Terra spoke with full authority, yet her tone was filled with a haunting comfort as she led Nina to her seat.

The ceiling of the dining room was an upside down parabola, a domed ceiling that was made of stucco. It was painted in pure silver, and all Nina found herself doing was staring up at it no matter how strange all of her surroundings were, including the guests. The domed silver ceiling seemed to be calling her name. Singing to her in a long echo.

Terra walked down to the other side of the table toward where Isaac was sitting and turned to face her guests. "Bridget, what should I play before His arrival?"

Bridget scratched her long chin with her cragged

hands far too long. In fact Nina and Isaac both thought she was going to cause bleeding before she stopped and shrieked out a loud chirping sound before speaking, like an injured bird pleading for relief. "Maybe you just play a little house music, High Priestess. Something heavy and slow pulsing to set the pace and tone."

"That's an exceptional choice, Tagati Magnus, wouldn't you say, Tagati Stone and Precious Rebecca?" Dr. Pinault spoke with vibrancy and excitement. The other two younger women spoke in unison. "That is truly an exceptional choice, Tagati Magnus. Please, please, Mistress, play the house pulse with all the house rules."

Nina wanted to know what in the hell Tagati meant, and Isaac felt the same way but was far too proud to show any hint of concern as his entire skillset in combat training was on high alert, though he wondered if it would do a bit of good with what was going on. He had felt the power of Terra firsthand. There was no telling what her gang of witchery could produce.

Before Terra responded to the music request, she walked back toward the center of the table so that each of her guests could see her on full display. She held out her arms to point at both Isaac and Nina. "To our newcomers. These are just formalities and formal titles we use, nothing to be concerned about. It's all part of being welcomed into a place and time that the world once thought gone, but we are here to show you that such a world is far from gone and is, in fact, the one that our Mother Earth is most in love with. This will all make sense later during the ceremony.

"Tagati Stone, I didn't thank you for bringing the cycle of the worms. You can bring that out when I signal you, just before His arrival."

"Excuse me," Isaac said. "What is going on here? I'd like to know, and I'm sure the young lady at the other end would like to know, too. No one's told you my name, by the way, but I'm Isaac."

Terra's Sabbath

His speaking up was almost exactly the cue needed from Terra's co-hosts sitting at the middle of the table. It was Bridget Magnus who spoke first as everything played out as if on stage, and on cue.

> **Bridget**: Oh stop it with such questions. Of course you know! And we were going to introduce you, you codgy dodgy pinky boy!

> **Janet Stone**: It's always been known. Right ladies? All of this has always been known. Our Priestess told us from the beginning. And she's right, you know, we were getting to you, Mister Santiago. No need for such rudeness!

> **Bridget**: She's never led us astray and she'll certainly never do so!

> **Dr. Pinault**: The newcomers are here to feast upon not only the morsels of the flesh, but of the bounties of eternity.

> **Bridget**: Bounties! That's the perfect codgefuddlement from our Tagatis and Doctor!

> **Rebecca**: When He arrives, our Priestess will make things so much better for you newcomers. You will see. You will see it all!

> **Janet Stone**: And after they see all there is to see, then they will know all there is to know!

> **Bridget**: Of course! Then the plan will unfold for that copper! That sleeky cheeky buggered boy! That copper needs a good

licking, to be sure!

Bridget, Dr. Pinault, Rebecca, Janet Stone in unison: Shemlemhafesh Tagatis! Shemlemhafesh!

Terra Drake takes a slow strutting walk around the enormous glass dining table, circling her guests and Nina and Isaac. Nina and Isaac look toward each other from across the table, locking their eyes and wondering what is going on. They watch Terra as she continues to circle the giant room and table and back to each other, back and forth they both look upon what is becoming a ceremony of sorts. They are confused, filled with anxiety and even fear, but also an exhilaration. Terra finally stops her circling and stands next to Nina, turns her back to her guests, stretches her arms out as a large movie screen opens from the floor and fills that side of the dining room.

Nina and Isaac did their best to lock onto each other's eyes as neither of them had a clue to anything that was said. They'd never heard such talk, such banter, and were feeling more and more that they were in the midst of some kind of live theater with Terra directing them into something so unknown they had to stay and watch the finale. They also both felt the need to blurt out some kind of retort before Terra cut off their thoughts.

"In our welcoming to you both, I shall present to each of you a story of your lives, the pasts that you have lived, but more importantly the dreams that you have also had, at one point or another, only to see those dreams bashed out of existence. Which is why you're here. It is why you're here with us...with *me*...where those dreams can become your new realities, your new futures, with powers from eternity. It is also why we await His arrival who you'll soon witness. Do not speak during these presentations. Try not to even move if you're wanting to.

"And now, as I've been suggesting, please welcome The Master of the Order of the Fly. As we've been waiting he has now arrived. Let us make merry as the grand order takes place."

A heavy gothic instrumental began playing in full Dolby 7.1 Surround. Both Isaac and Nina knew it was nothing like what had been suggested to play by the others. Or maybe it was, as nothing was making any sense. The music had a pulsing rhythm that was a mixture of night club house music and bizarre religious chanting.

From the entrance into the grand dining hall walked a man who stood at least seven and a half feet tall, wearing a mask that was designed like a harsh cartoon outline of a massive fly's head. What looked like iron crosses that leaned to the sides of the mask's base were designed as antennae. They were wet and glistening. The face of the mask was designed as an abstract fly's mouth with two elongated mandibles that hung grotesquely to the side of the mask, quivering as if alive. The man wore a long flowing massive gown in deep blues and blacks that complimented the mask. The hands and feet of whomever it was in the frightening apparel were hidden as he moved across the dining room, pushing a large wooden cart with a large cauldron that sat in the center of the cart. Large brass goblets were also placed around the cauldron, six of them.

"Please welcome to the Dinner Ceremony, Adramelech! Our dear Cain!"

Adramelech, aka Cain, aka Adrian Kane, pushes the large wooden cart—with cauldron— across the grand dining room and toward the far left corner of the room. He says nothing, as he moves more like a phantom than anything human. Bridget Magnus looks across to her partners in near hysteria.

Bridget: Shemlemhafesh! All my codgy Tagatis, ring it so loud and true! Goddamn the damned and fucked, ring it true! Shemlemhafesh!

Dr. Pinault: Oh, how agreed, Tagati Magnus! Shemlemhafesh! This is the time of our discontent to be soothed so graciously. This is our time, Tagatis.

Janet Stone: Our dear Houston officer won't know what to do after everything's been finalized tonight!

Rebecca: Oh, how true it is! I wish you could have all been there that night when he came into the diner so filled with trouble. So confused. So weary so soon! All part of the plan!

Bridget Magnus: Hear, hear! Now is our night!

Bridget, Dr. Pinault, Rebecca, Janet Stone:
Shemlemhafesh Tagatis!
Shemlemhafesh to our Priestess and Majestic Lilith and Adramelech!

Kane pushed the cart to the side of the giant dining table and just behind Bridget Magnus. He then picked up the cauldron as if it weighed nothing and placed it in the center of the dining table, between Bridget and the three others sitting on her opposite side. No one made a sound as the music was lowered to a simmer while Kane took one brass goblet at a time, filled it with whatever was in the cauldron with a matching brass serving spoon, eventually placing a goblet in front of each guest.

Both Isaac and Nina watched the enormous figure of Kane in more than just horror as his mask quivered in lifelike twitches when he moved around the dining room from person to person. To Nina it was the most repulsive thing she'd ever seen, causing her to gag. Isaac had seen plenty more gruesome accounts on the battlefield, but whoever this Kane was made him feel dirty inside and violated. Neither said a word.

Terra kept her distance as Kane completed his rounds, and when completed, she directed him to walk to the far East corner of the dining room where he then faced everyone in silence with his arms folded across his massive body, the gown draping from the arm sleeves as well as elbow creases. He was closest to Isaac, giving Isaac's inner radar such a sounding alarm he didn't know if he'd be able to contain himself from screaming. Because it was screaming that he wanted to do. Kane was a hideous figure, and such an imposing figure that gave off a presence of evil that Isaac only believed possible during some of his most harrowing tours of duty when he had seen firsthand the rape and pillaging of everything that moved. Isaac was a trained soldier and killer, yet everything inside him whisper-shouted in his ear that Kane could do more harm to him than he'd ever dreamt possible.

All Nina could do is stare back and forth to Kane and Terra as her body trembled as if freezing to death in a car or hidden room that had been long forgotten.

"Drink your drinks. Everyone." It was more an order from Terra than anything, a command.

"What is it?"

The four regulars had eagerly followed Terra's every syllable, but stopped with goblets to lips when Nina spoke, as if what she said was utter blasphemy.

"Nothing that you'll be opposed to, dear Nina Frost.

You may even find it the most desirable drink you've ever tasted, and certainly something that will help you digest everything going on this evening."

"What if I don't want to drink it?"

The room continued in silence other than the background music, which then sounded muffled. Terra slowly walked over to Nina, arms behind her back, then stopped right beside her. "All I ask of you is that you give this a chance, that you at least *try* to enjoy yourself. I assure you that you're safe. In fact, Nina, you're safer here with me than any other place in the universe right now."

Nina looked up to Terra and took in every word being said. Terra's tone of voice penetrated and soothed every anxiety Nina was feeling. She let out a deep breath and nodded in humble surrender to Terra. She was young and had nothing to do on a Friday night, and the stunning woman before her had padded her checking account quite handsomely. May as well let this show play out.

"Good. Now...shall we continue?" The room suddenly held an overall sense of relief.

Isaac took his goblet and nearly drained it as if to answer Nina's question. "It's good. You don't need to be afraid." He was speaking directly to Nina in as much reassurance as he could offer.

Terra giggled in throaty mockery. "See, there's no reason to be afraid!"

The giant theater-size screen directly behind Nina that had suddenly risen from the floor came alive with swirling images of chaos and grandeur.

"Let's begin, then." Terra walked away from Nina and gestured toward the screen as if to give a presentation. The theater screen's opening images soon morphed into images and scenery that Isaac or Nina never expected from any movie, not even the highest quality 3-D movie setup. Isaac had been on the streets and homeless long enough to know that whatever was being played on the screen during whatever the fuck it was that was going on all around him, no matter how sinister in nature, no matter how much more freakish and weird as he'd seen or experienced on the streets or even on the battlefield was something for which his starved soul felt famished. *Push through. Fill up the tank.* He'd never seen shit like this, and it was as exhilarating as it was overwhelming. It also was just enough intensity to keep his mind from Kane in the corner of the room. He also believed his attempt to comfort Nina was another plus. If he would do his part, there was nothing to worry about, and whatever he had drank was quite delicious, as he motioned to Nina to go ahead and take a sip.

Nina did and felt more relief as her drink *was,* in fact, quite nice.

Nina's seat turned toward the giant screen on its own even though she knew Terra was controlling it somehow as Terra remained next to her. What was being played on screen was everything that she remembered when she was only a few years old, not yet a toddler. She always had felt her mind was something quite unique in that she could remember so far back at such an early age. In fact, because she could remember the details of events when only two or even younger, had been the cause of a lot of stress. Hers was a mind that constantly remembered too much. Events like the birth of her baby brother, not the birth itself but her parents coming home with him in her mother's arms while she was sitting on the living room floor with the babysitter. That exact event was being played on the giant screen in such vivid detail that it was more virtual reality than anything she'd ever seen on the best Oculus VR headset. In fact, she'd purchased one for herself just a few months back to take her gaming skills to the next level.

But this was not that.

Nina could smell her own diaper and feel the beat of the child's heart drumming in anxiety, as it did when she was a toddler, not at all the beating of her own heart, right then and there in her own terror that began to increase.

When the film stopped suddenly, there was a single image splashed in front of the witches' audience: the eyeball of her infant brother's was displayed in its full goopy detail, filling to the edges the theater-sized screen. Nina wanted to scream as she looked at the mammoth image where she could see strange light that had penetrated the cornea, even the cells of the cornea that were pulsing in grotesque bubble-like movement, the endless black pitches of the pupil where Nina knew she was seeing an endless array of newborn knowledge that was infinite in a bizarre and confusing attempt to understand everything that ever was.

Bridget and the younger ones cackled in glee.

Terra hissed at them to silence as she placed her long taloned hands on Nina's shoulders and gently massaged them as she spoke. "I am the architect of all the code, and all the coders follow my blueprint. Think that one over, as there is no meaning to anything you ever knew was meaningful. I control the language. Every one. Every zero. Every combination.

"This image, for example. My dear Nina, don't be troubled. I'm here to give you a future that you've only believed possible in your dreams. The future that is personal to who you have always wanted to become. Settle in and let's continue."

The awful image of the infant eyeball disappeared from the screen as new images and scenes and stories and full chapters of a life that Nina had, in fact, daydreamed about all throughout her high school years began to play out like a full-featured Spielberg film. So deeply personal were the scenes being played that Nina moved her body toward Terra, shifting out from beneath Terra's taloned hands that had become too heavy.

"What is this? How did you do this?" Nina's voice

was barely a whisper, as she was almost hypnotized to what she was seeing on screen, as all scenes and characters were in fact Nina herself in places and activities that had never happened and were years and years into the future.

Terra signaled for the film to stop. When it did, the screen was filled with another single image, one of Nina who appeared in her early 50s surrounded by wealth and power and the most fabulous niches in all the world of fashion had to offer. She was also in full control over all of it.

Terra's voice was just above a whisper and filled with as much comfort and warmth as any voice Nina had ever heard, as if she were being spoken to by an angel. "This is my gift to you. Everything you see before you is *all* for you. Every facet of it, every piece of understanding. None of it will ever be taken from you. I won't allow it."

At that moment, regardless of how convincing everything felt to Nina's very spirit, regardless of the show's immortal display of power, she knew she had to make a stand. Everything that was shown and everything that had been going on during the evening pushed her into a place where she never believed she'd ever be pushed. Something deep within her believed that nothing could ever be given to her in such a way. She found a strength so quickly it took her breath away, for which she was grateful. A strength that whispered to her that everything being shown had to be denied, at whatever cost.

She had to make a stand, but she also knew such a stand couldn't be made on the spot. She had to keep it to herself, and knew that if she didn't she'd be killed, a sudden knowledge that also took her breath away. Any outward resistance would end in her death. She had to play it out, whatever *it* was, get back to her car when it was over, and drive away as fast as she could from the endless waves of hell that were coming down on her so fiercely—regardless of how gorgeous the façade was to mask the truth—she wanted to scream as badly as Isaac had wanted to with Kane over his shoulder.

"Okay." That's all Nina said as Terra's grin increased to a wicked slit that made her face distort surreally.

"Isaac. Let me come to you, as yours is next."

Both Isaac and Nina felt simultaneously how awful the silence had become from the ladies sitting at the center of the table as well as the continued silence from Kane in the corner. Only the music could be heard, but it sounded more like it was far away and in another room all together.

As the theater screen came down from Nina's end of the room, another one the same size appeared behind Isaac as his chair turned toward it. He was more than anxious to see what his screen would present. Like Nina's film, Isaac's began with images and scenes of memories he thought he had lost so long ago they didn't even seem real any longer. Unlike Nina's, Terra never stopped during the presentation. By the end of it, Isaac had also been shown full chapters of a future life that was filled with power and authority, images and scenes that became embedded into Isaac's mind so deeply rooted that what was shown to him as his future felt like it had already taken place. Also, unlike Nina, Isaac had made the choice long before his film ended that he was going to accept with pure gratitude everything that Terra Drake had shown him. He made a personal vow to even worship the woman if she so asked, and he knew that she would. He even made a vow to kill for her.

His was a world that had gone terribly South, and what was being offered was something he could never reject.

When Isaac's screen vanished and both Isaac and Nina were facing each other from the distance of the dining table, the others began to murmur a bit, saying only incoherent mumblings. The lights dimmed to a point where the dining room was almost in darkness when both of the theater screens were produced again, facing each other giving the dining room an enormous and brilliant ambience of a double-screened futuristic AI drive-in. The dining room ceiling's massive transparent curved dome began to shift as if it were the top of a giant globe.

Janet Stone then left the table and came back soon after with a few large bags of worms, placing the bags on the table, one bag to each side of the cauldron. A movie began to play simultaneously on both screens, a movie that showed what Nina and Isaac both believed was some kind of representation of the Biblical Garden of Eden story from Genesis.

Dancing around the Garden of Eden were two women and one man. Clearly Adam and Eve, but the other woman looked queerly familiar to Terra, only with blond hair. The music increased in volume and intensity as Terra leaped with panther-like agility on top of the dining table. She took a few steps back and forth and around the cauldron, then stepped out of her fitted royal purple dress, walking slowly up and down the table, wearing only a black leather thong. She reached beneath the leather straps of the thong with index finger and thumb and pulled out two small nipple clamps with a thin gold chain that hung from both. She gently clamped them on her taut nipples as the gold hung to her muscled core.

Terra's back had a large serpent that was either painted or tattooed that stretched from the base of her neck to the tip of her ass. As she moved, the painted snake moved with her body.

Nina and Isaac watched her dance in utter fascination and awe; Nina watched with just as much horror as did Isaac in more raw lust than he'd ever felt even as a young boy when first experiencing the thrill of seeing a beautiful woman naked for the first time. Both were overtaken by whatever their drinks had laced in them.

Bridget, Janet Stone, Rebecca, and Dr. Pinault looked

up to Terra, their hollow eyes following her every move in a complete trance of worship and not uttering so much as a peep. Terra's dance and movements across the giant table turned into something fierce and furious, her arms and hands writhing up and down her body like extensions of the painted snake on her back. She moved her hips and torso in slow gyrating circles, keeping her arms and hands in perfect unison as she whipped her head from side to side. The heavy gothic instrumental was soon accompanied by thick drumming that had boomed in the power of a John Bonham solo. No one could take their eyes off her no matter how vivid and bizarre the events unfolded in The Garden of Eden film.

That is until Satan appeared to both women in the garden, a Satan who appeared in a black gown with long flowing black hair and lavender eyes who engaged with both women to tempt them with the ends of the universe and all its offerings as Adam watched on in odd curiosity and confusion.

That's when the blonde woman left Adam to the inferior Eve and joined Satan in ecstatic hedonism, a scene that unfolded with Terra ripping open the bags of worms and turning them into snakes. Snakes that grew in size as Terra picked up a few and continued to walk up and down the table in the same rhythmic movement, her head moving side to side, more slowly matching the movements of the snakes' heads, her tongue outstretched to meet the snakes' tongues.

The longer she danced with the snakes the more Isaac and Nina felt a powerful hypnotic effect begin to overwhelm their senses. Both knew whatever they had been drinking from the goblets was too powerful to resist or overcome. Nina wanted to shout out to Isaac that he said it was safe, that it was okay, when nothing was.

The four regulars began to chant in unison.

Terra's dancing began to increase in its intensity and

speedy movement.

The snakes slithered around the cauldron, across the table, some falling to the floor.

Kane remained silent and stoic.

The music increased in volume to concert level.

The mock Genesis story ended with Adam and Eve banished from the Garden, leaving Satan and the blonde Terra dancing around the Tree of Life.

Nina fought against the drug's effects with as much willpower as she possessed, unable to take her eyes off of Terra. Isaac went with the drug's power as he also went with his carnal lust, keeping his eyes locked on Terra's every move. He was savagely hungry for her but knew he could do nothing but helplessly watch the dancing demon holding the snakes that had grown to python size.

In her peripheral vision, Nina thought she saw children sitting at the corners of the dining room, playing with large frogs. They had needles for teeth. Isaac thought he saw them too, but paid them no attention. Nina's mind almost begged her to scream, but her body melted into a jelly-like state with the music, lights, theater screens, as Kane walked toward the table with his arms stretched out as if to welcome the hellish ceremony into his massive gown. It all blended into a single kaleidoscopic swirl of cacophony when Terra stopped dancing and stood directly in front of Nina, her head tilted down, with one of the snakes draped around her neck and covering her breasts.

"I told you I wouldn't keep you past your bedtime, my dear Nina Frost. Bridget, take her back to her car and make sure she's conscious enough to drive." Terra turned toward Bridget Magnus and then back down to Nina. "Maybe this isn't for you."

With that, Terra strutted down the table toward the centerpiece cauldron and the other three. "You, my lovelies, get Isaac on the table and have your way with him. He's wound up perfectly. He'll make the perfect distraction for our fine officer."

Bridget followed Terra's orders.

Nina knew she'd blacked out when she came to and was sitting in front of her steering wheel with Bridget standing over her with the driver side door opened. She felt in a state of shock as she believed she'd just lived through Dante's nine circles of hell and was stuck in the ninth and final one, Treachery, where Satan lived with Cain planning out their strategy to rule the world.

"You run along now, little missy. You'll come around soon enough, you little codgy one! And if you don't...well, we shall see."

Bridget shut the driver's door and walked off into the woods. Nina leaned over the steering wheel, watching Bridget disappear and wondered why the hag didn't go back inside the treachery of Terra's home. She took deep breaths to gather her composure, started her Subaru and drove away as slowly and carefully as she'd ever driven, refusing to look back, praying for safety in a prayer where she begged God for mercy and for strength.

***

While pampering herself for Sunday evening, Terra was singing in mockery of a God she'd grown to despise with as much glee as scorn. Though it was just the start of summer, and one she planned to heat up with pure mayhem, she sang loud and vicious a few altered Christmas lyrics she had found utterly delightful, as she felt rested and alive from Friday night's Newcomer Ceremony.

"God rest you also, women, who by men have been erased. Through history ignored and scorned, defiled and displaced. Remember that your stories too, are held within God's grace. God rest you, queer and questioning, your anxious hearts be still. Believe that you are deeply known and part of God's good will, for all to live as one in peace, the global dream fulfilled."

Her rewrite of a popular carol took place the previous year's Christmas when she attended a Midnight Mass in Odessa. It was a deathly quiet evening. Her godless world where deceit ruled every strategy, she decided to go to that Saturday Mass, as it had been quite some time since attending for her own research. When rising from her pew and walking down the church aisle to face the priest with wafer in hand, she stuck out her tongue as long and harshly as possible before swallowing the wafer in aggression. When the priest asked her if she was okay, she asked him where was the goblet of wine to wash it all down. Seeing that she'd taken him completely off guard, Terra leaned in, grabbed the priest behind the back of his neck and pulled him in, kissing him, forcing her tongue inside his mouth. The priest was too visibly shaken to continue the Mass that night, which gave Terra the inspiration for her Christmas rewrite.

The memory caused her to laugh out loud as it was finally the evening to light things up for Marion. She knew Isaac was on board and his part was set. She couldn't worry about Nina. Not yet. This was the Sunday night that was to become a sabbath she'd been planning for Marion since discovering he was a more formidable opponent than she'd anticipated. Terra's Sabbath to be exact, and one the cop would never forget. One she knew would tap his full resources.

It was the club scene she desired. That's where she'd lead Marion to next. A loud and vibrant club scene where she could make an appearance that would begin her attack. She would capture his attention with a much hotter approach than the terror she assaulted him with at the Duncan Maze with her demon children.

That Sunday evening after the Newcomer's Ceremony, she was slowly enjoying the inside of her home's massive halls and twenty-foot-high ceiling and concrete marble floors. She felt secure and lofty in her windowless cavern-like ancient ship while strutting about admiring one of many grand rooms where there was a centerpiece that was a stunning iron spiral stairwell that went downward some fifty steps into an underground palatial ballroom. All concrete floors that sported a massive concrete stage. It was the last place that she'd seen Marion before the death of his brother. They'd both ventured out during New Year's Eve just as she was about to sacrifice the all-important child slave she'd once chosen as a part of many wicked rituals she'd been practicing since her betrayal of Adam. A ceremony that never played out because of the cop and his brother's interruption. She wasn't going to allow for any such interruptions ever again.

She began her routine pampering up and ready for a night of mayhem, and most likely murder. She had just the custom outfit for the occasion, one that she had designed herself, choosing the finest and richest black leathers and stainless-steel chains, gloves and boots—all her own cuts and designs.

She made sure to wear nothing she purchased from Nina.

The gig consisted of a leather one-piece bodysuit with a high French cut. Metal snaps lined up and down each side of the outfit, with a large metal ring that hung from a thick black belt. She'd designed a matching black collar that fitted around her neck, snug and wicked, with another metal ring identical to the belt ring, but a tad smaller. Leather and metal straps connected to the bust to display her ivory cleavage. To compliment everything, Terra also designed a pair of arm-length gloves that stopped just below her armpits. The fingertips of the gloves were designed as talons, with a leather belt and chain that strapped around her biceps.

The final touch was a pair of full leg-length high-heeled boots that stopped just below her crotch with leather and metal garter straps connected just below the metal-ringed belt. The boots fit her legs so tightly they made her legs look like they'd been painted black on stone white. Each boot had an assortment of metal rings and clamps inlaid into the boot leather. The outfit was a spectacular metal goth arrangement of stunning originality.

She decided to wear her hair down, perfectly parted down the middle, making sure she pulled enough behind her ears to show off a pair of studded diamond earrings. Finally, she carefully painted her lips a deep lavender to match her eyes.

More than satisfied, she went into her kitchen that was the size of any professional chef's with all the extras, poured herself a healthy few shots of iced Vodka, strutted into her concrete-floored living area and fired up a Rolling Stones compilation, selected "Bitch" from their *Sticky Fingers* album, turning it up several notches past what mortals could tolerate. She danced around seamlessly and seductively to Mick Jagger's ripping vocals about the ways and how's of sloppy drunk wild love. As soon as the alcohol hit her bloodstream with the soothing wave of solace, the Stones compilation cut into "Monkey Man." Terra slow danced in pulses of exaggerated hip movements with her hands and arms sashaying above and over her head and shoulders to the song's opening piano keys of a haunted world of drug addiction that filled Terra's imagination with all the reality she was ready to set in motion for Marion Paul to come out and play hard ball.

She wanted to fuck him up good and hard and quick enough to catch him so off guard that he would become just another plaything to her. He needed a touch far more raw and bloody than anything the newcomers had seen the night before with Kane's cauldron and demonic visions splashed all over theater screens where they stood no chance of resistance.

***

The club was Eternity 51 located dead center in Lake City, underground and directly across from the city's largest cathedral. It was built and designed by a group of local venture capitalists who hated the state and city's staunch religious views and decided to design something that was, in their opinion, exactly the kind of place the Anti-Christ could call home.

And she was about to.

The club's primary owner and general manager was Bartholomew Wilson, a man known for his fabulous wealth and extreme lifestyle of drugs, women, and men. Wilson had one donor who within the last year had fronted enough money to where the other original venture capitalists were no longer needed. Enough money was given to Wilson, in cash, to not only pay for the club outright, but also much of the surrounding real estate for plenty of add-ons if Wilson desired. But it wasn't Bartholomew Wilson's desires for such add-ons, it was the downright owner of Wilson himself, one Adrian Kane.

The club was designed as a series of different stage and bar areas that were built as five thematic replicas: a hospital clinic with waiting rooms for table areas; a cave with tunnels and dirt floors; an H.R. Giger room where the entire area was designed as the Alien creatures and ships that Giger had originally painted for the first *Alien* film with tables that looked just like massive unhatched eggs; a carnival-freakshow room with tables and chairs designed as obscene body parts; and the Graveyard room that hosted tombstones and coffins as tables and chairs. Each club room area had its own stage and bar designed to complement each room's theme.

Marion agreed to meet Terra at the club as she sent him a simple one-line text: Eternity 51 Sunday night. The moment he entered he felt an instant panic that things were not going to go well at a place he thought must have housed the finest of all the sickos he'd ever seen, which was saying a lot with every extremity he'd faced in the most awful shitholes Houston had to offer.

He walked around the place in utter fascination of the club's five thematic barrooms. He ordered an iced tea, no sweetener, when he decided to stay in the Giger area as he'd always loved the *Alien* films, especially with Sigourney Weaver as Ripley. For whatever reason he also knew it would be the area where Terra would come to meet him. He focused on the stage area and dance floor where everything was designed as if in the belly of the massive alien ship where Ripley ended up discovering hundreds of alien eggs before she faced the alien mother.

When the music blasted a techno rendition of Kiss's "Do You Love Me?" with the opening heavy drum sequence that was prolonged and sounded like cannon blasts more than drums, Marion saw Terra walking toward him dressed in a one-piece leather goth outfit that highlighted her ivory sculpted perfection. The entire scene of her walking, laced with the screams of an echo-effect Paul Stanley's voice, created such an alarming memory from his comatose dream that he thought he was briefly back in the hospital bed. He quickly snapped back to focus on the woman who walked right up to where he sat and looked down at him, not taking a seat just then.

"Glad you could make it."

Marion said nothing but stretched out his hand in a gesture for her to sit down.

She did, and took a long drag on her vape pen, held it just as long and let out an even longer breath that blew out insane amounts of white vapor. "I thought it was finally due to have a sit and tell, little facey-facey."

"Quite an entrance." Marion held her deep gaze, knowing it was going to be a long night.

"I know you're going to want to fuck me the longer

we're here, and we're just getting started. I say that to prep you."

Marion nodded, making sure to keep full composure. *Don't give this bitch an inch.* "So noted."

One of the club's hostesses came over with two sets of headphones and asked if they wanted to order anything. The hostess was dressed in a black rubber suit.

"These will help you hear each other a lot better as well as block out the background noise a bit. Plus they're cool as shit." The hostess giggled as she placed the headphones on the table. Terra ordered a red wine, Marion another tea; both put on the headphones.

Terra sat back in her chair with one arm slinked across the table, the other holding her vape pen as if it were a long cigarette. "Have you noticed, my dear street cop, how there's no backlash to anything anymore? I mean nothing. What I just said to you about wanting to fuck me more and more as the night moves on is just one small example. No retort. No push back."

"I'd said, *so noted.*" Marion was impressed with how the headphones worked. He heard Terra's voice perfectly as the club's astounding volume of background noise was indeed muffled. He felt as if he was inside a plane's cockpit.

"My point exactly, but let's take the bigger picture. Let's take...hmmm, let's take this place, for example. Ever seen anything like this nightlife? I mean, take a deep gaze at it. It's like it was built and designed to give birth to the likes of me."

"And what's that? Sickos and freaks?"

"Ha! Now, now, Marion. No need for insults. And certainly no need to be so trivial."

"Okay. Devils then?"

Terra took another vape drag and leaned in closer to Marion. Her sexuality was every bit as intoxicating as she said it would be. "Are *we* nothing but devils? Have we become nothing but monsters and witches and demon whores? I know nothing of these devils you speak. And if I did, what would you do about it? Then again, maybe I'm the mother of harlots."

"I see the resemblance, and don't underestimate me."

"Quite the contrary! I'm absolutely *counting* on you. Hush now. I'm going to tell you a story. You've been privy to more of it than you know. Like what you saw the other night in the back acre of Bridget's place. I was there, but I'm sure you suspected that by now. Maybe not. But you interrupted the ending of that ceremony. Or the end *to* it. The transformation never took place and it needed to.

"You see, maybe you've never believed in stories of monsters...real ones. But the real ones are much more terrifying than what we've all seen in vampire and werewolf and witchcraft tales and films. They're more terrifying because their presence is so much more subtle. Because they come upon you when you'd never expect it. You never see the real monsters coming. Until now.

"A wolf in sheep's clothing. Wolf and man, for example. But before I get to him, remember one thing. Real monsters come at you with what's nearly pure truth, with just a sprinkle of lies. Coming at you with this kind of mixture is almost impossible to see what's real and what isn't. Back to wolf and man. What you saw the other night. Was that a man I had on a leash? Or was it a wolf who had me on one while pulling me?

"Don't answer. Not yet. Not before I finish my story with the Order of the Fly. What it is and what it isn't. You see, Marion, I am the designer of all that is weird and manufactured that has replaced anything that was considered normal. I am the blueprint of everything lifeless and unearthly. I am *the* human deep fake. I am the lover of all contrived and artificial, for that is the new reality that I have created. I use this platform at the highest level, and no one will challenge it because everyone is terrified of the

Dean Patrick

consequences."

Marion settled deeper into his chair, took a drink of his tea, massaged his neck with both hands, trying to consider what she'd just said. He leaned in to Terra as she paused and took another deep puff on her vaper with as much seduction and power that Marion had ever seen from such a simple gesture.

"What the fuck are you talking about? What consequences?"

Terra didn't answer, as the hostess was back with her red wine. It was served in a blood transfusion bag that came with a complete setup of infusion pump, blood warmer, rapid infuser, and pressure device that had a smart button used to alert the bar for another round. Marion stared at it in disbelief but smiled, nonetheless. *Now that's a drink.*

"Thank you, dear." Terra's politeness was quickly overturned when she waved her hand at the hostess in dismissal.

"Where were we? Yes...consequences. You don't see them? Ha! Surely you do! The world is a walking contradiction of bizarre and obscene twisted fuckery, and no one whispers a peep in resistance because they're afraid of being erased. There is no courage to have an identity. The best that any of these sheep can ever hope to obtain is a world of limbo where the wait is for nothingness. The abyss of hopelessness because it's easier that way."

Marion leaned back and ran his hands behind his neck one more time. The headphones were assisting an oncoming migraine. The music also increased in volume and tension even with the headphones on. Maybe his set was faulty. But he pressed on. "Well that ain't me, lady."

"Nooo...no, no, you're a different breed that way. You're a breed just like your brother. He wasn't as genuine, but his addiction was a bit fiercer than yours. Or, maybe not."

"He's dead, isn't he?"

"And you're an adrenaline junkie. Just a matter of time before that kills you, as well."

"Don't be so sure about that."

Terra held out the palm of her hand in dismissal, as she was moving her body perfectly to the rhythm of the heavy industrial house music that felt produced just for her. "Please. Tell me, officer, what does a woman like me do to a man like you? Hmmm? What does someone like me do to all those thoughts that are stored inside your sick mind like a rotted cave? Or how about the good doctor? Are you telling me had you not just come out of a comatose pitch that you wouldn't have allowed her to suck every last drop out of your sleeping nut? Or better yet my young starlet Janet with her lashing tongue?"

Marion just stared at Terra, completely uncertain what to say or how to act as he sipped his iced tea.

"Little Rebecca at the diner at the end of the world? All my thieves of fuckery? Well...let's face it, I'm sure Bridget's not your cup of brew, but the others could have had their way with you had they put in a bit more effort. Could have tongued you dry."

Better say something or I'll be out of the game before it's even made it to the second fucking inning.

"And I guess that's where you come in."

"You're saying something different, officer? Isn't that your crack? Am I not the pipe you've sucked on year after year? Please. I've got you so tightly wrapped around my long middle finger you can feel it up your ass right now."

Show some fucking balls, goddamn it!

Marion put up his own palm, face outward in defiance. "Maybe. But I'm not my brother, lady. If you know so much, you fucking know that bit. And let me say this without your constant interrupting. Half the time I don't know what the hell you're talking about. You contradict yourself. You may not think I notice, with you being such a distraction and all, but you're a walking contradiction. Maybe a fire breathing one, but still. All your nonsense about sheep in wolves clothing, not expecting what's coming next because it's too masked for anyone to ever notice, but here you are right in my face not hiding a goddamn thing, showing me everything."

"How nice. What gumption! More points for you there, officer. Even when you slopped out of the coma bed you had more inside the tank than your town-drunk brother. Maybe that's why Mister Strange Love paid you such an early visit before the show *really* gets peaking."

She's gotta be talking about John...she knows about John. Of course she does.

"I think we're done here. Wait, no we're not. You said you had a story. You think I'd forget with all your nonsense, but you said you had a story."

Terra let out another stream of white fog. She chuckled. "Can't get anything past you, that's for sure. Okay then, yearbooks and body parts. That's the story I want to tell you. You're the perfect audience for that one."

"I'm sure I am."

"How many times have you had the chance, whether it's been part of your job or not, to sit and look at old yearbooks from people and places that you've never known?"

"I don't know if I ever have."

"I'm sure you've looked at plenty of photo albums when you were digging around people's haunted pasts, though. But yearbooks are different. I had this dream once, and I don't dream often, had this dream where I was in a large room with stacks of old yearbooks. I started looking through them, really looking at them. Yearbooks have such a creepy feeling to them. Page after page of young people's photos, the events from their high schools captured in timeless shots that are supposed to give the reader some magical glimpse of nostalgic history. But if you look at them long enough you can't help but wonder what was really going on.

"I ended up looking at one from the 80s. Such a grand time. Big Hair Bands. Girls doing their best to make their hair match their favorite rock star's. And I came across the picture of your brother, Steve. Had his hair the same way, mind you. Must have permed it. He looked so somber and morose."

"Maybe he was."

Terra put up her hand, palm out. "Don't interrupt me. You wanted the story, here it is. I'm telling you this because that's when I started following your brother, only he had no idea until it was far too late, as we both know. In the dream, I shut the yearbook and walk into a room full of arms and legs and torsos hanging from the ceiling of whatever room I'm in, and I realize all those hanging bloodied body parts swinging around in their personal gore represented all the different people that Steve wanted to be as he could never find out who the fuck he really was.

"That's the moral of the story, officer. No one knows who they really are when I come into play. Then it's too late."

Marion rubbed his neck again, not taking his eyes off Terra. "Who the fuck are you? Tell me this story of your dream about my brother and yearbooks and shit? How it all ties together. You know what I think?"

"Oh, do tell me. Can't wait to hear this one."

"I think you're full of shit, that's what I think."

"Wow. How clever." Terra winked at Marion and licked her lavender lips long and slow. "Tell you what, copper. Allow me to use the Ladies Room and continue for a bit when I'm back. Maybe there's a surprise in it for you. Where else do you need to be tonight if not here with me making merry?"

Of course Marion had no place to go or be, but he knew he'd about had enough of the demon woman for one night. Still, he made a promise to his brother to find out what the fuck had happened. Truth was he'd never been so intrigued, nor exhausted so quickly.

May as well hang in here, god knows I also wonder whether she'd kill me or not. Keep it the fuck together.

"Fine. But maybe let's lighten things up a tad when you're back."

Terra stood from her chair and their table while looking down at Marion. He could not keep from staring at her figure, and knew he couldn't hold a stare into her lavender eyes. "I won't be but a few, my dear officer." Terra took off the headphones and placed them right in front of him before heading toward the Ladies Room.

He wanted to tell her to cut the officer shit but just stared at her as she walked in a way he knew was designed to cause every head to turn—man, woman, or beast. He took off his headphones and crimped his eyes as a few more hard riff songs blasted throughout the club far too loudly, as his ears needed to adjust. Just before he considered buying a real drink while getting irritated at how long Terra was taking, he instantly caught in the corner of his eye a large Spanish man who looked as if he'd just decked a few patrons out of sheer mania.

Marion's focus became laser sharp. He could see the man was covered in blood, like he'd bathed in it. The bloodied man easily moved away from others who were beginning to gather around him to see what was going on, when he darted past everyone and took off in a full sprint toward the first exit he could find. Just as quickly Marion pulled the Beretta out of his belt, ready to take aim. The Spaniard was far more swift and crazed than Marion expected, and suddenly the man tossed a handgun right at Marion. His athletic reflexes were lightning in response as he caught the handgun the Spaniard had tossed without accidently shooting him. Marion instantly knew the Spaniard's was a .38 revolver, Smith & Wesson older model, probably from the mid-60s.

"You're gonna have some fun with her now, tipo duro! Cabron!" The man dashed through the exit before Marion had a chance to figure out what the fuck had just happened. Next thing he saw as he held the Spaniard's gun was a group of women screaming in hysteria that Marion knew exuded more horror than fear. He looked around with his cop eyes to see if Terra was anywhere around the area.

Because she sure as fuck is behind this mayhem.

It took only moments before the group of horrified women turned into a mob scene, the exact kind of shitshow where Marion was at his finest in all human senses both physical and mental. He tucked the revolver in his front pocket in a single motion while walking over to the crowd with his Beretta outstretched just a foot or so, ready for any fucking thing that would come at him.

He could smell the blood all around the area so thick he could almost make out the blood types of all that had been spilled. He waved the Beretta to completely take over the scene. "Back up. Back away. Everyone back the fuck away and settle the fuck down. Get management or whoever runs this fucking place. Do it and do it now! And call nine-one-one!" He picked out one specific frantic woman and made sure she was the one who heard every word as loud and as clearly as possible, some hottie dressed in all black goth, wearing barely a thing, but the one who had the most blood on her. Except for the Spaniard. Marion figured she'd be the one best to call for help as she looked like she needed it the most.

He screamed at her one more time, then got physical with everyone around the Ladies Room entrance area before heading into the restroom where he saw a slaughter had taken place.

There were restroom areas in each of the five thematic rooms, and the one where the horror took place was the Giger room; the Ladies Room of this area was a replica of inside the spaceship Nostromo from the first *Alien* film.

The walls and ceiling made Marion feel such isolation it was hard to breathe. That and the enormous amounts of blood that covered everything from the floor to the mirrors to the stall doors to the corners of the ceiling and walls.

There were four women whose bodies were so blasted to pieces it looked like each of them had been slung through a giant cheese shredder. Not only were their bodies shredded, but what was left of their flesh was filled with gaping massive holes from what Marion knew were far too damaging to have come from the six-shooter the Spaniard had tossed. The walls and mirrors were also covered in chunks of flesh debris and bone. Ligaments and even veins looked to have been splashed everywhere like giant bloody spider webs attached to everything from top to bottom.

But it wasn't the saturated gore that shut Marion speechless. It was the torsos of the victims that were laid out across the long hallway of the restroom. On each torso was a slaughtered pig's head placed on each ruined torso so that each woman's torso with a bloodied pig's head attached was facing the restroom's massive vanity mirror. To enhance the awful effect, and because the restroom was designed with mirrors all around the walls and ceiling, whoever had done this had placed everything just so to create an effect where the massacred victims both human and animal, could be seen for eternity.

It was all a bit much for Marion's calloused senses, as he knew the moment he entered the restroom that there was too much blood to have come from only four women's bodies. He saw that such vast amounts of ruined flesh and guts had also come from the pigs, but there were no pig bodies. After scoping everything as long as he could stand—and knowing he needed to get back out to the club—he covered his mouth and nose and went back out.

The music outside the restroom was suddenly at an ear-shattering level as he looked around the stunned patrons who were clearly in shock, as just moments ago, they were screaming. The club's strobe lights were firing so frenetically that they looked more like razor blades being tossed about in glimmering neon purples and oranges. It was then that Marion caught Terra in his peripheral on the Giger stage that was just to the corner side of the bar. She was strutting back and forth slowly to AC/DC's "Dirty Deeds Done Dirt Cheap." Marion's pure cynic cop humor almost caused him to laugh.

Almost.

Terra stopped in the middle of the song's fierce guitar riffs, looked down and across to Marion, took a bow, and blew him a kiss.

Then she was gone as the crowd around Marion prevented him from doing anything other than controlling things as best he could.

He fired the Beretta, round after round, into the club's strobe lights, knowing *that* would get management's attention far more quickly than the goth chick he had directed in violent shouts. Sure enough, all nightclub lighting of neon beauty cut off exactly as all white ceiling lights cut on in a blast of instant pain.

The place fell as silent as a concert that had just ended with everyone mumbling in drunken and drugged slurs of nonsense.

Not knowing what the goth chick had done, or who'd she tried to reach, Marion picked out another patron, a young man who looked no older than eighteen, but who had clear enough eyes that Marion trusted on such chaotic instinct. "You! Call the fucking police now! And I mean scream at nine-one-one to bring every fucking working stiff they got. Everyone!" Marion remained in control of the entire crowd with the Beretta just a foot or so in front of him, ready for one wrong move from anyone or anything. "Everyone else stays right here until first responders arrive and tell you you're free to go. Stay right the fuck here with me."

It took less than thirty minutes before an entire CSI unit arrived on the scene. First responders began roping off the area, and patrons who witnessed anything were blocked off for questioning. There had to be twenty or more, including Marion as he led the efforts before Lake City Police took over. First responders immediately began providing as much assistance as possible, and keeping things as orderly as possible since the bloody mess had created more chaos than anything Utah had ever seen. Marion also believed the entire EMS team for the entire state as well as all fire department personnel had arrived.

He continued to eyeball with laser focus any hints of Terra before a Detective Jay Raskin ended up talking to him. Raskin had with him someone who Marion knew was a civilian. Rather large man, way too soft, dressed in a blue silk suit.

Probably the club owner, no doubt.

Being a detective himself, Marion eased right into the conversation.

"This is Bartholomew Wilson. He owns the place. Mister Wilson, this is Marion Paul, cop outta Houston who first saw the fuckery in the restroom."

Marion reached out to shake the man's hand and made sure he shook it with enough grip to let Wilson know he'd never forget it. He immediately noticed the club owner wearing a ring with a familiar cut and design when Raskin cut off his thoughts.

"So help me out here. And I agree with you completely, by the way. With every fucking thing in that bathroom, I find it hard to imagine it being done single-handed, but you're saying that it was somehow the woman you met here tonight? Or could be? Tell me more."

Marion let out a long sigh and breath. "Well...for starters, and before we get to that, it wasn't a fucking thirty-eight six-shooter made those holes in those women."

"Yeah. No shit. So why did the Mexican have it on him and why did he toss it to you?"

"Who knows? Distraction, clearly, but this is something else altogether."

"Yeah, you're telling me. Straight out of Charles Manson's dreams. Okay, what about this woman? Tell me about her."

Marion let out another deep breath. One of a few hundred over the past hour as he'd been going over what had happened just after Terra left for the Ladies Room. He also eyeballed Wilson just as closely as Raskin. "The woman I met here has had some history with my family. My brother's dead because of her. And no, I can't prove that. Yet."

"Go on."

Seeing that Raskin wanted to hear him gave Marion a bit of relief.

"Last year I met up with my brother because he'd told me this woman was dangerous and that he was in danger. I ended up finding him on New Year's this year up at Snow Crest City where we went to her house. We went inside and found her with another woman. They were performing some kind of sick ritual on a young girl. Before I could do anything about it, next thing I remember was waking up from a coma I'd been in for four months at the Odessa Hospital. My brother was found dead at the Odessa Hotel. I've been investigating what happened to him and living at his place, since he handed everything he owned over to me, and while digging into his computer and reading notes and files and what not, I've discovered evidence that makes me believe she had something to do with his death. Since then, over the past many weeks, this woman has been...I don't know..."

"Stalking you?"

"Feels more like *hunting* me."

Dean Patrick

Wilson let out a silly giggle that instantly enraged Marion. "You think that's funny, you pudgy fuck? Keep it zipped or I'll slap that grin off your face!"

Wilson's flabby cheeks turned bright pink.

"You keep your fucking comments to yourself or that's exactly what I'll do, you copy that?"

Wilson's entire body shook. He clearly wasn't used to being spoken to that way. In fact, no one had ever spoken to him so viciously.

Raskin paid no attention to the club owner as if he felt the same way as his new friend, Marion, felt.

"Hunting you. You think she wants to kill you?"

"Possibly. But you know as well as I do there's nothing solid to stick her with. Nothing physical, that is."

Detective Raskin chuckled. "You think this isn't physical enough?" He swept his hand to the gore.

"Yeah, maybe for the bloody Spaniard. His shit is all over this scene."

"But you think she orchestrated it."

"Possibly, and framed him. Yeah, I do. She's daring me to catch her, and that's exactly what we shouldn't do right off the cuff, as there's no probable cause to bring her in."

"*We?*"

"I'm certainly not going anywhere. *We* can work this case together, but I plan to go to Houston next week because there's plenty I've read that I need to check out about this crazy bitch. You need my help."

Raskin nodded in agreement as it was certainly warranted protocol to work with other departments from other cities on such a brutal crime, especially if the brutality could be traced from elsewhere. "And you've never seen this Mexican before?"

Marion could tell that Wilson wanted to say something but thought twice about it and remained silent.

"I doubt he's Mexican, but no. Never seen him—"

"I have." The voice came from a young woman clearly dressed for everything Eternity 51 had to offer: mini skirt, rayon tank top, leather boots—all stylish and expensive. She was in her early thirties, dirty blond hair, five-foot-nine, toned and clear-eyed, though Marion instinctively knew she'd had a few drinks.

"Oh? And who might you be?" Raskin asked as both he and Marion turned to the woman. Wilson had his arms folded across his body as if to protect himself from her.

"My name's Nina Frost. I happen to know Isaac. To be fair, I just met him the other night. I've overheard what you've been talking about."

Raskin jumped in. "His name is Isaac?"

"Yes."

Marion and Raskin both looked at Nina with a light that went on only cops could see. Another officer came over to interrupt, a detective, Patrick Hill. "Jay, I've got a hit on that suspect. She's right. His name *is* Isaac Santiago. Former military. Marines. Three Afghan tours. Homeless for the past few years as far as we know. Has some theft charges, some drug shit. DUI. Nothing like *that* fuckshow." He tilted his head toward the restrooms.

"Thanks, Patrick. Everyone, this is Detective Hill."

"Well, there you have it." Wilson couldn't help himself, and Marion knew that, so he did nothing, regardless of how much he wanted to make good on his earlier promise.

Raskin ignored him. "We don't know what he did in war though, right? Probably something like this."

Marion stopped him. "With pig heads? And where are the fucking pig bodies? Doesn't seem warlike to me. Not this kind of war. And not a word from you." Marion's direction to Wilson made Raskin all the more wanting to join forces with the Houston cop.

"Let's find this Santiago asap. Put out the APB. On the woman, too. What's her name?"

"Terra Drake."

Nina cleared her throat and spoke up with a courage that impressed the hell out of Marion. "You're not going to find her, won't matter what you do. And she's not alone either. She's got a whole band with her. Especially some giant named Adrian, or Adramal...something, I can't remember. There were drugs involved. Drinks with drugs."

Wilson couldn't help himself again as his primary donor came to mind. "Are you serious? You think it's Adrian? You were drinking drug-laced wine?"

"I never said it was wine, and yes, Adrian something..."

Marion stepped into Wilson's personal space. "You know this Adrian she's talking about?"

Wilson took a step back, keeping his arms crossed. "If it's the same Adrian, he's the chief investor in this place. But she can't be trusted with what she just said."

"Your business partner?" Raskin stepped in just as curious as Marion.

"I wouldn't say business partner, per se. He just fronted me most of the money to outright buy the club and the property. Look, just because this young girl—"

"Woman, thank you very much," Nina said. "And all I'm saying is that I saw this guy at Terra's place the other night with Isaac and some others, and his name was Adrian, I think—"

"Whatever. Miss Frost is it? That's fine but—"

"Stop. Let's just stop right here," Raskin said, so as to not lose control of the conversation. "I don't care about this Adrian...whatever his name is. What I do care about—"

"Wait! I know an Adrian, if it's the same guy we're talking about." Marion's cutoff of Raskin made everyone silent. "I saw him a while back, standing on the bridge by my place when there was an incident out there. A truck had been driven into the creek behind my fence. He was there just looking on. Scary fucker, and as tall as any basketball player I've ever seen. Taller. I ended up talking to one of the deputies on the scene about him. Jim Evanston."

"Really?" Raskin was deeply curious now.

"Know him?"

"Yeah. He's good."

"Anyway, Evanston ends up telling me that this guy now owns the property next to my place. It used to belong to a Stan Smitts, but he was also found dead last year."

Raskin rubbed his chin in thought. "I remember it. Don't know all the details, but all this tying together seems a bit fucked up."

Wilson, yet again, couldn't shut his mouth. "This speculation is all just fine and dandy, but there is a bloodbath in my club that could be this Isaac fucker's fault and the woman that you met here, Mister Paul, but I don't think my investor should be bothered about any of it. I don't care where he was when Nina saw him. *If* she saw him, or that you may have seen him standing on some bridge over a creek."

Raskin cut in. "Doesn't really matter what you think, Mister Wilson. We're here to do a job so that *we* can help *you*, so if you don't mind...let us do just that. And it isn't just you, it's the whole fucking city that this will affect." Raskin turned directly to Marion and Nina. "Miss Frost, there's a lot to do around here, so leave your contact information with one of the detectives. We'll get you to come down to the station and make a statement. Let's have Detective Hill handle it with you."

"I don't want to leave right now, to be honest, and I can't drive because I've been drinking."

"I'll take you some place," Marion said. "In fact, we can go to the station together, if that makes things easier."

Nina nodded in agreement.

Wilson grumped. "I am *so* happy that you two are going to hook up."

Marion had enough, stepped forward, and grabbed

Wilson by his jacket lapels. "I'm done with your shit."

Wilson recoiled in overdramatic fashion. "Take your hands off me."

"That's enough!" Raskin shouted. "Marion, please. Take care of Miss Frost. Patrick, help me out here. I'll call you later. Mister Wilson, I want you over there with my team and I will get to you shortly. Right now we are getting an APB out on Santiago and the Drake woman."

Nina said, "You're not going to find her."

"Oh, and why is that, Miss Frost?" Raskin was clearly at his limit.

"Because it works the other way around. She'll find you when she wants you. Wouldn't you agree, Mister Paul?" Nina spoke directly to Marion.

He looked into Nina's eyes, knowing that she knew more about Terra than he had ever known or felt. "She's right." Marion inched closer to Raskin. "Terra will end up coming to us. She's long gone for now."

"Okay. Let's just get on this, Patrick. "Nab Santiago. We know what he's wearing. Shouldn't be hard to spot with all the blood on him and shit, but about Drake...what's she look like?"

"A fucking demon is what."

Nina slowly nodded in agreement at Marion's description.

Chapter Twelve:

Adrian Kane's New Home

Marion awakened a few mornings after the Eternity 51 bloodbath, feeling shaken and worn down. The club was the epitome of all the weird he'd ever experienced combined into a single gathering place. But what had happened after Terra left him was something he'd never seen, which made the club all the more frightening. What was the reason behind the murders? Why that place of all places? Where would she strike next?

Who was a better question.

He knew Terra had everything planned exactly in a way that was beginning to make more and more sense to all the madness his brother had gone through, and what he himself was now deep into.

He'd been weight training as well as running sprints and hitting the heavy bag since the day after he took over his brother's place, all of which he thanked God for, as he didn't think he could have survived without his body being as strong as his mind.

He also woke up that morning more and more intrigued with Nina in all the ways good that was such a relief to all of Terra's bad. He'd taken her down to Lake City for her statement to Raskin, which she handled like a champion. He also helped her get back to her car; she'd left it at Eternity 51 that night and followed her home to make sure she was safe. All of this, on top of his loneliness, was producing quite the attraction and longing for such company. It didn't hurt things, either, that she was such a beauty. He also knew she'd gone through something terrible at Terra's place, but hadn't pried enough to get any details. Marion knew it was just a matter of time before she'd open up more and more.

He wanted to call her but turned on the television as one of the cable news channels was actually celebrating an event that took place in Orlando where a drag queen show had one of their performers giving birth on stage. Giving birth to God knows what. All the performers were dressed as gobs of human mutations. It was a sickening display of obscenity but one that caused Marion to find the clip on YouTube and watch it over and over again, as it felt so similar to what he'd dreamt while in a coma. It was more than just a clue to all that he'd seen since living in Duncan. It was somehow an affirmation to everything he'd seen with Terra. He flipped around more channels to see how much coverage the Eternity 51 butchering was getting, as it was being dubbed the Lake City Pig Slaughter.

Never mind the women. It's all about the fucking pigs.

The women hadn't been identified yet, but Marion knew that would come soon enough. That was the hope, anyway. What was just as disturbing was how quickly the story was fading. With so many murders taking place all over the country, along with story after story where it seemed everyone and everything had to push out something more and more freakish, only the local news still had what happened as the top story, and even their coverage was slimming down.

He showered up and dressed, then sent Nina a text to see how she was doing while on his way out to check the mail. He was going to meet Raskin, since he'd just found out Isaac Santiago had been picked up.

When Marion looked across the massive driveway of his neighbor's property, he saw none other than Kane himself outside, walking around a killer black Chevy pickup truck, long bed, single cab. Walking around the truck like he didn't know what to do next. There was the man who deputy Evanston and Bartholomew Wilson and Nina had spoken about, the same tall cowboy standing over the bridge that day when the entire Duncan police department was trying to fish out the white pickup from the creek. But what was so striking to Marion was the man's look and appearance while seemingly walking around his truck as if he didn't know how it got there or who parked it there.

Maybe something's wrong with the damn thing.

Who Marion saw was certainly a tall man, a wiry and even powerful man, but not a gunslinger.

Guy's gotta be near seven and half feet tall.

He wore a pair of silk trousers that were perfectly cut and draped even more perfectly around the hips and legs. A stunning golden color, and tailor cut, easily a grand a pair. The shirt that matched the slacks, also silk, was a bright light blue, long sleeved and open four buttons down, exposing a flat wooden chest. His shoes were alligator, also tailor cut. But it wasn't the clothes that struck Marion as such a difference in the man he'd seen leaning over the bridge railing with a cannon of a six-shooter on his hip and a dangling cigarette.

It was his face and hair.

He had a face that was as chiseled as Marion remembered but looked more like it had been neatly cut and polished from a piece of finished oak; his hair was a washed-out navy blue with white highlights, wavy thick and deeply parted to one side, equally chiseled as if cut from the same block of wood. With a soft air-blown look to it as if just tussled. The man's eyes and brows looked saddened and effeminate with a hint of eyeliner and heavy blush. The right side of his face was painted in a rust-color makeup. His rich eyebrows were painted in the same color and highlight as his hair. His entire appearance was one of deep somberness, if not dread.

"You must be my new neighbor." His voice was deep yet soft and too elegant. It took Marion off guard for a moment as it cut through the distance as if he was standing right next to Marion's mailbox. He'd always remembered his brother telling him how voices carried in the mountain air from the farthest of distances. He skipped checking the mail altogether and walked toward the towering man, walking around the wooden fence that separated their properties, across the driveway and right into his neighbor's space.

Didn't expect to tackle this problem right after Terra's bloodbath, but why the fuck not?

"That's right. I'm Marion," he said quickly enough to show no one else could ever see his guard had been lowered. Marion immediately extended his hand for a shake. When Kane accepted the gesture, Marion couldn't hide his surprise. The man's grip was as powerful and overwhelming in its restraint as when shaking John's hand at the alien diner. His fingers were impossibly long as they engulfed Marion's entire hand and felt as strong as cable.

Christ. I'd have to pump him with a full magazine to take him down, if at all.

"That's quite a grip you've got. Can tell you could just keep on going with that one."

"Adrian Kane, and the pleasure's all mine," he said, completely ignoring the compliment as they released hands. Marion took note that both the man's hands had that same wood-cut look as his face and hair. Everything about him was overproduced to a point where Marion felt more off guard, but a feeling he was getting more and more accustomed to with all that had slammed him since stepping foot on the hospital floor. It was all about adaptability.

There were a few raids he'd been on in some of Houston's worst parts with some of the most violent and fierce gang killers when Marion could feel the hairs on his arm prick his skin like tiny needles. There was even a time when Marion and his partner once blasted through a door with a SWAT team and battering ram where they'd found in the living room a dozen young boys hogtied and whipped bloody. Standing over the boys was one of the FBI's most wanted human traffickers looking back at Marion and the team with a sloppy grin on his face as if what he'd done was nothing more than stealing a candy bar from the local grocer.

How Marion felt then was what he felt in front of Kane.

"There's something fucking off about you, fella."

"Didn't I see you a few weeks back over by the bridge? With the truck that was lodged in the river behind my place? The creek? Wouldn't call it a river, but folks around here seem to think things are bigger than they really are."

Kane took in a deep breath, the back of his hands on his hips with palms and fingers outward, and looked up to the sky as if trying to carefully remember something. "Possibly. I certainly remember the truck in the drink. Ever find out what happened? Terribly strange to see that around here. I certainly didn't recognize the vehicle, and I know pretty much everything around this town."

"Is that right? Interesting. Well, one of the deputies who was helping out happened to mention that you've only just moved into this property. That you're as new here as I am. How is it you know everything?" Marion decided not to ask about any relationship with Bartholomew Wilson or the club. Certainly not Nina or the Friday night she'd spent at Terra's place where Kane could have been.

Kane was still looking up at the sky when he first spoke, then looked down to Marion. His eyes were strange pinpoints. He licked his lips. "Did he now. Well, my good neighbor, as you probably know, this town's small enough to learn quite a bit in a quick and hurry. Used to be your brother's place, yes?" Kane nodded over to Marion's house.

"Yeah. That's right. Still getting used to the fact it's now mine."

"How true that must be. I know bits and pieces of your story. Was on the news and all." Kane yawned and looked up to the sky again.

He was easily a foot and half taller than Marion as Marion looked up to the man's eyes holding contact with laser focus.

Hold this fucker's stare no matter what.

Kane's eyes had something behind them that created a sense of deeper unease. In fact, everything about the man made Marion feel like he needed to walk away. He certainly wanted to walk away. There was a masked stink about him that reminded Marion of the hospital room and Janet Stone's living room.

Stay cool, just stay cool.

"I've heard that a few times. I was in the hospital for a while—"

"No need to explain. No need at all." He pronounced it *a-tall*." Kane flipped his hands in dismissal.

"I once had a therapist tell me this saying that's always stuck with me. 'Don't explain, don't complain.' That was his motto when it came to relationships."

The interruption bothered Marion, but not as much as everything else about the man. Especially his voice. What Marion first noticed in its depth and clarity had turned to one that was hyper-pronounced in a way that seemed like an attempt to mockingly sound like a sophisticated woman. Yet the more he spoke, the more Marion thought it wasn't mockery. There was nothing about Kane's voice nor his strikingly manicured clothing that matched his huge physique.

"This isn't a relationship. Let me clear that up. Listen,

Adrian. I've had a hell of a past few days, and I've gotta get back to some things—"

"Oh come now. I've seen what's been going on. News and all. Seems you're all over it yet *again*. Can't seem to stay out of trouble, can you?" Kane giggled in a way that caused Marion to crimp his eyes.

"No. Seems shit keeps following me around. Wrong place wrong time and all." It was then that he thought about asking Kane about the Friday night at Terra's but continued to hold back. Intel gathering was still the most important thing, regardless of how much he wanted to begin interrogating his neighbor.

"I understand, I really do. Hey, how 'bout something more fun, if you will? Why don't you come with me and have a look around my property. Get to know each other a bit more. Neighbors and all. I mean there's so much here that I *myself* haven't even seen, to be perfectly honest. I'd love to show you around. New neighborly chats are such a rarity these days. Come, come, let me take you around the place. I'm sure you can put everything on hold for just a few, right?"

Marion let out a long breath, clearly irritated. "Sure, why not." He immediately regretted not having the Beretta on him.

Knife will have to do if it comes to it.

He realized the best thing was to be as cordial as possible. He felt everything was off about Kane, from his clothes to his voice, to his stench, to his purposeful look of confusion.

"Oh good! I'm so pleased. This way, let me show you this first garage area. More like a garage shop, if you will."

"How'd you end up buying this place? You'd think there'd be a will that left it to the family or something."

"So clever of you, so aware of things. Of course anyone would think the same, but alas. No. Mister Smitts had no one, and I happened to just get lucky, I guess. Quite lucky, as all of these buildings you see are what he had built himself. So I was told. I was needing a place like this where everything is here for whatever is needed. There is so much needed, so much that needs to be done."

Marion had no idea what Kane meant but nodded in agreement as he walked alongside the man, still in awe of his overall size and appearance. From what Marion could see, the property consisted of the garage-shop building that Kane was walking to, a much larger garage building kitty corner and behind his own property, and a variety of custom-built wooden stall buildings that could have been used for horses, but clearly had been used for storage of whatever Stan Smitts had needed or wanted to store.

Kane opened the side door of the garage and held it open in a gesture for Marion to enter first. "Each of the buildings out here were all loaded up with cars, motorcycles, and more tools than you have ever seen at any service station. Smitts even had a nice ski boat and a motorhome twice the size of a school bus. Fucker had every goddamn toy you'd ever want. But I didn't need any of that nonsense. Useless to me. I've also had every toy known to man, dear neighbor, I've just been around long enough to know what's needed and what isn't. I mean, this guy must have had several million sunk into...*stuff*, and he still ended up gutted at the local drinking hole. With his throat slit wide open. Mercy."

Marion stopped and stared at the man. "Yeah..." He spoke uneasy and began to wonder if Kane was on something with as much as he rattled off and how quickly he'd changed his tone and language.

Maybe he's just not had company for a while.

He'd known the story of Stan Smitts' death as far as his brother had known about it, but nothing had ever been completely proven as to the cause of death. That was one more piece of all that his brother had gone through that Marion had also planned to continue digging into. He also wanted to go over it with Raskin and pick his brain. Learning as much about Kane would be more food for thought.

"You know his death hasn't ever been confirmed as to the exact cause that night he was killed. Smitts', that is."

"Ohhhh, that's right. I keep forgetting. You're big city police. I've known plenty. You guys always have open questions that are never answered. Probably the exact thing going on right now with Lake City and all. Awful stuff."

Marion kept the conversation focused on Stan Smitts. No way he was going to get into the other, even if he believed Kane was trying to bait him. "I don't think that has anything to do with it, I was just stating facts."

Kane tilted his head in curiosity and stared at Marion then let out a long breath, completely changing the subject. "The one thing that couldn't be sold is this full-service hydraulic system. It's a dandy. That Ram you have ever need any work we could put it on these racks and take a look right here and then. Check out the whole underbelly to see what's made it sick."

Marion stared right back at Kane and let out one of his own deep breaths to mimic his neighbor for a reaction, creating a brief staring contest that caused Marion's eyes to water.

"Let's go. Let's walk over to the big garage. It's impressive."

The building was fifty feet or so across from where they stood, and indeed was by far the biggest personal garage Marion had ever seen. Easily over three thousand square feet, it was the size of most homes in the immediate area. The massive building sat a hundred feet or so away from his own property and was something he had wanted to see inside since he'd taken over his brother's place.

Kane opened one of the solid steel side doors and turned on a massive track lighting system that made the place look even bigger. That, and the fact it was also

Dean Patrick

completely empty. Kane's voice disturbingly echoed off the solid steel walls and the solid concrete floor when he spoke. "Something else, isn't it?"

"Land a small plane in here."

"Ha! Such wit. I'm starting to really like you. Let me ask you, neighbor, what's your take on Duncan? This tiny town in general."

Marion thought about it for a second. "Interesting question. Strange is what I think. I've seen nothing *but* strange since I've been here. And it seems to have led me to even more strange, as you've seen the news and all."

Kane ignored the slight mockery. "True. So true. Small towns have that unique power to swallow you whole. Is that the kind of strange you refer to? No need to answer." Kane raised his enormous hand in gesture to not speak, flicking it with more queer effeminacy as he paused and looked up to the giant steel ceiling. "You hear things at night out here that you'd never hear in places like Houston, or any other big city. Other night for example. Almost a few weeks ago or so, did you hear music in the distance? Heavy rock and...chanting...voices? Like a surreal concert in the distance?"

Marion paused for effect. "Maybe."

Best just to see where this can lead, as he knows a lot more about every goddamn thing that's—

"No. Not maybe. Part of what swallows you whole in small-town America is the reality of such noises. The striking sounds in the dead of night that cut through any clutter. And visuals. I'm sure you've seen some *other* things here, am I right? Sounds and movements and chilling nuances that tap at your nerves. Unknown movement in the night sky...tell me what you've seen. Tell me what you've heard."

Marion didn't know where to begin but also knew Adrian was probably being rhetorical. He refused to talk about the massive UFO that night on the way to the freak diner but decided to mention Eternity 51.

"That butchering at the club in Lake City has certainly been a new one for me. That level of violence was disturbing. Decapitated pigs *and* women is truly fucked. But that kind of shit happens in big cities. I've not been privy to all of it just because I'm HPD. Big cities back when Manson had Sharon Tate and company carved up, that was decades ago and still as fucked up as anything. But if you're talking about small-town America...*this* town...yeah, I've seen some pretty weird shit. Still gathering more intel—"

"Stop. Please. I know far too much of everything. Mine is a world of absolutes. It's also one of chaos. Mayhem. I'm sure you've sensed it. You and I are cut from the same cloth, neighbor." Kane paused and looked all around the spacious building. They had both walked toward the center of the massive concrete floor. Marion hated being cut off again.

"I don't know what the hell that means, but you're the one asking questions."

Marion had kept enough distance to continue checking out his new neighbor for every single pinpoint detail that could provide some kind of edge. In the middle of the spacious garage, Kane's size and presence looked like a bizarrely lit giant candle where every shadow was controlled by his words and actions.

"I know I can be a little rude. Just part of who I am. Who I've always been." Kane turned to Marion in just enough of a threat that Marion patted the knife in his front pocket and wished again for the Beretta.

Kane's eyes noticed. "Easy, neighbor. We're just chatting. Back to small towns. It's like hunting. Another slice of small-town power. It's like a slow hunt. Have you been hunting, Marion? And I mean the kind of hunt that all of this brings." Kane spread out his arms as if to showcase his warehouse garage and his land as if it were representative of every small town in the country.

Marion stayed laser focused but said nothing. His breathing was getting heavy.

"To hunt out here, you've got to have incredible patience and understanding, which builds and creates trust. It's a long process of quiet and serenity, achingly so, then boom! The deal is sealed. You've found yourself in a blood-oath atonement. That's Duncan. And maybe you're its next big game cat as everything all ties together."

"And what would that make you, *neighbor*?"

"Ha! That's the spirit, my good fellow! That's what separates the gunman from the bow hunter. Enough of the banter." Kane put up both his hands in dismissal, clearly wanting to change the subject. "I'm considering a stage built in here with an arena-like seating arrangement. Place is far too big to just store things. I love the stage, arenas, and large halls for gatherings. What do you think, detective, have any thoughts on such an addition?"

Why the fuck would he want an arena in here, and for what?

"Honestly, I don't have any thoughts on anything you've been saying, as you're flipping around the channels way too frequently for my liking."

Kane stared at Marion again with that same stupid look that Marion was growing to detest. He wanted to smack the giant queer-face hard enough to knock the manicured wooden look into something more chipped and common.

"Tell you what, my good neighbor, I'm having some guests over this coming weekend. Maybe the following, haven't sealed the date yet. At least I was thinking about it, and it would be so nice if you'd drop by. Still working out the details and all."

"I'll be out of town. Heading to Houston for a week or so."

"Of course you are. Well, thought I'd mention it, and

you may be back in time, who knows? If not, I'm certain there'll be other opportunities. Why don't we go inside the house? I'd like to show you a few things. I can see the 'show and tell hour' out here has come to a curtain call. May I show you inside my place for a minute? Have a drink or a coffee? I promise to mind my manners more."

Marion breathed in deeply to think it over. He certainly didn't want to keep tensions building with Kane but knew well enough that it was best to keep going as long as there was an out, which there always was when things got nasty. Telling Kane otherwise would just force another time to sneak in and take a look around, and Kane was making things easy in that regard.

"I tell you what, I'll go inside and keep talking as long as I get to do a little more of it myself. Deal?"

"That's a deal, good neighbor."

Kane had to duck under the door entry to go inside his own house then Marion followed him down the first corridor that led into a spacious living area that was attached to an indoor swimming pool room. The walls of the living room were adorned with large brass crucifixes and paintings of strange and twisted portraits of bewitching women. The crucifixes themselves had not the Christ nailed down, but familiar women. At the base of each of them was an etched image of worms and rats. The crucified figures looked familiar, but Marion couldn't be absolutely certain.

Here's what he was certain of: things inside instantly felt worse than outside. He wanted the Beretta so badly he almost turned to leave.

The fuck is all this?

There were four 85-inch TVs hanging on four primary walls, an over-sized glass and iron coffee table that was highlighted with oversized picture books that made no sense to Marion, as he'd never seen the likes of the cover images. Sitting in the dead center of the grand table, centered between the picture books, was a long thick rubber index finger that looked to be suctioned to the glass. A veiny rubber index finger that had to be a few feet in height. It was unnerving, to say the least, and Marion was about to comment until he saw what was standing in the far corner of the living room, with purple lighting showering down on it.

A wax figure the size of Marion himself stood in a corner that looked like a biker who seemed lost and confused. Its hands were placed under its chin as if struggling to hold the weight of its head.

"That's the weirdest fucking thing I've ever seen in a house. What is it?"

"Him?" Kane gestured toward the disturbing figure.

"What else would I be talking about?"

"Well, there's the finger and all. That one normally gets folks talking. But...that's Ace."

"You say that as if it's real."

"It is! Well, he is." Kane giggled again, far too cheerfully.

"Right. Well, takes the prize for weird, no doubt. That and the finger, like you said, on the coffee table."

"I found that at a slave auction a while back. There was one of those just last year that your brother may have seen. But the one I'm talking about was many years ago. Ages ago. It was a prized possession of a plantation owner in New Orleans. Phelps his name was. Said he had a slew of the phallic fingers placed in areas of the slave quarters to remind them that they served under his finger's rule and would never have a thread of hope for things to change. Ever."

Marion cocked his head as he wasn't quite sure he heard what came out of Kane's mouth. "What the fuck are you talking about? Do you even realize how insane you sound?"

Kane's wide and wooden face suddenly grew a slightly twisted grin as if someone carved it in with a butter knife. He said nothing, but Marion refused to turn away as he looked into his neighbor's set of wild eyes that dimly glowed in perpetual insanity.

"What do you expect me to say to that, Adrian? Because I've got nothing."

"And I sure as fuck don't have my gun to put you the fuck down."

"Have you figured out what's wrong with this town yet? The root cause of it, that is?" Kane spoke as if Marion hadn't said a word.

"I don't know. What I do know is that you...never mind that. Maybe you're just a fucking nutcase like everything else that's going around. I reckon it's the same with everything."

"And what do you think that is, my good neighbor? With what you've seen." Kane's continual ignoring of anything Marion suggested or said was just one more tidbit of madness, and it was wearing on Marion's last nerve.

"From what I've seen, it's the Devil. The Devil has this town clamped down just as every other goddamn one of them, big or small. He just seems to be a little too close for comfort around here."

"And who is the Devil, Marion? Who do you think the Devil is, and has been all this time? I'm genuinely curious." With that, Kane's demeanor changed yet again. He looked as curious as he said he was.

Marion chuckled nervously. "I gotta hand it to you, neighbor, you know how to keep someone on their toes. Points for that. Let me say this, I think there are many devils. I'm just not sure who the ringleader is. At least not lately."

"Although you seem to be in line for the job."

"I don't buy that, detective. Not with your skills and thinking. Devils and demons galore, you say, and I'm sure of all the many tales of witchery that have unfolded, you're still finding yourself in the dark. Not a chance. Why don't

you take a seat in here. I know I could use a sit down."
Kane was pointing to the kitchen area that was more an
attachment to the living room, with an enormous kitchen
that would satisfy any top chef.

"Thanks, but standing's fine."

"Suit yourself, Detective," Kane said, but instead of
going to the kitchen area to sit, he walked over to the wax
figure he called Ace. "Maybe you've danced with The
Devil, personally that is, and found yourself just a tad
overwhelmed. At least that's the word on the streets, and
what, with all that was unloaded on you the other night in
Lake City? Understandingly so. You know what they say
about the devil in the details and all that jazz. Used to be
the case that when you'd least expect something to come at
you, what you never expected to come crawling your way
was what did it for the truly dark side. That's not the case
anymore. I'm sure you've noticed how fast things have
sped up. So fast that when you fall nighty night and then
come wakey wakey, the whole goddamn world's changed
yet again. Exponentially so. There are days when you turn
on the news, and the whole world has put on an entirely
new dress. The days for watching your back are gone. She
wants to be right in your face, squared up and ready. Giddy
up." As Kane was speaking, he was also admiring the wax
figure, almost as if he was speaking to it rather than to
Marion.

Marion thought about what Terra was spouting off
about just before she left him, how similar it was to what
Kane just said. He was about to call him out on it to
connect him to Terra when Kane quickly walked away
from Ace and over to one of several oak dining tables that
connected the living room to the kitchen. He pulled out an
equally impressive dining chair with yet another gesture for
Marion to join him.

Marion decided to oblige him, but instead of sitting
down, he walked straight up to Kane, looked down at him

but said nothing. Even sitting, Kane was still almost able to look Marion dead in the eyes.

"I make you nervous, detective?"

"Yeah, you do. But I'll use that to my advantage."

Kane then reached over the oak dining table to pick up a remote-control device. When he clicked on one of the giant wall televisions, each of the other three turned on a few seconds later until all were in unison. Another recent murder was the highlight reel, splashed on the screens of Kane's massive living room in 4k detail.

"Yike! Yet another mass killing?! My, my, and what a shame to see someone with so much promise being arrested for butchering *college* students. It's even more a shame to see it now taking precedence over what just happened around here. Ugly stories fade away so quickly. Tsk, tsk, tsk. Such a shame. So much promise. Not like that Santiago animal, that wartime criminal. And I know about promise. Promise and loss, I know them all too well. *Crazy* how many brutal killings are popping up all over the place, right, detective?"

Marion looked at Kane with more than just curiosity as the spacious living room began to feel like it was closing in by invisible gears behind the walls, the television screens growing larger and larger. Kane's voice pitched higher and higher to where he was beginning to sound like a little girl.

"Kane, the killer of the college students is no better than Santiago, regardless of what you think. Yeah, I think it's a lot more than just fucking crazy that's going on. And you know something? Huh... Strangely enough that guy looks a lot like you."

Kane turned from the televisions and just stared at Marion as Marion was looking at the televisions, noticing that the killer of the college students—alleged killer—who'd been arrested could have been Kane's twin. Minus the height and size.

Marion stared right back at Kane.

Keep it together and hold on with this motherfucker.

"Detective, I'm sure that's not the most recent picture since this all just happened, but...the resemblance *is* weird, I would have to agree with you. I mean, it's *uncanny*. If you were one of the local boys, you might find the need to cuff me. Ha! But, alas, no need for such a thing, since it looks like the locals up there in I-dee-ho have stepped in to catch the dastardly creature. Probably just a creature of habit, to be honest. Much like this Santiago beast."

Kane stopped talking and continued to stare at Marion, causing more and more discomfort that began to borderline on fear. Kane then stared back at the massive screens. "Fascinating, neighbor. A bit uncanny indeed. All of this fuckery that's afoot. The whole world is burning down to skinny little timbers. I'll say this, makes one want to be as prepared as one can be. Physical, mental, armed. The whole bit. Speaking of such, don't you know a Burke Macey at Macey's Martial arts down there in Odessa?"

Marion stayed focused. Kane's topic-switching was as off as everything else going on. "I don't know him, per se. Met him once. Had a boxing lesson from him a few years back. Steve set it up for me."

"Did he now? Well, I've been thinking of paying Burke a visit myself for a lesson or two."

"Something tells me you don't need a lot of self-defense training."

"Ohhhh, how kind of you, detective. How kind of you. Such silly sentiment."

Marion finally had enough, as his head began to spin to the point where his stomach was turning. The walking around the property, the bizarre discussion in the large garage, Kane's distorted and effeminate different tones of voices, his shockingly different apparel from when he'd first seen him on the bridge, the distortedly overproduced way his face and hair looked like they'd been cut from a block of wood, the absurdity of the enormous rubber index finger, and the wax figure should have been enough. But the way Kane watched the breaking news story of a new possible serial killer and the astonishing resemblance did the trick. Marion's entire inner radar was screaming "Get. The. Fuck. Out."

Instead, he continued playing the game of cool. He needed a quick break is all.

"I need to use your restroom. Do you mind?"

"Not at all, detective. Need to go potty, do you?"

I swear to Christ I'm going to kill this sick fuck.

Marion didn't respond to the ridiculous comment.

"It's just up the stairs. You'll see it to the left just past some of the open rooms."

"You don't have one down here?"

"Not usable, no. Up the stairs. I'll fix us a drink. What would you like?"

"Any diet with caffeine is fine."

"Nothing stronger?"

"Diet and caffeine. Thanks."

He walked up a stairwell that was all carpeted and looked plenty worn. The hallway Kane mentioned led deep into the back of the home's second floor. The hallway ended and connected with what looked to be the master bedroom. Marion saw that the door to the master bedroom was fully open. He could see Kane's giant four-poster bed; it was much larger than any king-sized bed he'd ever seen. "Had that one custom made, no question." Marion made sure to whisper as he knew voices carried inside such a house just as clearly as they did outside.

His cop instincts took over as he avoided the bathroom all together and took a few steps inside Kane's master bedroom where he saw the walls were painted in several massive fly heads. It was hard to comprehend at first, but as he panned the room, the more detail he picked out. Enormous fly eyes were painted on both of the walls to Marion's left and right. It was like he was re-watching the scene from *The Fly* where Jeff Goldblum's Brundle has discovered a housefly trapped inside one of the pods just before teleportation, where Brundle's computer is zooming in on every vivid detail of the fly's composite. Eyes, antennae, and mouthparts were painted in extraordinary detail on both facing walls so much so that Marion felt a sudden urge to vomit, but he snapped out of it quickly enough to keep scanning the awful room.

The ceiling was made of an entire screen of some type. Whether it was a monstrous computer monitor or television screen, Marion couldn't determine. He also couldn't see any cable inputs or outputs, no computer ports of any kind. Just a black screen that mirrored everything in the room, including Marion, in a frightening kaleidoscope of Kane's master bedroom furniture fused together with the hideous fly murals. The stereo system from the first floor suddenly boomed to life with The Cure's "Fascination Street." Robert Smith's tormented voice and guitar filled the upstairs with a terrifying echo that led Marion one step closer to the endless cliff of madness.

To his immediate left was a massive leather La-Z-Boy recliner and ottoman. Sitting on the ottoman was the gun belt and six-gun shooter rig he knew he'd seen Kane wearing the day of the creek incident. Behind the recliner, in the far corner of the room, hanging on an oak coat rack was what looked like a religious gown typically worn by Catholic priests. Its size matched something that would fit Kane. Next to the giant gown hung a hideous mask that was turned inside out. Marion couldn't tell exactly what it was but thought it could have been a large mask of a pig's head. He knew he had no time to check it out more thoroughly, but the thought of the decapitated pigs' heads that were placed on the butchered torsos at Eternity 51 blasted him like a fire hose of blood. What hung on the coat rack was familiar, but he had to focus on what he could do. *Can't call for an A-fucking PB because of a mask that's inside out, and I've got no fucking authority here anyway.*

He'd seen enough as he walked softly out of the master bedroom and into the restroom Kane had directed him to go to in the first place. Regardless of the music's volume, Marion wanted to avoid his footsteps making any impressions that he was moving around upstairs.

He had no intention of using Kane's toilet, he simply needed a mirror to gather his composure. It was a technique he'd always used when stress hit him the hardest. Look at himself in the mirror and speak out loud that he was okay and that everything around him was okay and that he would fucking get through whatever it was, which was always as bad as it could get when he needed to use the technique.

He leaned in close to the bathroom's vanity mirror, taking deep breaths, staring into his own eyes. "Keep it together, keep it together, it all ties together just keep it the fuck together, there's nothing you can do right now just get the fuck out of here."

He flushed the toilet, washed his hands for the perfect coverup, and went back downstairs. He saw Kane using the remote as the music turned down a few notches.

"Just in time, officer Paul. I found you a Diet Coke and have iced it up nice and frosty for you."

From what he could tell, Kane hadn't moved from the kitchen chair he'd been sitting in. He ignored Kane, refused to take the drink and decided to walk over to Ace the Wax Figure all the while keeping his eyes on his neighbor.

No way I'm leaving until I see this thing up close, no matter how fucked up his room is or how much I think he's part of every goddamn thing that has hit this town.

"You know something, neighbor, I think I'm getting tired of your bullshit in all honesty. Real tired of it."

Kane kept a close eye on Marion's every move. "I guess you're not thirsty. I understand."

Marion wanted to lean on the figure or at least touch it, but decided to just look at its face and body. The figure was astonishing in its detail. Everything from its skin to boots to jacket to eyelashes and piercing sky-blue eyes was as much a marvel as it was an absolute disturbance. When it winked its right eye and smiled, Marion jumped back in a jolt that quickly overwhelmed his senses. But just as quick was his ability to instantly recover and take action.

Marion shuffled back with both feet simultaneously, did a quick boxing L-step to make sure he'd clear any forward movement from the newly alive Ace, and drilled the man with two jabs and a straight shot, which knocked him down to the floor as fast as dropping a sack of flour. Marion then whipped out the Spyderco knife, and turned to face Kane in a single move. "The fuck is that!? Who the fuck are you?!"

Kane remained seated and let out a small giggle. "I remember saying he was real."

"Fuck you did, you sick fuck. Who the fuck are you?" Marion moved the knife back and forth toward Kane and back to Ace.

"I told you his name is Ace. Now you tell me, detective, knowing how hard you just pummeled him, do I need to call a paramedic?"

"Call who the fuck you want. I'm out. It's your mess."

"But you're in my home."

"Let's see who this ragtag police force believes. One of their own, or this sick shit."

"Point taken. And noted. I'm sure you can see your way out."

The man called Ace, who Marion had just knocked senseless, began laughing while doubled over on the floor. He turned to his backside and lifted his head to look up the best he could toward Marion. Ace was bleeding from the nose and corner of his lip but was clearly taking some pleasure in the insanity.

"Fuck you laughing at? I should gut you right here and now."

"Not so fast, not so fast." Ace spit out blood between his sickening giggles. "I knew your brother. I knew him as well as I could, anyway. Your neighbor didn't tell you as I've been listening the whole time, as you now know." Ace then propped himself up and rested his elbows on his knees, gathering his composure. "We were in jail together years back. Strange account even by our standards." Ace then held out his arms in a gesture of Kane's living room and home and every fucked up thing about it. "Strange account indeed. One so out of the ordinary I'm sure he never said something about it as we talked about bikers who knitted and church leadership I met at the Lake City Library one day, my drawings I wanted to show your brother when he so rudely cut me off just as I was trying to get to know him—"

"Shut up. Shut the *fuck* up, you fuck!" Marion leaned over a bit toward Ace with the knife toward the man's face. He did recall a story Steve once told him many years ago about how he'd had a cellmate who was a biker, who late one night, began to tell Steve the bizarre story of how he—Ace—used to meet up with the church president at the time and talk about knitting, and how during that discussion Ace went through some type of freakish transition from biker to demon queer. The story had chilled Marion when he first heard it. Looking down at Ace, Marion saw that everything was far more than just chilling.

He backed away a few feet from Ace and looked over to Kane, who was still sitting with his hand cupped over his chin like a giant child.

Kane didn't need much prompting as he stood up and walked over a few feet toward Marion and Ace. "As I said, it's time you leave. For now, that is. It's time you get out. There's plenty of time for this to continue. I'm sure you know that, and I'm sure that you know it will..."

"No, you're right. This is far from fucking over." Marion stepped back a few steps, keeping the knife outward and ready before he left Kane's house. Those last words spoken from Kane were not those of the effeminate façade, but from a voice that was deep and booming with all the control of a harnessed thunderstorm. It was the voice he thought he would have heard from the gunslinger he'd seen on the bridge that day when the local police were fishing out the pickup truck.

Chapter Thirteen:

Title Fight at Macey's MMA

Marion was done with Duncan for a few nights. Maybe longer.

As much as he wanted to head back over to Kane's with Beretta in hand to get nice and ugly with him and his boy-toy wax figure come to life, he was done. He quickly packed an overnight bag and headed to Odessa. Of all places, he decided on the Odessa Hotel where his brother was found dead. It was as good a place as any. It was also a place that he knew would keep his senses razor sharp.

He checked in and crashed the moment his head hit the bed sheets. The next morning, he thanked God Almighty that his body and brain had shut down for a recharge.

He showered up, dressed, and began flipping through the channels. Eternity 51 was still on every local channel, but it wasn't the top story nationally. *That* spot was occupied by the College Student Killer. Kane was right. Marion also wondered what in Christ's name would it take to make non-stop national news if not decapitated pigs' heads on four decapitated women at a Utah nightclub. He was also anxious to get down to Lake City County jail, meet up with Raskin, and talk to Santiago, since he had been booked in. Maybe Santiago had things to say that would connect everything.

With all that Marion had seen at Kane's property and

home, his cop instincts suddenly picked up on what Kane had said about Burke, that he wanted to pay Burke a visit. After all that Adrian had spouted off about, for whatever reason his mentioning Burke couldn't be a good thing.

His brain felt overloaded, so he decided to call Nina first and foremost, regardless of how much the Burke comment was nagging him. The Lake City Pig Slaughter, whatever had happened with Nina at Terra's place, and the carnival that lived right next door to him made calling Nina seem like the exact slice of peace he craved most. Then he thought twice about it. She'd most likely be at work, but then again it was just past 8:00 a.m. so why not? Retail normally started later in the day.

Back and forth his thoughts bounced like a game of pong. He smiled at the thought of the video game that started it, all so many moons ago. Just as he was about to send Nina a text and head out for Lake City, he dialed her number instead. *This other shit can wait.*

> **Marion**: Hey. Wanted to check in. How are you?

> **Nina**: You're funny. Checking in? Is that cop shop for asking how I'm doing?

> **Marion**. Something like that. I didn't know if you'd left for work or not, or even what time you do leave, so here we are.

> **Nina**: I leave in a hour or so to open up. Store's not open until eleven, but I like to get things ready and have some quiet time. And I'm doing okay. How are things with...I don't know, the case? Is that how to ask it?

> **Marion**: It's one way, sure. I'm going down to Lake City later. Well, right now, but I wanted to see how you're doing.

Nina: I'm glad you did. You meeting that Raskin? I don't know about him.

Marion: Oh...why's that?

Nina: Couldn't tell you anything specific, just a feeling.

Marion. I see.

Nina: Don't let that bug you. I may not read people the same as you, but you'd be surprised how much you learn after years in retail.

Marion. No, no. I trust your instinct.

Nina: Call me later? Text me or something?

Marion: Yeah, of course. Listen...let me know if you need anything. Seriously. I'm always wired in. You've gone through a lot, and all of it may not have kicked in yet.

Nina: I know. I really do, and I'm sure you're right. But I'm dealing with it. It helps that you called and were thinking of me.

Marion: I was, and I want to see you again.

Nina: Okay then, I'd like that, too.

Marion: Have fun at work.

Nina: Have fun at the jail.

When Marion pushed the red hang-up button on his phone, the fondness he'd felt for her the moment she first walked up to Raskin and him was certainly reaffirmed.

But she was in danger, and there was zero point in telling her. Regardless of his attraction, he didn't want to get too attached too quickly. He needed his edge, and women had a way of dulling it. The last week had turned his nerve endings to frayed threads. A romance could cause a crucial oversight.

I'll take it slowly and get through this shit, and there'll be plenty of time for something different.

Before he left the hotel room, he gave Burke Macey a call. No answer, of course, because Macey was probably teaching a class or giving someone a private lesson. He'd spoken to Macey a few times on the phone and thanked him for giving the hospital the letter and his brother's laptop, that it was nice to know there was someone local who'd given a shit. They talked briefly about Steve, guns, things to do in Utah to break the ice and Marion certainly made plans for some serious training at Macey's MMA.

***

Indeed, Burke missed the call as he was just finishing the cleanup of the jiu-jitsu mat and getting ready to do a full cleanup of the entire gym when he heard someone outside, laying on the horn incessantly. He opened the warehouse door that opened up the entire gym floor to see a black Chevy truck idling at a thick rumble. Single cab with a long bed, it looked like it had the power to take off and spin the wheels for a full minute without moving but a few feet. Then it did.

When it did, Macey didn't bother to lock up as he raced down the concrete steps to his own truck, an older model silver Tacoma, and tore out of the parking lot to chase the maniac in the black Chevy, as Burke saw the truck had not yet turned at the corner light to head down the main street to the freeway.

He was in one of those moods where his patience had already hit the wall, as a few of his students from the morning's class were not listening to what he was teaching, something martial arts instructors never appreciated.

"Who's this fucking guy?" Burke whisper-shouted but remained focused on the black Chevy truck. When the light turned green, the black Chevy roared to life; Macey followed it for a good five or six miles, both trucks racing down the main road that would spill onto the freeway entrance that led back to Duncan. Macey's limited temper was prepared to follow the black Chevy, even if the final destination was the shore of the Pacific Ocean.

Instead, he followed it into the parking lot of one of Odessa's largest churches. Just before the black Chevy pulled into the church parking lot, Macey had pulled back a bit to make sure he would maintain a good distance before confronting the driver.

When a giant of a man exited the Chevy, Macey pulled up closer, but much more slowly. The man was dressed in a cowboy rig: gun holster, ragged black cowboy hat and even more ragged boots, torn black jeans and what looked like an ancient leather vest, no shirt underneath. The gunslinger didn't pay Macey a lick of attention as he walked around to the passenger side door; he towered over the truck as if it were a toy.

Still, Macey had the stubborn gene and refused to go quietly. He took out his own handgun he always carried with him, a Glock .9 mm, and pulled up closer to the giant cowboy. "Particular reason you were at my gym, honking your horn like a fucking idiot?" Macey had his window lowered as he pulled up closer, handgun ready.

Instead of opening the passenger side door, the giant cowboy walked back to the drivers side to face Macey, putting his massive hand on the butt of what looked like a Colt .45 six-gun hand cannon. The man's face and hands looked more like chunks of brittle wood. He smiled with an open mouth filled with the most awful teeth Macey had ever seen. Before Macey could think things over on what was going to happen next, he heard someone else's voice, either a priest or a church worker who was walking hurriedly toward them, calling out to the giant.

Kane turned toward the church worker, then back to Macey. "Looks like Lady Luck just came your way. Take advantage of it." The giant cowboy's voice sounded like ragged sandpaper.

Never one to mince words or back down from anyone or anything, regardless how high the odds were stacked against him, Macey kept the Glock in hand as he slowly drove past the giant and his black Chevy truck. "Stay the fuck away from my gym."

The giant just stared down Macey as the church worker continued to call out that things could all be brought into the chapel, or something along those lines.

Macey rolled up his window and left the church parking lot to head back to the gym far more rattled than he ever expected.

***

It was later that following afternoon when Marion was on his way down to Lake City to meet Raskin for the Santiago interview at county, when Raskin called with a change of plans. It was Marion who canceled the interrogation the previous morning when he realized he just wasn't in the mood. He ended up calling and chatting with Nina again, then walked around the Odessa Hotel thinking about his brother, ordered some takeout, and fell asleep early, not realizing how much he needed the rest.

Raskin: Marion, glad you picked up.

Marion: Morning, what's up? Just on my way down there now.

Raskin: Yeah, glad I caught ya. Not going to meet up with you until tomorrow. Something's come up.

Marion: Case related?

Raskin: No, my daughter.

Marion: I understand. She okay?

Raskin: Hard to say, really.

Marion: She still live at home with you?

Raskin: No. She left for a new fold a few years ago. She's twenty-two and thinks she knows all there is to know. I'll fill you in because it could be case related as I've been thinking about it. But look, you're still free to interrogate the shit out of Santiago if you'd like.

Marion: I'd like it better if we both did. I'll head back to where I was staying, thanks for the heads up.

Raskin: You're not at your place?

Marion: Negative. Needed to clear my head and get away for a few days. Had a strange fucking run-in with Adrian Kane, of all people. First time I'd met him at his place. Weird as shit, I'll fill you in on that one.

Raskin: Can't wait to hear it. Didn't think he'd be home...well, what do I know?

Marion: What do you mean?

Raskin: I was thinking more out loud and maybe what's his name, Eternity 51's owner may have spooked Kane.

Marion: Wilson.

Raskin: Right. We'll sync up tomorrow and tag team Santiago, need to take care of this for today.

Marion: Later.

Marion knew all about daughters, as his own, Casey, was close in age to Raskin's.

Close to Nina's, for fuck sake, but whatever.

He hadn't seen Casey in a few years and, of course, hadn't spoken to her since last year just before Steve came to visit.

He suddenly missed Casey terribly.

He turned into one of the emergency U-turns off the freeway and headed back to the Odessa Hotel. He called Macey again, and again with no answer. "Where the hell are you, pal?" The comment Kane had made about paying Macey a visit continued to nag the shit out of Marion's conscience.

"Fuck it, your place is close enough to the hotel. I'll just stop by and see if I can catch you there."

***

It was that same time in the afternoon, around the exact same time Burke had chased down the giant cowboy the day before, when an athletic couple walked right through the lobby area of the gym and into the gym area without saying a word as Burke Macey looked at both of them in amazement. His professional fighting career had seen him against a variety of opponents who were formidable in their specialties. Whether a fighter was more skilled at boxing or with a strong ground game in wrestling or jiu-jitsu, Macey had gone up against the best plenty of times and won plenty of matches.

He'd never in his life seen anyone like the beast of a man and quickly wondered if the towering figure was somehow related to the cowboy giant he'd followed to the church parking lot, as this guy looked far different. It wasn't his height or overall size, it was his presence. For one, he had such an awful stench that it gagged Macey. Second, the man looked more like a seven-and-a-half-foot deviant mannequin mutant, plastic wooden skin and features. And lastly, he walked into the gym wearing what looked like some religious gown.

He'd also never seen anyone like the woman who was with him. She walked in like she owned the place, wearing a one-piece red leather bodysuit, black leather pumps, and a black felt cowboy hat. As Macey followed the two of them into the gym area, she was also one of the most perfectly shaped women he'd ever seen, and that was saying a lot, considering he'd trained plenty of gorgeous athletes.

Inside Macey's MMA gym were two ringside setups: one, a full-sized cage fighting ring, and the other a full-sized professional boxing ring. The woman had taken one of the visitor's chairs, placed it right in front of the cage fighter ring and sat there with her legs crossed and hands behind her head, leaning back, her lavender eyes just as striking as her partner's size.

The man dropped the strange gown, revealing he had on long shorts and a tank top. Boxing gear, to be exact. And why the fuck was he wearing it? He walked up and down the gym, inspecting both of the rings.

Macey, perpetually confrontational, found himself speechless at first, but knew he needed to say something. It was his club, for fuck sake. "Anything I can help you with?" That was the best he could do under the circumstances of the strangest entry he'd ever seen of any potential customer.

"It's you who'll need the help," the woman said. "You're in for the fight of your life. The fight *for* your life, to be exact." She spoke with full command of the place, same as Macey always commanded regardless of the class size, regardless of what special occasion, regardless of *anything* going on. It was his livelihood and business that he'd built from the ground up with a fourteen-year run of success. He needed to take back full control over the woman's clear attempt to disrupt his thoughts more than he'd ever remembered.

"Who the fuck are you?"

"I'm Terra."

"And who the fuck is he?"

"That's your opponent, Kane."

"What the fuck do you want?"

"You followed him down the freeway the other day, don't you remember?" Terra ignored Macey's growing anger as he looked closer at the towering Kane and his strangely wooden body. Macey realized she was speaking the truth—it was the maniac who was honking the horn incessantly just the day before, the maniac cowboy gunslinger who had some kind of fucked off church meeting.

Only the man who stood in the gym wasn't the ragged gunman, but something entirely different that caused Macey's skin to crawl.

"What's a pro MMA fight? Three five-minute rounds?" Terra continued to control the conversation. Macey nodded while he looked Kane up and down, but remained silent. "This fight will be a single round for as long as it takes. Or as long as he wants it to go. Chooses it to go, that is." Terra moved her hands in the direction of Kane and the cage ring.

Macey scowled. "What's your role here, cheering squad?"

"Don't I look dressed the part?"

He looked back and forth to Terra and Kane. Not sure what to say or do, he did what he knew best: accept and get on with it.

"Let's do it. Let's go. I'm not sure I've got any gloves

his size. Your size." Macey turned to Kane with the partial query. "Wraps will have to do; I'll get us some."

"Double set for me." Kane's voice was flat and dead.

Macey jogged out to the pro shop that was down the hall past the lobby, grabbed three sets of hand wraps, one for him, two for the stilts, then jogged back out to the gym. He walked up the three steps that led up to the cage ring, opened the cage entrance door, stepped in and pulled off his shirt, signaling Kane to come in.

After both men wrapped their hands, Macey began to walk around the ring to get a long look and feel for the man he was about to tune right the fuck up. Kane followed suit.

"What's your wi-fi password? We need to get this place lit!" Terra's glee matched anything Macey had ever seen in the most raucous mosh pits of some of the most violent events, and he'd seen plenty.

"Macey's MMA, one word all lowercase no apostrophe." Macey and Kane kept circling the ring, sizing each other up as Macey gave out the password.

The sound system at the gym was built for the ultimate experience, wi-fi connected for remote device control. Setup was a Marshall half stack that stood on a four-foot metal tripod that hooked into a Bose S1 Pro Multi Position PA system. A Rockville RPM209, 12-channel mixer powered everything to concert-level volume.

Terra, using her phone, played an extended version of Black Sabbath's "Zero the Hero" from their *Born Again* album. The song was filled with deep, heavy power chords and background noises of harrowing grinds and bangs that were produced with distortion-pedal driven bells and concrete thumps.

The entire gym roared to life as if a fire-breathing dragon was walking around the place, looking for something to cook up for dinner. Macey's heart raced at the thrill he felt just before every pro fight, except this one didn't have a ring entrance with a song of his choice, and there were no fans cheering for his victory.

"Pro MMA rules with no breaks. Fight!" Terra's command blasted into the cage ring with as much fury as the music.

Macey wasn't about to waste a single breath of precious air. A key to every fight, regardless of the level of experience, was breathing and how to control breathing for maximum focus and endurance. He was always a fighter who gave any opponent instant inside pressure to set up an uppercut or quick body shots; that was the exact game he'd have to bring to someone as tall as Kane.

The moment Macey drilled into Kane's body with an attempt for a takedown, Kane wrapped his own arms around Macey's torso, picked him up a few feet into the air and slammed him to the ground. Macey quickly maneuvered to get back to his feet, or to shoot into Kane's knee for a leg-lock takedown and to open up the fight for a grappling opportunity. But as he did, Kane landed a ferocious jab into Macey's face and jaw.

Burke Macey's entire skillset as a black belt in three different martial arts forms, with five Golden Glove tournament wins, vanished with a hit that he'd never believed he'd ever suffer. Kane's hand felt more like a slab of concrete. No one had ever hit Macey with such a devastating first punch. Kane could have easily connected with another, or even landed a kick to the ribs, but instead moved away from Macey and circled the ring with his head jolting side to side, his tongue hanging out like a thirsty dog's, his body moving in sync with the controlled screams of Ian Gillian's sandpaper vocals about a hopeless loser who would never amount to anything other than some vagrant on the street, eating raw liver.

Macey knew he had to get up immediately but also knew he needed to keep some distance while planning a new strategy. He couldn't sustain many more of such punches, or the giant would kill him. Macey jolted to his feet but stayed low to shoot into Kane's body. As soon as he did, he planted a fake-and-spin move in an attempt to reach Kane's back side, but instead pivoted to a more comfortable distance while keeping his hands high and outward toward the giant.

Kane kept his arms low and to his side but turned his head to follow Macey, continuing to shake his head from side to side with his tongue out. The two fighters circled each other again, Kane with arms lowered, Macey with hands out in a high guard position to keep as much safe space as possible.

When he thought Kane's arrogance finally gave way to an opening, Macey moved in quickly for a hard jab and hook combo but failed to land either as Kane easily dodged the strikes. Macey was in top shape, almost pro-bout shape. He'd fought some of the best boxers and martial artists in the country and had never seen any opponent so effortlessly maneuver around his shots. As soon as his hook missed, Kane again fired a jab that knocked Macey to the ground. He was bleeding and had a tooth knocked out, maybe a few.

But there was no fucking way he was giving in to the freakshow who'd walked in with the red-leather model. It was the woman who Macey looked to as he struggled to get back to his feet. She was smiling almost as if in laughter, legs still crossed, cowboy hat pushed back, lavender eyes that were hypnotic. When she locked his stare she began to dangle the pump on the foot that was crossed over.

"The fuck you smiling at? Shit's not over." Macey had hoped his voice would sound a lot stronger as he thanked God at least his courage was.

"It will be."

He couldn't hear Terra's voice over the music, but he read her lips loud and clear. He rose to his feet while spitting blood, not caring how much of a mess it would make on his ring mats. He knew not to panic, to never show any hint of defeat or weakness, but as he began to circle Kane again, Macey knew the towering man was toying with him. Macey then relied on what had always pushed him through the most violent of matches: anger. Controlled anger to unleash with all the physical and emotional force he could deliver.

He charged Kane with deliberate fakes and L-steps and pivots to where he believed several openings were there for kicks as well as jabs and elbow strikes. Kane dodged everything Macey delivered and responded with several body shots that broke Macey's ribs. Shots so pummeling that Macey dropped to the floor again. He knew this time he wouldn't be able to get back up.

Suffering severe internal bleeding, as the blood came to his throat and out his mouth and nose, Macey looked up to Kane from the floor. "Fuck you, motherfucker, whatever the fuck you are. And fuck you, lady."

After that last defiant cry, Kane drilled Macey with full standing force, laying out the pro fighter to his chest and belly, legs sprawled open, making his body look as if it had landed from a free fall after a suicide jump.

At that same moment, while Macey believed he'd been killed, Marion kicked in the door of the gym, Beretta out and ready as he blasted into the cage ring area. He fired several shots into the air and then aimed directly at Kane. He couldn't shoot him, as the caged walls could cause a severe ricochet, which could deflect a bullet into Macey's lifeless body.

Marion kept Macey in his peripheral vision as he focused on Kane and Terra, keeping his gun out and ready, both elbows locked in.

"Get the fuck back! Get the fuck out of the fucking cage now!"

Marion walked around the cage ring, ready to empty the remaining cartridges in the magazine. He motioned again for Kane to get out of the ring and eyeballed Macey's lifeless bloodied body.

Terra stood up and took a step forward.

Marion swiveled the gun to her. "Not one more fucking step."

Terra smiled. "You better think this through. Nothing was forced here. Nothing illegal. What's your plan? Gun *him* down? Your next door neighbor? Gun *me* down? For cheering on an MMA match that was consensual?"

"Doesn't look like a fair fight."

"What's it look like, officer?"

"An execution."

Terra slowly shook her head. "Everything here was consensual. Everything that happened. We're leaving."

"You're not going anywhere until I get him some help."

Terra nodded. "We are walking right out that door while you call for paramedics. You've got nothing but an injured friend. Maybe worse than injured, so time's not your friend here. Friend."

"Wrong. I've got Freak Show here telling me the other day he was going to pay Macey a visit here. It's premeditated—"

"Ha! Listen to yourself! You're a fucking cop, and that's what you're going to tell the local police? He's a professional fighter, well known around here." Terra pointed to Macey's body in mock sympathy, then back to Marion, placing her hands on her hips. By that time Kane had stepped down from the ring, pulled on his gown, and walked around the back of the cage ring where it led to the lobby. He didn't so much as make a whisper, completely ignoring Marion and Terra's faceoff.

She's right as fucking rain. No way I can do anything here but give this endless fuckshow a pass and chock it up as another goddamn loss.

Marion kept his gun on Terra, even though she walked right up against the barrel of the Beretta, inching her body to where her tight abs touched the gun's tip. Marion didn't budge, using the tip of the gun to apply pressure to Terra's body.

"Keep pushing me, lady, I'll empty this magazine into that fucking red leather."

"We. Are walking out. Of. Here."

Marion thought she was going to kiss him on the lips when she leaned in to say it. He pressed the gun into her with more force and could tell her body was as hard as Kane's. "You're part of everything. Fuck, you're the goddamn architect. I'm talking to Santiago soon enough, curious to see what he's got to say, knowing that he's back in until the cows come home unless he talks."

"Really. Santiago? That's your next play? Some street lunatic back in jail, this time for mass murder?"

"How about the DeMille case in Houston. Dead of course, but there's intel there. I've got a date with Butch Macintire, maybe he's got something to say, and maybe Santiago has something to say about *that*. The porn ring with a psycho named Eddie Henrickson, maybe you've heard of him."

Terra didn't so much as bat an eye in any surprise.

Of course not.

"Stop. Please stop. You're so far out of your league here I just can't bear to have you embarrass yourself any further. You know nothing, Marion Paul. Absolutely nothing."

"That's why you'll lose. Your arrogance. We'll see what's nothing."

Terra leaned in even closer as if to embrace the penetration of the gun barrel. "You're not your brother, I'll give you that." Her whispering cut through the background music as if it were the only sound in the building.

And with that, she walked away, cut off the music, and followed Kane to leave Macey's MMA in the black Chevy truck that caused Marion to break into the gym the moment he saw it parked next to Macey's Tacoma.

Marion called out to her just before she was out of sight. "Wait."

She turned her entire body toward the cage ring floor, giving him her full attention as she raised her cowboy hat an inch back. "Yes? Is there something further?"

Marion was on his knees next to Macey, his right-hand cradling Macey's neck and head. "I'm far from fucking done, lady."

Terra winked at him and tipped her hat, then turned to leave the building with Kane.

Marion called 911 inside the cage ring with his hand still on Macey's neck, continuing to check for a pulse. He took note there was just enough life left for a thread of hope.

PART THREE

"It is true, we shall be monsters, cut off from all the world; but on that account we shall be more attached to one another."

– Mary Shelley

Terra's Sabbath

Werewolf of Duncan – Raskin's Daughter – Terra's Visit to Santiago – The Henrickson Interrogation – The Final Interview – Chess Match in Monday Town - Last Call to New Orleans

Chapter Fourteen:

Werewolf of Duncan

O dessa police and its EMS arrived around ten minutes after Marion's 911 call. Several of the first responders knew Macey quite well, as he'd trained many Odessa cops over the years in high-level self-defense. Sergeant Shane Morris ended up getting the story from Marion.

As soon as Morris ordered Macey taken to the Odessa Hospital, Marion was having none of it.

"No way. What's the other hospital around here? The other big one."

Morris looked quickly irritated. "Big one?"

"You know what I'm talking about. Jesus. There's another major hospital around—"

"You mean The Gordon Center. Sure, but what's wrong with Odessa? It's—"

"I've had some serious issues with Odessa, and I don't want him taken there. That alright with you?"

"Yeah, well, we happen to know—"

"Can you just fucking trust me on this? Please? Look, I know you don't know me, and this guy's your friend. I get it. But I'm not telling you...*asking* you to take him to the other place for no reason. I have a good reason if you'll just trust me."

Morris looked over Marion and could see the desperation.

"You know, seems lately you've been in the middle of

shit when everything's going right to hell and back. Eternity 51, now this—"

"Call me lucky."

"I'm not so sure luck's got a whole lot to do with it."

"Can you just go with me on this one, please?"

"Fine. Let's get him to Gordon." Morris directed the EMS crew then pulled Marion to the side. "Oh, and here's more luck for you. I know you said there's an APB out on the woman. But it must have been pulled. Just got word, so what gives? You want to fill me in on exactly what the Sam Hill is going on?"

Marion thought it over a second and wondered why Raskin would pull it. "I don't know. Best guess is there wasn't enough evidence to pursue her. There wasn't enough to begin with, to be honest."

"But she was here with the monster who fucked up Macey, so I'm putting another one out."

Marion shook his head. "Fine. Whatever. It's not going to make a shit's difference. I'd think it through before you do that because regardless of what happened here, nothing was done illegally. This doesn't have anything that'll stick. I think you know that. But never mind. Just get Macey to the Gordon facility."

Morris nodded slowly in half agreement. "Not a problem. Look, you know the routine, but this is a small place compared to Houston. You can give me more at the hospital or come by later for something formal. And I'm not meaning to give you any shit. I'm glad you came when you did. He could have been killed. Everyone around here knows Macey's as tough as they come, so his condition is extremely upsetting."

"Yeah. It is. I'll come by later. You've got my number."

Marion called Raskin immediately when heading back to Duncan. He had to know why Raskin had changed his mind, regardless if it was the right play. When he got

Raskin on the phone it was just as he suspected. The Lake City lead detective knew that any kind of APB on Terra was useless, that it was best to try and nail down something solid from a fierce interrogation of Santiago. Marion agreed and decided it was time to get some rest, but then again rest, he knew, was just as pointless as trying to book the demon woman, who seemed to have an endless access to anything she wanted or needed in order to sustain a pressure he knew he could never sustain.

Marion felt alone and completely outmatched.

Before he let any desperation creep in, as soon as he planted himself on the leather sofa, he called Devon, the one person he'd grown to trust more than anyone, other than Nina. He said as much as soon as Devon answered.

Devon: What's up, boss?

Marion: Honestly, Devon, I don't trust anyone else to talk to.

Devon: Whoa. That's a tall order out of nowhere.

Marion: I just wrapped up another fucking crime scene. This one down in Odessa at Macey's MMA.

Devon: Christ.

Marion: Yeah. Christ wasn't there, and I wish to God with all that's been going on that He was, to be perfectly frank.

Devon: Okay, well, I'm not the Lord Almighty, so what can I do? I mean, how can I help?

Marion: You know what's going on around here, you have to. I'm talking about Duncan now. It's all related, I know it from the core of my fucking feet to the top of my hair.

Devon: Hmmm. I think I get it. Let me ask you this, how much did you see over there?

Marion: Can you be a bit more vague?

Devon: Sorry. Bridget's place. How far did you see, or...I don't know. How much did you see?

Marion: Interesting you'd go there. Your asking tells me you've seen things over there, too. A lot of things.

Devon: Yeah, lot of people have.

Marion: But you gave me fair warning. And now you're asking me, so what gives? Talk to me. I called you out of trust. Every time I've called it's been trust. What have you seen?

Devon: Honestly...I've seen gatherings over there. Men gathered in the back. Women, always women. I've never stopped to really look. Maybe you did that night, sure you did. But I haven't. I've just slowed down enough to see weird shit in these gatherings. But there was this one time it was...I don't know what it was. Something.

Marion: What was it? What did you see?

Devon: Believe it or not, it was like a giant wolf. And I do mean giant. Not an exaggeration. But I can't be sure. It was dark. It wasn't like any wolf I'd ever seen. In the sense of normal. Looked like it was standing on massive hind legs and severely hunched over, like it was in pain. Always seems I've seen things over there in the dark. But what I saw looked like some kind of weird process was taking place. It was fucked up. I felt my heart stop.

Marion: Process? What do you mean?

Devon: I don't know, Marion, hard to say. It looked like it was going into convulsions, or coming out of them. One or the other.

Marion: Was it alone? Just roaming or something?

Devon: No, it wasn't. Funny you should ask. In fact, there was something else near it. Something in the field. Something...

Marion: Something? Something what, Devon?

Devon: Hard to say. Something a lot more frightening than the creature or wolf. Maybe it was a bear for all I know, but we don't have any bears out here, at least not that I've ever seen or heard about. But the other thing I saw—

Marion: What do you mean more frightening than the creature? Just tell me what you saw. Take a few deep breaths if you have to.

Devon: I will. It looked like something in a burgundy glow, something that had beauty but also the power that could...not *could*, but was in complete control over the creature.

When I kept driving on I thought it looked like a... You know what an incubus is?

Marion: Yeah. I know what it is.

Devon: Are you into gaming at all?

Marion: I was at one time. In fact, with police work it was the only thing that took my mind away from the shit that was my reality.

Devon: Then you know there are some pretty wicked games out there. Especially if you've seen some of the newer ones with AI headsets, like Oculus. Anyway, I played one recently, demon game. Warlocks and witches and shit, heavy shit. The main villain in that game is an incubus. Incredibly hot woman, I mean, whoever designed her, this incubus, created something that's just as beautiful as it is terrifying. Easy to get hooked on it, let me tell you. Well...in my rearview mirror, when I was driving on, that's what I saw. The incubus from that game, and that creature was waiting for...direction or something. I know that makes no sense, and you probably don't believe me.

Marion: I believe you, Devon. Can you remember the name of the game?

Devon: No. But here's something else. I've got a fiber optics internet connection. The fastest. I can download a gig file in just a few seconds. The download for the game was around six gig or so, should have downloaded in a flash. But it ended up taking hours. And I stopped and started the download over and over many times to make sure I didn't have a bad source file. It was useless. Took forever and then when it finally finished, the file was considerably smaller, smaller than being zipped.

Marion: Where are you going with this? I'm not sure that means anything—

Devon: Maybe not, but I don't think so. Maybe. But I think it was something else. Because the file is now gone. Wiped from my machine. And I know what I'm doing. I write code in Perl, Ruby, Python.

Marion: Well, look, I take that back, and what you're saying is interesting. I haven't told you this yet, but I have told you about the woman whose been fucking with me. It's a lot more than that, and what I haven't told you is that she was there with me the night of the murders at Eternity 51. She's even a fucking suspect but there's no way to really tie her to any of it. Point is...I don't know if I should say anything.

Devon: Oh please! You've gone this far...and you called me, by the way. So spit it out. If you trust me then you've got to get it out. You called me for a reason. Your turn to take some breaths if you have to.

Marion: Touché. Something you said about the game with the incubus reminds me a lot of her.

Devon: What's so stupid about that? You don't think the people who create these games haven't come across real demon shit for inspiration? Look, Marion, gaming is no different than what people had years and years ago with dungeons and dragons, or even long before that. The world's always had demons to overcome. The media has changed, but the stories remain the same all the way back to The Bible. Goddamn devil was right there from the beginning. If you're dealing with something like this, you can't do it alone.

Marion: Right. You're right. And there's something else, too. May as well spill the whole fucking bean stack.

Devon: Hit me.

Marion: There's a woman I've come to really like, and I think she's in danger. She was at the club that night, too. Night of the murders.

Devon: Jesus man, how much shit do you have going on?

Marion: Exactly. Look, what are you doing a bit later?

Devon: Nothing. I'll be doing a lot of nothing, but suddenly that doesn't seem to be completely accurate.

Marion: How 'bout I buy you a beer. Shoot a game of pool. Talk this over a lot more, because that's the thing. There's a lot more.

Devon: I bet there is. Sure. In fact I was gonna head over to The Oak Post later.

Marion: Thought you said you didn't do anything.

Devon: I wouldn't call The Oak Post doing anything.

Marion: I'll see you there. Eight or so?

Devon: Sounds good. Peace out.

***

Marion had driven by the local Duncan watering hole a few times, one of two bars in the town. He was sure that his brother had spent all kinds of wasted time there, but Marion loved shooting pool, and Devon was the only person other than Nina that he had any trust in.

Once inside the bar, it didn't take but a second before he found Devon smack in the middle of a situation between the hillbilly thugs who greeted him at the Duncan Maze just before he met the demon woman herself for the first time.

They were dressed in cowboy rags, suspenders, torn boots, filthy t-shirts, cheap cowboy hats. Devon was in so far over his head that Marion almost felt a sense of instant fatherly protection. But it was his fierce cop protection that was mandated.

"There seems to be an issue here, Devon. You pickin' on these shit-heels?"

Devon clearly didn't understand the sarcasm, as being ambushed by the two hillbillies was scaring him right to his scalp.

"Never mind." Marion put his shooting hand behind his back ready to pull out the Beretta as he walked directly into the hillbilly's space. Their stink was nauseating. "You mean boys think this is cute? Ganging up here on young

Devon."

"Whooo eeee. You that punchy boy from awhile back, come out to play! My my my—"

"Shut it, you dipshit hillfuck. And you keep yours zipped. I will fuck up your already wrecked faces right here right now. I am praying for a reason."

The hillbilly Marion had warned to keep quiet spurted out in near glee, "You come in all hard and giddy up and cow—"

Marion stepped in close and drilled a jab into the hillbilly's jaw before he finished his comment, knocking him back into the bar itself where he hit it so hard he bounced back. Marion caught him a second shot right into his kidney, dropping him lifeless to the ground.

"Stay the fuck down," he said as he faced the other hillbilly squared up. He pulled out his Beretta to take full control. "I changed my mind. Pick up this sack of shit and get out of here. Test me and I'll shoot you both dead and let the locals sort it all out."

The barkeeper came out from behind the register. "What in the Sam Christ?! What's going on in here?" He looked at what was taking place as if he'd never seen such a thing in all his days of tending to bars and drunks.

"You know these two?" Marion pointed at both hillbillies.

"I do, in fact. But I don't know you."

"Thing One and Thing Two were in this young man's face. I took care of it, but I don't want to continue with it. This is your place, your problem."

"Devon? That true?"

Devon looked back and forth a few times to Marion, the hillbillies, then back to Marion, trying to figure out what was the next best play. "Yeah. Marion stopped them. These two, whoever the hell they are, came at me like rabid dogs."

"Ewwwww Eeeeee. Mister name caller! Mister insult

boy!" The hillbilly Marion had dropped spoke in bursts as he rustled himself off the ground to face Devon and the others.

"I ain't seen the two of you my damn self, so it's best you get on. Now. Get on out of here and but good."

Marion looked across the bar floor over by the single pool table that was notoriously tilted from where the voice came that quickly cut through all the mayhem. He recognized her those months ago in her hospital bed and wondered why in the name of all the hell that had surrounded him that she was there.

"Alice?" Marion quickly remembered thinking back when he had left the hospital that it was possible he would need Alice in some way, but when he saw her sitting at the lone table, he knew he'd been wrong.

Alice looked into Marion's eyes and nodded. In the darkness of the bar, she didn't look as haggardly as she'd been when rocking back and forth on her hospital bed. Marion nodded back and turned again to the hillbillies and the chaos.

"You heard the lady, and I've had it with both of you. I'm sure you're fine with it, too, Barkeep?"

"Fred Pendelton's my name."

"Okay, Fred, we done here?"

"Yeah, I'll take it from here."

The hillbilly that Marion knocked down rubbed his face and lips with both hands and spit into one. "You think you've seen the last of us, copper? It's all just itchin' to come right up your poo hole and out youse yakkety yak, best assure it!"

"Das right! Das right! He's not yanking any chains, but your chain's about to be yanked to never never land!" Hillbilly Two's chime-in made it clear to Marion that both of them would go down in any ship regardless if the ship was total insanity or total annihilation.

"You're both on Terra's train so, checkbox to each."

Fred Pendleton stepped up, as if he sensed Marion was about to get it on again. Devon had stayed put in silence but remained focused on every movement from everyone and everything.

"Devon, I'm going to go talk to Alice over there."

"Yeah. I know her."

Marion scoffed. "Of course you do. Whew. What a night so far. You good?"

"Yeah, I'm good. How do you know Alice? Another one of those things you were gonna go over tonight?"

Marion shook his head. "No. Another unexpected bit. You'd think I'd be used to them by now, but every time I turn my head seems a new thieve of fuckery is there to greet me. She was in the hospital when I came to. Long story, I'll fill you in. Just gonna say hello. Order what you want and get me an iced tea, cool?"

"Yep."

Marion made sure that Fred the Barkeeper was, in fact, handling the hillbillies and that Devon would be able to settle in and order some drinks before Marion walked over to Alice. She was sitting at one of the few tables of the bar and grill that only seated two.

"How's it going, Alice? Quite surprised to see you here, of all places. Alone." Marion pulled out the other chair that sat across from her as he took note of utensils, and a glass of water was where he now sat.

"Oh, I'm not alone. Friend of mine left the building when the shakeup started with your young friend there." She nodded over to where Devon was sitting at the bar.

"I won't stay long, Alice, but I had to come by." Marion looked her over carefully as he sat down, making sure to sit forward in the chair, giving Alice his full attention, but also ready to pop up quickly at a moment's notice.

"How have things been? When were you released?"

"Ha! Like I was a prisoner!"

Marion quickly raised his eyebrows but kept quiet to see what was next. She was far from the fragile creature he'd seen in the hospital after he'd come out of his coma. The woman he saw in front of him seemed far more sure of herself, but also far more disturbed.

"You're lit up on something, Alice. Maybe you've hit Wonderland, after all."

Marion cleared his throat. "Well...I won't keep you. It's good that you're out and about. You're not driving, are you?"

"Thank you for caring so much, but I'm fine. My friend will be back in shortly, I'm sure."

He stood up from the chair and placed it back in position then reached out his hand to her. She rubbed her face awkwardly, then took his hand and squeezed it with far more strength than Marion anticipated.

He let her hand go as easily as possible. "I'll be seeing you, Alice."

She allowed for the release of his hand, and then placed both hers in her lap as prim and proper as Marion had ever remembered his mother doing when at home or in public, a trait he loved remembering. Alice bent forward and looked up to Marion with eyes that were glassy and sloshy. "Be careful, Steve's brother. Be careful. You suffer with that depression, don't ya? Hmmm hmmm. Can see it all in your skin, crawling around and digging in."

Marion tilted his head back quickly but tried to not show so much surprise. She was right. Cops battled depression throughout their careers. It was part of a policeman's DNA, and managing it could mean the difference between sanity and unemployment, or in some cases, life and death. His brother's cross was the drink, and his own had always been the weight of dealing with the worst of the human condition, sometimes so sickening that it did its best to put him down for good.

But how the Christ does she know anything about it?

"Depression? I'm a cop. It comes with the territory. You're looking at an adrenaline junkie, Alice. Open your eyes."

"Just you be careful is all I'm giving you."

Marion nodded in full understanding and went to sit with Devon.

"What was that all about?" Devon took a long drain on his beer.

"Not sure yet, to be honest. Told me I was depressed."

"She said that?"

"Said she saw it in my skin or some shit. Think that's true? You see me that way?"

"Not really. Are you?"

"Not exactly. I've dealt with it before, from time to time. All cops do. Strange she said it the way she did. Everything about her seems...off. How long have you known her?"

"I don't know. Few years maybe. And it's not like I know her well, just know of her. Small towns, bro. You say she was at the hospital when you came to?"

"Yeah. She was the first person I saw."

"Any idea why she was there?"

"Not really. But the whole affair when I was walking around after waking up was rather one long fuckshow. It's nice out. Want to grab a seat outside?"

"Lead the way." Devon took his beer, peanuts, and napkins; Marion grabbed his glass of iced tea, and they walked out to a log cabin patio area that faced the front of a stunning mountainside that overlooked the entirety of Duncan.

It was just the two of them, as Marion guessed Fred the Barkeeper had done his due diligence with the hillbilly thugs.

"All right, boss. Let's hear it. All of it. You just now mentioned depression and what ever the hell Alice said sparked whatever it was that was rattling when you called me. I'm all ears." Devon finished his beer all the while keeping his eyes on Marion.

For the next half hour or so, Marion laid it all out as Devon ordered a few more beers and listened like a student at his very first college class where every word from the professor was mandatory in order to pass the first pop quiz.

He first told Devon of the visit Steve made to Houston, how Steve had been tormented by this demon woman, how his brother was terrified of her. He then went into Dr. Pinault and her control over the hospital when he first awakened. The endless nightmare he seemed trapped in before he awakened, the stage and audience of the dream with Terra preaching fire and brimstone just before he was swirled into the surreal dining room with the demons sucking on the gory creatures. The ride to Duncan with Janet Stone, the frightening living room scene and her serpent tongue. The first time he saw Kane leaning on the bridge rail. He went over the details of the notes and files that his brother had left him. The maze and his first meeting with Terra and the freakish building with child demons and Terra's descent into the building. He told Devon the details of the murder scene that the media never discussed. His visit at Kane's house and all the weird shit Kane had, and the miracle of barely saving Burke Macey's life.

"That leads us to where we are right now, and why I think I have to go to Houston again. Have to go there anyway and work things out with the department. See my daughter. Shit like that. But there's a bigger reason, I think. Plus Nina told me earlier that she's going to New Orleans for work, so hanging out with her is out."

It was a lot for Devon to take in, to say the least. He took in a deep breath and exhaled as he turned toward the mountain view. "Soooo... Christ, I'm not sure what to say. Or think for that matter."

"Just getting it all out to someone makes it all seem like some endless carnival fuckshow. But I'm glad I did.

Had to, and I know it's a lot. But I sure as hell couldn't tell Nina about all this. At least not before she's about to head out of town on business."

"Why not? I mean I doubt she'd get too freaked out, right? She was there the night of the murders, and clearly she knows more about this woman than you may think with whatever she saw the night before. Didn't you tell me she was at the woman's house that same weekend?"

"Yeah, yeah. Still, not the coolest thing to drop on anyone's lap before a business gig. I didn't press her on it while going through all the statements and so on. Don't know her well enough. I don't know. And you've been kinda my go-to since I've been here."

"I get it. Appreciate the trust. You forgot about Bridget, by the way. When you were talking about her earlier on the phone, it seemed you left some pieces out, am I right?"

Marion nodded, clearly disturbed by the thought of Bridget Magnus and what he saw on the side of the freeway, or the dreadful mock religious ceremony straight from purgatory where, briefly, she seemed the architect. "Right you are. Not sure if I wanted to go into that bit just yet. But you said you've seen gatherings over there before. I saw one too. And it was beyond fucked up."

"Yeah, well, everything about Bridget is fucked up. Everything. Where she lives, what she wears, how she smells. She's a goddamn train wreck all around. But from everything that you've told me up to this point, she's also simply a pawn, or a thug, of this demon woman's, right? Part of her gang?"

"Right again. Seems this whole town is an all-around train wreck that's subservient to this bitch."

"I think it's a lot more than just this town. With all that you've seen, that's an understatement. The depression or not, you should be a basket case by now." Devon paused and looked at the mountain view in deep thought. He scanned the landscape while scratching his head and taking another drink from his cold brew. Marion knew his friend was young, but also smart and shrewd for someone without a lot of world experience.

Devon's eyebrows raised in sudden alarm, and with a hint of urgency he turned to Marion. "Hey. Marion. Look up over there. Look." He was suddenly whispering in panic. "What the fuck is that?"

Marion looked across the base of the mountain and saw what Devon meant. Not sure what he was seeing, nor did Devon have a clue, a figure was walking across the field area that led up to the mountain base that moved with effortless agility, especially for its size and height. Marion couldn't see what it was wearing exactly, but thought it looked like a robe with a hood and a pair of aikido hakama, although the night caused everything to blend.

When the figure stopped and dropped all its clothing, Marion stared in shock. He darted his eyes toward Devon then back to the figure. He knew they both couldn't turn away from the Kafkaesque metamorphosis that began to take place.

That Marion knew the figure was indeed a towering man who had to be Kane was superseded by the reality of what looked like an excruciating transformation from man to beast. The man's body twisted in jerking motions that were obscene and violent. The bone structure in his shoulders and back cracked and groaned as the bones themselves grew and punctured through the skin in larger girth and sharpness. His head stretched forward as if being pulled apart by invisible vice-grips. His knees buckled and violently crimped backwards and opposite of normal human knee movement, his hands and arms grew in length and size in the same awful pulling apart his head was undergoing.

Marion thought he saw the different characters and appearances he'd seen in Kane—from the ragged and leathered cowboy to the board-like manufactured queer state—all come out in distorted, putty-like arrangements of gore as the metamorphosis continued in a full-blown lycanthropic birth.

Devon kept his voice at a whisper when he grabbed Marion's wrist. "Jesus Christ, Marion, it looks a lot like what I was telling you about on the phone. *What in fuck's name is it?*"

Marion focused on his own breathing as much as the frightening change that was taking place out in the open field of the mountain base. "Let's stay as quiet as possible, but I want you to take note without looking over to where I parked. That's our next move."

"Okay, okay, but are you seeing what's walking over to the wolf thing? Are you seeing *that*?" Devon's eyes were open in shock as he turned his head to Marion. "I swear to Christ that's the incubus I was telling you about. *How* can that be?"

Marion watched the other figure walking down and across the field area toward the hideous metamorphosis. Much smaller, completely tranquil, and clearly a woman with an amber glow, dressed in a golden-colored formal evening gown. A striking glow of authority and contrast against the deep mountainside horror.

Marion knew exactly who it was.

"Devon, listen very carefully. That's her—"

"*Who is it?*"

Marion tilted his head in irritation. "You know goddamn well who. I need you to keep it together and focus because this is really happening. I need you to stand up slowly and back away from the table. Keep crouched low while you head to the parking lot and my truck. I'll be right behind you. When I say run, you haul ass because she's about to turn that monster loose on us."

Devon was giving his best to indeed not go into shock, as everything was happening way too fast for what he believed he could handle. "How can you know that? Marion, I can't—"

"You've got to keep your shit together. You can do this, Devon. Do as I say or we'll be killed right here. This is our best chance."

"*Killed*! How the fuck do you know—" Devon was hissing when Marion cut it short.

"Because I know, now get up slowly and move. Keep it the fuck together, and we'll get out of this."

Devon followed the order to a T as Marion saw Terra point in their direction, telling the wolf beast exactly what Marion said would happen. It took off toward them in a blast of power and fury.

"Get to the truck now! Fucking *run*, Devon!"

Devon jolted from the seated area, moving as fast as he could all the while looking behind him to make sure Marion was right there.

Marion kept focused, as he'd been in situations where running was mandatory, knowing that looking back only slowed things down.

"Don't look back! Get to my truck. I'm right behind you!"

Devon followed orders but not before he had a solid glance of the grisly beast that was running on all fours. Or at least trying to. It was a beast like nothing he'd ever seen, its arms and legs moving in distorted and twisted vibrations as if still undergoing the metamorphosis while on the run. Its head was a fusion of a ravaged wolf and human that was clearly possessed and tortured, either from the awful transition taking place, or out of pure rage. Its body was stretched in gnarled chunks of human flesh that looked plastic and fused with sinewy, hairy muscles that were bleeding and torn.

Marion's truck was fifty or so feet out into the parking lot area, and Marion had the doors open and engine fired up with the key fob just as Devon nearly smashed into the passenger door. He was in with the door slammed home just as Marion did the same while slamming the truck into drive.

Devon looked on in horror, as he was trying to prevent shock from setting in. The beast was within twenty feet or less when he heard gunshots right next to him.

Marion had rolled down his own window and had the driver's door flapping wildly open to have his body outside the truck while holding the steering wheel with his free hand. In what was the most athletic move Devon had ever seen anyone perform, he briefly turned his head to see what was happening with Marion's right hand on the steering wheel while his body was outside the truck, his left-hand firing round after round at the oncoming beast.

Devon turned back to watch while leaning over and gripping the seat. Though the beast seemed to have slowed down, it was not enough as it leaped forward just as Marion had slipped back into the driver's seat to gun the engine. The driver's door slammed shut with the takeoff.

The beast had enough force with the leap that it was able to grab the top of the truck's bed railing and maneuver itself onto the truck's bed. It was screaming and roaring in sounds that neither Marion nor Devon had ever thought possible.

Devon also screamed at the top of his lungs in absolute panic and fear. He said nothing as he continued screaming while the beast smashed its forearms and clawed fists through the Ram's back sliding windows.

"Marion! Marion! Holy fucking Christ. It's going to kill us!"

Marion remained focused on the task at hand, which was to whip the steering wheel back and forth as violently as possible to catch the beast off balance and throw it from the truck's bed. He could feel the beast had as much power and force as the truck itself, but also knew that he'd put a magazine full of bullets square into the fucker's body.

Motherfucker has to feel some of that shit.

"Hang on! We're getting this fucking thing off our back!" Marion then cranked the steering wheel as far to the left as it would go while gunning the engine for all it was worth. The Ram's V8 Hemi burst to a roar and thunder that matched the beast that was trying to overturn it. In the rearview mirror, Marion could see the beast was trying its best to hold on with one aberrant arm and clawed hand while simultaneously smashing and pounding into the truck's roof and cab area with the other. Its enormous jaws that were filled with shattered chunks of bone and shredded gums were tearing into the truck's metal as if it were fresh steak.

When Marion thought the Ram was about to roll over in the direction he'd cranked it, he used all his strength to jolt it in the opposite direction, keeping the pedal to the floorboard.

Just as Marion and Devon thought the beast would devour and destroy the truck and themselves, it was unable to hold on as the Ram careened in the opposite circular direction.

"You got it, Marion! You fucking tossed its ass! Holy Christ!"

Marion remained laser focused on the task. "We're not out of this yet." He could see the beast wasn't done as it scrambled—popping up from its back—toward the truck; it had been thrown to the ground in such a way that it somersaulted a few times before popping to its feet for yet another go at them. Marion knew he needed to straighten out the truck to gain speed and momentum, which was far easier than the circling that allowed for an escape.

"The fuck! Marion you did it! Oh my God in Heaven!" Devon continued his hysterical accolades when to his astonishment, Marion slammed on the brakes and jammed the shifter into park, jumped out while dropping the magazine out of the Beretta and near simultaneously loading another one in, which he had in a back pocket, took aim at the beast with both hands on the gun, and emptied the entire mag within a few seconds. Every round hit home into the beast's body and shoulders, slowing it down plenty, but clearly not killing it.

Moments later, he was back in the driver's seat and slamming the Ram into drive again. Devon remained speechless in awe, his eyes peeled open.

Marion briefly looked over at him then back to laser focus on the road ahead. "It's far from dead but we have some breathing room."

It was another thirty seconds or so of racing down the back road from the Oak Post that led to the freeway entrance when Marion's headlamp brights revealed yet another obstacle standing in the middle of the road next to the 2-Way Stop just before the turn that would take them back to his house and property.

"Fucking hell," Devon shouted. "Is that Bridget Magnus?"

Marion ignored the question that sounded so puzzled all he could do was skip the obvious answer and decide whether or not he was going to run her down, as it was indeed the decrepit hag he'd first met at the Exxon station, then seen in her backyard during the freakish cult ceremony with trashcan fires, red painted children, and saintly men dressed in suits and strap-ons.

"Don't look at her. Let's see if we can get out of this shit in one fucking piece."

Chapter Fifteen:

Raskin's Daughter

oth Marion and Devon knew that it was best to avoid Marion's place. If Marion was right, then Kane was most likely the beast that had just tried to kill them. It was Devon's place first as Marion also knew the Ram was terribly damaged.

They went to Devon's place for a complete regroup.

It was a duplex area in Duncan where small units could be rented, something not common in Duncan County, but where thousands of them were built all over the greater Houston area, giving Marion a more familiar footing.

Devon's rental was adorned in ragged carpet, cheap particle board shelves that housed a fabulous stereo system that was all wired up to the latest 65-inch Sony Quantum Dot OLED television. It was clear that every dime Devon earned went to electronics.

Both men were still catching their breath, Devon far more so, as Marion was planning what was next.

"I can't drive my truck around that fucked up and I've got a lot to do in trying to connect all the dots to this whole motherfucker."

"Dickey Barlow. He's just down the street. Best mechanic in the whole state."

Marion sat down on the one piece of furniture that he could see, a couch just as ragged as the carpet. "Great name, Dickey Barlow. Done. What time's he open? Or the shop he works?"

"I don't know, man. Nine or so I'd say. He's a drinker. Alcoholic. But he's so good at his job that the owner lets him sleep it off each morning, so sometimes he gets there later than usual."

"Dickey Barlow the drunk. Nice."

"It's the best we've got."

"I trust you. I need to crash here until I take the truck down."

"Couch is yours, my man." Devon was pacing back and forth with his hands on his head. Marion knew he just needed to process it all. "What the fuck was that, Marion? Holy Christ."

Marion was scratching his own head. "Hard to say."

They sat up and chatted for a few more hours. Devon drinking cold beers, Marion drinking cold water and staying focused on what was needed. He made a list in his mind that consisted of the following:

1. *Getting the Ram to the shop with Dickey for a loaner swap*
2. *Calling Nina and checking on her*
3. *Going to Raskin's to find out the latest*
4. *Interrogating Santiago*
5. *Flying to Houston for a Huntsville Prison date with Henrickson to get his take*

All of it in that order made him feel far more organized as he laid back on the ragged couch after Devon polished off his last beer and went to his room to pass out. When he slept he did not dream.

***

Dickey Barlow was everything Devon said he was and more. With hair and beard sporting a complete Billy Gibbons of ZZ Top look, Dickey's clothes were plastered in black oils from years of use. He stood a few inches shorter than Marion at five-foot-nine, was wiry and rugged with a breath that could have lit up the entire mechanic shop if Marion had struck a match.

"What happened here? Haven't seen damage like this." Dickey walked around Marion's Ram, looking completely perplexed.

"Something tried to eat it."

Dickey chuckled. "Interesting."

"Listen, Dickey, I'm in a rush. Devon said you'd have no problem with a loaner."

Dickey nodded and pulled on his beard. "There's a set a keys in the front office you can't miss. Ram like yours, only older. Nineteen eighty-nine model. Nice Cummins. It's the one out front you probably saw. Maroon with white trim. I'm not sure how long this'll take, not even sure if we can fix all this shit."

"I'm sure of that, just do what you can. Nice to meet you, Dickey, and thanks. I'll stay in touch."

Dickey just nodded as he continued looking over Marion's damaged Ram.

First things first, Marion dropped by his place to pack another overnight bag. Before going inside, he made sure to give a brief once-over of Kane's area. There was no sign of his black Chevy, no sign of life anywhere. Regardless, Marion decided he would stay at the only hotel in Duncan located just a block down from the Exxon where he'd first met Bridget.

After he checked in, showered and shaved, he called Nina. She was in a hurry to get to work and couldn't talk much.

Marion: Are you ready for your trip to New Orleans?

Nina: I'm excited. Upper management invited me through a LinkedIn message, of all things.

Marion: LinkedIn? No personal call or email?

Nina: I know. Pretty cryptic. I've never been to New Orleans.

Marion: It's a cool place. Wild as hell, but fun if you stay away from the weird shit, which is everything.

Nina: Hey, you're going to Houston in a few days, right?

Marion: Yep.

Nina: Why don't you meet me?

Marion: Well, that's one idea.

Nina: I'm staying in the French Quarter. It would be fun.

Marion: Let me see what's going on when I'm in Houston. How long you in the Big Easy?

Nina: It's a week-long event. You could meet me the last few days or so.

Marion: Let me just see.

Nina: Don't you want to?

Marion: Of course I do, Nina, I just need to nail down some things. There was some wicked shit that went down last night—"

Nina: What happened?

Marion: You said you couldn't talk a lot and I'm about to see Raskin. I want to spend more time with you so we're not rushed.

Nina: But you do want to see me, right?

Marion: Very much. I'll stay in close touch, deal?

Nina: Deal.

Marion tapped the red phone icon on his iPhone and was out the door of the hotel lobby and in the loaner Ram on his way to Raskin's house, as Raskin wasn't on duty until much later in the day. Marion had made it clear that he was in a hurry.

He arrived at Raskin's in less than thirty minutes. It was in a Lake City neighborhood that was quaint and simple, a regular Barney Fife model. Marion knocked on the door and Raskin opened it, giving Marion an instant feeling of unease.

"Marion Paul, my new Houston comrade. Please. Come inside."

"Raskin." Marion nodded and entered Raskin's house, then Raskin shut the front door hard.

The home had a smell that Marion couldn't quite decipher, but it seemed familiar, like something rancid that had been covered up for years.

"Come on in to the living area. We can chat there. Things have gotten a right tad nickety nick and caw caw nutty. I mean, they've done gone busted right through the goo machine."

Marion looked into Raskin's eyes for a few seconds while slowly moving his hand to the back of his belt to feel the Beretta. "What are you talking about?"

Raskin slapped his own face and shook his head. "Never you mind, Houston."

"Are you...what's wrong with you?"

"World's gone more awry than a boxed-in rat, and all that ever happens is even far more the cock-eyed slant."

Marion stared at Raskin, waiting to see where such

nonsense would lead.

Raskin then cocked his head oddly as if he'd been struck. "Come. Let's talk in the chatty chat room."

The living room was no different than hundreds Marion had seen over the years while rummaging over case studies, perusing crime scene photos, private debriefings of the most sensitive nature, and every other goddamn thing in between. A few couches, ottoman and chair, coffee table on a wooden floor. Even a small piano in the corner with a nice mountain view outside. A few pictures of family on the walls, bookcase with large TV.

Still, *everything* was off simply by way of Raskin himself as he sat on the couch next to the piano. Marion sat opposite to face him on the La-Z-Boy and leaned over with his elbows resting on his knees. "Raskin? Everything okay around here?"

Raskin had his legs crossed, closed-crossed style, both arms to his side, his head cocked oddly. "There's nothing okay, detective. With this last batch of murders, the openings of the end of everything are right smack in our faces, wouldn't you say, Big City? The bowels of fuckery are dancing wildly. I see no end in sight."

Marion could see that the fully confident and assured lead detective that had taken over the butchery of a crime scene at Eternity 51 was not the man sitting in his own living room.

He's got more than a few screws loose, no doubt about it, so maybe this is my cue to bolt.

Marion huffed. "That's certainly one way of looking at it."

Raskin stared at him with hollow eyeballs, all color gone.

To avoid a staring contest, Marion stood up and stretched and gave a deeper look at his surroundings to find some kind of clue as to why his feelings had gone from unease to nearly disturbed. His own eyes stopped dead on one of the family portraits with Raskin's arms around a girl who Marion assumed was his daughter. Just the two of them.

"Yes indeed that is certainly one way of looking at things." Marion whispered it as he walked closer to the portrait as he recognized the presumed daughter as the woman gunslinger he'd met at the freak diner that night. He needed to make sure it was indeed Rebecca as well as to make sure not to give his revelation away.

It was her.

"Something wrong, detective?" Raskin's question startled him.

"Yeah, there's something wrong, alright."

As Marion turned back to Raskin, someone walked down the hallway. Almost running was more like it. Marion couldn't see who it was, but his entire body began to scream that it was time to leave. He put his gun hand behind him and rested it on the butt of the Beretta.

"Listen...I've got a lot going on, and I think you do, as well. You mind if I go talk with Santiago on my own this morning?"

"I think that's a fine idea. I think that's best. I do indeed have my hands full here." For a moment Marion could see in Raskin's eyes that he was making an attempt to go back to how things had been as he nodded toward the hallway in a gesture that it was best to leave. But also that Raskin was in trouble.

Marion couldn't worry about that as he left Raskin's, jumped into the loaner Ram, and headed over to Lake City jail to see if he could find out what the fuck was going on.

Chapter Sixteen:

Terra's Visit to Santiago

Inside Lake County Jail was nothing Marion hadn't seen before. The place couldn't hold a candle to Harris County. Still, it had the same presence of hopelessness as every big city jail. As soon as the massive iron doors slammed home, there was an impending doom that couldn't help be felt even if for just a visit. Visiting and having the privilege to question a murder suspect who had become as high profile in such a short time made him feel that much more dreadful.

He walked through the metal detectors with a darkness hanging over his every thought and move. Never had he felt so outgunned in his life. Not just outgunned, but outmatched. Terra Drake was step after step ahead of anything he'd ever faced. Still, he had to stay far above any level he'd ever pushed to as he completed check in.

The jailers had been briefed about his arrival and visit with Isaac Santiago. An area free of any inmates was prepared that looked and felt like a tank of walls and bulletproof glass that had been built to house the worst of the worst and then completely dropped off and abandoned at the end of the world.

Sitting on the other side of the bulletproof glass, dead center of the entire frightful area was Santiago. No guards anywhere in sight as Marion knew he'd have the place to himself for a few hours, that the DA had been asked a favor to have all audio recording turned off. Video still ran—just in case—though that meant nothing, as nothing on earth could happen to either of them. Unless Terra or God decided otherwise.

Although that wouldn't surprise me in the least.

Santiago's public defender also didn't object to the meeting because Santiago agreed to it, and because he also knew the public defender worked hand-in-hand with the prosecutor and judge and could give a shit less what happened to him.

Marion sat on the iron stool to face Santiago who sat on the same. Bulletproof glass was all that separated them with slits carved in a small circle that would allow them to hear each other.

Santiago's eyes looked like they'd been peeled open with invisible pliers.

He clearly hasn't shaved or changed his oranges since the moment he'd been booked and processed in.

"Why'd you toss the gun to me? What was your play there?" Marion asked the question fully aware that Santiago would talk about the obvious setup; he wanted to dig in early for the unknowns.

Santiago looked at him as if he'd been asked the same question a thousand times. Marion stayed patient and waited for a response, the two of them sizing each other up in an opening stare-down.

"You know there's no way I did what happened in that bathroom. Every-fucking-body knows that."

"That same *everybody* also knows you tossed the gun to me, as it's on the goddamn club footage. So my question sticks. Why did you do it? Because there's a lot deeper fuckin' reason than an impossible setup, and she was with me during the time you were in the restrooms."

"And you think long enough to have done the shit with the pigs? The fucking pigs and the fucking heads? You think—"

"No. I don't. Clearly that had taken some planning.

But there is nothing on tape that shows or suggests anything other than you being in there with the women who were butchered. Women who've been identified and targeted before they were murdered."

Santiago laughed in a disturbing manner that led Marion to see he was either lying or so completely detached that he cared less about his case than any points the public defender could make.

"And I'm sure you've already been given the intel about all video being cut off from the other entrances from the back areas. That the video you've seen is the only video, so you don't really have a clue what the fuck went down or how."

Marion in fact had not been told such intel. He thought there'd be other footage but wasn't privy to it.

Keep at it. I'll get more. It's just a matter of time.

He decided on a different route.

"You know something, Isaac, and I'm quite sure you do, she owns you. She put you here. And she'll let you rot and die here. She must have promised you the fucking keys to the kingdom. That she'd even let you fuck her as long as you'd be a good little bitch."

"You don't know shit about her, copper. Not a fuckin' bit, Gringo!"

Marion had gotten under his skin more quickly than he'd anticipated.

Keep the pressure on, fast and dirty.

"I may know her more than you realize, but why don't you fill me in here on what you know. I figure your life has been one train wreck after another, one warm beer and filthy fix to the next, just to pass out for a few brief hours of chemical naptime, then back at it on hands and knees until, whack! Woman straight out of your sickest wet dream fetches you off the ground and promises—"

"She's not a woman. You won't stand a chance if that's your strategy."

"Then what is she?"

Santiago looked around his claustrophobic area as if afraid Terra was right there next to him ready to scream Boo! into his ears with her endless force. "She's the dream weaver. Least that's what she first said when I was... Never mind. The whore of Babylon, that's who. And you best know this shit's Biblical." Santiago had lowered his voice considerably. His entire demeanor had changed from the wild child just a few moments ago to a somber, humbled vagrant that was homeless before Terra had had him raped and pillaged.

Marion made sure to show no sign of any surprise or even curiosity. It was always best to keep absolutely stoic, regardless of how awful or insane anything ever sounded coming out of the mouth of any killer or rapist or anyone in between. "So she produces this fabulous array of gore and mayhem and sticks you smack in the middle of the main event?"

"Maybe you're the main event. That's what they talked about anyway."

"Is that right? Why don't you tell me what happened the night before the murders when you were over at her place?"

"That little homecoming beauty tell you all about it?"

Marion said nothing.

"Don't blame you for having eyes on that one."

"Tell me about the pigs, because I know you know."

"Look, copper, you don't know what this is. I was taken in under some kind of black magic spell. The homecoming beauty... Well, she wasn't gonna partake. And when that demon cunt saw it, she had her removed. Then she had me. At first it was what every man ever wanted. Endless pussy of the highest order. But it turned...I don't know."

"How'd it turn?"

"Like I was being devoured. Every last drop of

humanity was sucked out of me, and they just kept going on at it no matter how much I screamed. Like they had the ability to eat my spirit. Then the screaming stopped. I had no more left. They still kept at it. Then that fucking monster had the pigs brought in and the witches slaughtered 'em and fed their guts to that beast—"

"Just hold up. Stop. Let me clear up a few things. This monster you're talking about. Did you see his face?"

"Not at first. Had a mask on with the gown he wore. He took the mask off when the witches brought in the pigs."

"What'd he look like?"

Santiago shook his head slowly as if thinking it over. "Oblong. Stretched. Fucked up. I was drugged and raped, so that's the best I can say it."

Marion scratched his head. "Then the pigs were slaughtered and fed to him? Is that what you're telling me?"

Santiago nodded.

"Then what?"

"Then the pigs' heads were stuffed into giant duffle bags, and I passed out."

"I'm sure you did."

"Next thing I remember, I was in the restroom of the club with the dead women and pigs' heads."

"And what about the women? What about their heads?"

Santiago snickered.

Marion couldn't quite hear it, as the sound between the dividers was muffled, at best.

He was snickering as his demeanor changed once again. "That I can't tell you. I remember the duffle bags in the bathroom. One of 'em had the gun in it, one I tossed your way. Whole blood infested mess is nothing more than a twirly twirl, as I was even doped up more than the night of the witches."

"And you knew I'd be there."

"I think we're through." Santiago then fell dead pan as he pressed his forehead to the bulletproof glass in a gesture for Marion to lean in closer. Marion did.

"Forget about telling that other copper who got you in here to chat. I'm sure you know he's already part of it now."

Marion stood to leave as Santiago began to laugh. He wanted to say more to the Spaniard, to get in one last lick, but knew it was pointless as he left Lake City Jail, got online on his phone and purchased the very next roundtrip ticket to Houston, which would leave at 1 a.m.

***

Marion was most pleased with himself that he'd already had enough in his overnight bag so there was no need to go home for anything. He had plenty of cash on him and could get plenty more at any ATM.

He tried calling Nina several times but no answer. None of his texts went through either, so reaching her was out. He called Devon and they spoke briefly about the Santiago interview and what had happened at Raskin's place. Devon was always the listening ear. Next on his list was calling Burke Macey's wife, Kasha, to get an update on Burke's condition. It was still critical, but her gratitude was heartfelt.

What Marion really wanted was peace and quiet from everyone and everything, so he headed to Lake City National Airport many hours early to get online and browse for nothing but mindless news, his Twitter feed, and anything else that wouldn't tax his brain for more than a few seconds.

Raskin tried calling a few times, but Marion was having none of it. However, Terra had gotten to him somehow. Whether it was through his daughter, Rebecca, or a combination of whatever fuckery she was in with Terra and the others, Marion had had enough for however brief the moment he'd have in the airport before flying into Houston.

Thinking of daughters, he decided to call Casey. Though the trip was for the sole purpose of meeting with Henrickson at the Huntsville Walls Unit, he called her anyway.

"I'll make time for you, Case, if you'll have me."

He called several times with no answer. "Isn't anyone fucking home?" He was certain that airport travelers were looking his way as he talked to himself, but his care was a shit's less about anything, so those who looked over his way could fuck right off.

When he texted Casey, he nearly crimped his neck when she responded right away. It was a one word reply of irritation: What?

He texted back: Please pick up the phone.

Another text came right back: Fine.

He dialed her number again.

Marion: Hi, sweetie. Thanks for picking up.

Casey: What can I do for you? I've got a lot going on.

Marion: Jesus, Casey. What can I do for you? Is that really—

Casey: Dad, what is it? I mean, I've not heard from you in nearly a year, and mom tells me you were in a coma and then came out of it, but that was weeks ago and still not a word. So what do you want from me? Pretty goddamn lucky I agreed to pick up.

Marion: You're right, and that's fair. I don't know what to say about it except I'm sorry and—

Casey: You're always sorry.

Marion: Right. Well, I still am. Look, I called because I'm flying down.

Casey: When?

Marion: Right now, in fact. Well, the red eye. One a.m.

Casey: I'll be asleep.

Marion: Yeah. Of course. I mean I'll be there later, or early in the morning. Point is I'll be there for a few days, and I thought maybe—

Casey: I've got things going on, dad. I won't be around.

Marion: Like what? I mean—

Casey: Hey, wait a minute, you don't have any right to ask me that! I've got something going on. I mean what right—

Marion: Okay, okay. You're right. I'd just like to see you, is all. I've missed you. I miss you, that is. I miss you, Case. Doesn't that count for anything.

Casey: Not really.

Marion: Jesus. You win, Case. You win.

Casey: For Christ's sake, dad, it's not about winning! Listen, I'm not gonna fight with you right now. I'm glad you're coming down and all, and I'm not gonna keep hammering you like the bitch you think I am. But this was an exciting invite for someone important to look at my artwork.

Marion: I don't think you're a bitch.

Casey: Fine. But I am. And did you hear what I said?

There is a long pause on the line as Marion can hear his daughter take struggled deep breaths and sighs. He is hit hard in the stomach with the reality of how awful it feels for being so estranged from her, how badly he wants to instantly repair all the damage over the years as he watches plane after plane pull up and take off from their respective gateways. His heart aches with a pain that cuts through all the horror that he's faced since walking the hospital floors before Janet Stone would unveil the true evils of the world.

Marion: Yeah, I did, Casey, I don't know what to say. I'm happy someone's wanting to see your work. What I do know is there is nothing I can say to fix anything right now. But in time I hope to. Who are you showing your work to?

Casey: Art dealer out of Moscow.

Marion: Russia?

Casey: No, the little podunk place here in Texas.

Marion: You're on a roll here. Art dealer out of Moscow. Sounds ritzy.

Casey: Who knows, but I have to at least

Dean Patrick

entertain it. Invite came by way of social media, so who knows?

Marion: Seems that's how a lot of things are being communicated lately with business.

Casey: Listen, I've gotta run. Glad you're coming to town, but I don't see it happening this time around.

Marion: Yeah. I love—

Click.

Marion looked at his phone long enough to go into a trance. He had wanted to say so much more to her, wanted to make some kind of headway, but knew at the same time he'd fucked things up royally for so long that it would most likely take just as long to even begin the healing process.

He walked around the airport terminals for a few hours, stopping in the book shops and souvenir shops, then taking the walkway escalators over to the international section of the airport, as all that area's shops and dining were open 24/7.

At just past midnight, he headed back to his terminal and gate. The flight was half full, which was always a relief. He was the only passenger on his row for even more relief.

He decided to take the window seat just as his phone buzzed again with Raskin sending him a video with a note: Footage I think you should see, from your Santiago meet.

Marion was logged into the plane's wi-fi, which had plenty of speed to download the nearly 10-minute video. "I was in there a lot longer than ten minutes," he whispered as the video opened on his phone's browser.

The video had no sound, of course, per the agreement of the meeting. Marion watched the surreal interrogation of

Santiago while thinking of the horrors that the Spaniard had spilled.

When Santiago jolted back during one of the questions—Marion couldn't remember which one—what suddenly appeared next to Santiago was a transparent apparition of a torso with neck and shoulders and a face that looked up to the camera, mouth wide open in a scream of rage, and lavender eyes that looked to fire small tracers directly at the camera that was recording the interrogation.

It was gone the second it appeared.

Marion's back pressed firmly against his seat as the plane roared to life.

Chapter Seventeen:

The Henrickson Interrogation

He watched the video over and over again on his phone, then sent it to his laptop to catch more detail when he zoomed in as far as his screen resolution would allow.

He watched it on the laptop almost as long until he was certain the image of Terra was burned into his brain. Whatever had happened at Lake City jail would most likely take place at Huntsville. "Depending on her fucking mood, I guess."

"Excuse me, sir? Did you need something?"

Marion cocked his head instantly at the flight attendant. "No. Sorry. Just talking to myself."

She giggled. "Oh, I understand. These late flights can do that to anyone. If there's anything you need, please let me know, but we are landing soon so you might want to put away your electronics."

Marion just stared at her.

She turned away and walked back to the front of the plane when she'd had enough of the no response.

Houston's International Airport, also called the George Bush Intercontinental Airport, was quieter than Marion had ever remembered, and he'd taken plenty of redeye flights.

Rather than think too much of it, he quickly hit the rental car area where he treated himself to a Dodge Charger, hit the freeway system he had raced around his entire career, and was at his condo in less than thirty minutes.

Grateful that his ex-wife had taken care of the place—or had someone take care of it—he took a quick shower, shaved, and freshened up. He was back out the door within an hour, racing down the I-45 freeway toward Huntsville before the 6 a.m. traffic had the entire freeway system shut down.

***

The Huntsville Unit of the Texas Department of Criminal Justice was nicknamed the Walls Unit, the oldest prison in the Lone Star State. Home of the Texas execution chamber for both men and women.

Marion had been to the facility several times over his career, and every time he walked up to the facility's main entrance he thought of the photographs and images of Auschwitz. Though nothing like what happened at the concentration camp ever took place in the Walls Unit, it was built as an ominous brick structure that had far too many resemblances of Auschwitz's entry that always caused Marion's bones to chill.

This was the place where Eddie Henrickson had spent every day of his life since the brutal murders he'd bathed in with Dean Corll, the infamous Candy Man serial killer of Houston. It was Henrickson himself who killed Corll, and it was the Walls Unit where Henrickson would die, too.

Marion had spoken to the warden of Huntsville, Kassidy Strongarm, in order to get permission to speak to such a high-profile inmate as Henrickson. He had tried to reach Butch Macintire many times with no luck as he wanted the cop's take on everything in general since he'd been so instrumental. Now that Marion was walking through the Walls Unit with his head down, he started to wonder what in the fuck he was doing there in the first place.

What am I going to ask this fucker? What am I going to learn? Do I hit him right between the eyes about the demon woman? Was she part of the child trafficking ring that Henrickson ran? Was she the fucking architect of it all, and what in Christ's name—

"Hello, Detective Paul." Strongarm's detached and toneless voice cut off his thinking to the quick, and quick was what Marion needed with the woman. Known as hardcore as any warden in the country, Strongarm didn't take shit from a single source who ever thought they could give it. She stood as tall as Marion and was just as sturdily built. With a haircut that looked like someone placed a bowl over her head and trimmed it around the edges, she was standing in the middle of the facility's main hallway where visitors would check in or come to pay the commissary. Her voice echoed as did Marion's when he responded, "Warden."

She got right to the point. "Just what is it that you hope to accomplish here, detective? Henrickson's been here for fifty plus years. This is his fucking burial place, too, so you can't expect any kind of truth or wisdom from him."

Marion looked the warden up and down and let out a deep breath, not realizing how anxious he'd become.

Get your shit together quick and in a hurry.

"There's a case up in Utah where I'm assisting the Lake City team. As I mentioned to you on the phone."

"Yeah, you did. And so what? What you didn't tell me was what Henrickson has to do with any of it, because he doesn't."

"So thoughtful of you, warden, to protect him."

"Cut the shit, Paul. I want you to give it to me straight, or I'll have this whole thing canceled right here and right now. I've spoken to your lieutenant. I've talked to Boggs, and you haven't been active all year."

Marion knew she meant every word, as much as he

knew Lieutenant Hayden Boggs hadn't been completely onboard with the whole thing. Marion had to really grease him for the visit. Marion also knew he'd been one damn fine detective over the years and had busted more sickos and shitbags than any other detective over a five-year stint. Marion had made Boggs look good when Boggs needed it most, so the favor was owed. Still, he knew he had to pass Strongarm's test, regardless of what arrangements had been made.

"Warden, you're right. Henrickson doesn't have a thing to do with what happened in Lake City. But are you aware of what happened up there? The grisly murders at the nightclub?"

"I saw a few clips on the news. Like every other damn thing, it's gone in a few days and replaced by the next one."

"Yeah, true. But this one was particularly fucked up. And the guy they have in jail and have charged him with felony after felony...he's not exactly the Henrickson type, but I think he's been inside the same framework that Henrickson was part of. I simply want to connect a few dots, if I can."

Strongarm looked at Marion like he was completely out of his element. She folded her thick arms and hands around her thick body, one of her shoes lightly tapping the lobby's concrete floor in sharp echoes. "What kind of dots?"

She's gonna send me home if I don't seal the deal right now.

"There's a woman involved."

"Ha! Isn't there always? Are you serious, Paul? Are you shitting me?"

"Please. Stop. Just hear me out. That's all I'm asking."

Strongarm bit her lower lip gently but with clear irritation. "Go ahead."

"This woman, like I said, is part of what happened up

there, and I think she was part of what happened in a case here, in Houston, the Robert DeMille case back in '07. I've done a lot of work on this bitch, and I think I can trace her work back to what Henrickson was involved with in Dallas and that child trafficking ring. Not her exactly, but she's been part of all of it. Orchestrating. Those are the dots. And I'm asking you to please let me try to make a connection." He wasn't trying to brownnose her, as Marion wanted her to know he really needed this. Marion was also careful in what he said about Terra as to not frame her as someone who'd been doing this kind of shit decade after decade after decade. He knew the warden wouldn't buy it if framed too bizarrely.

"Because women don't do this kind of fucked up shit, only this isn't a woman, dear Warden Strongarm, no ma'am we are talking about the goddamn devil in a fucking blue dress."

Strongarm stopped tapping her shoe and biting her lip, but her arms remained locked around her thick frame.

Marion kept her stare.

"Fine, Paul. You've got your meeting. You know the drill. Turn in everything you've got on you, and the guards will come retrieve you. You'll be on the same floor as Old Sparky was, of all places. Fitting, right? That's all I could get on this kind of short notice."

"Old Sparky" was the nickname that the Walls Unit had given the electric chair at Huntsville, an area of the prison that Marion had seen more than a few times.

***

When the metal barred doors slammed home after Marion had surrendered the Beretta, his Police Spyderco knife, wallet, the works, he thought it was the sound of hopelessness making itself perpetually comfortable. He'd been inside many prisons and jails, but regardless of how many there had been, the sound that closed him off inside the Walls Unit, the unforgiving steel casings and iron doors was one of the most unnerving sounds he'd ever heard.

The two guards who'd come for him were the standard bearers of all prisons. Big men with big bellies with small paychecks who didn't give a rat's ass about anything other than causing as much turmoil as possible to those they ruled over. They were Officers Dan Higgins and Wayne Olgeby. Early thirties, semi-illiterate, who'd spend their entire careers inside the walls of the abandoned.

The room that Warden Strongarm had arranged had a concrete floor with concrete walls four feet thick. There was one barred door that acted as a screen to the iron door that kept it secure. A large bulletproof glass slat allowed for the guards to see everything inside, and cameras were placed in the corners of the room. There were two sets of track lighting with bulbs that were just about to burn out. A single folding table and two cheap metal chairs were placed directly in the middle of the room.

Marion took the chair that faced the barred door.

"We'll go fetch him for ya. Just you make yourself comfy. Want some shitty cold coffee or some hot tap water while you wait?" Higgins let out a ridiculous laugh after he said it. Olgeby was the more serious of the two and kept his eye on Marion, doing his best to give off a sense of toughness and authority.

Marion stared at both of them, knowing he could take them in seconds if it came to it. "I'm fine, thanks."

"Suit yourself, *de-tech-tiv*." Higgins spit it out as he left to retrieve Henrickson. Olgeby stepped outside and waited for Higgins to return. Within fifteen minutes, it was Olgeby who entered the room with Henrickson, walked him over to the table, sat him down on the metal chair facing Marion, and left his hands cuffed behind his back.

"That's not necessary. We'll be fine. Right?" Marion looked right into Henrickson's eyes so the killer would know he wasn't fucking around for one second.

Henrickson held Marion's stare for a moment then looked up to Olgeby.

"Suit yourselves." The guard uncuffed Henrickson. "I'll be just outside the door if you need anything. We'll be watching the cameras and all."

"Thank you, officer." Marion nodded that it was okay for them to be alone, then looked across at the man who'd killed Houston's Candy Man as well as participated in the murders of twenty-seven or more young boys, as well as being the architect of one of Dallas's most vile child trafficking rings in the city's history.

"You know I don't have to say a goddamn word to you if I don't want. You know that, right?" Henrickson's eyes were glassy and fogged over. His hair was long and strung out. His face so deepened with harsh wrinkles they looked more like someone had carved them in with a steak knife. He had only a few teeth and hadn't shaved for a week.

"No, you don't." Marion would play this out by using every technique of calm and cool that he'd ever learned. He knew he'd need it. He sat back in the cheap metal chair and even reached behind his back out of habit for the Beretta that he'd surrendered. "My name's Marion Paul. I'm a detective for HPD. I'm working a case...actually helping with a case up in Lake City, Utah."

"That murder bit that happened at the night club? Pigs' heads and shit?"

"Yeah, that's the one. Try not to interrupt, okay? At least while I'm giving you a little history?"

"Ohhhhhh, bit on edge, are ya?"

"A bit."

"So what do you want from me? Want me to tell you how I'd figure that one out for you? Come here to have me do your job? Fuckers always coming in here to get some kind of inside shit."

Marion stared at him with mild curiosity. "You might say I'm working a case where I may need your...well, as you so eloquently put it, 'inside shit.'"

"That's what I thought."

"I'm sure you know it all. Sure you know just about everything there is to know, regardless of the subject. But listen up, you fuck, I know all your case files and everything there is to know about the Candy Man fuckshow. But also the porn and trafficking rings in Dallas. I know the whole—"

"Whoooooo Eeeee, whoa! I'm shakin' all over here. You know me like my mammy's tit. But so what? Where's that have us? You think you can make anything worse or better for me? Ha!"

Marion put his elbows on the table and tapped his fingers together on both hands.

"I'm sure it's something you'd never even considered, to be honest. Or maybe you have. In fact, my bet's placed on the second option."

Henrickson sat back and rocked back and forth on the cheap metal chair's back legs, scratched his filthy hair and head, and rubbed his face. "I've got nothing better to do, copper, so let's get into it. Show me your cards. Let's play."

"Okay, Henrickson. Let's. It's my thinking that the one in charge of your crime ring was out of your league. So out of it I think you don't even know what you don't know."

"Is that right!?" Henrickson slammed the front chair legs back down on the concrete floor and leaned way into Marion. "What makes you think that?"

"I think it was a lot more than just grooming little boys and selling 'em off. I think it's possible you were one of the originals to be groomed and highlighted and sold to the lowest fucking bidder."

Marion paused as Henrickson remained leaned in over

the table as he clasped his hands together. He was breathing harder and his lips were quivering. Marion could tell the strategy was beginning to take hold, but he also had to edge in that fine line of empathy and sympathy to a Lifer with no parole who had lost any such attachment to humanity years ago. Marion would need body language along with verbal skill to move the needle.

"So...who was she? Because I know you know who I'm talking about."

Henrickson sat back in his chair with his hands remaining clasped more tightly.

Marion pulled back with an easier tone. "Listen...I think, if I said I know who she is, too, you'd not think I was out of my skull. I think if I told you that the cat up in Lake City also knows her, that you'd...probably understand what he's going through."

Henrickson unclasped his hands and rubbed his face, then lean back over the table with a gesture that he wanted to tell him a secret. "What do you know about her, copper?"

"You first."

Henrickson took in a deep breath and let it out. "Okay. Let me tell you a story. Maybe it'll be worth something to you."

"I'm all ears."

Henrickson leaned a bit more toward Marion. "Tell me, do you hear eerie operatic music in the background? Or chanting?"

Marion paused to listen because he thought he could hear many different sounds coming from the prison walls, but also knew such inmates as Henrickson would say anything to keep things off pace.

"Let's keep to the story."

Henrickson cleared his throat in a ragged effort. "I had this dream before the whole boy-toy thing started. I was walking around an old...ancient is a better word...an ancient graveyard. And I mean graveyard. You know, the ones that ain't cemeteries? I was stumbling around, not drunk or nothin' but...confused. The gravestones were big chunks of broken granite. All of 'em. It was awful dark. Misty. I could hear large insects bickering, if that makes sense. Suddenly, in front of me walked this woman pushing a wheelbarrow that was filled with severed fingers and dicks. Looked like thousands of 'em, as many spilled over and onto the muddied ground.

"I looked at the woman's face in a sense of pure befuddlement. I was about to ask her why she was hauling such a horrible load when she stopped, set it flat, and put her own index finger to her lips to silence me. She told me she was carrying all the sins of all the kings whose finger's she had cut off so they could never give orders again. That she'd also done so when they were not yet kings but still boys, that her purpose from the beginning of time was to destroy such destinies while still young.

"That she was the destroyer of children."

Marion stared at Henrickson as if he'd not completely heard him correctly. He also had to think quickly enough to make sense of it so as to not lose Henrickson's wisp of brief trust.

"You think this woman was the same woman who turned you into a killer? Who gave you the curse and all its sick twisted fucking rituals?"

Henrickson tilted his head to the side slowly. "Of course it was. But of course you know that already, copper, am I right?"

"What does she look like?"

"Like a purple-eyed serpent whore."

Marion ground his molars. *"Nailed that one, pal!"*

"Your look says it all, copper. She's into everything. But you know that, too. Just maybe not as much as you thought. You've connected the dots, as you said. Or you wouldn't be here. Picking at my wet noodle. Everything.

And I mean everything. Silver tongued attorneys and sack-clothed judges. Whole fucking legal system. Filth in politics. Filth in religions and false prophets. The silt and shit in schools. The seduction and disease in whorehouses and bathhouses. Every flesh hole that's been plugged with every cancerous cock. All of it tied to her. She's got the tips of her talons tickling it all like her personal ivory keys. With access to any resource no matter the cost. Tickle, tickle, tickle, drool and dribble. She's up inside your sphincters all around and deep, I can see it. She's found something personal to ya!

"But never mind that because in the end, she'll roll her load of bloody fingers and dicks right over everyone's sleeping bones!"

Marion jolted up from his chair, knocking it over. The banging of the metal and concrete echoed longer than was normal as he braced himself on the hard plastic tabletop with both hands gripping the edges. "We're done here. You've given me all I need to know."

"But have I given you all you need to do? That's the real question, detective."

"Guard!" Marion had had enough. He needed time to think through all the dots.

Henrickson leaned back in his chair as the iron door opened and both prison guards entered to take him back. They said nothing to Marion as they placed the cuffs on and walked Henrickson out. But not before he turned for one last pitch.

"She's got something personal on you, that's easy to see! But don't think she'll stop there as she gets in deeper. Everything close to you, she'll fuck it all up!"

"Alright, that's enough, ole boy, time to get you back to your crazies." It was Olgeby who spoke as he looked at Marion. "Hope you've found what you're looking for, de-tech-tiv."

Chapter Eighteen:

The Final Interview

Marion called Casey the minute he left the prison. Everything that Henrickson rambled on about, regardless of its insanity, made sense in one specific area: that everyone who Marion cared about or loved was indeed in danger. He just didn't know the devil in the details.

No answer from Casey. The text messages he sent right after the call were of the green color. She had an iPhone so that meant her phone was either off or that she was out of range. Or that she blocked him. "Christ I hope that's not the deal, Casey. I really need to talk to you." He spoke quietly as he fired up the rental Charger and raced back on the freeway toward the airport.

He ended up calling his ex-wife, June, who had quite little to say, that she had no idea where Casey was or where she would be and that she didn't have anything to talk about. When Marion pressed, he knew it was a terrible idea.

> **June**: Jesus Christ, Marion, it's enough that you were never around when her brother died! Now you want to come back creeping into her life?
>
> **Marion**: My son, June. And thanks for that.
>
> **June**: Oh, don't even start with that shit.

Dean Patrick

Really? You're gonna go there?

Marion: You know...it's always so nice to—

June: Goddamn it, Marion!

Marion: Okay, okay, okay. Look, can you just listen to me for a minute? Please just listen.

June: Oh for fuck sake, what is it?

Marion pauses before saying anything further off the cuff, as he has to think carefully what to say next. He knows June will hang up on him and may not answer the phone for six more months. She knew how to hit every nerve to push him to his limits within less than a second. Bringing up the death of their son, Jeremey, always did the trick. It also instantly put him in a frame of mind where he couldn't think straight. The accident Jeremey was in was no one's fault. But not according to June. Still, he'd tell his ex the bottom line regardless of her reaction, as the freeway before him turned surreal.

Marion: Just be careful. And tell her to be careful as well. She's going to some art thing or something—

June: I know all about it. Woman who contacted her is quite well connected and I'm happy for her! And what do you mean be careful, Marion? Do you think I need this shit?

Marion: Woman? What woman?

June: What do you mean "be careful?"

Terra's Sabbath

Marion: I need to know about this woman, June.

June: Oh Jesus Christ. It's always something with you. I'm done with this conversation.

Marion: June just tell me—

Click.

And that was it. Just like that, as fast as June came back to life, she was once again dead, as her comment about the woman who'd apparently contacted Casey left his stomach instantly wrapped around his throat.

He couldn't do a thing about it. One of the greatest skills he had ever learned as a cop was that when the absolute knowledge was there about any given scenario and there was nothing that could be done, it was always the best strategy to let it play out and unfold. Regardless of how difficult. Marion knew this was such a time as he decided to catch the next flight back to Lake City.

***

It was a few days later or so, and the July 4th Duncan Parade was just around the corner, and all Marion could do was think over the endless world he'd awakened to where the witchcraft of Terra Drake had consumed him to the point where he'd lost his appetite to the point he could see an unhealthy weight drop.

He continued staying over at Devon's place as well as the Odessa Hotel, only driving by his place to grab items he needed. He simply didn't need the loneliness while trying to keep it together. The calls back and forth with Raskin had become as insane as everything else, from Janet Stone to Bridget Magnus, and he certainly didn't need another encounter with Kane. Not as a next-door neighbor anyway. He couldn't reach Casey, and Nina was in New Orleans, but he hadn't been able to reach her either.

The morning he received Terra's frightening message to his LinkedIn profile, of all places, a profile that he rarely checked, but had notifications turned on in his phone when he was alerted, his heart felt like a large stone that dropped to the bottom of a filthy pond. He felt his blood turn white as he thought of Nina telling him that LinkedIn was the exact same way she was contacted about her New Orleans gig, that she had never been contacted by anyone from her work or her company that way before. Moreso, he thought of how Casey had been contacted in a similar way.

His hand gripped the phone so tightly it was like the device was his final thread on a rope that was barely keeping him alive.

Keep it the fuck together.

> Hello, Marion. I was perusing your LinkedIn page and immediately thought this to be the best place to reach you. I have your daughter. And Nina. Not in my clutches exactly, but I know you know what I mean. To save them there is a process that I'd like you to follow. There is a production warehouse where I'd like you to begin this process. Everything's about procedures, Marion.

> It's a place that most folks around the area have believed to be the future. A fabulous warehouse for the creation and production of new parts for aircraft that have been traveling across the ages. But that's not important. Dr. Jaquelyn Pinault will do your intake. The warehouse is an enormous place just off the freeway inside Odessa's city limits. I'm sure

you've seen it. When you arrive, she will lay everything out for you in detail. You will have an invite sent to your email within 24 hours of this message. When you arrive you will meet a production team of dazzling and psychedelic transients who I feel need someone to redirect their thoughts so that all may understand and see the vision I've never once forsaken. I know that you'll reply, here, which is something I'm looking forward to reading. Or maybe not. The choice is yours, but your ladies' choices are running out.

Marion responded to Terra after carefully thinking about what to write, or how to write it. The first thing he wanted to do was shoot her a text but realized that anytime Terra had called or texted that the number always displayed UNKNOWN CALLER. He followed her direction with a quick, "I'll be there." He had to use every single skill he ever learned or experienced in the field to stay razor sharp.

***

The meeting itself strobed its way *into* Marion in the form of an office inside the massive warehouse that was larger than his own Duncan home. The office had to be several thousand square feet. Decorated with mood lamps placed against red brick walls, blacklight posters that hung ominously over the red bricks that popped the walls off as if Photoshopped on with fancy backdrop shadows, nestled brilliantly in thousand-dollar antique frames, brass or silver. Posters of Jimi Hendrix, Led Zeppelin, The Doors. And crucifixion scenes that Marion remembered being hung on the walls of Kane's living room and hallways.

As for the mood lamps, he'd always called them such. Those inexpensive, six-foot tall structures screwed together in sections. Cheap iron. Upside down bowl-shaped finishes at the top with submerged 40-watt bulbs that dimmed by turning an imitation brass knob. But the lamps inside the office were far from cheap and looked morphed and molded only for the elite.

In the center of the spacious office rested a solid oak coffee table cut to an exact square—six feet each side, at least eight inches thick with carpentry work from Michelangelo himself. Etched into the wood were characters from Chaucer's *Canterbury Tales*. Or maybe from Poe. "Mask of Red Death"? "Tell-Tale Heart"? Marion couldn't see them clearly enough to determine. Plush chairs—black velvet most likely—were placed at each side of the table. Floors were mahogany, deeply stained and heavy. Also hanging on the walls were blueprints and illustrations of aircraft that he'd never seen, or even thought were possible.

Dr. Pinault was sitting behind an office desk that was designed to match the coffee table.

"So glad you could make it. Please. Have a seat." Pinault stood up and walked out from behind the desk to gesture to Marion where she wanted him. She was dressed in a white bodysuit with blood red stilettos, her red hair dyed deeply enough to match the shoes and pulled back tight, her nails the same shocking finish.

Marion was filled with anxiety and hunger to reach over and grab her by the throat and demand to know where Casey and Nina were being held, but he had to play it out.

As the actual interview began, it felt more like a screen test for a Kubrick film. Marion's mind began to race when Pinault rattled off, "On a scale of one to ten, how afraid are you right now?"

He leaned in. "I don't know. Never been asked such a thing. My anxiety's in full tilt, but I'm not sure if that's fear. I'm here for my daughter and Nina, and you fucking well know that."

No response as Pinault stared at him for a full minute or so. Her green eyes were ablaze with insanity.

Hold it together, that's all that matters is holding it all the fuck together.

"If you were to see your mother here, sitting across from you, and she was grading you on this interview, what do you think she'd say?"

Marion held her stare. "She'd probably say I'm scared."

Dr. Pinault made some notes in a thick spiral notebook. Without looking up she asked, "What do you think about the black lighting in here? The posters so popularly used decades ago that welcome the false light so vividly? Some of the posters from a time long long ago. And the blueprints? What do you think of the plans?"

Marion looked at the wall hangings again to demonstrate he was doing as he was told. "My brother and I grew up on these bands, but as for the other scenes and those spaceship-looking designs, at least that's what they look like to me, I don't know what to say. I'm not entirely sure what *these* posters are, but they're far more than just posters, as you've placed them in frames that create a feeling of something that's as fucked up as everything else about you and your gang. I'd say they're probably the best part of this interview, wouldn't you say, doctor? Why don't we just cut the shit and you tell me where they are."

"All in good time, Marion. I think you were told to follow this process through, am I right? At least that's what I think is the best course."

Marion let out a deep breath of as much irritation as exhaustion. He had to surrender. "Fine."

"Good, let's continue then. If you knew that a colleague was doing something unethical, or illegal, and he or she was also your boss or supervisor, would you create a fake social media account and say terrible things about them, like they download illegal porn on a regular basis?"

Marion tilted his head and blinked slowly. "I'd arrest the fucker myself."

Pinault let out a long healthy laugh, one that highlighted her throaty voice. "I have loved your resilience since the moment I saw you talking to Alice in the hospital, during one of her Wonderland moments. She's here, you know."

Marion continued staring at the doctor. "I knew that you'd do whatever it takes while on this ship when you were prying into the why's and how's of her rocking back and forth on her bed. Anyway, let's get back to it. Here's the next one for you. If you're caught looking at porn on your work machine, at the police station, mind you, and because *everyone* looks at porn, Marion, everyone, but if you're caught with it at work, would you continue looking? As to not lose your hard-on? Or would you slam your laptop shut as if you're leaving, or taking a break to rub one out in the nearest bathroom? Hell, right where you're sitting for that matter?"

All Marion could do was go with it. "I don't look at porn at work. At many places you get fired for it."

"But that's not an answer to the question now, is it?" Pinault spoke with abrupt spurts, her eyes wigged around. "The question requires an answer to *if* you are caught. Being caught is the main ingredient here. Will you continue looking or will you *shut down*?"

"I told you I don't look at porn at work. That's my final answer. I've given you my thinking, and apparently this one isn't going anywhere, so why don't we just move on from the porn. That a deal? I'm sure this fuckin' place is filled to the brim with every Tom, Dick, and Harry getting their rocks off. Maybe Alice, too. But I'm losing my patience."

"Now *that's* the spirit! That's what we're after! Listen, Marion, everyone knows why you're here. But I want you to think about something, considering all that you've been through so far. Think about this place. That it has the outward appearance of something that you were told about in the initial message that brought you here. This is a special place. This *can* be a highly emotional operation once you've been given the golden handcuffs and keys to the kingdom. Quite emotional indeed, to be honest. We're doing things here that will change...well, let's just say we're doing things here designed to change the fabric of time and space.

"Now, you've obviously heard such nonsense spewed all over the media endlessly, am I right? But that's the point Terra wants to make. All that you have heard is nonsense. What you're being offered here is a chance to save your precious ones, yes, but it's so much more than that. I'm about to let you proceed with the process for *that* chance. We're quite aware of the stress factor you're under. I have nothing more, Marion. And I really don't need to hear any of your own questions, to be frank. I'd like to take you over to the warehouse floor and let you see everything."

***

When entering the warehouse floor, Marion's eyes instantly flashed across the ceilings and walls as if they were fastened on the base of a multi-lens fashion-camera: rapid panoramic shots that soaked in every inch of the thirty thousand square foot facility. The massive entrance was a profound and overwhelming hall with ceramic ceilings forty feet high, walls at least three feet thick of fancy chiseled natural stone. He'd never seen such opulent work inside any home, much less a warehouse. But this certainly wasn't just a warehouse. He felt he'd been launched into something vast and fascinating beyond what he'd experienced thus far from Terra or Kane.

As he continued scanning the entire physical vision in awe, Dr. Pinault was right by his side but remained silent, allowing Marion a full appreciation of an initial walk through. The ceilings were adorned with fabulous track lighting, each piece designed in an eight-foot, deep silver aluminum case that encapsulated massive LED bay lights. The fabulous lighting burned a hue of blues and purples across the entire floor that slowly danced in an aura that glowed over every machine and machine station that was built and housed on the main entry floor.

The floor itself was designed to look like a massive flag of some kind, made of pewter-like stone. Celtic perhaps. In fact, he wasn't so sure the whole floor wasn't solid pewter. He lost count of how many LED casings lined the ceiling. The grand floor was also double storied with fabulous iron stairwells on each side that led to a second tier of even more impossible stone design. Cobblestone first came to mind.

"Spectacular, isn't it." Dr. Pinault's deep voice broke the silence like a hammer hitting a brick of ice.

"Yeah, it's something else. Where are they?"

Pinault ignored the question. "It's our Sistine Chapel. Our Last Supper, if you will. We're doing marvelous work here, as you can see. No expense has been spared. It's her vision, as I'm sure you're now aware. Walk with me."

Dr. Pinault continued as Marion walked alongside her. Her white suit became such a contrast to her hair and stilettos that she had the appearance of being as manufactured as anything such a warehouse could design and produce. She stopped and slowly twirled around with her arms out in a display in what seemed more in awe of herself than anything she was showing.

"All of this came to her one night as she was pondering life and death. Her own, that is. Let me rephrase that. Her life *or* death as far as such eternal perspective plays into things. Can you imagine such things, Marion? How life *overcomes* death. Resurrection, for example. Terra is a visionary, as you know. She has studied with so many of the great ones, walked with them in their every thought and action. Seduced them to their very core.

"You see, she was suffering at the time when she had her most profound event. She wanted to let go of everything and give up. I know that's hard to believe, and every condition would never allow giving up. Not in the physical sense. It's been that way since the beginning. I'll explain a bit more in a minute. One night a terrible dream of great bursts of fever ravaged her. Nothing could soothe the ravaging no matter what she guzzled or pumped through her body. Something your brother submitted to, yes?"

Keep it the fuck together.

Marion wanted to wrap his hands around the doctor's porcelain neck.

Dr. Pinault's eyes bore into Marion with large glassy pupils, wildly dilated as if she had just sucked down all the chemicals she spoke of in a single drink.

"It all came to her during that night of extreme fever. She dreamt of a time...of *that* ancient day, of that fateful night in Jerusalem. She had the dream before she was there, and she was, you know. She was right there the whole time. But she was higher than the others who were part of that awful and glorious event. She was high upon an area where she could look down to witness the ferocious beating and mocking that was taking place at a ruthless pace of brutality.

"She had placed...instructed really...a group of demons who surrounded the accused during the mock trials, the scourging, the crucifixion. Demons who were far more barbaric than the Romans who had thought they were the ones who led the events. Demons surrounding the entire blood bathing scene. *She* directed the demons, Marion, more clearly than the brutes ever could who continued to administer hell to the man who said he was God's son. Demons that looked as if they were walking on inches of bloodied ground, where the blood was several inches thick. They were dressed in long, draping death shrouds. Their arms folded within their robes to hide any flesh, or whatever demons use as hands. She's been the author of all countless stories of atonement. For all mankind and the gobbledygook.

"She wanted something far, far different. After the Christ Figure was flogged and nearly ruined, after the cross was forced on his back, and as he started to make his way to the hill of crucifixion, our dear Lilith directed, in even *more* horror, a transformation that took place within the actual body of Christ himself. From the waist down, an abhorrent and sickeningly massive, insect growth began to protrude from Christ's lower spine. A gargantuan half-body of some moth-like creature. The wings of this abomination looked to be made of long, jagged shards of rusted metal. As the dying Christ pressed forward, his legs all together disappeared and were replaced by shattered, yet still functional large ropey veins that acted as legs, but burst at the seams, spraying blood with each step so swollen and engorged with abscesses they were. She directed what was perceived by the demons as a half-man, in this case half-God, half monstrous insect creature where the legs looked more and more like the metal jagged wings, which started to wither and erode in a melting heap of rust and bolts."

Dr. Pinault stopped as if her train of thought was lost before catching herself and looking up and down Marion's body.

"What kind of story is that? What's the *fucking* point of such a story? Is this still part of the procedures to check my reaction to any panic or dissent? You don't think I've seen enough by now that I no longer have any fucks left to give in what takes place next? You know what? I have no idea what to say, doctor. What am I supposed to say to something like that? A story like that. I'm here to face whatever it is to save my daughter and Nina. And, believe it or not, I've got a feeling that Terra, or Lilith as you've called her, puts some kind of value on that, as remarkable as that may sound."

Dr. Pinault took a few steps toward Marion until she was inches from his face. "No need to say anything. Listening is enough. And you're right. This has become such a showdown. She believed that God Himself had been trapped in her own condition. She directed the demons that fateful day to place upon God Himself the reality that such a perception would one day come to fruition in our everyday life. And hasn't it? Isn't such a distortion of truth splattered on every canvas from paper to tablet every minute of every day? Are you following me now?"

"Yeah. I'm following you, lady. Every word."

Dr. Pinault let out a long, saturated breath while looking up to the ceiling. "Good. Then it's time to move forward. This is where I say goodbye for now. Walk through those doors." She pointed toward a large door entrance and walked back toward the front office.

***

Marion entered an area that looked as massive as the warehouse main floor itself. He looked up and around in awe that such a place was part of what he'd just seen. It was divided up into different thematic areas which, for a brief moment, reminded him of Eternity 51's design.

The first area he walked through was a wax museum that resembled the best of any Ripley's Believe It Or Not, where the first display was a mid-19th century saloon—with the bar itself built to attach perfectly with a cowboy barkeeper who leaned over beautifully polished oak wood, cleaning rag in one hand placed on the bar in such a way that it made the figure look like he was buffing the wood in small circular motions. The figure's other hand braced against the bar's edge to hold his weight after a 14-hour shift.

Marion looked past the wax barkeeper to the many,

and various, booth-like setups where the next one over was a police station entrance designed from a 1950's camera shot that jumped to a lead story on the six o'clock news. He couldn't tell if it was New York or Chicago, or even Houston.

Marion continued walking forward as he next saw a vintage 1990s Ace Hardware get up. Down a few more an 80s Dairy Queen, then a 70s skating rink. He couldn't tell how many of the thematic areas had been built, but he decided to go back to the first one with the barkeeper, as something there reminded him of what happened at The Oak Post just before the wolf creature rushed him and Devon. There was music in the distance, but he couldn't tell what song was playing. When he reached the bar room, he could hear quietly in the background the sounds of billiard balls cracking and racing across unseen green and red felt tables.

The wax used to create and build everything from the bar to the barkeeper to the chairs and everything in between was so meticulously carved and painted that Marion wondered what kind of purpose it all served.

Whatever the fuck she's got planned, I've got to get Casey and Nina out of here, if they're here at all.

There was also something frightening in all the familiarity. The cowboy was dressed in a pearl-colored shirt with white enamel snaps, silver cufflinks, tied off at the neck with a brilliant red and black bandana with a black velvet rim hat, massive leather belt with custom buckle, spray-starched deep blue jeans, and two Colt .45 six shooters. *Hand cannons.*

Marion leaned in for a closer view to study the details of the barkeeper's forehead lines, mouth and lips, eyeballs and eyelids—all put together with majestic and intricate care.

He then took a step back and realized before his skin froze what was happening when the barkeeper winked at him.

"I'm sure Kane's close by, you fuck." Marion's voice was just above a whisper.

He laughed the same high-pitched squeal that Marion remembered the first time in Kane's living room right before he knocked Ace to the floor.

"Something else that you've remained so calm. Makes this job worth its time and price in gold. But goddamn it, boy, you look like the devil himself just reached through your grill, inside down into your guts, and raked over the raw nubs of your pecker bone."

"How 'bout if I come over and reach down your guts."

"Is that really your next play here?" Ace stood up as stoic as if everything going on was a typical day at the warehouse.

Marion remained where he stood. Knowing he could pull out the Beretta and gun down the freak certainly helped. "I'm not sure of the next move. But if I need to go through you, best know that's not a problem."

Ace stiffened up. "Let me say this. She's my boss, but I'm sure you know that. It's all tied to her, and had you not known that already, you wouldn't be here."

"And where's *here*, exactly? Seriously. What's the purpose of all this?"

"Cranky, are you? That's natural. Especially since everything's so unnatural."

Marion was beyond agitated but had to press on. "Yeah. I do. Never felt anything so unnatural, but still, what is it I need back here? Or from you? Or do I just need to tell you to fuck right off so I can get on with the finale?"

"Do whatever you want, Marion. Say whatever you want. Makes no difference to me or anyone else, for that matter. Just head down these aisles and try to keep an open air to everything. That's your best route. That's your road less traveled by. You head on down there, now, dear boy.

Head on down the yellow brick road and make sure you keep your wits about you, follow me? You may just need every last one."

With that, Ace leaned back into his original position where Marion first saw him and believed him nothing more than fabulously poured, carved wax. Much like he'd believed when in Kane's living room. All the lighting instantly turned to a deep hue of burgundy that Marion had never seen. A sudden burst of dread he knew he'd never felt soon followed.

He also knew there was no turning back and that Nina and Casey were all that mattered.

They're worth my own goddamn miserable life.

He took a few steps forward and away from the bar.

The burgundy lighting deepened in color to royal purple, then to a depth of blue so vivid and paralyzing Marion felt his lungs struggle for more life, that his heart skipped a beat or two. His lips turned salty and parched, his tongue dry and achy. Almost blistered. Music suddenly burst into an aura of life from every inch of the walls and ceiling before him as if a single alien lifeform birthed a freakishly fused tune.

At first, it was Eric Church's "Give Me Back My Hometown" where the singer wailed in anguish about what was and what can never be again. The haunted tale of lost high school football nights, the endless agony of lost innocence. The song faded away as astonishing as it opened. Newer...harder...fiercer house techno began to pulverize in such intensity that Marion felt the floor moving as if gently shaken by a mild earthquake.

The thematic areas he first saw vanished into bizarre and distorted cave-like structures that looked what he envisioned black holes must look like from the new Webb Space Telescope. Vacuumed shadows of impossible density that stretched apart ever so slowly as if possessing an endless strength of reverse tension certainly not of this earth's understanding.

Make sure you keep your wits about you...you may just need every last one.

He placed one foot in front of the other as carefully as if he'd just learned to walk as a toddler. A stench blasted all throughout the area with even more intensity as the pulsing insanity of the techno music sped into such a frenetic chaos, he could no longer follow its rhythm. It was the stench of gore, of shit and piss, of rotted meat laced with maggots and fly juice. A stink so vile and angry that Marion's nose gushed in heavy, bloody runs. His face became such a mess, he felt he was fighting for every last breath. The heavy gore stench and murderous techno created a hopelessness and fear so overwhelming, he wondered if he was dying, if everything was finally going down in what Terra had surely designed specifically for him.

He fell to his knees, cupped his violated ears with all his strength to soften the furious rhythmic blows, wiped his face into his now-soaked shirt, not sure how much blood mixed with sweat he was wiping. He'd never felt such soaked exhaustion after his harshest workouts. To no avail, he began to weep.

"Why? Why am I crying?" he pleaded to no one at all, then rocked back and forth on his knees for quite some time before gathering the strength to stand again and press onward. In what seemed like half a mile or farther, he reached the first cave-like black hole structure—more an acrid suture cut deep into space-time. He was shocked into even deeper panic and anxiety when he leaned against the thing, and it held his weight. Briefly relieved, Marion leaned on it with both hands to catch his breath, to find some source of physical and emotional stability to find more oxygen. But all air still seemed completely out of reach.

Suddenly, flashing across in rapid bursts of black on

white lettering on dozens of theater-size monitors that hung on the walls were sentences that screamed in all caps all the sins Marion ever committed. Every wrongdoing. Every lie. Every deceitful, angry, lustful thought. Every broken promise. Every betrayal. What was Marion's entire life-long legacy of hidden secrets became exposed reality that flashed relentlessly and repeatedly on the monitors, creating such a mixture of words, sounds, and smells he was certain both a stroke and heart attack began in their crippling infancy.

It was an avalanche of sustained horror that shattered Marion's spirit. He fell to his knees again in utter exhaustion as he looked around to see the entire floor became a vast room of emptiness where only painful white light pierced and pressed into every inch of his failing soul.

He felt such heaviness of regret and sorrow he couldn't decipher what was real and what was being inflicted upon him by the demon woman herself. He felt the consequences of emotional turmoil that he lived through for nearly forty-five years. Utterly alone. Abandoned and left to manage an atonement he could never sustain.

Keep going, get them out of this, that's all that matters.

Marion stood up yet again in a sudden resolve that there was nothing left to combat that could possibly face him. His head hung from his shoulders as if every muscle in his neck collapsed in atrophy, and he wanted to walk again.

Just as his tears swelled and fell down his face, a large swinging door perhaps fifty feet directly in front of him opened outwardly. Terra Drake stood just inside the opening dressed in an opulent pewter fitted bodysuit with black alligator full-length boots. Her hair was bleached blond and ratted into a blast of chaos, her lavender eyes lit with controlled insanity.

"Come with me, Marion. You've done well, and you

don't want to miss this."

"What's going on with your eyes?" It was the best Marion could muster as he willed himself to hold Terra's stare.

"Think nothing of it." Her voice was dead but filled with authority as she turned away from him and walked into a spacious area of the main warehouse that Marion was certain wasn't there when he first entered. The lights and design looked far more like the insides of a massive aircraft of some kind, most likely something from the strange blueprints he'd seen in the office with Pinault.

As she had done from the moment he first met her on the fields of the Duncan Maze, her body moved with such ferocious seduction he found his mind once again focusing on her rather than the ordeal he'd just pushed through.

He took a deep breath and held it as he followed her toward a stunning ceramic stage that was built to either host large events in obscene extravagance, or to comfortably seat just as many for some kind of journey.

Kane stood on the stage dressed in a bizarre ritual gown, burnt orange in color with a bleached white hood. Dr. Pinault, Janet Stone, Rebecca, and Bridget Magnus stood next to him dressed in black silk dresses and black berets. A podium was placed in front of each of them, podiums designed as wooden, rustic altars. An elaborate tracking system-conveyor belt was built in front of the stage and surrounded the immediate seating area. Arranged inside the tracking system were rows and rows of empty seats that completed the overall setup and design that not only felt disturbing to Marion, but somehow strangely familiar.

The fuck is this?

Marion could only stare in disbelief as the conveyor belt started. The sound of it created an echo of ratchets and movements that cascaded after one another in crisp pings that were distant and hollow.

Terra walked up to the stage in front of Kane and the witches and motioned for Marion to come closer. When he was at center stage, looking up at her, he felt the dream he'd awakened from while in the coma flash before him. But everything in front of him and surrounding him was far more clear and far more organized.

"'It is true, we shall be monsters, cut off from all the world; but on that account we shall be more attached to one another.' Do you know who said it, darling Marion?"

Marion felt himself finally releasing the air he had been holding. He'd never felt so outmatched and wished he'd taken Devon with him. Even the comfort and familiar feel of the Beretta that was ready for action seemed pointless.

"I'm surprised you didn't. Now where's—"

"Never the shortage of wit. That's been quite the trick you've been able to pull off. Through it all, you've never disappointed. You've been a formidable opponent. Mary Shelley. Though I thank you for your attributes and cunning, Mary Shelley is the one. The Frankenstein Lady."

"How fitting."

"Ha! Yes it is! You know her story, of course. Her monster. And now you also know my vision of God as an insect. It is the monster who cuts us from the world, make no mistake. Monsters, that it is, and when it happens why do you think we are all attached as our beloved Mary said? Give me your answer!"

Marion continued to look up at Terra. His focus remained solely on her every move and gesture. Regardless of the monstrosity of Kane and the others on stage with her, he knew that this was a life-or-death moment for not only Nina and Casey, but himself. He licked his lips and scratched the back of his head with both hands in exhaustion. Then: "Because if it really is evil, or the monsters as Shelley said, that cut us at the fucking knees, then we are left to do one thing, and that's help each other.

That's how we're attached."

Terra slowly clapped for a full minute or longer before placing her hands behind her back. "That is a remarkable answer. Almost sounds divine. Bravo, Marion Paul. So very sad your brother could never face what you face with such clarity."

"Where are they?"

Terra placed her hands on her hips in a gesture of reprimand. "Have you learned nothing?"

"You told me that they'd be—"

Terra lifted her right hand to her throat, palm down with fingers together as she gestured for Marion to be silent. She walked to the very edge of the stage, looked down to him and shouted, "Since when has the devil ever spoken the truth!?"

Marion jolted back a few feet as Terra's voice hit him like a fleshy heat wave.

"We are not finished, Marion Paul!"

On the conveyor belt that circled the seating arrangement, Marion could see it was moving severed fingers and cocks. He pulled out the Beretta in a move that was more than second nature, aimed it directly at Terra's head with both hands firmly wrapped around the handle.

"Maybe I'm finished with you! Maybe I'm finished with all of you." Marion moved his body with gun in both hands from Terra to Kane, to the witches, back to Terra, keeping the bright red barrel site dead on her forehead. "It may not kill you but it'll sure as fuck feel right."

"I will tell you when we are finished, especially if you ever want to see your precious ladies again. Best put your little popper away." Terra turned to Exit Stage Left, her taloned left hand pointing to nothing Marion could see as suddenly the entire walls and ceiling began to move in a circular motion with lights that beamed up and down and across not only from the walls and ceiling but also from the flooring. It was as if the aircraft's look and feel Marion sensed came to life in a swirl of high-tech futuristic machinations that turned into a single holistic object.

Marion put the Beretta back behind his belt and placed his arms outward to brace himself from the immediate onslaught of vertigo. He felt his entire equilibrium shift his entire being. The spinning motion became too much as he fell to his knees. Just as he did, the entire light show from the instant machine shut off, and Marion looked around in a completely empty warehouse.

Whatever Terra had done had shut off and vanished, leaving him to look around in silence.

Except for an echoed tapping of hard heeled shoes he detected coming his way. As he stood to his feet again he saw Bridget Magnus walking toward him with a cane in hand.

"Monday Town, you codgey copper you! Monday Town is your last test!"

Chapter Nineteen:

Chess Match in Monday Town

Marion raced back to Duncan in the loaner Ram from Dickey Barlow's shop and had Devon on the phone as soon as he entered the freeway. He'd gunned down Bridget Magnus but knew she would survive, so that was one more mark against him not knowing what kind of outcome would take place.

Not that any of it will make a fuck's difference anyway.

Marion: I shot Bridget and have no idea what the fuck to think as I was there inside the building, Devon, when Terra had everything fucking disappear. Either that, or some kind of technology that she controls. Hard to say what happened at the end, to be honest.

Devon: Whoa, whoa, whoa! Hold on, boss, what do you mean you shot Bridget?

Marion: Doesn't matter. Had no choice, and she's just fine, you can bank on that.

Devon: Jesus let's not talk about it on our cell phones.

Marion: Really, Devon? You think...never mind that. I'll be up there in twenty or so.

Bridget hackled something about Monday Town. I have no idea what the hell that is.

Devon: Well, wait. What about the technology you mentioned. What happened?

Marion: The inside of the place looked like an aircraft of some kind. Spaceship as insane as that sounds. But it couldn't a been, right?

Devon: No idea. But no stranger than anything else. Remember you telling me about the night in your corral when you ended up at the diner? What you saw in the sky?

Marion: Yeah, yeah. All of it seems to be connected in some *fucking* way, that's for sure.

Devon: So what kind of disappearing were you talking about?

Marion: The area of the warehouse where I ended up suddenly changed into some kind of swirling machine that vanished as soon as the lights were cut off, then I was left standing in an empty warehouse that looked as if it had just been built. Except for Bridget. Apparently she was left there same as me and started walking toward me with all of her bullshit.

Devon: Christ.

Marion: Yeah. Something else, too. Just before I saw Terra. I was in another warehouse area that was designed as wax houses. Best way I could describe it. I saw my neighbor's freak fuck of a friend. The whole thing was one giant head fuck.

Devon: Okay, so what's the plan?

Marion: What the fuck is Monday Town?

Devon: Monday Town...Monday Town. Yeah, I don't know much about it, but I tell you who does know, that's Dickey.

Marion: You go with me to see him? Think he's up?

Devon: Of course. Yeah, of course. Christ. If I'm in this, it's all in, and I'm sure he's up drinking as usual.

Marion: Bank on another thing. I'll get you out of this. You have to trust me.

Devon: I do. Get up here, and I'll call Dickey right now.

Marion: Got it.

Marion focused on the freeway ahead to not speed or drive chaotic as to get pulled over by any state trooper, as they were always on the hunt for ticket handling. Before hanging up, Devon had proceeded to tell him all that he knew about Monday Town, that it was a massive mountainside area just across from Bridget's property, that a small town or village had flooded in a severe way, years back in 1983, when all the snow melted far too quickly and came rushing down into Duncan, flooding basement after basement, causing the creek itself that was behind Marion's place to turn into a wrath of chaos. All of it taking place on a Monday so the town of course nicknamed the mountainside area accordingly.

The mindset of a small town always amazed Marion

as compared to places like Houston.

What's more amazing is the fuckshow that it's turned out to be by lovely Terra Fucking Drake.

By the time he pulled into Devon's driveway of the duplex, Marion had collected himself back to complete focus. To his surprise Dickey Barlow was also there. Drinking, just as Devon said.

The three of them stood in Devon's small living room, both Devon and Dickey waiting for some kind of word from Marion about what was to go down. They both saw clearly that he was still trying to shake whatever had just happened.

"Listen, the only way you're getting anywhere tonight up into Monday Town is by horseback." Dickey was dressed in his usual oiled pants and plaid shirt getup he seemed to work and sleep in. He took a pull from a leather wrapped aluminum flask that smelled of something hard, the kind of smell that Marion remembered far too often with his brother. Dickey had probably started drinking in the early afternoon.

Maybe even a few shots first thing in the morning to keep his hands steady so he could trim his neck.

"Okay...I'm guessing you have a plan?"

"I've got two horses, not just a plan. You ride?"

"Not for a while, but I have. Not an ace at it, but I know how to move with a horse."

Devon looked at Marion in curiosity. "Is there anything you haven't done in the cop world?"

"With all the latest entries from Duncan, I doubt it. Speaking of towns, Devon tells me you know a lot about this Monday Town. Anything there that's particularly...I don't know, more fucked off than usual?"

Both Dickey and Devon chuckled nervously as Dickey pulled on his long beard. Marion could tell Dickey was thinking things through before answering, one of the things that Marion had grown to like about the alcoholic mechanic as he also took another pull on the flask.

"Well...let me think. Hmmm. Yes sir, there's a place up there, an abandoned place. Way up the mountainside up some steep trails. Wouldn't think anything of it in any other situation. But from everything Devon's told me up to this point sounds like fucked up shit has been on your heels for a minute."

"That it has. So what gives? What's up there that Bridget would have been so adamant about? And what's up there where she could have my daughter and Nina, that's the real fucking bit." Marion folded his large arms and hands across his body in genuine interest. Both Dickey and Devon could see the stress over the past few months and how everything that came down had aged the big city cop several years.

"Best way to describe it is that it's an old abandoned wreck of a place that was built in the early eighteen hundreds. Before pioneers trekked out this way. What's left of the place is, I think, a brick-and-mortar chimney that was probably inside the house, but that's all that's left. It sits in the middle of an area of the oldest mountain trees that ever grew in these parts. There's also a giant well that sits next to the ruins. Way up the piedmont in an upland area. Whole place is creepy as fuck, so if there's any place in Monday Town that batshit Bridget was talking about, or where this demon bitch would have your women folk, that'd be it. Like I said, horseback's the only way up and in."

"No concern of property owners and such? Fact, who does own it?"

"Don't worry about that. Monday Town's been a mountain range for hikers since the pioneers pulled handcarts up and down it."

"You said the chimney and well ruins were older."

Dicky pulled on the flask again. "Everything's fine, Big City. Can you just trust us? You want us to trust you, yeah?"

Marion looked over at Devon and back at Dickey. "You're right. Where are the horses?"

"I've got 'em pastured just beyond Bridget's place, of all things."

"You're shitting me."

Devon folded his arms over his wiry body. "No, he's not. But I think she's the last thing to worry about since you laid her out."

Devon's logic made perfect sense. Still, Marion had no idea what his chances were, but what he saw in the two men who had become his friends gave him at least a tad of comfort. "I guess Devon you drive us, then Dickey and I will ride on through."

Devon nodded as the three of them moved out of Devon's living room and jumped in his old Ford '72 long bed. The ten-minute ride through the deep mountain night saw the three men in silence. Far too silent for Devon as he turned on the old Ford's custom stereo with Grace Slick wailing through "White Rabbit" and how Alice was ten feet tall as well as small and how her Wonderland made sense of it all.

"Just the tune to keep things in check," Marion said just as Devon passed Bridget's property and into a field area with a few low-grade horse stalls.

No one said a word about Bridget, but Marion couldn't help but wonder if the hag was wandering around in her endless madness about to change into the monster that ate dead carcasses off the side of the freeway.

Within minutes, Marion and Dickey were sitting on Dickey's two horses, Dickey on Trixie, Marion on Angus. Both were American quarter horses, six years old, Trixie a golden brown, Angus as black as night.

Devon slowly followed Marion and Dickey as Trixie and Angus slowly trotted past the Magnus property a hundred feet or so as they turned east into a deeply gashed entry into Monday Town, which was a region of the

Wasatch Mountains known as the Wasatch Back that overlooked Duncan County.

Devon rolled down his window and looked up to Marion. "I'll be here waiting for you, boss. You stay alive. Thanks, Dickey." Devon tipped his hand to his forehead to both riders.

Marion waved and followed Dickey as Trixie moved alongside Angus, both horses quite intimate with the terrain. They gently rode in and out of the backcountry on trails that looked to lead into an abyss of deep mountain loneliness.

Guided only by the crescent moonlight, they rode through the silence and darkness. It felt overwhelming until Dickey stopped Trixie. Angus followed suit without Marion having to direct him.

"Wanted to see how you're holding up. It's been a while since you rode."

"Thanks. I'm fine. In fact...I think it's best I take it from here. Alone I mean."

Dickey pulled on his beard the way he always did while thinking things through. He pulled out the flask from his back pocket and took a deep pull. "You sure about that?"

"I'm sure that what's up there is something I need to face solo. I'm plenty armed but I doubt that's gonna mean a thing. How much farther to the ruins and the well?"

"I'd say another mile, no more than two. Keep Angus on this backtrail. It's easy for these parts to swallow you whole."

"I don't know when I'll be back."

"Kinda figured that. We'll be waiting, doesn't matter how long. You've become someone that kid has really looked up to. I can see why."

"I appreciate you. Especially Devon. Let him know, please."

Dickey nodded and turned Trixie to head back down

toward Devon but stopped the horse just shy of the tree-line. "Hey, Marion." Dickey made sure not to speak too loudly. He was getting drunker by the moment, but he knew enough to keep things down in such deadly silence.

"What is it, Dickey?" Marion was anxious to push ahead, but he could tell Dickey needed to say one last word, much like his own brother liked to do. *It's the alcoholic's way, I guess.* Marion moved Angus closer to Trixie.

"Look, I'm sure this ain't the best time to mention this, but truth is your brother went on and on about this crazy bitch you're about to face up there. And I know all that you've been through with her since. Fact is, he and I did some serious drinking together, and at the end of things, well...I knew he was truly scared. It weren't no joke. No amount of drinkin' could settle his nerves about her."

Marion took in a deep breath of the cold mountain air and let it out slowly as he looked over Dickey. "Yeah, and things didn't work out too well for him, I know. I get it, and I know she's no joke. She was there when he brought me into this deal, and I've been in it neck-deep since the first part of May, so what is it, Dickey? If you've got some kind of insight that will make my odds against her better, then spit it out."

Dickey nodded as if he was trying to follow every word that left Marion's mouth, but Marion could also see he was doing everything possible to think things through in his drunken state.

Just be patient. What ever Terra's got planned can wait. She's going nowhere.

"I don't want to end up like your brother, that's what I wanted to say. And I don't want you to end up like him. Dead that is. Your brother loved you. I just wanted to tell you these things. Come back, okay? Come back."

Marion nodded. He knew there was nothing left to say and that it was best for Dickey to get that out without any reply. Just two men understanding each other, as Dickey needed. With that, up toward Monday Town Marion went as he led Angus up deeper into the canyon trails toward the abyss.

***

It didn't take more than just a few minutes before Marion felt utterly alone. When a few more minutes began to feel like a few hours. The darkness itself moved in and out of the backtrail like thick tubes of black fog that felt not only endless, but hopeless. Angus seemed as distraught as Marion as they continued to climb upward and outward into the vast mountain range where the entire geography was covered in massive trees and boulders.

Angus whinnied in anxiety.

"Easy does it, boy. Easy does it. Let's just keep on keeping on." Marion's whisper even sounded too loud. The quarter horse's shoes clicked through the silence like hammers tapping away at concrete slabs. The backtrail had finally spilled into an open area as Marion looked around doing what he could to adjust his eyes in the darkness for an attempt at any clarity. Suddenly, Angus stopped and reared up, spooked but just short of bucking. The black quarter horse would go no farther, and there was no amount of prodding Marion could do that would convince him otherwise.

"What is it, boy? What's up a head?"

The horse whinnied and shuffle-stepped backward.

"Alright, easy now." He knew he'd have to get down from Angus and walk the rest of the way on his own. After he dismounted, he tied the reins to a tree branch and patted Angus's shoulder. "Appreciate you getting me this far, Angus. I'm gonna check this out, you just hang back here."

The horse nickered and huffed quietly in agreement as he clearly knew things were not right. "Wish me luck."

A few steps down the trail, he spotted the faint glowing ember of a light just ahead. It didn't take long before his eyes could decipher what Dickey had described back at Devon's place. He saw the ruins of what used to be a brick house. For all he knew it could have been the remains of many houses. It was the chimney remains that were nestled inside a broken wall structure that looked as if it had been blasted by cannonballs. The massive well was also there, in front of the structure with dozens of ancient trees hovering over the entire area, protecting it like mythological Roman Silvani.

The glowing light that Marion first saw was, in fact, burning embers from logs that were stacked on what he thought was a rusted metal grate. It was more of a haunting strobe that danced around under the crescent moonlight as an eerie shadow that wanted comfort from the trees.

"Hello, Marion."

The sound of the voice was unmistakable but still shook him to his core as he looked all around to locate Terra. She came from behind one of the giant arching trees to Marion's left, carrying an iron lantern in one hand, and an old leather draw-sack in the other. The lantern glowed with similar burning embers as the fire pit. She wore a deep red satin robe with a white satin sash wrapped several times around her waist. The robe hung on her loose enough to where Marion knew she wore nothing else. Her hair was bleached golden blond and was braided in thick ropey strands that hung around her head like Medusa's snakes. Her lavender eyes were more striking than ever in the fierce night. More frightening than Marion had ever seen them.

She walked over to the well and placed the lantern and sack down on the ground to provide light to the well itself. Out from behind the ruined chimney wall came Rebecca, Janet Stone, and Dr. Pinault, all dressed in similar robes as Terra's, but in black satin with black sashes. Each of them had their hair dyed the same golden blond as Terra's, knotted up in tight Egyptian buns.

Marion eyed all of them as best he could, and then Kane made his appearance, stepping from behind one of the massive trees opposite to where Terra entered the scene. He was dressed in the same ragged cowboy gig he'd worn that day on the bridge when Marion first saw him. A cigarette dangled from his lips. He looked a thousand years old, his face beaten and swollen, his hands torn and blistered. He carried a folding table under one arm, and a large game board under the other. He proceeded to set up the table and board next to the well, a chess board, of all things.

"Looks like every bullet I fired into you didn't do the trick." Marion kept his voice firm and under as much control as possible. Still, he thought it quivered a bit.

Keep it the fuck together.

Kane ignored the comment and walked over to the three witches dressed in black. Terra walked in front of the chess board and table. She bent down and reached into the leather sack and pulled out the chess pieces to set up the game.

"Do you play?"

Marion moved his eyes with measured control back and forth to everyone surrounding him as he tried to figure out what was going on and hoped a play came to mind. "Do I have a choice?"

"I didn't ask you if you had a choice, I asked if you played chess."

Marion cleared his throat. "Of course I do."

"Yes...of course you do. Now to answer your question, there's always a choice, dear Marion. But for this match you at least must choose to play in order to either save the ones you love, or to save yourself. Take a look."

Terra pointed her taloned index finger into the woods where Marion saw two life-sized holograms suddenly appear from the ground. One was of Nina, the other of his daughter, Casey. Both women were absolute replicas so vivid in reality that the first impression for Marion was to run over and hold them. They stood six to nine feet apart from each other. Nina was dressed business formal as he'd seen her a few times when she got off work. Casey was dressed in a halter top and blue jeans, as casual and fancy free as he'd always seen her. His heart and breathing raced wildly, but he held it together, knowing the holograms were only more of Terra's black magic at work, which seemed to have no end.

"Where are they, Terra?"

"Sssssshhhhhh. Hush." Terra hissed as she put her index finger to her blood-red painted lips. "We're going to play for them. You win, I let them live. I win, their souls and lives belong to me."

"No. You win, I go with you. I win, you free the child slaves and leave my family the fuck alone."

Terra giggled deep and throaty. "How noble of you, but—"

"Terra." She was suddenly cut off when someone else stepped from behind yet another one of the massive trees in the immediate area, clearly unexpected.

She turned away from Marion and shuddered as if she'd been stung by a Vipertek stun gun.

John walked into the light. He was dressed in the same cream-colored suit he wore at the nightmare diner when he arrived to give fair warning.

Terra remained silent.

Kane stormed directly into John's immediate personal space. "You have no right to be here." His voice was as ragged as his gun belt and boots, yet his towering figure and presence had no visible effect on John.

"Of course I do. Not only do I have the right, I have the authority. Go back to where you stood by the others. Those three in black."

Marion watched in astonishment as Kane obeyed him. John looked over all the players, slowly and carefully, nodded to Marion before focusing on Terra. "Doesn't look like the fairest tournament I've seen. Thought I'd even the odds a bit."

Marion's slight grin was filled with as much exhaustion as it was relief. He looked at Terra's deadpan expression, and with John in his peripheral, he leaned over the chessboard and started the game with a King's Knight Opening move.

Chapter Twenty:

Last Call To New Orleans

In the low light of Monday Town, Marion and Terra continued exchanging move after move as the holograms of Nina and Casey remained, an omnipresent reminder to Marion that their fate was in his hands.

"Be nice if you could make those goddamn things go away, John. Makes me nervous."

Marion grappled with the memory of Henrickson's last rant at the Walls Unit Prison. *"She's got something personal on you, that's easy to see! But don't think she'll stop there as she gets in deeper. Everything close to you, she'll fuck it all up!"*

She sure had fucked up Henrickson's life, and my brother's.

And they both believed she was at the root of it all.

Maybe she is, maybe she isn't.

After the first several moves, Marion knew that Terra was doing nothing more than mirroring his own play. He'd move a pawn, she would move hers. He'd move a knight, she would move hers. She wasn't playing to win, he realized, she was playing to torment him.

Marion was truly exhausted, but all the while, with his head down focusing on the chess match, he considered exactly what John had said, that he wanted to make sure the odds were evened out. Not only that, but also what he said about *having authority*. Authority from where? *Over* what?

Terra's Sabbath

Doesn't fucking matter, Terra seemed silenced by him, and the monster Kane obeyed him. That's good enough for me.

"Maybe the odds are evened out a lot more than I realize," Marion whispered to himself, not realizing it as he was about to move his queen.

The silence from Terra and Kane became too much. It was the whole goddamn scene of witchery that remained in silence, which was beginning to fray his last nerve endings. He looked over to John before continuing the game moving the queen. It didn't seem real that John had such authority...and the witches, they too didn't seem real, especially the stoic Kane, so out of character, and deadpan Terra Drake, not a hint of seduction in her lavender eyes, just a cold stare, and more so, the holograms meant to instill fear and high stakes. None of it felt real.

Marion's face felt suddenly hot with suppressed rage. Looking back at John, Marion wondered how he was going to play it all out. John nodded as if understanding and agreeing with Marion's current thinking.

As one who had the privilege of understanding authority, Marion felt a sudden empowerment and new clarity.

Suddenly, wicked humming cut through the silent mountain scene, which jolted Marion's senses to full alert. He looked over to the three witches who were humming in unison. The tune ascended to a shrieking madness, then plummeted to a low-pitched chant. "Shemlemhafesh, shemlemhafesh, shemlemhafesh!"

Marion looked again at Terra. It never ceased to amaze him how intoxicating her beauty and seduction had been, regardless of how severe the situation or how dangerous her illusions appeared.

Or how fucked up this shit has become, and she still has the power to arouse.

He snapped out of it, quickly, as her continued silence

gave him even more clarity, and he instantly detached from her power of allurement.

He needed to make a move to prove that his thinking was correct, that his brewing plan would work, that he needed to rely on all that he'd learned over the past two months and use this revelation to his advantage and challenge what he thought was her endless power.

I'm betting it's not endless, that her world is more fucking illusion than anything real, and I'm about to fucking bet Nina and Casey's lives on my next move.

When he was convinced she wouldn't speak, Marion kicked over the table and chessboard, which caused all the pieces to look as if they exploded into the air and rained all over the ground. "I'm done with your games! Done with *this* fucking game, for sure! And I'm done with you and your psycho sidekick cowboy *fuck*!"

Terra stood speechless, her lavender eyes in a rage like he'd never seen them. But she was powerless, or so it seemed, as she made no move or threat. She just stared. Kane, on the other hand, appeared to take offense to the insult and stepped forward, hand on his six-shooter and feet spread.

Marion thought to pull the Beretta from the back of his belt and pump Kane full of hollow points, but he knew from experience—wolf creature or not—it would be a waste of good bullets. Then he thought to attack Kane with fists and feet, give him a taste of Houston street fighting, and hope to get him down before he pulled his gun, but he remembered the beating Macey took, so that was out.

John stood by the well, shook his head slowly, and Marion got the notion that there was meaning in his expression, that perhaps he hadn't learned a fucking thing.

Is Kane and Terra's menace all in my goddamn head?

Steve had taken the bait, as did Macey, and the consequences were catastrophic.

I need to walk away...that's my fucking play here.

Marion's play felt terrifying to pursue. Nothing he'd faced since the coma dream could match what his mind and body felt as he walked right into Kane's immediate space and looked up to his endless black eyes. "Go right to fucking hell where you belong."

Terra stepped forward.

Kane pulled the hand cannon from the holster, but Terra signaled for him to put it back.

Marion scowled. "We're done here."

"You're right..." She said it in a voice that sounded as hollow and empty as it did assertive. She stepped a foot closer, her eyes continuing to pierce Marion's. "About hell, that is."

"I *know* I'm right. And about all this *fuckery* tonight, as John said, everything's evened out." Marion nodded to John who kept his stance of pure authority. Dominance.

"But don't you think to dare walk out of here," Terra seethed. "They'll die. Your precious ladies. I. Will rip. Their fucking hearts out."

Marion kept at it as he felt the tide turning. "Henrickson was right. We had a little chat at Huntsville prison. He told me you're connected to every goddamn thing from child trafficking to a porn ring, to DeMille, to Dean Corll, The Candy Man, to the slaughter at Eternity 51. That you're the evil that lives in all of us, since the time of Lilith, the Garden of Eden, the snake, the sin, and you manifest yourself through those who'll do your bidding, but not this time. The fucking hell I saw firsthand at your warehouse, that hi-tech shitshow, and every goddamn thing in between meant to deceive and convince the weak and afflicted to bend to your will.

"Not this fucking time. Henrickson let you in, as did Corll and Bundy and Berkowitz, *they* all let you in. All of them! I didn't. You sought *me* out! From the moment I woke up from the coma and had to deal with those psycho fucks!" Marion pointed to the chanting witches.

"And Bridget Magnus. Christ. John knew it, that's why he's here, to show me you've got no power over me. Only the power I let you have, the power my brother let you have...but it killed him. You're *not* killing me. Not Nina. Not Casey."

Terra's eyes glowed more fierce, as if she were feeding on his denial of her, her smile grew more wicked, more alluring. "Don't be so sure of yourself, my dear Marion Paul." Terra said it in a voice that was sickeningly one of comfort, of all things, as she stepped closer to Marion. "I've been here, rooted in humanity's shit since the beginning of time. I fucked Adam, goddamn it!" She moved into his immediate space like a panther, reached her arms around him, pulled him into her hardened body and kissed his lips as if they were lovers. Then: "And I can certainly fuck you."

Marion turned his head and spat on the ground. "Fuck off, lady!" He said it with as much effort as his throat would allow, as her sexuality felt overwhelming; still, he pushed her away.

She lashed out, backhanded him across the face with such a blow that he felt she'd broken his jaw as he went down and landed hard on his tailbone.

So much for fucking illusions.

He looked over to John and back to Terra, wondering if he'd be able to get to his feet, when suddenly, out of his peripheral he saw Dickey Barlow ride into the light on Trixie. She reared up and whinnied, giving Marion an instant sense of victory.

"Looks like you need a ride outta here." Dickey's voice was slurred and filled with the drink, yet heroic, nonetheless.

Marion clambered to his feet and felt his jaw to make sure it wasn't broken.

Kane remained stoic, his eyes locked on Terra.

Marion saw that John had walked away from the well

and was walking out of the light and into the darkness from whence he came, his right hand up in a gesture of goodbye. The holograms of Nina and Casey dissolved. Terra clasped her taloned hands together just below her breasts. Her robe had opened fully, her naked beauty aglow with the power of evil within anyone who would answer her call.

The three witches went at it again. "Shemlemhafesh. Shemlemhafesh. Shemlemhafesh."

"Nice group you've got gathered here, boss, but I think it's time to call it a night." Dickey had moved Trixie close enough to Marion so that he could jump on back and hold on to Dickey's greasy jacket. "Let's go, Trix." He spurred the horse around and down the dark trail.

"Where's Angus?"

"Down yonder where ya left him. He's smarter than me and more stubborn than Trix."

"Hurry her up. I've got some phone calls to make." Marion hoped they'd been safe and sound all along.

***

Dickey and Marion rode back down the Monday Town trail until they reached Angus where Marion hopped on the black quarter horse and continued following Dickey until they reached Devon's truck parked on the roadside. The three of them put away the horses, then dropped off Dickey at his place.

Marion walked him to the front door.

"Thanks, Dickey. For everything. Were you behind me the whole time?"

"Close enough. Figured it weren't the event to go it alone, after all." Dickey pulled on his beard again.

Marion could smell the alcohol coming from Dickey's pores, reminding him all too well of his brother. "I heard what you said before it all went down. I mean I really listened to you, Dickey."

Dean Patrick

"Yeah. Maybe it were Steve that nudged me to stay close to ya."

"Maybe."

With that, Devon drove to his place, as Marion was too exhausted to deal with his Duncan Ranch neighbor. He plopped himself down heavy on Devon's cheap sofa. The sun would be up soon, and though exhausted, he knew he couldn't sleep and took out his cell phone.

Devon sat on one of the kitchen chairs that faced the living room. "You gonna call your daughter first?"

"She'd never answer. Constantly angry with me. Besides, not even sure where she is as she never told me where she was going on her trip."

"Shame you two aren't closer. I'm cracking a beer." Devon stood and went to his fridge. "You want one?"

"You know I don't drink. Sure as fuck won't start now. I'm calling Nina. She's in New Orleans, probably up and getting ready for her business meetings." To Marion's great relief, Nina picked up on the third ring.

> **Nina**: Hey there! Wow, I was just about to call you.
>
> **Marion**: Is that right? Are you okay?
>
> **Nina**: I'm fine. Why wouldn't I be?
>
> **Marion**: I'm *so* glad to hear your voice.
>
> **Nina**: Wow. Why?
>
> **Marion**: I was worried, to be honest.
>
> **Nina**: Worried? Worried about what?

Marion listens closely to her breathing. His heart begins to settle down as he thanks God above that she picked up. That Terra didn't get a hold of her, just as he suspected. He feels Casey's safe, too.

Terra's Sabbath

He can tell that Nina has immediate concern in her voice, but he thought it best not to tell her what happened, though she'd probably pry it out of him someday, one of the things that he's grown so fond of, one of the many things.

Nina: Why so quiet, Marion? Are you sad? Relieved? I can't tell which.

Marion: Relieved to say the least. I am just so glad you're okay. I worry about you when you're gone.

Nina: Well, maybe you should. Hey! Guess what. You will not believe this. I was going to call you to tell you your daughter is here. I shit you not.

Marion: What? In New Orleans?

Nina: She flew in last night and she found me, of all things, in the lobby of the hotel we are both staying at, can you believe it?

Marion: I'm not sure I can. How did you know it was her?

Nina: Always the cop.

Marion: Yeah. But how?

Nina: There was a note that one of the folks at the front desk gave to me that said a Casey Paul was looking for me, that she was here to meet me, of all things. That's your daughter, right?

Marion: The one and only. She never said she was going to New Orleans, and she sure as shit doesn't know you.

Nina: Stranger things have happened. In fact, she's here with me right now. We're going to have breakfast together. Want to say hi to her?

Marion: Wow. No, no, no. That's okay. I don't want to bother her. Wow, again. Jesus.

Regardless of how strange things sound, Marion's heartbeat speeds up as he's suddenly filled with more hope for his relationship with Casey than he's had in ages. He feels exhausted yet exhilarated.

Nina: It's no bother. Come on.

Marion: She doesn't want to talk to me, besides, I'm spent. Got to get some rest. It's good enough to know she's alright, too. Please take a picture of her, text it to me. It's been a long time since I've seen her.

Nina: Okay, will do. I'll call you later. We will call you later. Funny how things work out, right?

Marion: It is. Talk soon.

Nina: I miss you, Marion. Talk soon.

He hung up, stunned to his core. "Devon, you're not going to fucking believe this?!" Marion stood from the couch and walked to the kitchen where Devon was draining his second beer.

Devon's phone rang and began slowly spinning on the kitchen table from the vibration. "What the hell?" He picked up the phone and examined the display. "Fucking Unknown Caller. Hate those." He silenced the noisy intrusion.

UNKNOWN CALLER? Marion remembered the last time he got such a call. It was Terra. His phone dinged in a text from Nina, showing a picture of Casey. "My daughter...my daughter is in New Orleans with Nina, and I just got a picture of her. Can you believe that shit?" He stared at the photo. Her hair was pulled back and she was smiling as her fingers pinched the pendant on her necklace.

"Wow, boss, shit's really looking up, right?"

Marion kept staring at the picture, and the more he looked at the pendant, the more his grip tightened on the phone.

"Marion? Right?"

He peeled his eyes away from the picture and raised his head to look at Devon standing at the end of a long dark tunnel.

"Boss? What is it?"

He looked down at Casey's photo again, at the pendant she wore, and he turned cold inside, as if all blood had drained from his body.

This isn't over yet.

Be sure to read Dean Patrick's
The Lady Mephistopheles

Stephen Paul is a raging alcoholic whose addiction suddenly manifests itself, one cold Utah night, in the form of a beautiful woman. Terra Drake, at first, seems warm and inviting, but she soon shows him the horrors she'd beset upon his small town, the murder of his next-door neighbor, the bewitching of his hairstylists, the freakshow the county fair had become, and the damnation of his priest in the new Church of Flies. She's in cahoots with another demon, the Hooded Darkness, who stalks him at every turn, and the more he drinks, the more horror he sees and the more he blames them for the misery that has befallen small-town America. As his warnings to citizens and friends go unheeded, he strikes out on his own to defeat this ultimate evil, to save the world before hell itself comes calling.

Dean Patrick was born and raised in Houston, Texas. Educated at The University of Houston with Masters Degrees in Professional Writing and Literature, he works as a writer for a Houston-based orthopedic center and for software technology companies in the Salt Lake City area. He lives in Morgan, Utah, on a small ranch with his wife, Lisa. To this day, he considers his sobriety his greatest victory.

Dean Patrick

Enjoy more novels and short stories from

www.twbpress.com

**Science Fiction, Supernatural, Horror, Urban Fantasy,
Thrillers, Romance, and more**